The Whumpboratory

Kailey Alessi

THE WHUMPY PRINTING PRESS

To the scientists

Contents

Introduction

For WPP's third anthology, I decided to let the people choose the theme. Out of many fine options, the theme "lab whump" won the vote. Talented writers from across the globe submitted their stories for this anthology, and I'm ecstatic for you to enter *The Whumphoratory*! This book contains twenty-seven stories of unethical experimentation and whumpy goodness. Be warned: these stories are dark and contain some unsettling content. Content warnings are included at the beginning of each story.

Now sit back, relax, and enjoy these whumpy stories with a splash of science.

Your New Lab Rat: A Guide for (Whumpers) Scientists

Kailey Alessi

CW: Lab whump, dehumanization, implied captivity, torture, non-sexual nudity, and restraints

Whumpee: Unspecified, Whumper: Unspecified, Caretaker: N/A

Congratulations on your new lab rat! This is a big step in any scientist's career, and in this helpful guide I'll walk you through getting your subject prepared for experimentation. I know you're excited and want to jump right into the science, but trust me, the proper prep work is essential.

First things first, you need to call your lab rat something. The following are some of the most common names, but feel free to be creative!

- Subject (my personal favorite)

- Specimen

- Asset

- An ID number

- Their species

Did you pick out a name? Excellent! The next step is to strip away the rest of their dignity. I know this might seem a bit harsh, but it's the best way to ensure your subject cooperates, and you need their cooperation to get that sweet, sweet data you're after. Take away all their possessions, even their clothes. You can give them some scrubs or a hospital gown if you want, or you can just leave them nude. If they argue or cry, just ignore them. There's always an adjustment period when a subject enters a lab, it'll pass quickly.

Your next steps will vary based on the temperament of your subject. If your subject is docile, you might not need to do anything further in preparation and can jump right into experimenting. However, some subjects exhibit aggression, which is unproductive to data collection. You will have to tame them. There are a wide variety of techniques that can be used, so consider the resources at your disposal. Note that you do not want to cause irreparable harm to your subject at this stage. Here's a list of popular disciplinary techniques to consider:

- Shock collar

- Withholding food, sleep, etc.

- Isolation/solitary confinement

- Stress positions

- Sedatives

And of course, give positive reinforcement when your subject completes a wanted behavior. Most subjects are eager to please once they understand that they will be rewarded for cooperation. Your subject will be behaving themself in no time!

Finally, it's time to start your experiments. Stick to the scientific method, and remember results must be replicable to stand up to peer review. That means that you'll need to run the same experiment on your subject multiple times, and preferably have other subjects to compare them to.

A note on safety: even the best trained subject can act out if in pain. I always recommend the use of restraints during experimentation for your own safety. Additionally, always make sure you are wearing the proper PPE. Gloves, safety goggles, lab coat, hazmat suit, etc. Make sure you protect yourself!

Science is hard work, but by preparing your subject beforehand it will be that much easier. Whatever your research goals, I wish you and your subject good luck!

About the Author

Kailey Alessi is the founder and editor-in-chief of the Whumpy Printing Press, a publishing company whose mission is to publish the work of the whump community. She is also the author of the Of Vampires and Men dark fantasy series, and her short fiction has appeared in numerous anthologies. She is an archaeologist by day, and by night she writes all sorts of dark fiction. You can find her on tumblr @whumpy-writings

Control

KL Massey

CW: captivity, medical theme, implied drugging, Stockholm syndrome, abuse, past trauma

Whumpee: Man, Whumper: Woman, Caretaker: Woman

Daniel jolts awake from the dreamless void, alert as something calls to him from beyond layers of consciousness. A burst of static energy crackles through the air and hisses out of existence. Hairs tingle at the back of his neck and a shiver runs down his spine, making ripples where cool air caresses exposed areas of skin. He tugs roughly at the hem of his t-shirt and stretches it down to cover the pale, vulnerable flesh of his stomach, instinctively self-conscious. Everything feels tight, his muscles tense and claustrophobic within the too-small, too-new clothes.

Daniel stares up at the ceiling and scans the limited horizon. Everything is grey and the dull colouring settles over his mind like a comfort blanket, tempting him to remain motionless. He blinks slowly as if that might shake something loose and reveal the truth of his predicament. Tentatively moving his eyes to take in his surroundings, he finds dull panels of concrete scarred with gleaming flecks of metal and glass that reflect coldly in the stark overhead light.

At first he thought he was alone, but now he freezes, alert and uncertain. He has no recollection of this place but holds tight to the certainty that this is not somewhere he recognises. Fear spills up into his throat and he swallows it down, but it leaves behind the bitter aftertaste of isolation.

His heart beats loudly, reverberating within the blank space of the room. A wry smile flashes across his face but doesn't reach his sea-glass green eyes. How fitting it is, that this exterior so neatly matches how he feels inside. A blank space within a blank space. The familiar dull ache tugs at his core, reminding him of the emptiness that he carries wherever he goes.

Daniel's pulse quickens, anxiety forcing him out of inaction. His muscles flex against the fabric of his shorts as he moves to a seated position. The sagging mattress beneath him screams in protest against the action. Sweeping his gaze in rhythmic arcs, he occupies himself by noting details. The room holds little: the shallow bed frame, a solid steel door with a simple panel above it. He dismisses it all, there is nothing that can help him.

Ragged breaths assault his lungs, escaping in desperate gasps. He is edging dangerously close to a panic attack, terrified of being left alone again. He tears at his unfamiliar clothes, hoping that they might reveal some sort of clue, but they offer him nothing.

What has he done to end up here? How did it happen? He must have done something to deserve it, but he struggles to understand. He fails to pick up the pieces and reason deserts him. He is left alone with his thoughts.

***

His heart had been broken so many times that he came to expect it; this was how it always was. With bittersweet desire he peeled back the layers of himself and stripped away anything that had once brought him happiness, knowing how easily it could be ripped away. He gave up on his wants and needs, discarded them like well-loved childhood toys, convinced that they must be holding him back now that he was a man. Starved for connection, he offered himself as a willing sacrifice to anyone who would take him. Temporary use kept him going, dreaming of the one who would want to keep him.

***

A velvet voice oozes from the intercom, drips down and covers him.

"Greetings, Subject," says the disembodied female voice.

Daniel stares fixedly at the speaker panel as if it could project a vision into the room. He waits expectantly for the message to continue, straining to hear every single word. His leg bounces erratically, mirroring his impatience.

"Welcome to the Cell. Everything you require for the duration of the test period will be provided for you. You have been provided with garments which you will wear for the duration of the test period. You have been provided with a collar which you will wear for the duration of the test period. Anything that you do not receive, you will not require. Do you comprehend?"

Daniel's breath catches in his throat, pressure building there. He paws with weak confusion at the collar that encircles his neck. How had he not noticed it before? The metal surface has warmed to body temperature, in perfect synch with his biology. Running his fingers along both sides, he pauses to investigate a bulky section on the left, strangely hollow-sounding when he taps on it. He strains but cannot bend his head at the correct angle to see it.

"What?" he whispers, as his fingers continue their journey. Meeting in the middle underneath his chin, he flicks at a small metal loop located in the centre, moving it up and down in a mindless rhythmic pattern.

"Commencing test protocol."

A sharp sting pierces his neck and he scratches at it pitifully, unable to place his fingers underneath the tight loop of the collar to find relief. Flooded with confusion his muddled thoughts fall in and out of position, none finding the right fit. The itch burns like nettles, and he claws at it around the unyielding metal.

"What is this?" he pleads.

"First dose complete, the subject is active. Subject, please state your name."

"Daniel," he says in a whisper.

"Good. You are ready to begin your test, Daniel. Please pay attention and follow all instructions. You are to rise and stand in the corner of the room."

An additional light flickers on and illuminates one corner; the question that rose to his lips vanishes before he can speak it. Tentatively, he stands and takes the few steps to reach his destination. Bathed in the bright light, he huddles with his back to the wall, waiting for whatever is to happen next.

He suppresses his thoughts before they get a chance to start roaming, forcing them into an empty state. Open and ready to receive. He slows his breathing, making it steady and even, finding strength in identifying something that he has control over.

"Good, Daniel. The dose you have received is now working its way into your system. You will feel the effects, beginning with your breath becoming slower and deeper. It will ease every part of you, relaxing your muscles and your inhibitions. You will become compliant and receptive to all instructions. Do you understand?"

Daniel feels the way his breathing has altered; follows the suggestion that this is spreading to his muscles, reaching into his mind. Relaxed. Calm. He is only doing what he is told to do.

"Yes," he answers.

"Good. Stay right there. All responses will be monitored. Procedure initiated."

In his relaxed state, Daniel is unprepared for the downpour that hits him, ice-cold water streaming from above. After the initial shock subsides, he is grateful for the pressure on his tired muscles, rejuvenated by its invigorating impact. Daniel closes his eyes and accepts the treatment, slowly breathing in and out. He is focused on waiting to hear her voice again.

The stream of water persists, flowing through him and sending a chill into his bones. He crosses his arms protectively over his chest, vainly attempting to conserve heat, but there is none left to be saved. Lifting his head under the torrent he glances out, seeking something that he knows cannot be there. The rough concrete walls tower over him. Tears fall down his freckled cheeks, lost in the downpour. He leans against the wall, the gritty surface scraping through the drenched t-shirt that covers his back. Grateful for the distraction that the pain provides, he presses harder, willing himself to endure the torment to the very end.

He imagines that she is with him throughout this ordeal. She must be watching him somehow...didn't the voice tell him that everything would be monitored? He straightens, a sudden rush of fear forcing him to stand upright, skin prickling with the sensation of being watched. The test has not finished yet and he has not received any further instructions; he must wait to be told what to do next.

Numbed by the thud of freezing water, his mind takes him back to a place of endurance, a place he has been to before. Here he can outlast the physical torment, shutting down until it is over.

Eventually the shower ends, pressure lifting like so much weight that he carries with him. Silence creeps around the room and he remains rooted in place, needing to hear her voice again. Seconds pass, but they stretch painfully until the click of the intercom signals his attention.

"Procedure complete. At rest, Subject."

Daniel heaves a sigh of relief and his mouth gapes open, teeth chattering uncontrollably. He reaches up to wring icy droplets from his long hair, unnaturally dark under the saturation of icy water. Small rivulets run down his neck and gather on his already soaked clothing. He glances around the room, despite knowing its contents, and confirms that there is nothing he can use right now. No towel, no change of clothing.

Eyes cast downwards, he walks the few steps towards the small bed and lowers his body onto the thin mattress. He lies shivering on the blanket-less bed, lacking cover and comfort. Wet fabric clings to his shaking body, holding him in a tight embrace. He is thankful for its touch. Rubbing his fingers over his chest, he tries desperately to return some heat to the core of his body, but the cold has already found a home inside of him.

Daniel closes his eyes, shedding silent tears from beneath his dense lashes. Exhaustion wins and sleep claims victory over him.

***

He had learned that other people could see his emptiness, immediately under-standing that he was different fromthem. If they noticed him, they inevitably regarded him in one of two ways. Some would radiate with disgust, desperate to avoid him lest the damage was transmittable and he infected them also. Others -- fewer, but enough -- watched him with gleaming eyes, hungry for the power they could hold over him. He wasn't sure which was worse. At least when he was being hurt he was being noticed. He became useful when someone needed him. He existed in those moments; their gifts of pain made him real.

***

He doesn't know how much time has passed. He stares unseeing, creating dis-tance from reality. His head is empty except for the pounding silence that fills the room. A tangled mess of feelings squirm inside him, knotted and writhing in the chaos.

Daniel jerks his head in the direction of a loud click and sees the door standing ajar. The gap is wide enough that he could pass between it, but he automatically recoils, shrinking away from the change in his environment and trying to make himself physically smaller. Maybe that way he can disappear, and he will finally be safe.

Her voice sounds over the intercom. "Subject, please move through to the adjoining chamber."

Fear evaporates and he responds instantly, swinging his feet off the bed and standing quickly to attention. Dizziness clouds his vision, but he continues to move anyway. His clothes have dried out as he slept, and they crease uncomfort-ably against his tender skin in response to each movement.

He passes through the doorway and walks past a small toilet, crossing the room in a few hurried steps. He stands before a single chair set at a slim metal table that appears to be fixed to the floor. The table is laid with a cup of water and a plate holding a meagre meal of plain white meat, sticky rice and green beans. His stomach twists in anticipation but he is too anxious to be tempted by his hunger.

A long mirror is set into the wall above the table, and Daniel cannot avoid witnessing just how pitiful he looks right now. His sandy red hair is in tangles around his shoulders, and the ill-fitting clothes are drawing attention to his awkward posture. His hands hold each other, seeking reassurance. He is crushed with the realisation that she must be behind the mirror, out of sight and out of reach. He knows there is a trick you can do to see if a mirror works two ways, but he can't recall the method now. He doesn't need to check though; he is certain she must be watching him.

Daniel flinches away from the mirror, not wanting to look at himself, wishing he could see her instead. He waits with urgency, and the desperate need to hear her command pulses inside his brain.

"Please be seated, Subject. You must eat."

A flood of relief washes over him and his stomach turns to liquid. He hurries to the chair and sits. He notices a spork that had been placed next to the plate, lifts it delicately and begins to eat methodically, taking small bites and chewing thoroughly before swallowing. He barely notices the taste, but his stomach growls in appreciation.

"Very good, Subject. I suggest you drink up and use the facilities while you have the chance, you will return to the Cell shortly."

He snatches the cup almost fiercely and gulps down mouthfuls of water until it is drained, empty. He feels better now, comforted by the simple meal and the security of her unseen presence. Rising from the chair he turns and starts towards the toilet but stops abruptly. She will see everything. Shame rushes over him, and hot blushes bloom on his tear-streaked face. He must do this, and he must be quick. He finishes and stands, feeling disembodied, like he has stepped outside of himself.

"Please return to the Cell, Subject."

Her voice carries him over the threshold, and the door clicks loudly as it shuts behind him. He is grateful to return to his quarters, already feeling safer now that he is not faced with the mirror.

"That's far enough, stop there."

His movements are interrupted by her voice and he halts to pay attention. Another stinging sensation rises beneath the collar, the injection delivering his second dose and spreading prickling heat. The wave of relaxation returns and he is ready to receive the next task.

"Notice how quickly the relaxation spreads through your system. You are a willing and compliant participant. All responses will be monitored. Procedure initiated."

Daniel's lungs strain and he lets out the breath he was holding onto, unsure of what he had been afraid of. He stares blankly, relaxed and ready.

"Kneel, Daniel."

His body drops like a dead weight, knees buckling in his haste to fulfil her order. He reaches his hands out to brace himself against the hard floor and hears a sharp intake of breath that is not his own.

"Not like that, Subject. Place your hands on top of your thighs, palms up."

His hands move into position like a puppet being dangled from strings.

"Do not move from this position until you are instructed to."

Daniel takes shallow breaths and nods to himself gently in understanding.

"Stay."

The intercom falls silent.

Head lowered as much as the collar allows, he gazes into the dull grey haze that surrounds him and becomes lost in it.

Quivering with the sustained effort, his nervous energy surges upwards and gathers in his throat. How long would he have to wait for her? He is no stranger to pain, but this torment is new. She is there, out of reach, and she is concerned with what happens to him.

Aching aeons have passed since he last heard her voice and he longs for the sweet touch of it. He imagines her coming to him, rewarding him with a single kind word. His jaw strains with concentration, rosy lips parted to focus on the simple act of breathing, keeping him focused on his goal.

He wants to be useful to her, to prove that he can do what is needed of him. If he doesn't then she will leave him, and he cannot bear to be alone again. His brow furrows and he drags a clenched fist over his forehead, as if he could erase the thought by force.

An abrasive screech travels across the room, the sound of stone grinding against metal. Fresh air breathes into his quarters from the newly emerged doorway in front of him. A concealed panel has retracted, revealing a corridor out of reach from where he kneels. Decisive footsteps approach, sharp as gunshots in the silence of the surroundings. They stop short just in front of him and he extends his head towards her like he is seeking sunlight.

She stands with perfect posture, her slender neck elevated above straight-set shoulders. Soft curls of auburn hair settle on her collarbones. Her dark eyes pierce his thoughts.

"Pathetic creature," she says, and her voice sounds like the one inside his head.

He looks up at her through the shield of his eyelashes, feeling impossibly small under her icy gaze. He does not dare to respond.

"You moved from position. That leaves me with no other choice; the test is terminated."

Confusion builds to panic. He opens his mouth to deny, to defend himself, but she does not permit him a voice.

"Stand."

He rises to his feet, eager to recover from his mistake and repair the damage he has caused. He knows he always does this, he is always a disappointment. Memory projects a showreel, replaying highlights of all the times he has been made to feel less than, othered. His mind is not a safe space, and in a clenching wave of sickness, he understands that pain will always find its way to him.

Daniel shuts his eyes, retreating within himself to avoid her scrutiny.

She is close enough to touch him, and a metallic click echoes in his left ear as she activates part of the collar. He keeps his eyes tightly shut, fearful of the harm she could cause. A familiar hot flush returns, the needle tattooing pain onto his delicate flesh. His veins burn and he clamps his jaw tight, trapping the moan that rushes to escape him.

"There, that should do. I have manually adjusted your dosage and expect to see better results."

"Yes," he says, in barely a whisper.

"What was that?" she says sharply. "Look at me while you speak."

Daniel does as he is told and opens his eyes. She graces him with a cold, vampiric smile, teeth bared through her blood-red lips. He is taller than her, but she still manages to look down on him. He falls silent under her gaze. She notes his lack of response and moves towards the inner door panel, pressing buttons like dots of Morse code.

"Very well. We shall proceed with the next phase."

The sound of metal scraping against metal fills the room, setting his teeth on edge. Daniel clenches his jaw tighter against the discomfort of it.

Walking towards the open corridor, she addresses him over her shoulder.

"Take your place under the shower and kneel. You will not move from your position. Remember that everything you do here is monitored, and your compliance is vital."

She exits from his chamber and the door slides back into place as if it had never existed. Everything is moving so quickly and he does not want to fail, he cannot fail this time. He stretches his lean limbs as he moves mindlessly towards the shower area, flinching as he recalls the pounding cold of the water drumming onto his skin, into his mind.

She has modified this corner of his quarters, raising up rows of small metal studs from the base of the shower area in a uniform grid. Bracing for impact, he falls to his knees as commanded, and shooting pain from the studs burrows into his knees, his shins, the tops of his feet. It harmonises with the stinging glow of his neck and he is painfully aware of his body, how it aches, how it betrays him. He deserves this, of course, and now he must atone.

Shifting his body weight back and forth, he cannot find a place of comfort. He steadies himself and tries to welcome the pain. He kneels, back straight and palms placed lightly on his lap. His muscles burn in unison and the hurt pounds through to his bones. He can succeed, all he has to do is focus on the relaxation offered by the dose. Calm peace drifts into his mind and he thinks of her, watching him closely.

Time has slowed and the still air around him fills with the dull hum of blood rushing through his veins. Sweat beads at his pulse points coating him with damp, sticky heat, but his breathing remains steady and relaxed, just like she said it would. He is in tune with this place now, he knows what he has to do to survive and he will do whatever it takes to get through this.

Static crackles and his hopes are lifted by her words.

"Final dose administered."

Heat pools under the collar as the needle breaks his skin for the last time. His chest swells with gratitude, and a smile brushes his lips, softening the skin around his eyes and making him look younger in this moment. It's nearly over. He has done well this time.

The studs retract into the floor with a sound like knives being sharpened, and he cries out in relief. Blood rushes to fill the indentations, making angry red marks that will stain his delicate complexion with bruises. He stays kneeling, unsure if his legs would hold him if he attempted movement. He waits for her instructions, eager to complete his final task.

Light streams down around him, marking out the confines of the shower area. He flinches, shuddering with the unease of anticipation. He wishes she would tell him what to do, he is helpless now without her instructions.

As if she can sense his need, she speaks again.

"Remain in the shower area, Daniel. You may move freely but do not leave the light."

Daniel's legs shake erratically as the joints strain to extend, his range of movement restricted by the kneeling position he has held for so long that it has altered his physical form. He staggers upwards on unsteady feet, arms reaching out for balance. He moans softly, the pain transforming with every new movement. His upper body hangs limply forward and his legs tremble beneath him.

"Good, Daniel. Notice the relaxation returning to your body. The final dose is giving you an innate sense of calm, allowing you to comply easily with all commands. Your reactions will be monitored. Procedure initiated."

His lungs fill and expand as he holds onto his breath, tensing in expectation of the falling water. He sighs out deeply as the cold drops embrace his skin. The water washes away his concerns, leaving him clean and renewed. His pale skin gleams as the freezing temperature drains it of colour, bright white in contrast to the rest of the grey room. He raises his fingers and works them into his scalp, kneading pressure points and feeling the tension dissolve, melting away and running down the drain, carried along with the water.

Daniel slowly becomes aware of a change in the atmosphere, the droplets becoming warmer now, creating a light mist that diffuses the room around him and softens its hard edges. He revels in the sensations, turning to face the wall and slipping into bliss as the pounding heat massages his back. He offers silent words of thanks that he is spared from the torture of before, grateful for the warmth and the ease that it brings to his body.

Luxuriating in the gift of warmth, he dreams of her sharing this space with him. Imagines soap suds bursting from a porous sponge and spilling over his muscles as she lifts it to wash his back, arms, chest, washing away his sins. Scrubbing the delicate parts of his body, touching the tender parts of his soul. Ignoring the pains inflicted on him throughout the day's procedures, he aches only for her.

Heat rises and the temperature of the water increases, falling from above in a rain of fire. He cannot see beyond the blur of steam, blinded by the light in which he must remain. He rakes at his skin with his blunt fingernails, desperately needing to soothe the burn but only increasing the searing agony. Mouth gaping, he gulps at the dense air and heat penetrates his airways, lungs filling with dissatisfaction.

Unable to bear the layered misery, Daniel collapses to the floor in a crumpled heap, his saturated clothes clinging like wet bandages to open wounds. Laying on one side he draws his dappled knees to his chest and tucks his arms around them, shifting into a primal gesture of protection. Water splashes up from puddles on the floor and lands on his face, marking him as blood rushes to the surface.

Darkness descends as he closes his eyes and thinks of her. Thoughts of her cool touch and the low tone of her voice soothe him. He remembers her words and repeats them to himself, lips moving gently. He considers raising his voice and begging for release but thinks better of it. He can prove himself to her if he just holds on.

Violent red streaks are visible on his skin and shine through his clothing, turned transparent in the unrelenting downpour. He dimly wishes that he could tear the fabric from him and scrape his skin raw until there is no feeling left. He steels himself and waits for the pain to end, challenging himself to remove the sound from his cries as he empties hot tears into the drain.

The water finally ceases and he breathes heavily, panting in the suffocating steam. He remembers the gunshot sounds of her heels clicking towards him and a mirage forms through the clouds. She stares coldly down at him and spits out her words.

"Clean yourself up."

She drops a towel to the floor, and it lands next to him in a hushed thud.

He gropes for the towel and holds it to his chest, shaking gently as his body struggles to process the conditions it has been subjected to. His mind floods with so many emotions that he cannot choose one, he feels them all at once.

The steam is slowly extracted and his haze clears. He dabs at himself with the towel, drying himself roughly in haste to get the job done. He looks up at her and realises, stupidly, that he is still on the floor. He pleads with his eyes, not knowing what is next, not knowing what he wants. Knowing that she will provide for him, he looks to her for absolution.

Blinking slowly, she moves her eyes towards the bed frame. His heart lurches and a blush deepens on his already reddened face. He shifts nervously, unable to still his fidgeting in the endless moments until her next instruction is delivered.

She points one perfectly manicured fingernail towards a small stack of neatly folded clothing at the foot of the bed.

"Get dressed for dinner, and follow me when you are done."

She doesn't look at him as she strides towards the door panel. It clicks open and she enters the adjoining chamber, leaving him alone in his quarters. He mourns her departure but is thankful to be spared the indignity of changing in front of her. Her kindness is a blessing he does not deserve.

Shedding the dishevelled clothes, he runs his hands over the stretched and soaking fabric, marked with his sweat and tears. They are so far changed from their original state after all that they have endured. He cringes as he imagines his own ruined appearance. The records of his treatment are documented in the marks on his skin and the messy knots of his hair. His pale eyes shimmer with hopeful tears, yearning for salvation.

Putting on the clean clothes presents a new challenge; they rub against his sore skin and the raw ache makes him groan out loud. They are copies of his earlier clothes but fresh and new, the softness causing tears to spill once more as he revels in the gentle pressure that hugs his battered body. He lightly pats his hands over the creases from where the clothes had been folded earlier, lingering a while longer to gather his courage before he follows her into the next room. He decides he can wait no longer, his need to see her overriding his fear of being seen. He wants her to see him, to have her notice all he has been through to please her.

He treads lightly into the adjoining chamber, having learned to move quietly despite his size. She stands in front of the mirror, and he freezes in place as their eyes meet and she coolly assesses him. His heart beats heavily, shifting his centre of gravity higher as it rises to meet the heaving pulse within. Her proximity has him flustered but soothed, a confusing predicament.

She indicates with a fluid hand gesture that he should be seated, and he crosses to the chair. He sinks into it, receiving its support like a lifeline. Delicate scents waft up from the tabletop and he casts his eyes downwards. A stacked plate identical to his earlier meal, but almost double in size, awaits him.

Her voice reaches out, gently encouraging him.

"Eat, Daniel."

He eats, chewing the food mechanically. His throat presses against the collar with every swallow, so he takes it in tiny bites to lessen the pressure. As the meal progresses, his shattered nerves mesh back together. He can feel the nourishment being carried into his cells, working to repair the damage he has endured.

She watches him and he keeps his eyes cast downwards, focusing only on the plate and the task at hand. She has provided him with this meal and he is keen to savour every mouthful. Before today, he cannot recall the last time anyone prepared him a meal, and sadness washes over him at the memory of his home life. A tear falls, distorting the angle of his cheekbone.

"You suffer beautifully," she whispers. "It has been my pleasure to observe you."

He shrinks away from the compliment, unsure of how to react or if he should dare to speak at all. She did not request a response, so he gives none.

"You should know that the procedures are over now. All that follows from here is standard duty of care, to ensure that you are fit to be released."

He has paused to listen to her, and on noticing that he has stopped eating, she gently chides him.

"I told you to eat, Subject. Do not disappoint me now."

His eyes widen as he shovels the remaining food into his mouth in heaped mounds, forcing himself to keep going even though every bite takes him closer to the end. He cannot bear it. The spork drops to the floor with a tiny clatter, and he shakes with frustration. He shoves his trembling hands into fists and tucks them tightly against his chest, to still the motion and suppress the panic that is starting to rise.

"I see you are done," she says. "So be it. Stay there."

She walks to stand behind him and he peeks up to look in the mirror, wanting to see her and using the room to his advantage. Their reflected eyes meet and without breaking eye contact she lifts her hands with elegant precision. There is a metallic click, and in one single movement she withdraws the collar from around his neck.

He feels naked now, afraid and exposed without the constant contact on his throat. The air feels too cold and his head floats above the rest of him, lighter without the added weight. Daniel heaves a small sob from the pit of his chest, alone and uncertain without her guidance. Of course, the two were linked. The collar and the waves of relaxation provided by the doses. The commands and his willingness to follow. He was blank and empty once again, with no idea what to do next.

He breaks. Risking her displeasure, he quietly begs.

"Please don't make me leave."

"I must let all my subjects leave, Daniel. It is part of the process."

"I can't leave you. Please, please let me stay."

Hot, silent tears fall to the ground, punctuating his words. He raises his eyes to look up at her reflection in the mirror, praying that she will see the truth he is offering. He cannot leave her.

He watches fearfully, searching for an answer that doesn't come. She is immovable, solid, infinite before him.

Anguish tears through him, and he yearns for the calm relaxation of another dose. Closing his eyes, he sags out of the chair and falls on his brutalised knees beside her. He opens his mouth to speak again, only capable of uttering a single word.

"Please."

An eternity passes, yet she is not moved. He senses her still beside him and gathers strength from her patience.

"Please," he begs again.

"Tell me what you want, Subject," she says, in a jagged voice that does not match her usual poise.

"I want to stay. Please. Here. With you."

The words come tumbling out and he knows he has not said the right things. He should be telling her how perfect she is, and how he wishes to be like her, and how if he cannot be like her then just being near her would be enough to satisfy him.

He gasps as her hand connects with his jaw, a hint of movement lifting his chin so he is forced to look right at her. Her eyes burn through him, and he thinks that he could disappear if she stops looking at him. The way she watches him makes him feel alive, whole, purposeful.

Her pupils flicker and something in her softens. She loosens her grip and speaks gently to him.

"Do you understand what you are asking for?"

She stares at him expectantly, waiting for an answer but he doesn't have words, only feelings. He nods in eager response.

"Use your words, Daniel."

"Yes," he says, as that is all he can say. He will always say yes to her, will agree to whatever she wants so long as she wants him.

She moves away from him and he cannot bear it. He has lost her, and he has lost himself. He has nothing left, there is nothing he can give to her. He detaches from the pain as every part of him sinks into the ground. Subtle sounds bounce around the room, but he cannot focus on them. He cannot focus on existence without her.

His hair hangs over his face, tickling his ear and pulling at his scalp. He looks up, always up, at her. She is clutching his hair in her fist, pulling it away from his neck and inspecting the area that was previously covered by the collar. Her other hand gently strokes the tender flesh there and he melts inside, all of his thoughts floating away.

She tugs at his hair, pulling him towards her slightly and he manoeuvres his body to follow her movements obediently.

"Do you remember your procedures from earlier?" she asks.

He nods in acknowledgement, then remembers his words.

"Yes."

"You remember that they were initiated after each dose that you were given? And how the doses removed your inhibitions, leaving you calm and relaxed, ready to comply with my instructions?"

"Yes," he repeats, recalling the sense of calm that flooded through him, just as she said it would do.

"There was no dose," she says, and smirks cruelly, dropping her hold on him. "You were my control group, Daniel. Your dose was a placebo."

Confusion spins his memories into scrambled puzzle pieces. But he remembers the doses, remembers the calm, remembers the instructions. It had worked, hadn't it?

"It was all the power of suggestion. You had complete free will, just as you do now. You could have left at any time, but you stayed. You didn't even look at the door panel although you could have used it at any point. Your freedom was always within reach, and you didn't take it. Why is that?"

"I wanted to make you happy," he says. His voice is small, and he thinks she has not heard him.

"Come here," she says, and beckons for him to move towards her. Of course, he follows her command, it feels natural to do so.

She dangles an object from one hand, teasingly out of reach. The tangy metallic scent spreads towards him, so strong he can taste it, as she brings it closer.

"Is this what you want?", she asks, dangling the collar in front of him.

His eyes widen and he whispers the only word he remembers now.

"Yes."

She places the collar back around his neck, where it belongs. She fixes it into place, the seam becoming invisible once it is closed. With one hand she reaches for the small loop on the front and hooks a finger through it, raising him up.

"Welcome home, Daniel."

His body melts against hers, and she supports him, holding his head in her hands and lightly combing her fingers through his hair. He belongs to her. The broken parts of him clash against each other and she holds them steady. Eventually they will weld together, bonded stronger where they have mended.

About the Author

KL Massey resides in the beautiful city of Nottingham, England. Specialising in weird fiction, she crafts surreal and sensual short stories infused with deep emotions, mundane terrors, and layers of symbolism.

Nameless Tune

Kras Nebula

CW: Nonconsensual drug use, restraints

Whumpee: Man, Whumper: Unknown, Caretaker: N/A

He's strapped down. It's one of the few real things he can comprehend, despite the way reality seems to shift and shimmer around him. His brain wants to ooze its way protectively out of his skull. There's an IV this time— his thoughts are foggy, but he *knows* this isn't the first time— and every time he looks at the machines and tubes his eyesight melts and he wants to shudder out of existence. He feels raw, cut open, somewhere between a pinned butterfly and a slab of meat, and whatever they are putting in him **burns**.

Someone hums just out of sight as he tries to breathe— large, ragged gasps through his mouth, his eyes desperately closed. He doesn't know the song. Someone touches his shoulder.

"Shh," they say in response to his quiet, choked whimpers. "You're doing *so* good." The hand moves up to his brow, and he has a sudden, *violent* fantasy of biting it off. "It will be done soon."

A sudden pulse of pain has his eyes flying open, scream clenched between teeth, and the person murmurs encouragement and it's *too much*.

He can't move his head but he *can* move his eyes and he *can* move his jaw enough to croak out "H... help. Help me. *Help me.*" Over and over again until he's *screaming* it, begging the person with the kind hand and voice to *help him*—

"Increase the sedative," the person orders.

His world melts into a sensory kaleidoscope, and he's lost.

About the Author

Kras Nebula is a little guy who's been writing things since they were even smaller than they are now. These days they primarily write science fantasy and westerns and specifically science-fantasy westerns, as well as doing art professionally for a variety of projects.

Breath of Life

Mill Cohen

Abel clawed at his unbreathing throat, as if that would do anything to help. Not a whine escaped, the flesh of his trachea fused solidly shut, lungs screaming for air. The stupid things didn't know he was dead.

After a few minutes of this, he pounded at the wall in frustration and picked up the broom. At least Soe wasn't home today, and he could express his despair without her breathing down his neck. Must be nice.

Tears pricking at his eyes, he made as quick work of the laboratory as he was able. Soe was right, as much as he hated to admit it: he didn't *need* the air, at least not physically. He moved as well as he did in life, flesh itching at just the beginning stages of decay. Soe was going to have to top him up. At least she didn't tend to mess around when it came to that. If she let him go too far, she wouldn't have her slave anymore, after all.

His lungs burned. His grip on the broom tightened. He kept working.

When the floor and counters were clean and the potions and herbs were organized, when the very table he'd been brought to life on was cleaned of the ghastly remains of Soe's recent experiments—all of it a Sisyphean task considering how messy she left the lab every time she worked—Abel sat in the corner and waited.

He used to have other wants. He used to dream of freedom, of escape. After that dream had been crushed by flesh only Soe could stop from rotting, he'd moved on to craving some sort of dignity. Things to call his own, ways to entertain himself when his work was done, a necromancer who treated him like a *person* rather than animated meat. And after that still, when all hope had been taken from him, he'd yearned to return to the quiet, peaceful death he'd been stolen from.

He'd been denied it all and more.

Abel couldn't muster up the energy to care about such things anymore. Not with the entirety of his confused, half-alive body wailing for air he could never reach. It surrounded him, he could wave a hand through it and feel it brushing against his fingers. He could even walk outside if he wanted to, feel the wind on his skin—Soe didn't bother to lock the windows anymore. There was no point.

It wasn't long before Soe's key turned in the front door. Abel perked up like a trained dog greeting its master, hating himself for it, but he couldn't help it.

Soe sighed as she dropped her bag by the door. It was *torture*, hearing her breathe so freely, like she was flaunting it.

Abel sat quietly and waited.

"Oh, lovely. The lab looks perfect," she praised. "Just a moment and I'll give you your treat."

He couldn't respond. If even breathing was beyond his grasp, he couldn't hope to speak. Besides, he knew what was expected of him by now. No matter how desperate he was, bothering her would at best get him reprimanded, and at worst get his reward taken from him.

Abel sat quietly and waited as Soe put her things away, all the ingredients she'd bought at the market. He sat and waited as she went to her room to change clothing. He sat quietly and waited still as she started dinner he couldn't eat, chest twitching, fists clenched. At least he didn't get hungry in unlife.

Once the pot was left to boil, Soe deigned to come crouch by where he sat. "You did so well," she praised, her soft, warm hand coasting over his clammy cheek. "Good boy."

He grimaced at the praise, all of it. The *doing well* was almost worse than the *good boy*. He'd reduced himself to nothing but her servant, not even fighting anymore.

"Don't make a face," Soe scolded.

Abel didn't even need to try, the expression replaced instantly with fear. He'd done *everything* right. He couldn't get it taken away at the last moment.

"That's better!" Soe patted his cheek. "Alright, alright, here you are."

She breathed out, a long, deep exhale that felt icier than it should, and by the time she was done, Abel's throat had opened once more.

He gasped, sweet air rushing into neglected lungs, every breath taken like it was the last he'd ever be allowed. He couldn't get it in him fast enough, almost choking in his rush to get as much of it as quickly as possible.

"There you go," Soe murmured, petting his hair. He didn't even care. All that mattered was that he could *breathe,* the relief flowing through every cell he had.

Once Abel finally had enough that his breath was stable, *in out in out in out,* the endless need quenched, he spoke.

"Please," he rasped, "Please just let me keep it. I'll keep doing well, you won't even notice a change. I'll be better with it."

"We've been over this. You don't need it," Soe reminded him, like it was nothing. Like it wasn't *air*. "You do just fine without it, I've been very pleased. This is the only way for you to be good, remember?"

"I just need another chance!" Abel insisted. "You win! I'll do whatever you want, please just let me *breathe.*"

"You're breathing right now," she said simply. "I think things are fine just the way they are. Now sit quietly and enjoy your reward." With a final ruffle of his hair, Soe got up and went back to preparing her dinner.

Abel shut it. He knew that was it for tonight, that if he kept pushing, all he would get would be his time cut short. He closed his eyes and enjoyed his reward as instructed, focusing on the rise and fall, the way he could pull as much into his lungs as he wanted. It was heaven. It was *bliss*.

It couldn't have been more than thirty minutes before he felt a tap at his shoulder.

Abel opened his eyes, his dreaded necromancer standing before him. He hadn't realized he'd been crying.

"One hour?" he begged.

Soe sighed. "I'm busy tonight, I can't be keeping track of whether I've left your air on or not."

"You could just leave it on." Abel's voice was quiet now, none of that defiance left in him. He cowered back against the wall like a scared child.

Soe gave him a look that could have been pity on anyone else. "Are you ready?"

"No," he sobbed. His breaths picked up then, the final ones, the ones he knew would have to last him the night. Every breath was a great and powerful thing, rushing in–

With a quick pinch of her fingers that didn't even touch him, Soe manipulated his flesh as though it were clay in her hands. It was as if his trachea had disappeared entirely, and though he tried to get one last breath, nothing came through.

No, no, no! Abel clawed at his throat once more, mouth wide open and ready to gasp, if only it could.

"Oh, stop that, you act like you're alive," Soe chastised. "You'll have more tomorrow."

About the Author

Mill Cohen is a New York-based whump writer who explores the horrors a person can face when immortality is on the table.

Pristine

Ryan Breadinc

CW: An abstract kind of self harm

Whumpee: Man, Whumper: Woman, Caretaker: Woman

The tiles are white.

Jonas lays upon them in a tangle of limbs, unwilling to unfold himself from the uncomfortable position he's slept in just to see more of them. He knows they've already cleaned everything while he was unconscious. It's likely that his spare sock is gone too. A shame – it had little red squirrels on it. He likes the little red squirrels.

And now they've been replaced with white, like everything is in here.

The pristine tiles make his head ache.

"Forty-Seven? You awake?"

He doesn't answer. Answering would mean getting up, would mean acknowledging the white tiles, would mean acknowledging the bone-white lab coat and pale, spotless form standing somewhere behind him. Her hair is the same white as the tiles – perhaps she *is* part of the tiles, in some abstract way.

"Do you require food?"

Jonas doesn't respond. She sighs, a faint rustling coming from her position. He could guess at what she is doing (pressing her hand to her forehead in exasperation, or pulling out her phone to inform the guards that he's being uncooperative again) but he doesn't care enough to try. He's tired. Spent. But instead of the guards or food or even her leaving, she lingers silently. He'd hear it if she left, so she must still be there.

But what is the point?

"What do you need, Forty-Seven?"

Interesting question.

"The tiles," he croaks.

"The tiles?"

"Make them red."

A beat of silence, and then, "The next durability experiment isn't for a week."

"Yes."

"...this is really what you want?"

"Please," he manages. Anything to make the *clean* go away. Pain is nothing. Pain is an old friend with gnarled hands and a kind smile, with a different story to tell each time they meet. *Clean* is eternally unchanging, unmoving, ice-cold and burning.

"Very well," she says after a lengthy silence, and he hears the scalpel.

About the Author

Ryan Breadinc is a Western Australian author of odd little stories, both comic and prose. Find him on his website () or on Twitter(@breadincbooks)!

Rainbow Rock

Devin Oldham

CW: Body horror, eye whump, parasite
Whumpee: Man, Whumper: Woman, Caretaker: Woman

Part 1

The apartment was located in what Jack's dad used to call "junky isle", a towering block of four buildings flanking a small park called "Rainbow Rock".

Jack pulled his car into the mostly empty lot; he was greeted by a sculpture in the courtyard. The installation was a set of differently sized arches crossing over one another, they were rusty red but Jack vaguely remembered a time when they had been painted as a rainbow. Though worn and unwelcoming it stood in the center of the park like a bizarre monument to curved steel; an unintended reflection of the state of the buildings themselves.

Jack returned his eyes to the towers ahead and followed the hundreds of tiny windows towards the overcast sky. He produced a hastily scrawled address from his pocket and headed towards the second building next to where he had parked.

He crossed the lot and instinctively skirted the tiny park.

The entrance to the complex was a set of double doors, one of which was covered in plywood, the other smeared with some kind of yellowish grease. He could see inside neither.

He considered pressing his cupped hands against the cloudy glass, but opted to simply pull open the door. He'd be entering the building no matter what; Jack was out of options.

Inside the entry gave way to a musty, reeking hall. Decades of wallpaper peeled from centuries of paint, revealing the rotting wood and stained stone Jack assumed to be original to the structure. Even the brick looked decayed, like tightly packed sand, ready to crumble.

The hallway led to an elevator. Jack pressed the button to go up. It was sticky and he quickly withdrew his finger once the light turned on. He tried to wipe the residue on his thick wool sweater, but pulling his finger across the fabric only gathered an equally disgusting layer of fur.

"This better be worth it," he said to himself as the descending light stopped on the "G".

When the metal box's doors screeched open, Jack stepped inside. He was still vigorously rubbing his sticky finger on his sweater when the door chimed closed. The dissonance of the bell filled Jack with foreboding. The building, though empty, had an attitude he did not like. As if on cue, the neon light inside the cramped box flickered.

The smell inside the tight car was a mixture of human sweat and gasoline. It tingled the hairs in Jack's nose. He felt a bit dizzy, and swooned briefly.

Instinctively he covered his mouth realizing in horror that he had smeared some of the sticky substance from his finger onto his upper lip. He frantically wiped at his face with his clean hand, coughing with disgust.

"You sick too?" A voice crooned from the corner.

The smell made a lot more sense to Jack when he turned and saw the hunched old woman.

Between heavy breaths she inhaled from a plastic shopping bag; it left a green ring around the remaining skin of her protruding jaw.

"Excuse me?" Jack asked, unable to reconcile the words with the strange speaker.

The woman hobbled forward. The scent caused Jack to feel high again, like someone forcing him to sniff a dozen Sharpies.

She passed Jack, reaching for the button pad. For every floor the corresponding button had been pried off. All except floor seven.

The button to floor seven was pristine. It glowed with a brilliant yellow shine. Maybe it was the fumes, but Jack thought it beautiful, serene even.

"Do you hear it humming?" The woman asked, as her elongated nail pushed into the plastic.

The elevator swayed, and the slight G-force of its upward movement made Jack want to hurl.

During its lumbering ascent, the woman approached Jack and placed her hand upon the left side of his stomach.

"You can feel it?" Jack asked.

"She's a big one."

The lump under Jack's skin seemed to respond positively to the lady's touch. She had a glow about her too, a serenity: her own "button-ness".

She was the first person other than Jack to ever see the lump. No doctors could find it. Anytime Jack would see a specialist, there would be nothing to show. Even a half-dozen ultrasounds revealed nothing. It was as if the lump swam through Jack's body like a creature beneath a murky lagoon; knowing when to surface, and when to hide.

The woman tickled the lump from over Jack's shirt. It bristled. She slid her nail up, and to Jack's amazement and horror, the lump moved slightly, following the gnarled finger.

"She wants to get all the way, up there, to her home."

Jack stepped back. This was insane. He hadn't come to junky isle to be felt up by some gassed-up granny.

"Mine died in eighty-eight," the lady said, staring forlornly at Jack's own protrusion. "But it brought me here too, like the rest."

Suddenly the elevator shook to a halt and Jack was more than ready to get off. But the woman blocked his way.

She lowered her shirt collar, revealing a gnarled collarbone, and just above her left breast was a gaping hole. A pink and wet tunnel bore into delicate flesh.

"This is all that's left," she continued, now sobbing madly.

Jack tried to pass her but as he moved to one side she matched him.

"Look at it!" The woman screamed.

The cavity of scar tissue undulated, the inner meat constricting and relaxing.

Jack reeled backwards and finally threw up when he saw a white, withered slug-like thing squeeze itself from the hole.

It plopped to the grimy elevator floor and wriggled in a puddle of stringy slime.

Jack wiped his mouth of remaining vomit and barreled past the woman. He knocked her over and she hit the floor with an enormous thud.

Jack thought of her falling directly on top of the emaciated slug, splattering it, but his fear and revulsion overrode the concern. The doors closed and chimed a pathetic ding that rang tired through the musty hallway. He spit a final chunk of puke onto the carpeted floor and went on. He was alone, on floor seven.

Part 2

Jack lifted his shirt and checked on the lump. "What the fuck is inside there?"

He pushed a finger delicately into the mass, and felt it swim beneath the pressure.

It was born on his foot. He had come home from a two-day camping trip and spotted what looked like a tiny animal bite on the bottom of his sole.

After a few days he couldn't walk; he felt like he had an acorn in the bottom of his shoe.

Eventually it traveled upwards, growing in size. For nearly a month it lived on his left thigh. Jack refused to go to a doctor, afraid it was cancer.

Finally, one night the thing started to pulsate and a severe pain shot through his entire leg and into his spine, stiffening his back. He broke down and went to the emergency room, that was the first doctor to tell him that his lump simply wasn't.

Four doctors later, and Jack is here. In the Rainbow Rock apartments. Seeking the help of two home surgeons. "Experts" in illegal body modifications. The only people he could find that may be willing to dig around in there until they find something.

He walked to apartment seven thirty-four and knocked. He was shaking, panicked by the already fading thought of the woman in the elevator. It was so distant, like he had watched it happen in a movie, but the adrenaline wasn't forgetting as fast.

The door creaked open and a single eye peered beyond the chain lock.

"I'm here to see," Jack pulled out the crumpled paper upon which he had scrawled the doctor's name, "Spewn?"

The door shut, and Jack heard it unlock. When it opened the second time, he saw that the bachelor apartment had been emptied of all furniture, save for a solitary dentist's chair in the center of the room.

The man who let him in was in his sixties. He had long sweaty gray hair that stuck to his pallid skin. He wore tiny round sunglasses despite the dimness of the space.

It took Jack a second look at the man's face to see that he had a disced bottom lip, like something from a National Geographic documentary. It was red, probably infected and the skin there was purulent.

The guy stepped to the side and gestured for Jack to enter.

If the old woman in the elevator imparted a type of serenity to the lump, this couple did the opposite. Jack could feel little friend retract somewhere deep inside of himself. He instinctively felt for it, and as usual, it was gone. This trip had been an especially grotesque waste of time. They would simply refuse to operate on him.

Just then a woman came out from the bathroom area of the apartment. It had been sealed off with plastic and Jack saw that beyond the transparent sheet it actually looked relatively clean. She wore a surgical mask and Scooby-Doo scrubs.

She was remarkably normal looking. Except for what peaked out from her shoulder length black curls: tapered ears, sewed to look like those of a cat.

She spoke through the mask, her tone of voice and the way she carried herself made her out to be a doctor. Or at least, once a doctor.

"You don't look like you need your septum stretched, or ears clipped," she said on her way over to the tall hippy.

She placed a hand on the guy's shoulder and he gently closed the door, relocking the chain.

"Have a seat," she pointed to the dentist's chair.

Jack felt a vulnerability wash over him. She projected an authority that he'd attribute to any other health-professional.

"Are you Spewn?" Jack asked.

"That's what I am called here, and this is Brocca." She leaned against the curtained window, facing the chair. "So if you don't need cat ears or a nose ring than why the fuck are you here?"

"I have...a lump," Jack responded.

"Then go see a real doctor."

"It...well...I." Jack was struggling. "This was a bad idea," he said as he started rising from the seat.

"It moves?" She asked.

Jack stared at her in shock. He slowly lowered himself back into the chair.

"Where was the last place you saw it?"

Jack lifted his shirt and pointed to the left side of his stomach.

The woman placed her soft hand on Jack's bare skin. It felt nice to finally have someone believe him. And she was graceful, practiced, like a lump whisperer.

She rose from her crouch and spoke to Brocca in a language foreign to Jack. The man entered beyond the plastic curtain and returned with a box.

He placed it down on the surgical table next to Jack's chair.

Inside the box Jack saw many objects, none of which appeared particularly medical. A leather bound book, some rings and necklaces, all of it old, some ancient.

She dug through the bobbles for a moment and pulled out a chain, at the end of it hung a jagged symbol. It resembles a swastika, but the arms had their own set of arms. In the center of the shape, a triangle had been cut from the metal.

Spewn opened the curtains and the entire apartment was bathed in diffused sunlight. Brocca reeled back and instinctively removed his sunglasses. The doctor crouched back down, her face intimately close to Jack's now exposed stomach. Her head was low and Jack could see the courtyard beyond the window. He noticed the tops of the arches belonging to the rainbow sculpture, a constant reminder of where he was, and how he had gotten there.

The doctor, if she was one, pushed the metal sigil into where Jack had pointed. His soft, delicate skin protruded out from the triangle. "What are you doing?" He asked.

Spewn responded by pushing harder.

"Look, this is not what..." Jack began, but quickly closed his mouth.

The lump was moving. He felt it being forced out from somewhere around his spine. It almost felt like he could see what it saw. A liver or some other organ, blood, all the softness inside a person that is meant to remain within. But mostly he felt the lump's reluctance.

It was being drawn to the surface. "That's the lump!" Jack yelled despite the intense pain. "What is it?"

Spewn signaled to Brocca, Jack couldn't see what new thing he was bringing her, but assumed it was some way to treat the infectious bump.

When she didn't answer Jack asked again, or at least tried. But before he could speak, Brocca had, from behind, wrapped one arm around Jack's throat, the other covered his mouth.

Jack tried to scream. The lump throbbed like a second heartbeat, it was afraid.

The chaos escalated. Everything seemed frantic and Jack could not muster the strength needed to kick out. He still felt dazed from the hotboxing in the elevator, and his peripheral was blackening.

When the lump made complete contact with the metal of the talisman, Spewn pressed hard enough to force it through the too small triangle. She pulled the talisman up and forced it to the center of Jack's chest. It was nothing like when the old woman had guided it. The pain this time was unbearable. When Jack struggled too much from the pain, Brocca bore down on him and increased the pressure of his headlock.

Jack's will abated as Spewn dragged the mass up.

He distantly felt the thing being carried up through his neck. Hot blood spilled from cracking skin as the triangle pulled the inflated skin up Jack's cheek.

The sigil passed over Jack's left eye and the lump was drawn behind it. The pressure of the foreign object inside the ocular cavity caused the eyeball to pop from its socket; it hung swaying.

Jack was awakened from his shock by a banging at the apartment door, accompanied by shrieks of terror.

"Don't let them kill her!"

Was it the old woman?

For a moment Brocca let go. Jack felt life surging back into him. The pain, mixed with the fear, sent forth a burst of adrenaline fueled vigor.

"No! Hold him still! It's almost there," Spewn said, her tone still that of a professional.

Through his one functional eye, Jack saw that above the window was affixed a wooden poppet. Its head was the skull of a blackbird. And upon its stomach had been carved the same symbol Spewn used to guide the lump.

Jack kicked out and connected his boot with the doctor's mid-section and she flew backwards.

Brocca ran back from the door, leaving the crazed woman wailing on the other side.

Spewn held out a hand. "It's done."

Jack sprung up from his seat and screamed. He felt for his dangling eye and as he cupped it in his palm he saw his own hand. His forehead pounded with immeasurable agony.

Still buzzing with terror, he dashed for the door.

Brocca stopped him like a wall and gently guided him back to the seat. He pressed down on Jack's shoulders, pinning him in place.

Spewn drew a scalpel and carved a line in Jack's forehead.

The lump looked out. Seeing the world for the first time. A birth, like all births, without consent.

Jack too saw through it. And he looked upon some sister world. The serenity had returned. It now permeated his entire being. He didn't just feel serene, he had entered some fabled nirvana described only by mystics.

He dropped his left eye, letting it dangle; he no longer needed it. He saw the truth behind reality. In the sister world the effigy of the crow was not of wood, but made of flesh and squawked with glee. He looked at doctor Spewn, she wriggled and hissed, like a cat. Brocca looked much the same, but through the lump's lens Jack saw that he was merely flesh, stitched together by a skilled hand and given life by some glowing force beneath the skin.

Finally Jack looked out from the window, and when he laid his eye upon the arches of Rainbow Rock, he saw they were no longer curved, but perfect rectangles. They stood tall against an ebon backdrop, radiating all colours. A testament to their name. The sky hung low enough to greet them in the black horizon. And the starless sky drooped low enough to touch.

Jack extended a hand towards the new beauty before him laughing, and the lump, the slug, fat and healthy laughed along.

About the Author

Devin is a Canadian author who focuses on rural and small-town cosmic horror.

Cycle-stys of Despair

Nemesis

Castys thought endless torment as an immortal test subject would be a little more *exciting*. Not that he'd expected it to be fun, but it was just...boring. Every damn day was the same. They'd drag him out of his cell to the same room, strap him to the same table, cut him open with the same knives and take out the same organs. Well, no, the organs they took varied by the day. But he only had so many different ones, so at some point he'd experienced it all before. The tests, on the other hand, had a horrifically wide variety to them, but the common theme seemed to be Painful and Terrible and 0/10 Would Not Recommend.

He'd fantasize about being back on his pirate ship often to distract himself from everything. He'd imagine the sound of the waves, the feel of the spray in the wind, the smell of salt, his crew by his side...the thought of them made him happy and sad at the same time. He missed them all so much (except for Harris, he was a bitch), but the fact that he was here meant they were all safe and happy. Yeah, that was why he was stuck in this stupid place, those darned mortals and their tiny lifespans that he just had to get all sympathetic about and give himself up to these psychos so they didn't spend the rest of their little lives in misery. Instead, *he* was going to spend the rest of his much longer life stuck in-no, he was going to get out...somehow.

But how? He didn't have anything to pick the locks with. He was constantly restrained, either strapped to a table or chair in the lab or being manhandled from one room to the next by people who were ridiculously stronger than him. He'd tried to rush past the guards when they came to get him from his cell, but they caught him and chained his ankles together, making it nearly impossible for him to even walk. The short chain connecting his ankles and the muzzle they'd strapped to his face a couple weeks in were never taken off, just permanent additions to what it was like to be Castys. And if they took the muzzle off, it was just so they could mess with his mouth, and it went right back on afterwards, because why give food and water to someone who can't stay dead?

So it went. Castys started to forget what it was like to walk normally, to speak with other people, what it felt like to eat, to be touched in a way that didn't hurt, to be treated like a *person*. There was only the cycle of wake up, get dragged out, get sliced open, get poked and prodded and stabbed and studied, get dragged back, fall asleep and pray that tomorrow would be a little better, or even a little different. He could vaguely keep track of time by how blood-crusted his skin was, a way to tell how long it had been since the last time they'd hosed him down and chopped off his hair. The ship he dreamed of never went anywhere anymore, it was stuck, like him, because there was only here, wasn't there? Everything else was just a delusion. The boy had always been in a cage, the ship had always been in a bottle. The square of the sky he could see out the window was there to trick him into thinking there was something else out there, but he knew there wasn't. There was only here, and there was only the cycle.

The cycle, though, began to change, so slowly as to almost be imperceptible from one day to the next. Tests were a little shorter. Less organs were taken. They left him alone for a minute more. He hardly noticed it was happening until one day...they didn't come for him at all. At first he was alright with it, he preferred the loneliness and the quiet to the table and the pain. But not dying at their hands every day meant the condition of his body wasn't being reset constantly. Soon enough, hunger and thirst began to claw at him. Even if he had something to eat or drink, that muzzle was still stuck to his face, no matter how much he fiddled with it. Or maybe that was just a part of him, maybe he didn't have a mouth, and this was just his face.

Every three days. Thirst. Weakness. Dizziness. Death. Was it three days? Is that how long you could last without water? He tried to count, but the numbers got lost in the haze all too easily. There was no way to mark the stone, to keep track outside of his head, the blood wasn't being washed off him anymore. He had nothing, nothing at all, just here and himself and the unyielding stone. The square of sunlight would move across the cell, the only motion to break the constancy of everything else. It was the same day repeated over and over and over and over and over and it was the same just the same nothing ever changed, ever, ever, it was the same-

Something wasn't the same. The leather muzzle that had kept him silent for so long had been slowly rotting, and it finally fell off. For a moment he simply stared at it lying there on the ground, broken, dying, fading away. He opened his mouth for the first time in decades. And he screamed, because that *thing* got to rot away and disappear and he *wouldn't*, he would always be here, hungry and thirsty and alone and trapped and *alive* and it wasn't fair, not at all, and he screamed because it had been so long since he was able, he cried because it was all he could do.

The tears, at least, moistened his dry tongue.

He drew lines. Some were faint, and some were vivid. The vivid ones were good, they were brilliantly red, they tasted so sweet, they pulsed and burned like stars. He drew so, so many, and every one was new and different and brilliant. Little cracks in the never-ending cycle of monotonous agony. They let him feel for a moment like his thirst was quenched. The cracks widened, chunks broke off the sides, and then that constant feeling of hunger went away, too.

And so it went, drawing and sucking and biting and chewing in an attempt to satiate those cravings, but it was never enough, never enough, and he would wake up to unbroken skin, and the cycle could start all over again. Maybe he could have counted somehow, how many times it happened, but it didn't matter, there wasn't an end to count down to, there was just wake up and hurt and drink and scream just to hear *something* and wait for death so we can start again just wait just wait it's coming the ship is sinking in the little bottle but it always comes back up please just let me rest just let me *go* I can't do this again *I can't I can't-*

There was a new sound. A creak. Footsteps. They came back, old memories of something outside the cycle. There was someone-or was it some*thing*-standing on the other side of the bars. Its eyes were so white and empty, a color he hadn't seen in so long that he couldn't help but stare. It stared back, eyes narrowing and then widening.

"Castys?" He cocked his head. That sound, that word *meant* something, right? It did, it did, he was sure it did, but...what was it? And what...who was that? The more he looked, the more he was sure that there was something familiar about that silhouette. It was...distinct. Unmistakable. Unique. He didn't remember who it belonged to, just that he recognized it. It was a some*one*, yes, yes, not an it, not-an-it-or-I'll-tear-your-throat-out. So when they opened the door to his cell, when they came in, when they smiled at him, fangs flashing in the dim light, he wasn't afraid, even if he should have been.

"I finally found you."

About the Author

Nemesis, or Nemi, is the sadist your mom warned you about who enjoys the gorier, darker side of whump. She's a geologist by trade, though, and loves hiking, baking, and playing video games in her spare time.

A Song for Galatea

Vanessa Roades

CW: Consensual body modification

Whumpee: Woman, Whumper: Woman, Caretaker: Woman

Galatea isn't named after a hero in any traditional sense.

Not if the reader is looking for sword-wielding barbarians or battles of great wit. Orpheus and Heracles are better known for their travels to the Underworld, but what is Galatea besides an extended hand, a welcoming smile, to greet a mortal crawling from the brink?

Today, it's a young woman named Cassandra who Galatea brings back – back from the dark of the anesthetic haze, back from the fateful path she was once bound to. After the death of her inventor and his dreams for her, Galatea found that this role suited her best.

"How are you feeling, my dear?"

Cassandra blinks herself into the workshop; her brown eyes flick around the cozy operating room, landing on the table swept clean of tools, the framed harp strings on the wall by her bed, the display cases of polished flutes and oboes, and Galatea herself, smiling down at her.

"I don't – "

Cassandra grasps her throat like she's drowning, clutching at that aborted sentence. She shoots Galatea a panicked look.

"A little pain is perfectly natural. Now, how are you *feeling*?"

The pain never has any patience once the girls wake up. Tears spring onto Cassandra's lashes. Galatea can't feel pain, but she's gone to great lengths to ensure that her work has an easy recovery process. She wonders if humans are mostly brought to tears by the surprise of the pain, after so long in the dark.

Cassandra mimes holding a pen and scribbling.

"No, no, there is no need to write." Galatea sets her hand on Cassandra's. "Speak. It is the only way to make it better."

Cassandra scowls. Then she throws that expression aside, perhaps realizing that pouting at one's benefactor is not the best look for an aspiring ingénue.

She swallows haltingly and winces. Her fingertips tentatively explore the shape of her trachea beneath her pale skin, as if searching for the metal reed so carefully installed there.

Galatea says, "I put utmost care into ensuring that there is no change in the appearance of your throat. You could walk up to your own parents or an old sweetheart and they would not know the difference! Not until you spoke, at least."

It takes her a few false starts, tears sprinkling onto her cheeks from her rapid blinking, but finally Cassandra forces the words out: "Unfair. That it's ... so hard ... to h-hear ... myself."

"If you sing, then you will hear precisely what has changed." Galatea sits back from the surgery bed, giving her plenty of inviting space. "Sing for me, Cassandra."

Cassandra knows better than to argue – the job is already done and besides, with her throat the way it is, complaining will only hurt her more.

Breath scrapes through her larynx (it's bound to scrape, it's bound to hurt, that's the way it goes and what she was warned) as she takes a deep inhale. And then she sings.

How lovely!

Cassandra's voice was strong before (she sang at their first consultation so Galatea knew what to emphasize, what to trim away). Now the sound is worthy of being called *gorgeous*. Her voice has lost its rasp when pitching low; she soars effortlessly from note to note like a swallow.

Halfway through the folk ballad, a red bubble pops at the corner of her lips. More blood burbles forth. It draws bright candy stripes in the cracked lines of her lips.

On a sibilant note, tiny flecks of blood hit her hand. Cassandra chokes to a stop. She wipes her mouth, stares at the blood, and relents softly, "It doesn't … s-sound like me."

"*You* sound amazing. None of those big city fools will overlook you now."

"It hurts." She swallows blood and flinches. "Even speaking." She stares at her red-smeared hand. "What in hell did I *do*?"

They all know the risks of going under the knife, and still all of these girls are so surprised when they feel what the knife leaves behind. Worse hurts than cuts and stitches have led them here in the first place. Galatea will be patient – eventually, they all learn that this pain is worth never feeling rejected again.

"All of this is normal. The pain *and* the worry. I have seen this a hundred times." Galatea takes Cassandra's hand, covering it with her own metal one, showing her that the blood is no bother. "Continue to speak, continue to sing, and your body will understand that *this* is what you are. With all that plainness scraped away, here you are. Here *you* are."

***

May 19, 1927

AUTOMATED WOMAN AWES CONCERT CROWD

Arthur Corduroy's musical automaton stunned audiences with a surprise concert yesterday in Langley Gardens. The automaton is aptly named Galatea, after Greek mythology's statue brought to life for her desperate sculptor by the goddess of love. America's modern-day Pygmalion told the audience that she's almost entirely made of instruments and runs on complex clockwork to create a unique, personal orchestra. Each instrument has been precisely reconfigured to fit amongst each other, and to fit inside the form of such a beautiful, shapely young lady, sure to make the hearts of all the men sing and those of the women burn with envy.

***

For the first consultation appointment with Galatea, Cassandra arrived with her mother.

Her mother told Galatea all about the smoker snarl-rasp from a childhood full of coughing sickness, the pitchiness from her off-shaped septum that belonged to her father, and how the directors at the big city orchestra snubbed Cassandra because of them.

"She could train her whole life, but it wouldn't scrub away what she was born with," her mother moaned. "Fate's stacked against her!"

"I play the strings just grand," Cassandra had snapped, like that meant anything when she couldn't sing, the same way a caged bird could gleam and preen but not fly. "Doesn't that matter most when it's the *strings* I wanna play?"

And today Cassandra walked in, entirely alone, and pointed at Galatea's arm with its shiny silver strings in the soft skin and said, "That. Just give me that. It's all the same to me."

Now, here she is, waking up with a new violin installed in her arm.

It's too late for Galatea to be concerned. After all, she'd trusted the girl's intentions when explaining the procedure, when laying her down, when cutting her open. It's too late to wonder, *What changed? Did your mother sass you about your strings? Did another audition go badly? My poor, poor girl. This will prevent all of that from happening ever again.*

Galatea helps Cassandra drink some tea to wake and soothe her. She's careful to not nudge the wires that hook Cassandra into the lab equipment, convincing her body with pulse after pulse of electricity that the new instrument is a part of it and always has been.

'Fate's stacked against her!' is what her mother said. Galatea thinks of Pygmalion and how he was doomed to never have a proper woman, until he created someone perfect. Then he was doomed to never have her ... until power changed everything.

Galatea shows Cassandra her new arm. Work like this is *Galatea's* power. "The hollow needs some time to heal. The lining hides the most delicate parts from you, so please return and let me ensure that everything is progressing as it should." She takes Cassandra's hand and has her trace the inside of her left forearm. The lining is made of specially-treated oak and resin, a process unique to Galatea's innards and, now, Galatea's instruments.

"This is very important. Let me demonstrate." Galatea clicks open the compartment on the side of her own fiddle-forearm. She takes out the bow hidden inside. "Mine is made of wood, but yours is made of the majority of your radius bone, like we discussed. So you must be very careful while the bow is in use. Your arm is very delicate."

Cassandra copies Galatea's action with a flinch. Her bow is made of sinew and bone, carefully measured and carved for maximum ease of use, minimum obstruction to the fiddle body itself, and negotiable effects on her arm's stability in daily use.

"We will play together," Galatea says. "We will hear your first true song."

Galatea puts the bow to the underside of her arm where the steel strings are tucked. Galatea has been called a miracle worker, a magician, by countless women as they admired their new body in the mirror or heard the new thrill of their voice (they were *always* built for dance or song, they just needed a little coaxing from Galatea to fully emerge). But it's *this* sound that is the miracle, that is the magic.

After a few moments to understand the key and rhythm, Cassandra drags her own bow across her arm. Her teeth grit. The note is a scraping wail, partly from her arm and partly from between her teeth.

"It hurts," she says in her new melodious voice.

"It will always hurt at first."

"And it looks all wrong."

"We do not come out of the womb like this, now do we? It looks *better*. It *is* better. Think of all the girls who will go to that theater with nothing special about them, only to be shuffled away. You are better than them now."

Cassandra snorts. "I'm not normal."

"There is no home for normalcy anymore. This is the new era. Try again. Let the song move through you. For now it truly is *through* you, and that is incredible, is it not?"

Galatea plays with her, quickly moving off center-stage to accompany with only soft harmonies, letting Cassandra shine. Once her shakiness wears off, she presents the pure talent that got her in the big city with aspirations so gleaming and high, playing with conviction, even if she can't breathe through her teeth – even if she gasps through every scale.

The final notes tumble and scrape to a stop. Cassandra slumps. Her skin is raw and red, blood trickling out of the holes where the strings were screwed into the delicate inside of her wrist. The dying vibrations of the strings stir up foam in the blood, little pink bubbles that pool inside the wooden hollow.

"What is this?" she snaps.

"It is all a normal part of the healing – "

"No, all of this." Cassandra snaps her hand at the laboratory around them. "How do you keep your doors open? How many people do you shuffle through? What's the point?"

"Music, Cassandra. Music is the point."

"I could play just grand before!" She white-knuckles the bow made of her bone. "I was the best, y'know, best everywhere but this fucking city."

Galatea leans forwards, her voice gentle. "And what did that get you, being the best all the way out there?"

Cassandra bites her lip. After a moment, she says, her out-of-towner accent thicker in her anger, "Music is the point, huh ... I don't get it. Isn't the joy of music in the listening? So, what? Am I supposed to wait until someone bothers to listen to me? Is it all worth shit if no one's decided to admire me?"

I'm listening. "No, no." Galatea touches Cassandra's arm, feeling the warmth of the bloody strings through her sensitive receptors. "Do you not agree that there is also joy in the creating? In writing the music, in feeling it flow through you?"

"I don't write music. I perform it. I find it, and I chop it up, and it ain't even mine. I just repeat it."

"And still you love it. You are a beautiful, talented girl, Cassandra. Do you not sing in your room when you are alone? Do you not narrate the world around you when you walk somewhere beautiful? The joy is in the creating. I know it is for me."

Cassandra looks away and says, voice fragile in the way Galatea thought she fixed, "I did all this just to play someone else's songs."

Galatea has never had to convince a stubborn girl that she needs this. More often than not, she's convincing girls of the opposite – that being exactly like Galatea herself, entirely inorganic, should not be the goal. There's a line where it's too much. Galatea isn't sure where it is, precisely, or why that line exists, but she *feels* it.

Galatea says, pressing the bow into Cassandra's palm, "I will leave this room to put together your recovery packet, and you will play. For you. Remember what you did for what you love."

***

October 3, 1934
MODERN DAY "PYGMALION" DIES AT 89

Days short of his ninetieth birthday, one of this generation's most prolific and artistic inventors, Arthur Corduroy, died peacefully in the city that made him famous. Corduroy was best known as the creator of the musical marvel, Galatea, who has been touring to sold-out shows since her debut in 1927. The nuts-and-bolts starlet sat at his bedside all through his final days.

Not all aspects of this tale are so romantic, however. While Corduroy dedicated almost the entirety of his assets to various charities, Corduroy reportedly had not penned any documents regarding who would inherit Galatea and her future royalties. Investors were quick to follow the news of Corduroy's worsening condition with betting wars on Galatea (and the undoubted fortune she earns every year). Protestors gathered outside the manor belonging to one of the highest bidders, Sir Reginald Smythe, saying that attempting to buy Galatea is akin to buying the child of a widower.

"Arthur tricked the public all these years, making some of us think [Galatea]'s a real girl," says Sir Smythe. "She's not a real girl. You get too close and you can tell; the illusion is blown apart. And that's the point of purchasing her. We wouldn't be arguing about the sovereignty of a toaster, would we?"

***

A few months later, Cassandra returns to Galatea.

There's a new brightness to her that fills Galatea with pride. She knows there will be good news before Cassandra even says it: "They want me, they really want me!"

"Your orchestra, dear?"

"The orchestra of my dreams!" She bites her lip, gliding into the consultation chair. "There were more'n six auditions to pick us, can you believe that? But after the first one, they told me that I was only playing in the other five for appearances. I'd got the job. After one song!"

Galatea smiles knowingly. "With your strings?"

"And my voice." Cassandra goes pink. She was transformed in those months away, filled with a bright light that only dreams fulfilled and hope can give a girl. No more of that ugly negativity.

"I am so proud," Galatea says, and she is. "Would you write me a testimonial? It can be anonymous if you like. But this is the kind of story I want to give everyone."

"If everyone has it, then the story's gonna go stale, don't you think? I'll keep it to myself, thanks."

Galatea can't help it. She opens her arms for a hug. After a spot of hesitation, Cassandra dives in and then hugs her harder than anything. It makes Galatea feel like she's the girl's mother. The girl's provider from cradle to grave.

Galatea holds her at arm's length, looking into her eyes. "You deserve to have this dream come true. Thank you for finding me to tell me."

"No, actually, I'm here to book another."

"Another?"

"Yeah. I'm right, you know – people know you, and one day, they're all gonna have visited you, and my story's gonna be the same ol' story that everyone else has." She lifts her arm to indicate her singular instrument. "I want something no one else will ask for."

"Are the violin and the voice not enough?"

"They're enough *for now*. You never know when *they* are gonna ask for more."

"Who is 'they'?"

"Don't play coy; you know." *Do I?* Cassandra takes a deep breath. "So, this is my idea ..."

***

Galatea breaks Cassandra's legs.

The procedure has never been done, so they spent days workshopping how it could be done. Galatea unearthed her best inking pens and vibrant watercolour paints to design sheet after sheet of prototypes, taking care with the curves, the shine, the transition from skin to metal, the engraved decorations as intricate as those in Galatea's instrumental body. Cassandra wanted engravings that represented her old life out West, the life that gave her the rasp and the crooked septum she no longer has.

When it came down to it, however, the procedure was mostly about a measuring tape and a bonesaw.

After a good hour of bedrest and with plenty of recovery tinctures flooding into her veins through IV, Cassandra is allowed to stand. Galatea holds her hands, keeping Cassandra afloat so she can devote all of her attention to the awe that her new legs deserve.

With her calves reshaped into the feminine sways of a harp, she takes on the coy, secretive silhouette of a satyr or a nymph. Any other year, this would be too strange to win anyone over, but Cassandra's timing is impeccable.

A series of fantastical novels about forest spirits swept the country by storm recently; girls have been putting chemicals in their hair and winding the heat-curled locks up into elaborate braids to imitate the coquettish characters. They've been passing around their grandmothers' techniques for tying beaded twine into the shapes of leaves and flowers, then wearing them on their throats. They've been dreaming up new deities to call to. The papers decide which of these little crafts are the most beautiful of all.

Galatea anticipates that Cassandra may begin a whole series of similar procedures – unless the phase dies out too quickly. One can never be sure with these things.

Cassandra gapes at the mirror. She pulls one hand away from Galatea to push aside her surgery gown, to see the immaculate white of her thigh bending and adjusting with the natural instinct of a human body to keep her balanced. Her calf, leading into the fine-boned foot, is little more now than bone shards threaded together like those girls and their beaded necklaces, laid upon the spine of the harp with the outer delicacy of petals upon a flower, but the inner strength of screw after screw after screw. Her feet are permanently tilted; she must stay on tiptoe, so she is perfectly balanced with the curve of the instrument (Galatea suggested she lose a little weight before the procedure to help). It's no matter. In her profession, she'll be wearing high heels for the rest of her life.

Cassandra totters towards the mirror. Galatea holds her up – she buckles immediately and then tilts when she tries to right herself, for her legs can't bend like they used to. She cries out. Grits her teeth so tightly that Galatea can feel it where her head has fallen against her shoulder.

She steps and steps and the body is amazing, understanding naturally how to adjust and compensate, until Cassandra stands on her own before the mirror, involuntary tears from the pain on her cheeks.

From her hollowed-out knees (narrowed and smoothed during the procedure, because why not add little adjustments?), blood runs in calligraphy swirls into those carefully-considered designs.

"I would have wrapped them up to soak up the discharge," Galatea says, "but I wanted you to see as soon as you could."

"I have to play," Cassandra says, her voice a little hollow. "Give me a harmony, Galatea."

Galatea helps Cassandra teeter back to the bed. Cassandra insisted that they not anchor the steel strings in bone nor muscle because of how long it took the ones in her arm to stop aching. So the strings are dutifully attached to the harp metal as they're always meant to be. Cassandra must arrange herself on the seat in order to reach down to play (they also fortified her fingertips with the excess bone from her legs, so they'll never burn, never hideously callous from the strings), and it forces her into the loveliest of poses, a painting from the great masters come to life, capturing a beautiful woman reclining in her silks and dreaming aloud.

Galatea opens the panel in her own back, breathing in and adjusting herself to attach her pipe-organ lungs to their stops. She breathes out a single, sustained, gentle note.

Cassandra matches it.

The music her harp legs makes is so sweet, it brings Cassandra to tears.

***

The months roll by as well as the procedures, and pure, heartfelt music fills Galatea's world once more.

Cassandra always returns with stories. Most girls don't have stories – they come with what they want to change and ask for suggestions and that's all. Galatea reads their *why* behind their eyes. Cassandra is open with it.

"I need to bring them something new, or else they're gonna get bored."

"Another girl joined and she's got the same voice as me. That was from you, huh?"

"They just want *more* of me."

"You're my maker," Cassandra insists when Galatea hesitates too long at her demand to fix something else. It isn't said with adoration. It's resigned but full of trust, the way one hands their faith over to medicine or a god.

Cassandra begins to stay at Galatea's apartment after her procedures (tucked above the lab, too small to hold them both, but Galatea doesn't need to sleep or eat so she lets Cassandra have it all). She confesses – again, in that way of handing over faith with a heavy heart – that her mother doesn't respect what she's doing and she's sick of hearing the snide, sideways comments and the questions she doesn't know how to answer.

"The voice, the *voice* she wanted me to fix," Cassandra explains. "That one was her idea. She said it obviously had to go. But everything else isn't me. How's that her decision? Wasn't the voice *me* too? How's all of this *not* me?"

***

December 10, 1934

MUSICAL MAIDEN CLAIMS HER FREEDOM: YOU BELIEVE I'M REAL, AND SO I AM

This city made from lovers of music, technology, and freedom heard the news of a lifetime yesterday. Galatea, a clockwork instrument whose creator died in October, took to city hall to announce that she knows who will claim her in this headache of a bidding war: herself.

Galatea told the crowd that she has "held up a business for seven years on my own shoulders. I have a right to that business. You made me, with your belief and your love, into something real. So let me claim every part of that reality."

This matter has stirred up heated discussions in multiple disciplines. Critics liken her to household tools or the instruments she's made from. Philosophers have questioned what divides Galatea, with her apparent sentience and independence, from the rest of humanity. Some women's rights activists uphold her as a woman literally shaped by patriarchy against her own will, now reclaiming and redefining her purpose.

The legal decision will be handled in court, with the first hearing set for December 18th this year.

***

On a warm summer evening, Galatea attends one of Cassandra's shows.

Cassandra had given Galatea a ticket with warmth and gratitude, as if she was giving it to her own mother. "I want you to see what you've done for me," she'd said, "and you need to get out of this ol' lab!"

The venue is no less lavish for its intimacy. Drifting through the crowd, Galatea learns through eavesdropping that this is the estate of a governor, and Cassandra's troupe is headlining a benefit ball. Galatea can't figure out which charity it's for. She hasn't been around so many people, lights, smells, and sights since the law gave her full rights over her own self and she shut herself away. The disorientation is worth seeing Cassandra perform.

The troupe needs so few people when she's built the way she is. Her band seems to be there to merely decorate her and provide the gentlest of melodies. Her dress is stripped back everywhere it can be to show off her physique: the violin of her arm, the satyr harps of her legs, the stops and keys glimmering up the line of her extended neck, the cello giving her its curves and posture and deep, moving thrall. And of course her voice, the original way they unearthed the Cassandra who was always meant to be on that stage, soaring over the crowd.

She has surpassed me, Galatea thinks, only able to smile. *In a world where anyone can be like us, no one after her will be rejected ever again.*

At the end of the song, Cassandra grins and her bandmates clap for her. The ballroom fills with applause to the rafters. Even once they move on to present the other members, Cassandra is pink, knowing all eyes are on her.

One of the women at Galatea's table whispers to her companion, "Can't she step out of the spotlight for a *minute*? Goodness gracious."

Clapping politely, her companion lifts a brow at the audience. "Look at all their faces."

"She didn't do any of the work."

"Right, right, she's not the composer."

"Or the artist, really!"

"Or the artist."

"She's the tool. We all know why they're so excited about her. Lucky girl, huh." She chuckles, with a new, surreptitious edge to it. "Not all of us get to do that and reap the benefits."

Galatea excuses herself to no one in particular and wanders through the crowd until she reaches a bubble of air near the bar.

She slots herself a few steps away from a man. His eyeline follows Cassandra closely as she lifts from her third bow. Cassandra's smiling so hard it looks like her face will rip.

Galatea says to the man, "She is something to be admired, is she not? Are you thinking of a similar procedure?"

"What? No. Aren't you seeing her try to bow?" He points her out, tracing her luxurious shape from across the room. "It's such a shame. She's ruined, and for what? Just for us to ogle her?"

"It is so she can play the way she was born to play."

"It's so she can take all the attention, that's what."

"They demanded she be that way," Galatea says automatically. *They*, Cassandra had said, but Galatea doesn't quite understand what it all means. The man looks at her, perplexed, and then his eyes sharpen with a realization.

"Are you ... ? You can't be."

"Galatea. Arthur Corduroy's creation." She says it firmly. "I do these procedures now."

"That doesn't make any sense. I keep seeing these girls everywhere – no one with anything like her, but still, they're crawling into every job in the music industry. You're taking in these pitiful things and screwing them up."

"Am I 'screwed up,' sir?"

"No." He shakes his head, stepping out of this conversation. "You were *made* like that. It should be you on that stage. I'd pay you double what that shameless idiot asked for."

Galatea lets him leave. She weaves through the tables until she's right in the middle and Cassandra sees her. Those brown eyes are glittering with tears. Galatea claps hardest of all, even once the rest of the crowd has quieted.

***

May 23, 1927

'World in the Palme of Your Hand'

Interview with Arthur Corduroy's musical automaton, 'Galatea'

[Transcript begins at 00:04:53]

JOSEPH PALME: Tell me, Galatea, what's your favourite tune?

GALATEA: *Pure as Snow* by Fisher Phillips.

PALME: Wow, good choice. We were all moved to tears by your rendition at Langley's. Right, folks?

[Audience applauds.]

PALME: How does that song make you feel?

GALATEA: Can you clarify the question?

PALME: You *can* feel, right?

GALATEA: I have been given receptors that make me sensitive to heat, cold, and pressure.

[Palme and Audience laughs.]

PALME: Is that so? But I mean, do you feel through the music – the emotions, that rawness, that's a song that fills many of us with yearning for young love lost. What about you? What does it mean to you?

GALATEA: It does not mean anything.

PALME: Then why do you say it's your favourite?

GALATEA: The crowd likes it very much.

PALME: Hmm. Can you expand on that a little? Tell me what that situation's like in that pretty head of yours.

GALATEA: Gladly, Mister Palme. I like to play music because of what it gives to others. They expect me to play and like me best when I play. If no one was there to listen, I would not sing at all. There is a lot that people would not do if no one was watching.

PALME: Oh, really? What wouldn't *I* do, if I weren't here on the television?

GALATEA: You would not style your hair in that coif and would not have so many ladies doing your makeup.

[Audience laughs.]

PALME: You're right, you're right … Turns out I don't dress up on my lazy Sundays. Alright, ya got me. You don't enjoy listening to music?

GALATEA: I was not made to enjoy listening. I was made so *others* enjoy listening to *me*. I am here for them. I am made for them.

PALME: So, alright, you could say you do enjoy playing, at least in that round-about way. If you didn't play, others wouldn't get to enjoy it.

GALATEA: Let us return to your original question. *Pure as Snow* by Fisher Phillips makes me feel a yearning for young love lost. I will think of you when I play it next, Mister Palme.

PALME: You've got yourself quite the impressive little lady, Corduroy. A sharp mind in both of you!

ARTHUR CORDUROY: Thank you, that's very kind.

PALME: On last Thursday's STS broadcast *[Archivist's note: Science and Technology Showcase]*, you mentioned that Galatea is still a work in progress. What kinds of advances or debugs does she need, good doctor?

CORDUROY: Actually, your exchange with her just demonstrated something I'd like to fix. You see, er ... Galatea learns from what she's told. Her scripts are rewritten depending on what people say to her. This can apply to language, accents –

PALME: I did notice she's got a touch of your Northern twang.

CORDUROY: – and ideas. Ideas, yes. It could take one too many people telling her, you see, er, 'Galatea, you should be singing for yourself.' Or, 'Galatea, if you don't like to sing, stop trying to impress others.' And then she'll believe it. And then she won't do what she's made for.

PALME: I can speak for us all when I say that would be a damned shame. What's your solution?

CORDUROY: I'm working on training her to love her purpose. To believe that that love, er, that it came from *within* herself, not because I told her to or because people expect her to. One day, I'm not going to be here, and I want her mind to be firm and certain: she wants to play. She loves the way she is. Everyone should aspire to be her. No one can change that.

PALME: And will she believe that her wish to make you loads of cash came from inside herself too?

[Corduroy chuckles, pretending to shush Palme. Galatea laughs along.]

About the Author

Vanessa is a writer, artist, and editor located in Canada. From cheesy fanfiction as a preteen to sprawling fantasy novels now, she's always loved creating stories and helping others tell their own. She's a classical art, mythology, and folklore enthusiast, but can't turn down a good cliche-filled graphic novel or webcomic.

Part of You

Zi Trone

CW: drugging, needles, dismemberment, body horror, parasites cannibalism, brief animal death, murder, gore, infection, ableism, character death
Whumpee: Woman, Whumper: Woman, Caretaker: Woman

Chapter One

Happy New Year!

Genka and I have spent the whole day trying to recover from last night. The party itself was awesome — the repercussions less so. We may never learn our limits when it comes to drinking, but as long as we're here to take care of each other, it doesn't really matter, does it? (Pickle juice still works wonders, by the way. Even at our age. Maybe especially at our age.)

The kiss was as magical as ever, it was every bit as electric and wonderful as our first time. The way she made me forget about the crowd around us, the way she held my face and looked at me like I was her most precious treasure, it felt as tender as our wedding day.

She can just do this. She can just make me forget about everything but her.

There is no one I would rather spend the first day of the year with, taking turns in the bathroom puking and holding each other's hair out of the way. There is no one I would rather spend all the days in the year with. All the days in all the rest of our years.

And just so I have written proof of it when I turn out to be right: let it be known that my beautiful, stubborn wife is getting sick again. I told her not to sacrifice warmth for looks, but she didn't listen, and now I can hear her constantly blowing her nose in the other room. She insists she's fine, but we all know this is going to be one of at least three colds she will catch this year, as always.

I'm going to stop here. I think I'm going to get sick again.

20xx. 01. 01.

***

Amynta set the bowl in her lap, staring at the mixture she had made with empty eyes. She blinked at it like it was something foreign, something she had never seen before, despite the recipe being one from her "favourites" folder.

She felt so tired. Exhausted. *Heavy.*

Still, she grabbed her silicone spatula and started stirring, making sure not to overmix. Keep it light, keep it airy. Stir. Stir. Stir.

Gena used to love these banana muffins. She was the reason the recipe had ended up among the favourites, and Amynta was always ready to indulge her. Today, it felt like she was working in vain.

She kept stirring until the mixture looked smooth enough, then put the bowl back on the counter. She carefully scooped a couple spoonfuls into every well in the muffin pan, trying to get excited for the dessert. She had to smile a little. Genka always hated when she was sad.

She stopped halfway through, deciding she needed some music to lift her spirits. What use were the sweet muffins if her mood was always so sour?

She put her hands on the handrim of her wheelchair and pushed herself away from the counter, crossing the room to get her phone. She needed something upbeat, something that was loud enough to drown out the banging of her own thoughts, but something that didn't feel *too* happy.

She wanted to be happy. She wanted Gena to be happy. But right now, being happy felt like an egregious sin. It felt disrespectful, even *mean*, but then again, not being happy felt like self-victimisation. Smiling felt forced, but guilt and sadness felt performative.

Her finger hovered over her playlists, and she realised she could barely remember what each of them contained. It had been so long since she'd allowed herself joy. So long since that time she'd put on some music to dance with her beautiful wife.

They should spend some time together, once the muffins were ready. Maybe they couldn't dance like that anymore, but... Maybe they could at least reminisce.

She clicked a random playlist and went back to the muffins, filling the remaining five cups to satisfaction. She put the pan in the oven and decided not to wash the mixing bowl yet. Gena had always loved to eat the leftover batter.

She hummed along to the song as she grabbed some meat from the fridge, sliding it across the counter to the cutting board. It had been so long since they'd had a nice dinner together.

They both needed it, Amynta thought. Maybe she needed it a bit more than Gena, but in the end, she couldn't imagine she was happy with the way things were. They both needed a break. And they both needed some music and good food.

Chapter Two

It's been weeks. Nobody is willing to listen, nobody is willing to take this seriously. I'm telling them all that I can, and they're brushing it off.

Genka has never acted like this, not once in our ten years of marriage. She's snippy, angry, impatient... She's constantly ravenous, and I try to cook enough for her, but she's still losing weight. I don't understand any of it. People keep telling me I'm overreacting, that it's just a bad cold, but no cold has ever made her eyes bloodshot and her fever so high. No cold has ever led to her being hospitalised.

It doesn't matter. Doctors, nurses, none of them want to help. My poor love came out of the hospital in a worse condition than she had gone in, and I'm never bringing her back there. If they won't help her in or out of that ghastly building, then I'm keeping her home, where I can at least grant her patience and kindness.

I changed her room to be more... accommodating. I wish I didn't have to, I don't wish this on my worst enemy, but here we are.

Some days I wonder if it's the last one we'll get to spend together. I know I shouldn't, I know I should have faith in her strength to pull through until I can figure something out, but... Sometimes I just can't stop the thoughts.

I wish things went back to normal. That's all I ask for, every single day. I wish I didn't have to go to work every day and pretend everything was fine. How can I stand there and accept pats on the back for my 'accomplishments' when I can't even heal my love? I know she's suffering, and it's killing me.

20xx. 02. 19.

***

On any other day, Amynta might've been more patient. She would've kept politely insisting her colleagues talk to her instead of her lab assistant, she would've smiled through being cut off, or interrupted, or straight up ignored.

Today was not that day. Today, she was desperate and angry.

"Would you fucking look at me when I'm trying to talk to you?" she snapped, making her colleague *finally* pay attention. They looked taken aback, same as her assistant, but at the moment, she didn't care. "This whole time I've been trying to explain these stupid results to you, you haven't *once* looked me in the eye. Can you stop staring at Katie?"

"There's no need to be rude," they mumbled, clearly flustered. Being head of the department at least came with the perk of being able to yell at others with little to no consequences, even if they refused to listen to the actual words.

"You know what? There's no *use* being rude. I'm leaving."

"Excuse us for a moment," Katie said hastily, then *grabbed her wheelchair* by the push handles and attempted to physically pull her away from the confrontation. That was the last straw.

"Get your fucking hands off of me!" Amynta screamed, channelling every little bit of pent up anger into her voice. All those nights spent worrying, all those days spent working on a fucking cure no one else cared to even try to make, it was all coming out now. "What is *wrong* with you people? I'm fucking leaving! Don't you *dare* touch my chair again!"

Amynta didn't really have much to be proud of lately, but the way she had stunned them into silence at least gave her some satisfaction. Nobody stopped her as she exited the lab. Nobody even looked at her. They all pretended to be awfully busy as she left, taking the first bus home.

Her at-home lab wasn't nearly as good as the one where she worked, — *had* worked, most likely — but at least there was no one to condescend to her, no one to talk over her, and no one to fucking annoy the shit out of her every moment of the day.

Was it selfish of her? Was it selfish of her not to bite her tongue after the thousandth little thing? Was it selfish of her to give up potentially the only place where she had the proper equipment to do research into her wife's condition?

She let out a heavy sigh when she realised she'd left half of her papers on her desk at work. She'd collect them the next day, she decided. Maybe... Maybe just for an afternoon, she would rest.

Maybe if they didn't end up firing her, she would go back to biting her tongue.

Chapter Three

I understand now. I know why she's losing so much weight. I know what she wants. I know what she needs.

A couple weeks ago, I brought her some chicken breast. It was the only thing on her plate that she touched. The next day I brought her an array of different animal products, and she devoured everything. The next day, I found her on the floor in her room, hunched over the corpse of a poor bat. She was eating it raw.

She needs raw meat. I think that's the only way to sustain her now. I've been going to the butcher quite frequently, and my theory seems to be holding up quite well, but I still feel uneasy about feeding her things like that.

No, that's a lie. That's not what I'm uneasy about. I'm uneasy about the way she looks at me. The way she stares at me in a way that's so uncomprehending, almost animalistic. The way she snaps her teeth, almost drools at the sight of me.

I've been thinking about it a lot. About whether I could do it. At the end of the day, there's really no other alternative. Gena is my responsibility, and I'll do everything to keep her safe and fed.

20xx. 03. 25.

***

Amynta scooted to the edge of her seat, carefully reaching up to the lower shelf for her medication. She was starting a new bottle today.

The phantom pains that should've subsided ages ago were still very much present, and Amynta was inclined to believe that her skills as a surgeon left much to be desired. Who knew what sort of nerves she had cut into? What sort of tendons and muscles she had severed, what bones she'd left with jagged edges that dug into her flesh?

Maybe it was the lack of sleep, maybe she had pushed in the bottle a little more than usual, or maybe it was just her being distracted. The bottle fell from the shelf and onto the ground, the lid popping off with a stupid little noise and the pills flying everywhere. They were rolling across the floor like the tiniest little critters, rolling under cupboards and behind the fridge.

Amynta watched, frozen in time. All at once, her situation hit her.

There was no stopping the tears once they'd started flowing. She tried to wipe her eyes and quit sobbing, but it was futile. This was so *ridiculous*. Her life had been so *different* less than a year ago.

What did she do to deserve this? What the fuck did she do to piss someone off so bad that they'd decided to somehow curse their household? To make her wife contract a mystery illness that had turned her into... something else. Something so devoid of her beautiful, kind soul. Something that feasted on blood and flesh.

She gasped softly as a wave of pain coursed through her, starting from her legs. It was a sharp, stinging sort of pain that reminded her why she had to take painkillers every day. But as she stared at the scattered pills, she decided she wasn't about to put them all back in the stupid little bottle.

Her wife was suffering; she wanted to suffer with her. She was in pain, so Amynta didn't deserve the medication either. She was starving, so Amynta didn't deserve to be making three-course meals.

If she couldn't make her beloved's life be worth living by finding a cure, she didn't deserve to live either.

Chapter Four

When I first realised I would have to feed Genka pieces of my own body, I thought I would be able to 3D print myself prosthetics. I thought I would only have to part with some of my legs to buy her time. But she needs to eat human meat much too frequently, even if I supply her with animal products.

I don't have more to give her. Both of my legs are gone. I tried to ration it, I tried to make it so that it would last, but I can't anymore. Cutting off my hands would mean I would make research infinitely harder for myself, and I would likely need a caregiver, or someone who could help me around the house.

I can't let others in. They'll hear the incessant banging, the way my sweet Genka wails all day and all night.

I wish I could hold her more often. But I need to prioritise work.

In the lab, people are asking about my "surgeries." I joke with them, I tell them the stupidest stories about what happened to me. Sometimes I tell them the truth. "I cut off my legs to feed my wife." They laugh. I laugh with them.

I need to start looking elsewhere for her sustenance.

20xx. 06.16.

***

The devil's breath. "The most dangerous drug on the planet." It made the victim awfully suggestible, all the while they appeared perfectly sober. As soon as Amynta saw the article about it, she knew she would have to get her hands on it.

Using it was second nature by now. She sprayed it in the face of unsuspecting victims and waited for it to hit, then she simply told them to bring her home. She was just a little lady in a wheelchair, after all.

Please sir, won't you help me get home? The streets can be dangerous at night.

Amynta let the man push her up the ramp at home and opened the front door. She let him have his moment, let him feel useful, playing into all the dumb thoughts he must've had.

"Thank you so much," she said for the hundredth time. "You're a lifesaver. Not even the bus runs so late, and I was out all day... My arms are killing me."

"Of course. Happy to help." He looked around the hallway, probably wondering how she could afford such a nice place. Or better yet, how he could quickly rid her of her wealth. "Can I have some water before I go?"

"Sure thing. Let me grab you a glass." She rolled past him and into the kitchen, and she could hear one of her painkillers crack under her wheels. Another one she'd missed. "I'm sorry, can you grab that pill for me? I must've dropped it earlier, and picking anything up from the floor is such a hassle for me..."

The man grinned wide, happy to be useful. Dumbass. "Of course. No problem."

As soon as he bent down, Amynta slammed the sturdy bottom of the glass
against his skull. It knocked him out cold.

She rounded the man's unconscious body and grabbed her scarf from the hall,
— the one she only ever used for this purpose — then went back to him and got
out of her chair. It wasn't necessarily the easiest, but she'd long since learned that
being on the floor for this part was the most efficient way. She looped it around
the man's neck and began to strangle him, counting down the seconds until she
could be sure he wouldn't wake back up.

It used to be so difficult; now it was just another annoying chore.

Everything seemed so insignificant compared to her ultimate goal of finding a
cure. Every life seemed so worthless compared to Gena's.

Once she was done, she dragged herself over to the cupboard with the chop-
ping board and her knives. Gena seemed to require more and more food as her
infection progressed, but this body would last her a while.

At least she hoped.

Chapter Five

*It's getting harder and harder. We're at a point where she starts whimpering as soon
as she sees the needle, and honestly, I don't blame her. I've tried everything I could
think of, there were weeks when I had three new formulas ready to inject her with.*

Nothing is working. I'm... starting to lose hope, I think.

*I hate myself. I hate that I'm doing this to her. I just want to help, but who's to say
she knows it? I tell her every day, I try to get through to her, I try to calm her... It's
no use.*

I hate hurting her so much.

I'm afraid one of these things will hurt her even more.

I'm afraid of killing her.

I wish I could test them on myself. I wish I could take whatever has infected her and insert it into my body, so I could inject myself with these stupid concoctions.

I love her so much. I just want her to be okay.

20xx. 09. 10.

***

Amynta crossed the hall as quietly as she could. She knew Gena could hear her — the rattling started up again. Her poor love. Her sweet angel.

"I'm gonna come in, okay?" she asked softly. There was no response. There was never any response.

She turned the key in the fortified door, then opened it all the way. She hit her hand on the doorframe — *again*; she should really be better about this by now — and pulled it closed behind herself.

There she was, wrapped up in torn blankets, clothes, and entirely too many chains: the love of her life. She was thrashing like a wild animal, growling and snapping her teeth behind the muzzle Amynta had had to strap onto her beautiful face.

"I know," she cooed. "I know you hate this part. You know I hate it too. But it's to help you get better, love. I promise."

Gena whined, her frenzied eyes wide open and fixed on the tray in Amynta's lap. Or more like, the syringe on the tray.

"It'll be over before you know it, sweetheart. I promise. Just a pinch, yeah? And then I'll go bring you dinner."

She came to a halt next to Gena and grabbed the syringe, then set the tray on the floor. She scooted over to the edge of her seat and took a deep breath, taking her wife's restrained arm in her hand.

It was still so beautiful, even blackened and rotting. She was always so, so beautiful.

Gena screeched when she injected her, and she quickly went on to rubbing the injection site, trying to soothe the pain and make sure the medicine would spread faster. Pieces of her flesh tore off as she did so, the wound underneath oozing pus.

"It's over," she murmured. "It's okay. It's over. It's done."

The poor thing continued crying, and Amynta couldn't stop her own tears.

"It's gonna be okay, Genka. I promise."

Chapter Six

I don't know anymore. I don't know. I thought I was doing the right thing, but it's been almost a year and Gena isn't showing any signs of improvement.

I killed seven people in the span of six months. Her appetite is only growing. I don't know what to do.

I cut off my legs. Why did I do that? Everything would be so much easier if I hadn't done that.

Why am I keeping her here? I should've let the hospital take care of it. They would've found something.

No, the hospital has only ever made it worse.

I haven't left my house in months, besides to take people home and kill them.

Will they ever find this diary? Will they put me in jail? Who will take care of Genka if I'm not here anymore?

I don't know whether there's any point to taking care of her.

No one will find her fresh human meat to eat.

I want to disappear. I want to stop. I just want to rest. Why didn't I tell anyone?

A year ago everything was okay.

Maybe I should let go.

20xx. 12. 31.

***

There was no banging from the room as Amynta neared the door. She almost felt too drained to lift her arm and turn the key in the lock.

Another syringe. Another dose of experimental medicine.

She pushed the handle down and opened the door. She was mindful not to drop the tray she was precariously balancing on her lap, making sure to go slowly lest it slide off.

Dread pooled in her stomach for reasons unknown to her. Something felt off about the room, but she was too sleep deprived to look around.

"It'll just be a pinch," she mumbled, more out of habit than a genuine conviction that Gena could understand her. "Just a little bee sting."

As she approached the spot where her wife had been for the past several months, she could see the length of empty chains on the floor. It took her mind a few seconds to catch up and process what her eyes were clearly showing her. It took another few seconds to register what felt so awfully wrong.

There was no whining. There was no rattling of the chains.

It was quiet.

Too quiet.

"Gena!" she called, panicked, spinning around with no care for the tray or the syringe. She was just in time to see her pounce from the upper corner of the room, landing on her lap and making her topple over.

There were long, inhuman fingers wrapped around her throat.

She was being choked.

She couldn't breathe.

She was desperately feeling around for a weapon, anything she could use to get Gena off herself, and her fingers eventually brushed against the syringe. She grabbed it and jammed it into Gena's neck, making her howl in pain and let go to yank the needle out.

Amynta turned onto her stomach and started dragging herself away, and right now, she was awfully happy she had been too lazy to take the hammer back where it belonged. She managed to grab hold of it just when Gena grabbed hold of her torso, but she couldn't swing fast enough to avoid being *bitten*.

"Stop!" she screamed, flailing around to try and dislodge Gena's teeth from her side. "Gena, stop! Stop it! It's me, Mynty!"

There was no recognition in her bloodshot eyes.

One of her swings finally connected and Gena's skull cracked under the hammer. Amynta was finally free and high on adrenaline, and she hit her again, and again, and *again*.

Blood was splattering everywhere. There was nothing left of her wife's beautiful face. Her arm was getting tired.

Amynta only stopped minutes after Gena had ceased struggling. If she'd learned anything during those seven murders, it was that people could endure way more than others give them credit for.

If she'd learned anything during the past year, it was that Gena could endure way more than any human.

Amynta dropped the bloody hammer and collapsed onto the ground, next to the ruined mess of brain and bone that was her love. Even her corpse smelled different. It was nothing like the sweet scent of decay she'd come to recognise in humans — it was bitter, awfully, unbearably bitter.

But it was Gena.

Her Genka.

"Love?" she called miserably. "I... I'm sorry, I... Genka?"

There was no response. There was never any response.

"Genka?" She wrapped her arms around her all-too-still sweetheart, nuzzling up against her for one last time without the chains. She hadn't been able to do that in almost exactly a year. "Genka... I'm sorry... I'm sorry, I lied, I said it would be okay... I promised..."

Amynta held her so tight it would've been painful, had she still been alive. Rot didn't matter, decay didn't matter, disease didn't matter. Even now that she could finally see Gena for what she was, a corpse held together and kept moving by nothing but a parasite, she was still her Genka. She would never be anything else.

"I'm sorry... I'm so, so sorry... I should've done better... I should've saved you..."

Something slippery and wet crawled onto her face, and Amynta flinched back. She tried to get it off and throw it as far away as possible, but the thing was holding on tight.

Eventually, Amynta gave up.

It was the thing that had infected Gena, wasn't it?

She should've hated that thing. She should've hated it for taking away her beloved. And yet, as she stared at the abused body of her wife, the thing crawling towards her mouth felt like her only memory of her.

Her soul, almost.

She parted her lips for the parasite to crawl inside and tried not to gag as it forced itself down her throat.

She would always carry a part of her within.

About the Author

Zi Trone is but a humble fear enthusiast with a passion for writing. An undying love for scared and crying characters has been the driving force behind hundreds of thousands of words already written, and hopefully many more to come.

In Prison

Christina Nordlander

CW: Body horror, eye trauma
Whumpee: Unspecified, Whumper: Woman, Caretaker: N/A

When I'd sat out almost a year at Lily Towers, we were given the opportunity for volunteer service. Each tour shortened our term by three years. It was impossible to turn down that option, even when I crossed the court below the twilit sky and heard the sounds. They weren't screams. They were of something wrenching and snapping, and it brought me back to dentist's appointments when I was a kid, to hearing the sound through my jawbone.

We met a female inmate, escorted. She walked slowly. Her arm looked small beneath the bandage.

My file had said "eyes". I remember only discomfort when they fitted the translucent suction cup over my left eye. The optic nerve was severed with a little flash.

The implantation specialist injected the buds in my eye-socket, six glassy globs in different spots. They taped on a surgical eyepatch. That side of my face was just darkness.

"We'll summon you in a few days, before they have time to grow too big," she said as I was released from the examination chair. "You're just there to give them a good growth environment."

But they keep a watch on me, so that I won't be able to tear off the eyepatch, or scratch myself too hard through it.

I feel the new eyes growing from me. Sometimes I hope she's placed them too close, that they will drink one another.

About the Author

Christina Nordlander was born in 1982 in Sweden, and now lives outside Manchester, the UK. She has published about 25 short stories, most recently "The Cuckoo's Brood" in Tangle & Fen (Crone Girls Press, 2023). She also holds a PhD in Classics and Ancient History from the University of Manchester.

Nervous Intervention

APEX

CW: Graphic torture, gore, genital mutilation, referenced sexual violence (non-graphic)

Whumpee: Man (male referred to by they/them pronouns), Whumper: Man, Caretaker: N/A

The cold white walls of room 507 fluoresce under the sharp hospital lighting. In the middle of the room is a man, completely naked and strapped down to an operating table. He's deep under a carefully concocted mixture of sedatives and muscle relaxants. There's a helmet of circular pads and wires connected to his bald scalp.

"Unit 7, Department of Defence, Trial 1. This tape encloses the treatment of Subject 078. Male, 5'9, 186 pounds. No documented medical conditions. Blood type AB+. Transfusion available, if required."

Adler places the tape recorder next to the steel gurney. He adjusts the overhead lighting arm until the bright glare is focused on Subject 078's bare chest, their pallid skin glowing a sickly white. Thin black streaks of surgical marker cover their torso and limbs. Despite the inconspicuous appearance of these markings, they are in reality the result of hours of meticulous mapping of 078's body by a team of medical professionals. Adler inspects them with no small amount of satisfaction.

"Subject displays no nervous dysfunction. A subtherapeutic dose of compound Delta was administered on a 7-day time course to measure tolerance, no adverse reactions were noted. Head physician Doctor Adler will be performing and narrating the experiment."

A single electrode taped to 078's chest keeps track of their heartbeat. The monitor beeps softly in the background, and Adler briefly glances at the screen to ensure that the readings are acceptable. 50 BPM. Perfect.

"Due to Subject 078's near-perfect biological compatibility with compound Delta, upmost care must be taken to preserve their processes. Depending on the data collected, further testing will take place with 078 as our prime candidate. Future technicians utilizing this tape are urged to seek out the accompanying file on 078's medical history." Adler rattles off all the relevant background information like he's reading off a script. After seventy-seven of these procedures, he's more or less memorized the details.

If this was any other lab rat, Adler would be dreading the monotonous hour he'd be in the surgery suite, but this isn't any other lab rat. No, this is 078. Their golden goose. A perfect specimen in every aspect for Adler to collect the data that he so desperately needs. They've never had any other subject complete the time course for Delta without a single side effect.

If all goes well, this just might be the experiment that cracks the code on optimizing Delta dosage and finally unlocking its full potential. Adler is overcome with professional delight at the prospect– and maybe a bit of sadistic curiosity about what exactly makes 078 different from the others.

He picks up the half-full syringe sitting next to his surgical tools and taps it twice. The needle slips into the port in 078's IV line. Adler flushes the liquid out into the catheter.

"The experiment will begin in three, two, one…"

In the span of a half-second, the line on 078's heart monitor shoots from 50 to 110 in a sharp incline. They wake up with a shallow gasp. When their eyes snap open they're bloodshot, frenzied.

"What the hell."

Adler fiddles with the settings on the heart monitor until it displays the electroencephalogram on a separate screen. The gentle rolling of REM patterning has shot up into distinct peaks. 078 is experiencing panic.

"Subject exhibits anticipated confusion upon awakening."

078's eyes are darting around but room 507 offers no clues as to its purpose or location. They swallow hard, and when they speak, their voice is rough from underuse.

"What?"

Adler glances at 078 out of his peripheral. Flushed cheeks, wide eyes, excited pulse. All characteristics of Delta– or any stimulant, really. The *interesting* effects would take a bit longer to set in.

"Hello, Adam."

078 eyes shoot to Adler, like they just noticed he was in the room.

"Who're you?" Their voice has a hint of panic, either from the uncertainty of the situation or the drug rushing through their bloodstream. Adler guesses it's the latter. Given 078's history, they're not the type to panic. They wouldn't have survived in the field this long if they were.

Adler walks back into 078's line of sight and they follow his movement like a hawk.

"My name is Doctor Adler. I'll be conducting your tests today."

The metal gurney clinks as Adler unwraps his sterile equipment. 078's glare turns uncertain and their lips quirk down in confusion.

"What– what are you talking about?" Their muscles seize up tight as they try to jostle around in the restraints. Despite their efforts, their body stays still. "Why can't I move?"

Adler clicks his scalpel onto the handle. He puts it back down on the gurney. There will be plenty of time for questions after. First, he needs to build a rapport with his subject.

"Do you know anything about human anatomy, Adam?" 078 stares at Adler like he has two heads. Clearly, they had expected something more hands on, more violent. Makes sense given their background in reconnaissance and... unorthodox information gathering techniques.

"What?" They ask. Adler scoffs. He isn't going into this slashing and stabbing without a plan. Torture isn't an appetizer, it's the main course. He's a professional– he has a carefully curated way of breaking down a man, one more effective than mindless violence.

"Anatomy. I assume not, given your lack of education, but surely you know the basics. You did a good enough job with Sergeant Barnes– right through his femoral, hundreds of yards away. Consider me surprised. Your marksmanship scores aren't exactly impressive."

At that, 078's confusion melts back into that dissatisfied glare. They're an intimidating man with their array of battle scars and hard muscles, but in their immobilized state, they look like nothing more than a whiny toddler.

"Go to hell."

Adler smiles where 078 can't see him. He's a professional, but that doesn't mean he doesn't take pleasure in his work. The defiant ones are always the most satisfying to break.

"I'll take that as a no." He rips open a sterile alcohol pad.

"I have a proposition for you." 078's eyes shoot down to stare as Adler wipes down the vertical line on their forearm. Adler keeps talking.

"Unfortunately, I can't collect my data without your cooperation. Neurology simply hasn't gotten that far. The EEG readings are useless if we can't make parallels between nervous impulse and subjective subject experience."

078 looks at him like he's crazy. Again, Adler remembers that they haven't been briefed on any of this. He gestures broadly to 078 spread out on the table. If he

wanted them quiet, he would've just gagged them. Much less messy. Unfortunately...

"What I mean to say is, I need you to answer some questions for me."

078's guarded shoulders relax the smallest bit. This is definitely more planned out than any torture session they've endured before, and Adler takes pride in that. He's not a heathen. He's a scientist.

"And why the hell would I do that?" 078 asks. Adler gives them a polite smile.

"Because if you cooperate, then you get off with a clean record."

For the first time, 078 seems genuinely surprised. Not angry, or confused, but truly surprised. They open their mouth to say something then immediately close it. This is unprecedented. You don't just *get off the hook* after killing a Sergeant. That's life-ending.

"Witness protection and honorable discharge. Consider this your one-way ticket out of jail. All you have to do is behave." 078 raises an eyebrow.

"And if I don't?"

The *audacity*. Adler squints at 078. You'd have to be a real idiot to speak back when you've been offered an olive branch like that, but apparently their useless pride is stronger than their self-preservation instincts.

"Then we'll cut you open anyways, and you'll rot in jail until they give you the electric chair," Adler says. 078 opens their mouth but then the drug kicks in all at once, and their eyes shoot open. They let out a strained gasp.

"What the hell is this?"

Finally. It hadn't taken this long in the other subjects, but then again, 078 has always been an anomaly. Adler picks up a scalpel handle without a sharp on it.

"Tell me if you can feel this." He pokes 078's stomach with the blunt end, and their muscles ripple out from the contact in a strange wave-like motion.

"Don't touch me!" 078 gasps, their eyes wide. They seem more confused than angry. Adler pokes them again and they yelp.

"On a scale of one to ten, how intense would you rate your cutaneous sensations?" 078 gives him a frustrated stare. They're breathing hard, gritting their teeth together.

"My *what?*" they ask. Adler gives them another poke.

"Touch. How intense is my touch?" Poke. This time, 078's muscles seize up under the skin like a taut rubber band.

"Ten. It's a ten– fuck! Stop that!"

Adler backs off and 078 takes a huge breath. As soon as the scalpel handle clatters onto the table, their body relaxes down into the table. A thin sheen of sweat shines on their body under the hospital light.

Despite their clear discomfort, Adler questions whether a little bit of poking would really be a ten. While a normal person would have found it to be intensely overstimulating, given all the torture 078 has endured, they should be far more resilient than any normal person.

Maybe they just reacted explosively because they weren't expecting it. Or maybe it really *is* that uncomfortable. This is what Adler hates the most about subject involvement– you can't get something objective out of a subjective account.

"In the interest of collecting accurate data, you will be given all relevant information about my procedure. Please give concise and authentic responses," Adler says, tone harsh. 078 better not make this harder than it has to be. Adler's the one with the scalpel, after all.

"Oh, don't worry, I'll give you authentic," 078 mutters under their breath. Adler ignores them.

"You have been given a drug that enhances your nervous impulses." Adler picks up another syringe. 078's eyes train the movement in fear. "Normally, your brain will dull sensation once an adequate response has been generated, but right now you are feeling about five times the natural physical response, as your neurotransmitters evade reuptake–"

He flushes the liquid into the IV line and 078 lets out a frustrated hiss between gritted teeth as it shocks them awake.

"You're fucking insane!"

Adler pokes them again, this time with the tip of the syringe. 078 yelps. A small prick of blood wells up from the puncture.

"Please don't interrupt me."

He picks up the scalpel handle with the blade attached. When he turns around, the metal catches a glint in the light and 078's muttering ramps up to yelling.

"Wait– wait, back the fuck up. Back up!" Adler settles himself on his stool and wheels himself until he's next to 078's hip. "Seriously, don't fuck with me, man. I'll kill you. I'll fucking kill you!"

078 doesn't scream at the first incision. The pained grunt that threatens to escape is stopped by their teeth gouging into their bottom lip. Adler nods in appreciation. *This* is what they expected from a special forces' agent, not a whining, pathetic mess.

That's how Adler knows that he's broken past the nonchalance of 078's outer shell to their core. This is when 078's military training will kick in– where Adler can actually get usable data between all the screaming and begging.

After all, one of the hallmark effects of compound Delta is its capability to bring out repressed memories. The best way to bury sensitive information is to forget it. Normal torture might be able to break down those walls, but it's impossible to tease out something that can't be accessed. That's where Delta comes in. So far, even if the subjects can't tolerate the drug, it's had one-hundred percent efficiency.

"You know, if you weren't drugged up to the ears in sedatives right now, your heart would be beating too fast for your nervous system to keep up with it," Adler rattles off. He works best when he's talking.

"You'd have a heart attack, I mean." He keeps talking, even though he knows that 078 definitely isn't listening. Even as a seasoned veteran, the amount of pain they're experiencing would be enough to knock any sober person out cold. Delta is the only reason they're still conscious.

Adler uses a gloved hand to stretch taut 078's freshly shaved skin so he can get a more precise cut. The razor-sharp edge of the scalpel glides through fat and skin without any resistance. It pleases Adler to his very core how easily 078's flesh parts for him.

At the end of the day, humans are nothing more than animals. Sophisticated high-order machines of entropy and emergent property that defy categorization. Men like Adler– they seek to do the impossible. They seek to become Gods of their own anatomy.

The scalpel eats through 078 in little bites. Each swipe parts the almond shaped incision wider, the edges of skin blossoming out like a flowering bud. Bright yellow bubbles of fat bulge out from the lesion. Prickles of blood well up at the upturned edges of the wound and drip out over skin. Adler's gloved fingers slide on the blood until 078's thigh is a vivid mess of red gore, the gaping gash in their leg standing out starkly with its bluish veins and marigold fat.

078 is letting out stifled grunts from above. Adler reaches up with a bloody hand to adjust the light, slathering red all over the hospital-white ceiling mount in the process. He cranes his neck down to get a better look. The pungent smell of metal is overwhelming, eye-watering. Inside of the cut, severed capillaries throb out little rivulets of blood. Each squirt syncs with the feverish tightening of 078's muscles as they desperately attempt to worm away from an agony that is inescapable.

Pain is nothing more than nociceptor response. It's an extensively researched subject but the sheer magnitude of pain that 078 is currently experiencing is a gap in literature– when the human mind is faced with such uncategorizable suffering, its immediate response is to shut down. 078 cannot shut down. The drug in their veins keeps them sharp and aware.

Somewhere far away, Adler knows that he should feel remorse, the same way that he knows that this is unethical. Unfortunately, his curiosity overshadows any remnant of humanity that he may have.

He purposefully digs the tip of his scalpel into the gouge he's made in 078's thigh and violently jostles the exposed flesh. Little frothing pieces of bloody fat spit out onto Adler's hospital gown. 078 screeches like a skewered pig, their teeth grinding down into their tongue to mute the noise.

"On a scale of one to hundred, where ten is the hypothetical maximum for an average civilian, how would you rate your pain?" Adler asks. 078 lets out a pathetic whimper.

"A hundred," they rasp. Adler raises an eyebrow.

The problem with delving into an untouched part of human suffering is that you have to make new rules and scales for pain. A civilian's ten is going to be different from that of a service officer. Realistically, only the first eighty or so points of Adler's scale are usable– if 078 was really at a hundred, they would be screaming too hard to say it.

Adler looks up to see 078 splayed out on the table like a ragdoll, their eyes glazed over and their skin a slippery mess of fear-sweat. Blood and saliva pools in their mouth from their lacerated tongue. Their chest is rising and falling in a desperate attempt to get air into their lungs in between the choked screams, but they keep choking on their own spit.

Adler reaches up to knock their head onto its side. A gelatinous wash of bloody spittle spills out of their mouth onto the operating room floor. 078 makes a broken noise, like a dog getting run over.

"We can do this the easy way or the hard way, Adam. I'd rather do it the easy way." That's true– mostly. For documentation purposes, Dr. Adler would prefer to do it the easy way. The violent part of him, however, wants an excuse to dig his nail deeper into 078's insides, and he does exactly that– simply because he can.

He gets his scalpel in the cut and slides it right underneath the sensitive upper layer of skin. The metal bulges up from under the skin, shoved snug into 078's thigh. Adler digs and digs and *digs* until 078 lets out their first real scream, until they finally give an answer–

"Sixty! It's– it's a sixty." Adler yanks out the scalpel and throws it aside. It clatters onto the gurney, blood and wet flesh splattering onto shiny metal. 078 shuts their eyes as tight as they can. Adler can see their poker face slipping.

"Now, was that so hard?" Adler asks. 078 doesn't respond. They keep their jaw clenched and their eyes shut tight.

Adler gives them a moment to breathe as he sets out his cauterization pen and retractors. 078 braces tight when the retractor clips onto the edges of their wound and both ends scissor apart to spread the gash open like an eye.

Adler was careful to cut straight down from the exact location of the surgical marking. Something gauzy sparkles at the bottom of the cut. It's blue-tinted and translucent, and it gives away with craft paper to Adler's cauterizer. Fascia– and underneath, 078's sartorius muscle.

The acrid stench of burning flesh fills the air. 078 is hyperventilating, biting, growling, anything to hold back a scream. Their muscle fibers continue twitching as they're exposed to the air. Ruby red, corded, pulsating with even undulations like a mass of maggots. The burning hot tip of the cauterizer gouges into the mass and 078 gasps. Soft sizzles fill the air, not much different from a slab of steak searing on a grill.

Adler's hands shake the smallest amount when he puts down the cauterizing pen for his tweezers. This is it– the part he's been waiting for. This is when he finally gets to see the real power of Delta's nervous intervention.

"This might sting a bit..." Adler digs into the bloody, burnt wound with the tips of his tweezers. He roots around until he finds cords. Buried deep underneath 078's muscle alongside the artery and vein is his femoral nerve– thinner and more branched than the other vessels. Adler gets his tweezers hooked around the thick base of 078's nerve, and he *pulls*.

The noise that leaves 078 is neither a scream nor a shout. It's something raw and screechy, the sound that barn animals make when they're shocked with a bolt gun. Adler drags his tweezers along the nerve to rip it out from its cocoon of connective tissue. The vessel stretches out from 078's leg like a rubber band. Each swipe along its length with the metal tears another inhuman screech from 078. Adler plays them like a violin, stroking their strings until their screams choke up with tears.

"Why did you kill Sergeant Barnes?" And that's the crux of this experiment– seeing how much torture it takes to break a man who tortures for a living. 078 screams, and it's so visceral that Adler actually stops his assault for a brief moment.

"FUCK OFF!" The tweezers tighten again. Adler slides the teeth along the nerve and 078's screams start up again.

"On a scale of one to one-hundred, how would you rate your pain?" Adler asks. 078, despite all odds, *laughs*.

"Are you fucking kidding?" Adler is very much not kidding. He flicks his wrist, tangling the nerve around the tip of his tweezers. It strains with the effort of stretching past its limit and 078 lets out a high-pitched squeal.

"Oh god– okay, stop–" The tweezers freeze. 078's wet, bloodshot eyes squeeze closed.

"Eighty," they rasp. Adler smiles, making sure 078 can see it. That sudden anger from earlier is still stewing under the surface of their saliva-wet snarl. They glare Adler down as he gets up.

"I'm going to fucking kill you for this." Empty threats. These military types are all the same– the only defence they have against violence is more violence. In actuality, they're scared shitless, and it shows.

"You hear me? I'm going to *slaughter* you. They're not going to find a body. I'm going to grind your bones to dust." Adler scoffs under his breath. As if that could ever happen.

"I'd like you to try." There are men far more dangerous than 078 who want Adler alive, and they aren't half as forgiving as him. The things they would do to 078 if he so much as tried are too horrific to put into words. Next to them, Adler might as well be a saint.

Adler sits himself next to 078's torso and relishes in their panicked breaths as he starts in on their forearm. That cocky arrogance from the beginning is all but gone. Now, 078 *knows* what Adler is capable of.

"This one is less deep," Adler mentions. 078's head lays motionless on the gurney.

"You're one sick fuck, you know that?" they mutter, half-gone from pain. Adler ignores them.

"Of course, it's still dangerous. Arteries and nerves run parallel. One wrong move and you'd bleed out in seconds." To prove his point, Adler gets the body of his cauterizer underneath the bundle of vessels and pulls up. There's a wet squelch as they all tear up out of the pocket in 078's arm that they're nestled in.

It's a marvel every time, just how *flexible* arteries can be. Adler stretches them to their limit. 078 is sobbing openly now, their face a mess of spit and snot. They sob at the apex of the tension, then scream when Adler lets go, the artery sliding back into place with a snap. Blood splashes up onto Adler's cheek.

He leans in and 078 turns their head, like he won't be able to see them if they can't see him.

"Don't worry, though. I'm a professional" he whispers. It's true. By the end of this, 078 is going to *wish* that they'd bled out in the beginning.

Next, Adler goes back in with his tweezers. 078's eyes are still closed.

"You are part of something groundbreaking right now. What we're doing here is going to change the landscape of wartime reconnaissance forever. As an intelligence agent, you should be more appreciative of the bigger picture."

When you slit a pig's throat, it gurgles even though it only makes the blood flow faster. When you hang a man, he tries to breathe, even if it comes out as a breathless wheeze. 078 alternates between the noises of a pig to the slaughter and a man with a noose around his neck. Their breathing wheezes in a death rattle and their cries threaten to drown them in spit. A violent red flush has overtaken their face like an engorged tomato. Silent, choked, they try to speak through the pain.

"Please..." they whimper. It's barely recognizable as a word, with how hard they're sobbing.

"Please, what?" he asks. 078 gags on their pain, wet and disgusting.

"*Please–*"

Adler yanks. The nerve stretches desperately. 078 screeches.

"Why did you kill Sergeant Barnes?"

Come on, Adler thinks. *Come on*. He's so close.

078 shakes his head.

"Please, please, I can't–"

As soon as the metal teeth of Adler's tweezers touch the nerve, 078 caves with a scream of frustration.

"Okay– okay! I'll tell you." The tweezers withdraw. 078 takes a deep, shuddering breath, like it's the first one they've had for a long time.

"He disrespected me." A laboured pause. "I couldn't stand for that."

How laughably vague. Adler's eyebrow twitches in frustration. What could *possibly* be so scandalous that it'd warrant this level of secrecy? It's not like 078 has anything to lose. They've already been caught and prostrated.

"I struggle to believe that a distinguished man like Barnes would humiliate you unless he had an understandable motive." Of course, *understandable motives* are different from what may be considered ethically sound. From what Adler knows from 078's file, Barnes was a hard-ass– he lived for the mission. He respected his squad's skill and expertise, but he would have done practically anything to ensure a win. He was good at what he did. A perfect Sergeant. He had to be, to be entrusted with such an important mission, not to mention the level of classified information he was privy to.

But then again, up until now, 078 was supposed to be trustworthy as well.

078 is hyperventilating. Their broken body struggles to take in all the air it's been deprived of in the past half-hour. Adler gets up and leans over the operating table. The snarl on 078's face is vicious– the hatred of a man who's been wronged in a catastrophic way.

"Barnes is a sick bastard. He– he's a monster. I'm a killer but I'm not a goddamn psychopath." Adler sighs. He leans back and 078 starts breathing again.

"Must you insist on speaking abstractly, Adam?" he asks.

Still, it's progress. Adler breathes in deep. He can't help it; they've been brute forcing this trial for months now and they're finally getting something usable.

Hell. He deserves a chance to celebrate. Why not *play* a little?

"I'm a patient man, Adam, but you're pushing it," Adler warns. 078 watches, paralyzed and prone, as he forces two fingers inside the gash in their inner thigh. Bloody latex rubs up against the exposed nerve, and 078 lets out a whine of defeat.

"On a scale of one to one-hundred–"

"It was Amelia! He– he raped Amelia."

Adler's eyebrows stitch together. Amelia. Amelia... he knows that name...

"Stop, please," 078 chokes out. Adler looks up at them, and the shockingly human look of surrender on their face makes it all come together.

Amelia– or Agent Sanchez. Another special forces officer in unit Terraform. She's their rifleman, their sharp-shooter, a small, unimposing woman who becomes a nightmare behind a sight. There isn't a single kill-shot she's taken and missed– or at least, nothing on record. She is objectively the most skilled and talented officer in Terraform.

"Alright," he says. His fingers slip out of 078's wound and he wipes them down on their pallid skin. 078 looks at him like he's crazy.

"*Alright?* That's all you have to say?" Adler shrugs. Might as well keep prying. Adler won't be satisfied until he knows that he took 078 apart completely, mind, body, and soul.

"Clearly you aren't willing to make this easy, so we're going to keep going until you cooperate." He picks up his scalpel. 078 goes bug-eyed.

"What? I told you the truth!" Their voice doesn't hold a hint of their previous defiance now, as they realize that nothing will suffice other than pure honesty. Adler scoffs.

"Excuse me if I struggle to believe that a special operations officer would flip the handle at something as commonplace as sexual assault." After all, 078 has seen violence much worse than rape, and Adler wouldn't be surprised if they've enjoyed some of the *spoils* of war themself. Adler knows he would, if he had the protection and immunity of the special forces. It's one of the few perks of the job.

"She's my wife, you freak!" Adler raises an eyebrow. Well, that's interesting. Still, it's not something extreme enough to warrant 078 killing a Sergeant and throwing their entire life away. You need to have had an iron will and a flexible constitution to be a part of a special forces unit like Terraform. Someone that flies off the handle with such little provocation wouldn't have made it that far.

Adler's foot hits the locking mechanism on the gurney's wheels. 078's eyes widen when he hoists himself up onto the surgery table, the rickety metal creaking with his weight. He settles himself with a knee on either side of 078's knees. His white lab-coat pools on their thighs, soaking up the blood in their wound.

"What the fuck are you doing?" 078 panics. Their eyes dart around to catalogue anything in their limited range of vision that could serve as an escape route—an instinct that's crucial on the field, but useless here.

Adler doesn't bother with the bells and whistles. He's done playing nice, and he's done being professional. He's been in here for an hour longer than he'd scheduled for, and quite honestly, he's getting *mad*. 078 is hiding something from him. Nobody hides anything from Adler, not when he's got all his tools in the arsenal.

Delta is his child. It's his magnum opus. 078 must be a damn idiot if they think that they're getting out of this operation table without spilling their guts.

"No, no, wait, *wait*–" Adler's blade touches skin. 078 whimpers like a kicked puppy.

There's a horizontal line laying across the base of their flaccid penis. Every muscle in their body is held taught. Adler digs into the shaved flesh and his razor-sharp scalpel glides through like butter, down 078's skin to his fat then to his muscle.

It's just a shallow nick– a small down-stroke with the blade, but the cut floods almost immediately with frothing red blood. It bubbles up and spills down the shaft of 078's penis down to their thighs and the shining metal table. 078's crying has devolved into unintelligent, frenzied screams. Their pupils struggle down as far as they can in an attempt to make eye-contact with their captor. When they speak, their sore throat grates against itself to make a terrible, awful noise.

"Don't– I'll tell you whatever you want to know, just don't–"

"Why did you kill Sergeant Barnes, Adam?" Adler uses his free hand to grab 078's penis and pull it taut so that the wound stretches. 078 screams so hard that their voice gives out.

078's twin pudendal nerves are a mere few millimeters from the scalpel. All Adler would have to do is push. All it would take is a flick of his wrist. He could bleed 078 out with just a little bit of pressure, and *ruin* them all at once–

"It wasn't Amelia," 078 mutters. They sob silently, shamefully, the broken noises of a man who has been reduced to absolutely nothing. Adler barely hears it. All his blood is rushing through his ears.

"It was me," they finish. A wet cry bubbles up their throat, and they don't hold it back.

"It was me. He– it was me."

For a second, Adler is shocked. It's rare for a man to admit to that sort of thing, especially one so high up in the military. Rape of females, sure– but a man like Adler? 5'9 and built like a machine-gun? Most of them would rather take that with them to the grave, even if it means suffering along the way.

"Please, don't keep cutting," 078 whispers. Small, scared, juvenile. Adler basks in his victory. 078 scrunches their face up in pain.

"He– he raped me, then he castrated me."

"*Castrated* you?" That's impossible, given that Adler has his blade buried in their manhood as they speak. 078 sniffles.

"Me and Amelia... we were–" their voice catches. "We were going to have a kid. I don't know how Barnes found out. I don't know. But he did, and he–"

078 stops for a second. They open their mouth, but the words struggle to come out. Adler adjusts his grip on his scalpel.

"No. No, please. He– he drugged me. I woke up in the military hospital after. That's when they gave me the paperwork."

078 lower lip trembles. Somehow, the next few words seem the hardest to get out.

"For the vasectomy," they finish, and their eyes slip closed. They lie there, silent as a corpse, splayed open and gutted. They might as well be dead for everything they've let slip.

It makes sense. It wouldn't be good for Terraform to have its best shooter out for the count and honourably discharged on maternity leave, especially not if it'll be down a reconnaissance agent as well. That's tantamount to career suicide for Sergeant Barnes. He'd be laughed out of any room. The man who let his most prized pony get knocked up by a rowdy donkey.

But to Adler, that's not the part that's the most delicious about all of this. No, 078's suffering is sweet, but it's nothing compared to the severity of the secret that they've just revealed.

078 is not nearly skilled enough to make a shot like that. They couldn't do it, not on their best day, but Amelia could. Amelia, who has killed countless men and gotten away with it. Amelia, whose husband was just assaulted and sterilized. Amelia, whose temper is almost as explosive as her trigger finger.

078's most volatile, dangerous secret, on tape for every researcher in the Department of Defence to hear. That's the power of Delta. It turns Adler breathless, how *powerful* of a weapon he has in his hands. One small dose and it'll tease out anything. Even something buried as deep as this.

078 is still crying. They bite their lip to hold back their hurt noises, as if being quiet will grant them some sort of mercy.

"Please, don't hurt her," they beg. It's so pathetic that Adler almost feels bad for them. Almost.

"I can't promise anything, Adam, but I'll put in a good word. You seem like a respectable man."

Adler is, of course, lying. He isn't going to do jack shit about it. He wouldn't even care enough to report it, but whether he says something or not, his superiors will listen to the recording. He might as well cash in on his finder's fee. Amelia Sanchez is as good as dead. Maybe if Adler is lucky, he might even see her in the next round of trials.

The scalpel buried in 078's flesh pushes down. 078 gasps.

"What are you doing?" they ask, a deer in headlights.

Truth is, Adler never intended to let them go. There is no witness protection. There is no honourable discharge. There is absolutely nothing holding Adler to his words except his own virtue, which he has shown several times is non-existent.

"I told you the truth! I told you the fucking truth, you bastard!" 078 screams. *Screams.* Adler has seen angry subjects before but this is definitely the most violent reaction he's had. It's like having a rampaging bear strapped down to his operating table– of course, the bear wouldn't be able to do anything on the ridiculous amount of Delta it'd be shot up with, and neither can 078.

The cut is shallow but it doesn't have to be deep to reach the distal nerves in 078's penis. Two parallel lines, running down their shaft. Adler's grip on the scalpel shakes violently. The heart monitor is beeping loudly next to the gurney, trying to indicate that 078's heartbeat is dangerously high. Their ECG readings are a frantic mess of steep lines.

A particularly violent shake of Adler's wrist pushes the blade down into an artery. A spray of blood jets out of 078's limp penis. 078 makes a horrific, guttural noise, and Adler adjusts his grip.

"On a scale of one to one-hundred, how much pain are you experiencing?" he asks.

078 tries to talk through their screams, but Adler pushes down before they can get a word out. All at once, the heart monitor crashes to silence. The ECG lets out a loud beep. 078 goes lax and wordless on the table. Their pupils continue darting around behind their closed eyelids.

"Fuck," Adler mutters. He climbs off of the operating table.

There's blood soaking into his lab coat. It's thick and vibrant in the crisp white fabric. On the table, 078's half-severed penis is spitting out lines of blood in time with their stabilizing heartbeat. It's been cut all the way down to the stringy interior of the erectile tissue. There's no doubt that the nerves have been fully severed. The post-experiment medical staff will stitch them back up, but whether it'll remain functioning is a toss-up. There isn't exactly a large focus on keeping test subjects intact, mentally or physically.

Adler forces himself to take a deep breath. He wipes the strands of hair stuck to his sweaty forehead with the back of his bloodstained gloves, wiping a streak of blood onto his cheek in the process. The ECG has settled now, along with the heart monitor. Adler peels off the latex gloves.

"Subject 078 seems to have had a grand mal seizure. Heart rate has settled to 60 BPM, and EEG readings show brain activity consistent with unconsciousness. A blood transfusion should be administered as soon as possible."

Some part of Adler is disappointed. Not that 078 passed out– Delta is cutting edge but it still has kinks to work out. No, he's disappointed that he went so hard so quickly, because it'll be weeks, if not months, before 078 has recovered enough for another trial.

Though, at the end of the day, it isn't the worst thing that could've happened. 078 is still alive and they won't be going anywhere after what they've confessed too.

Adler hums as he stuffs the gash in their penis with gauze. There will be plenty of time for Adler to get his fill. After all, he still has to work out the perfect dosage.

About the Author

Vincent Schnecke (online pseudonym Apex Predator) is a horror-romance author who writes both original and fan-fiction whump on AO3. His work ranges from hardcore hurt no comfort to feel good fluff, with an emphasis on exploring concepts like sexual trauma and social stigmas surrounding gender/sexuality.

The Exchange

Midnight Blue

How has it come to this?

How has it come to you being strapped to the table -naked- by a madperson?

And why can't you remember your name?

Why can't you remember anything?

A strange scientist -white lab coat, black gloves, a predator's grin- whom you've never seen before -at least not in your memory- hovers above you and giggles. "I've been waiting for this for a very long time."

First comes the needle they inject into your neck.

A sharp hiss escapes your teeth and your body twists and writhes in a horrible, uncomfortable agony as whatever disgusting liquid contained within flows throughout your body.

Once they finish, you don't feel relief as the needle is removed from your skin, clattering to the floor.

Your body continues to shake.

You see them grab a long knife from the table.

They press a hand on your shoulder, holding you still as they stab you in the collarbone and pull the knife downwards.

Your shriek is ear-splittingly inhuman.

You thrash and blubber and flail, begging for them to stop.

They only stop once they're past your chest, then heave the knife out of the incision with force.

A warmth glides across you.

Nausea pools into your stomach and you begin to feel faint from how much blood -your blood- is slicking the table, dripping onto the floor.

With their own bare hands, the doctor pries open the incision.

Your vision goes white.

Are you about to die?

And if you did, would it be for the best?

You're not even able to begin processing that a small saw is cutting into your ribs.

One,

Two,

Three,

Four,

Five are taken out.

Now, the doctor takes a much smaller knife to your heart, cutting it out, slowly, meticulously.

You're surprised you haven't passed out by now.

You have nothing left to scream and no tears left to cry.

The doctor removes your heart from your own body.

Miraculously, you are still alive.

With a wicked grin, they hold your bloodied, beating heart in their slippery gloved hand. "Yes...it's beautiful."

Your heart is placed gently on the table, and the doctor begins to remove their own lab coat, their own shirt, and your eyes move just the slightest bit to watch them.

They grab another needle off the table and jab it in their neck, only they don't writhe and jerk.

Perhaps they're used to it.

You notice they're repeating all the previous actions on themself.

The cutting open of their chest, the sawing of their ribs, and finally, the meticulous, methodical removal of their own heart.

And they did it all with a smile.

"Isn't this wonderful? Now we'll each have a piece of the other!"

Grabbing a needle and thread from the table nearby, the doctor begins sewing their heart where yours once was, stitch by stitch, every pipe, every tube, fitting perfectly together.

Some of their blood pours inside your body.

You do not protest.

Slowly, you begin to feel a heartbeat again.

Not yours, of course.

With almost gentle fingers, the doctor sews your incision back up, seeming to haveforgotten about your ribs.

They giggle to themself as they begin to do the same with your own heart, sewing it into their chest, albeit awkwardly and clumsily.

Once they're finished, you wonder what's going to happen now that this experiment -you suppose that's what it is - is over

You think about the heart beating in your chest.

This heart is foreign to you.

You never asked for it.

So why should you be forced to have it?

"I love you so much!"

The doctor comes over to your side and plants a kiss on your lips, the skin from their open chest flapping about.

You don't fight back.

You have no fight left in you anymore.

You simply watch as your own heart beats in front of you.

About the Author

Midnight Blue is a normal, well-adjusted person, as clearly evidenced by their submission. Their love and fascination for mad scientists knows no bounds.

Transmission Received

Nox Spacey

CW: Alien abduction, environmental whump

Whumpee: Man, Alien Whumper: Alien, Caretaker: N/A

I had been so excited for my first independent mission. It wasn't a simple one, but I'd thought I was prepared for it. Everyone else had thought so, too, since they'd let me go by myself.

I was supposed to stay in this planet's orbit for one full rotation around its sun and catalog what I could about it in preparation for a possible first contact. It was strictly observatory for now, but I was expanding the limits of the known universe! It was exciting. Maybe eventually they would let me take samples up from the planet and do real experiments. I had a laboratory up here, after all.

I was trained in science and anthropology. I was eager to learn and study. I hadn't done it before, but... I knew all about how to do this *in theory*.

I thought I knew what to expect.

But as I approached the planet, I started hearing... noises. It *sounded* like a primitive attempt at language, softly whispered, and it didn't bother me too much at first.

It got louder as I got closer to the planet. More insistent. More voices. More sounds. More often.

I tried to figure out what they were. A good first step for my mission. There did seem to be a native species down there capable of intelligent communication and society-building. That's who we *might* be making contact with.

But as time dragged on, the noises kept tormenting me. I gave up and captured a specimen of that species. I wasn't *supposed* to–not yet, I hadn't been cleared to actually use the lab yet–but I needed *something* to make some progress. The Association wouldn't be happy about it, but I was well outside their jurisdiction. I needed this. I was good at learning languages, but...

I couldn't get the stupid thing to talk to me. They even had predominantly sound-based communication! Unlike most carbon-based megafauna species, which communicated through horrible smells, this one used sound. I also used sound! This should be working! Why wasn't it working? I'd tried our slates used to teach language–even larvae were capable of using them–but it always cringed away from me.

I needed it to talk to me. I *needed* to figure out the- the *anything*. I could barely think. If I could get this thing to talk to me, maybe I could figure out what the sounds were.

The noises continued to drive me more and more mad every day. It wasn't helping anything.

Back at it again at the Krispy Kreme let's go Hello? (And if the beat live) (B-B-Bankroll Got It) ayy Uptown Funk You Up Uptown Oh no (bang) oh no (bang) Hello? oh no no noNOW IT'S YOUR TURN TO ROLL Hello? How are you THE BIG GAME today? Did you hear about Stepped on a poptop blew out a flipflop what dad said Buy a Sunsetter Awning and save NO DOWN PAYMENT six hundred dollars FREE TRIAL NOW NO DOWN PAYMENT CALL 1-800-ALL YOU NEED FOR THE BIG GAME Fever dream high in the quiet of the night Hello? you know that I caught it I want you to stay 'til I'm in the grave 'til I rot away Hello? Nothing to stay when everything gets in the way WE DONT' TALK ABOUT

BRUNO-NO-NO-NO OOH-OOH TEMU all of my wishes came true SHOP LIKE A BILLIONAIRE OH-OH TEMU Did you see the video I sent you? Hello?

***

Sam was having the worst luck lately.

First his manager at the grocery store had gotten pissy with him, and then his second job at McDonald's had stopped scheduling him for hours, so he figured they were lowkey firing him. Then his girlfriend was being a bitch again, and then to top it all off, he'd been abducted by aliens.

He genuinely couldn't tell if there was more than one or not–he only ever saw one at a time, but he couldn't tell if it was the same one every time. It always came in and hurt him. The deep, thudding, booming sounds vibrated his organs and jarred his bones. Rattled his teeth. He was convinced one of these days his eardrums were going to blow out, or he would be liquified, or something. It was terrifying, and it *hurt.*

He curled up in the corner of the holding cell–it was empty except for some heavy, curved, uncomfortable furniture. It was too heavy to throw, or he would have tried to use it as a weapon by now. He was hungry and thirsty. There was a small trickle of water from a fountain in the back of the room, but his previous tasting of it had revealed it to be saltwater. He was going to die here, alone and scared and confused, and he couldn't figure out what it *wanted.*

The door to the cell *whooshed* open. Sam scrambled back in terror as the monster came back in. It moved across the ceiling and walls with the same ease it took the floor, and it maneuvered itself so the entire length of its disgusting, many-legged body trailed inside. A faint chittering and a wet squelching accompanied each twist of its purplish carapace. All the bulging eyes on its head and running down its body were looking at him.

Sam cowered. He'd tried pleading, threatening, bargaining, but nothing ever made it better. But what else could he do? "Please. Please, I- I don't know what you-"

The alien snapped its mandibles and the sound came. It *hurt*. It vibrated his bones, and he slapped his hands over his ears, but it still felt like his eardrums were about to burst.

"Please!" he cried. "I'm sorry! Please stop!"

The ringing in his ears didn't fade as the creature closed its mouth, or mouths, or whatever horrible noise-making thing it had. His heart pounded.

The thing let out a series of clicks, its antennae wiggling, and it slithered down the wall onto the ground. Its wispy antennae battered Sam's body despite how he tried to press himself into the corner.

"Oh God," he gulped. "Oh God, oh God, oh God."

As it got closer, he could see the fluid dripping from its curved fangs, the preternatural twist of its many eyes, the too-many-moving-parts of its mouth, its head, its neck, its whole body. It was a goddamn horror show.

One side of its many legs ferried an object up towards its head. Another one of those flat, iridescent square things. They looked a bit like a tablet, but it was ridged in a way that the thing's pointed graspers fit into.

The thing manipulated it with some rapid-fire motions of its spindly forelegs, and the device emitted a high-pitched screech that hurt almost as much as the creature's natural sounds.

"Fuck!" Sam wailed, curling up in a miserable ball on the floor. "I'm sorry! I'm sorry! Stop! Please stop! What do you *want?*"

The beast let out one final ear-piercing screech–this one more intense and louder than the rest, then tossed the device at the wall, where it clattered to the ground. The creature shot up the wall in a sinuous wave and peeled out of a hatch, which shut behind it.

Sam lay there with his ears ringing, eyes on the tablet. A faint buzzing sound emanated from it.

Why had it left it behind? It hadn't done that before. It'd thrown it against the wall, almost like...

Almost like it was frustrated.

Sam hadn't expected to be able to recognize any emotions in such an alien creature. He hadn't bothered looking, or thinking about it till now. He'd been too panicked, but–

But now, he recognized the frustration. That's what it was, right?

So was it... not hurting him on purpose? Was it trying to do something else, and failing?

He stared at the tablet, thinking very hard.

***

I paced the entire length of the observatory station, on the verge of a complete breakdown. Why wasn't it *working?* Why did it always just cower away from me? It should be *working* and maybe if I could focus I could get it to *work* but *who in the universe could focus with all this damn noise-*

Hi, how are you today? I'm Donald Trump and I approve this Message Hello? Never gonna give you Up this is a test Hello? this is a test I'm finna get this shit off my chest Hello? and lay it to rest THE BIG GAME Hello? THE BIG GAME Can we go on Saturday Hello? instead? I have to leave early on Sunday. if you or a loved one Hello? have been diagnosed with mesothelioma Hello?

I slammed my head against the hull, all my legs wrapping around myself, curling up like a juvenile. Embarrassing, embarrassing. I was an *officer*. I should be able to *do this.*

But the *sounds*. I hadn't been able to enter regular torpor at *all*. I was too exhausted to *think.*

THE BIG GAME My air conditioner doesn't Hello? work great. Hello? Working nine to five the building is really old THE BIG GAME Hello? Can you hear me? Hello? Bueller Bueller THAT'S FIFTY PERCENT OFF MEMORIAL DAY

SALE AT Bueller Hello? Good. She wants to It's been really hot lately go out for a movie for her birthday RING RING RING RING UP TO TWENTY FIVE PERCENT OFF We can meet there at three? Hello?

I started prying part of my exoskeleton off. It was a bad habit I'd managed to kick after pupation and eclosure, but this whole ordeal was bringing it back.

One of my distal eyes caught sight of something drifting closer in the porthole, just outside the craft, in empty space. I shifted so I could see it with my primary eyes.

A metal flower floated into view, a silver base with gridded black petals spread out towards the light. The sounds reached a crescendo, and I went berserk.

This was an observatory mission and I wasn't supposed to interfere. Hell, the craft didn't even have any weapons. But it didn't matter. I knew nothing except for the mad desire for silence and the primal rage to destroy to get it.

I was doing advanced kinematics in my head as I reached the control panel, calculating velocities, momentums, the arc induced by the planet's gravitational pull-

I aligned the ship properly, ejected an escape pod from an external panel, and watched through the porthole as the capsule shot out from the ship, floating, dream-like, and smashed into the satellite. The petals crumpled and snapped off; the base broke into two pieces and began to drift away, debris from the collision spreading out like a slow-motion explosion.

I had no way of knowing, but down on the planet, three million people had just lost their cell phone service, and just as many radios went dead into static.

Oh, but *nobody* was enjoying that silence more than me. I could finally *think*.

Which meant I immediately realized what the problem had been all along–of course, a soft-bodied creature like this species would use low-frequency radio waves to communicate. The planet was bathed in them–to me, it had sounded like a weak static, but of *course*, they would speak softer. They would-

...They would be *hurt* by the frequency and acoustics my kind used to communicate.

Oh *no.* I hadn't been *talking* to it. I'd been torturing it, just like its species' constant radio waves had tortured me.

Damn. Not the best start for the mission. But, well...

In the silence, I could finally think. Maybe I'd gotten it backwards. Maybe instead of trying to teach it my language, I needed to learn its.

***

Sam continued fiddling with the tablet. It was... difficult, with its design. His fingers were too fat, too greasy, too clumsy.

He couldn't understand any of the symbols on it, of course, and he suspected he was missing a huge chunk of information that he couldn't even see—maybe those things did part of the interaction by feeling the device with their antennae, or something.

But he'd managed to turn the volume down. That was a good start. He'd gotten the object to make an annoying, but not painful, pulse pattern that thudded in his hands.

The hatch in the ceiling opened again, and he dropped the object and fled to the corner again.

The creature snaked out, clinging to the ceiling and examining him with a series of low-pitched clicks.

Sam looked at it with his heart pounding.

The thing's legs moved in a wave as it came down and slid the device towards itself, examining it with its head cocked, all of its—he could only assume—*eyes* looking between him and it.

"S-sorry," he stuttered. "Um. I was just playing with it."

The thing picked it up and started manipulating it, sliding levers and flashing through screens. Its movements were less agitated, and it wasn't actively hurting him, so this was an improvement.

Sam swallowed. "Um... Can I go home? Please? Why am I here?"

The mandibles opened, but instead of the usual horrible, hurting noise that came out, it vibrated in such a way that softer, broken sounds echoed out. "H...ello?"

About the Author

Nox is a lover of all creatures and people in sci-fi and fantasy and loves stories about persevering through horrors to come out better on the other side.

Project Touched by an Angel

Kay Hanifen

CW: medical abuse/torture, body horror, cancer, dubious medical ethics
Whumpee: Unspecified, Whumper: Woman, Caretaker: Woman

From the decoded personal notebook of Dr. Kiana Thompson
07 May 2035
Location Redacted:

I've always found the label "mad scientist" reductive and unhelpful. If I ever say that out loud, though, people will just tell me, "that's exactly what a mad scientist would say" before readying their torches and pitchforks. The thing is, when people picture mad science, it's always Victor Frankenstein cackling "It's alive! It's alive!" Real life mad science is more mundane in its evils. The father of modern gynecology experimented on slaves and the immortal HeLa cells that have been vital in lifesaving research were taken from Henrietta Lacks, a black woman, without her consent. You'll notice a pattern here.

I've been thinking a lot about this lately and the ethics of experimentation. Back then, scientists experimented on people of color because they were seen as less than human. Even now, I know I'm less likely to be listened to by doctors because of my gender and the color of my skin. Because we can no longer openly subject humans to this kind of cruelty, we now use animals. It's more acceptable for them to suffer if it means we'll reduce the suffering of humanity overall, but even then, some are trying to speak for those who cannot speak for themselves. I wonder if people would speak for something not of this world with the same passion.

Specimen 1 appeared in Death Valley National Park after an explosion comparable to the Tunguska Event on 01 March 2035. All the sand surrounding Specimen 1 had been superheated to shards of glass. It laid in the center, bone protruding from a broken leg and bowels spilling from a wound in its side. When the first responders arrived, they watched as it pushed its bowels back inside and the skin heal over as though it hadn't been cut at all. The same happened when it set its leg, crying out in pain as it pushed it back into place. It waited calmly and quietly while the military collected it and brought it to this black site.

Specimen 1 is a bipedal humanoid with no discernable sex. It's entirely hairless, but that's the only consistent thing about it. One moment, its skin is pale, the next, it's obsidian and then every shade in between. Its eyes, too, change in size, shape, and shade from black to brown to blue and green. Its nose, cheekbones, mouth, even height and nail length are constantly in flux. I have not been able to determine a pattern in when or why these shifts occur.

The subject is remarkably docile. Despite canines indicating that it's an omnivore, it doesn't even eat meat. All day, it just sits on its bed in its cell staring at the two-way mirror. It's not very scientific, but I don't get a feeling of hostility from its gaze. I think it may be studying us with the same curiosity that we're studying it. To what end, I'm not sure, but it's been entirely cooperative. It allows us to draw whatever samples we want—blood, tissue, even bone. I don't think it's afraid of us or of pain.

I believe that its healing ability is something that can change the course of human history. It has the salamander-like ability to regrow any limb or organ within minutes. Even stranger, its organs and blood appear to be compatible with any mammal. In tests with mice, Specimen 1's blood was found not only to help hemorrhaging mice recover, but also made them more resilient to disease, reduced inflammation, and even promoted faster healing. The same happened with cats, dogs, and chimpanzees. The all benefitted from Specimen 1's blood. When exposed to a disease, the antibodies Specimen 1 produces can be made into a vaccine safe even for immunocompromised people. If the pattern holds, Specimen 1 may singlehandedly end all disease. Can you imagine?

Because we have seen zero negative effects of introducing Specimen 1 to the mammalian body, human trials begin tomorrow.

08 May 2035

Julia Hayes: age nine, suffers from a rare form of metastatic bone cancer. The doctors gave her weeks to live, and her parents are just desperate enough to try an experimental procedure. I understand that kind of desperation. My wife also went through chemotherapy. We're lucky we caught it early, but I'll never forget the dread I felt as the world bottomed out below me and I thought I'd lose the woman I love most in the world.

The marrow from Specimen 1's bones has been successfully transplanted, and Hayes is in a recovery room for observation. There is no sign of her body rejecting the transplant yet, and her pulse is strong, but we'll still monitor her and her treatments for the next few months.

Specimen 1 did not resist as we entered the cell and strapped it face down to the operating table. Its expression was difficult to read, but it seemed almost eager. We injected it with a general anesthetic, and it seemed to fall asleep. But, when the needle slid into its bone, Specimen 1's eyes shot open and it whimpered.

"Stop, stop," I said, "It's still awake."

Specimen 1's eyes, currently dark brown, met mine, and it shook its head.

"You understand what we're doing?" I asked it. We'd tried talking to it before, but it was unresponsive. We'd all assumed it couldn't understand us.

It nodded.

"Okay," I said, and then to the doctor harvesting the marrow, "I guess we'll proceed."

We resumed the operation, Specimen 1 biting back whimpers and cries of pain. A few minutes in, I took its hand. It gave me a grateful look before squeezing it to distract itself.

It's strange. All this time, I've been thinking of Specimen 1 as something entirely alien, but standing there and holding its hand while it went through a painful procedure for someone it will never meet, I think it may be more sapient than I first believed. If so, that adds a new wrinkle to the ethics of using the parts of this...being. I should probably stop referring to Specimen 1 as an it. They're intelligent enough to give informed consent. They agreed to this procedure, but a single procedure is vastly different from getting scrapped for parts for the rest of their life. I'll need to come up with the right anesthetic cocktail for them. I can't imagine being awake while my organs and bone stem cells are being constantly removed. There is so much we don't know about them. Where did they come from? They're clearly not of this world, but are they even from this plane of existence? If I were a religious person, I would call them a gift from God—a being with infinite healing ability that can help all of humankind.

I've received word that the patient is waking up. I will update on her condition.

08 May Continued:

I knew Specimen 1's properties were borderline miraculous, but this is much better than my wildest dreams. Over the course of a few hours, Julia's cancer went from terminal to practically cured. I will forever cherish the looks on their faces when our team announced that she's in remission. The slack jawed shock, the smiles, the tears. A little girl was given the gift of a future today. I shouldn't get ahead of myself, of course. We'll keep having her come in for tests to make sure the cancer doesn't come back, or her body doesn't reject Specimen 1's stem cells, but I have a good feeling. In Specimen 1, we may very well have a cure for cancer, and that's just to start. What other gifts do they have?

15 May 2035:

We've been trying different cocktails of anesthetics, but nothing seems to be working. Specimen 1 may appear to be going under, but as soon as needle or scalpel touches skin, their eyes shoot open. In two days, we are performing an experimental kidney transplant and I don't want them to be awake for that. Were it up to me, I'd slow down on the human trials until I know more about Specimen 1, but my superiors were excited by the results of the Hayes experiment, so we're barreling forward. It's strange. At this point, I find myself more concerned for the wellbeing of Specimen 1 than the patient. It's not that I don't care about the people we're experimenting on. It's just that, so far, no one has experienced any negative effects of exposure to Specimen 1. Julia, for example, is happier and healthier than ever. Her parents reported that she's now so energetic that they can barely keep up. It's as if she never had cancer at all.

Specimen 1, though, runs the risk of spending the rest of their days in agony, strapped to an operating table, their blood, tissues, bones, and organs constantly being removed to meet the demands of a needy world

If I look at this from a utilitarian perspective, then who am I to deny the futures of thousands, if not millions, for the sake of one? But they're just so innocent. In an attempt to make life more bearable for them while alone in their cell, I gave them one of our test rabbits. Specimen 1 adores him. Instead of sitting and staring at the two-way mirror, they now spend their time focused entirely on the bunny, petting him, playing with him, feeding him. This rabbit is not used to kind human contact, so he took a little while to warm up to them, but now they're inseparable. It would be so much easier if Specimen 1 was a mindless vessel, but I know that they're intelligent, that they think and feel and even love, and I hate that all I do is inflict pain on something that has never done harm to anyone.

17 May 2035

Kidney transplant was a success. Steve Zhao: age 36, a Chinese immigrant, widower, and father of three with kidney failure. After three hours of surgery, he's awake in recovery and appears to be in good condition. We'll keep him under observation for a week, but I am optimistic for his recovery.

We could not find an anesthetic that is effective for Specimen 1. We've tried general anesthetics, local anesthetics, hypnotics, dissociatives, sedatives, adjuncts, neuromuscular-blocking drugs, narcotics, and analgesics but they were still awake throughout the entire procedure. They mostly whimpered while the surgeons worked, only screaming once the kidney was removed. When they were wheeled back to their room, they ran straight towards their rabbit and sobbed into his fur.

Here I am, on the front lines of a scientific breakthrough that could change the course of history, and I'm just heartbroken. I'm heartbroken for the patients, that Zhao was so desperate to live for his three children that he signed up for a dubiously ethical experimental procedure because he otherwise could not afford treatment and I'm heartbroken for the medical miracle themself and the agony we're putting them through. No matter what happens, I'm not leaving the project with my soul intact.

27 June 2035

We've accelerated human trials, with each one a resounding success. We're performing a procedure almost once a day—a transplant, a blood transfusion, stem cell retrieval—but I'm beginning to think that no anesthetic will be effective. Specimen 1 is going to feel every needle and every incision.

I've tried to make their existence while not being poked and prodded a little more bearable. I've given them another bunny along with a pile of old stuffed animals. Their favorite appears to be a ragged cat Beanie Baby. Specimen 1 always brings it to the operating room and squeezes it while the surgeons work. The other members of the team think I'm crazy and growing overly attached to this alien being, and I wonder how they can be so callous. I can understand wanting to maintain some distance for the sake of objectivity, but this is still a thinking, feeling creature. Maybe I am letting my emotions get the better of me, but I'd rather err on the side of compassion where I can.

DC and the pharmaceutical companies have caught wind of this discovery. The corporations are panicking, which means the politicians are panicking. I've been so focused on the possibilities of it that I hadn't considered the implications beyond curing cancer and most other deadly diseases, but this could also spell the end of the medical industry as we know it. If Specimen 1 is the miracle cure-all I think they might be, then these very profitable industries will lose a lot of money. I don't think that the fear is enough for my superiors to pull the plug just yet, but corporate greed has a long history of undermining public good for the sake of profit. Just ask the fossil fuel industry.

In personal news, my wife is going in for a checkup with the oncologist. It's been five years, but the fear is still there. She's been coughing a lot lately and trying to be discreet about it. When she's asleep, though, I hear a faint rattling in her abused lungs. She tells me not to worry, but that's my job. I love her so much, and I can't stand the thought of losing her.

27 June Continued:

I was startled out of my anxiety spiral by Specimen 1 knocking on the two-way mirror. Once they had my attention, they pointed to the door. This was the most communication I'd had with them outside of holding their hand in the operating room. I didn't even think they knew they were being watched while in their cell.

Specimen 1 had never hurt anyone or anything, but my hands still shook as I opened the door. I'd never been alone with them before. I stepped inside, shutting it behind me. Specimen 1 took my hand and led me to the bed before placing both bunnies in my lap. They stroked them gently while meeting my eyes as though showing me how to do it.

"You want me to pet them?" I asked.

They nodded.

As I stroked the bunnies, I began to talk, to try to explain myself to someone I wasn't sure understood me. "My wife, Yuki, was sick once. Lung cancer. We caught it early, but I still can't shake the feeling of helplessness I had when we first heard the news. I think I was more panicked than her. She's a mortician, so her relationship to death is a bit different from mine. She accepts its inevitability, but I'm a doctor, a healer. It's my job to stave it off." I could feel the flood of tears pressing against the dam. "I'm sorry. I'm sorry that you have to suffer for me to help people, and I'm sorry that I'm the one inflicting it. And I'm sorry I keep doing it because in every patient's face, I see Yuki's."

As expected, they didn't say anything, instead resting their head on my shoulder. And suddenly, I had this feeling of warmth and peace, like waking up beside Yuki on a lazy Sunday morning. I knew this feeling wasn't my own. Somehow,

Specimen 1 was projecting it into my mind. Apparently, they were an empath. I struggle to be surprised by them anymore. I guess that explained them knocking on the mirror. They could feel my distress from the other room.

I was in there for an hour. When I came back, there was a tearful message from Yuki telling me to meet her at the oncologist.

28 June 2035:

It's back. And it's metastasized. I don't know what to do.

I need to focus. Today, we're getting a visit from the heads of the Department of Health and the FDA, John Barrowman and Lewis Crain respectively. They want to see Specimen 1 for themselves. I don't know how I feel about that. Specimen 1 has been trying to get my attention all morning—probably sensing my emotional distress—but I have so much to do before the government officials arrive. If it goes poorly, the project will be terminated. If it goes well, Specimen 1 lives a life of agony they don't deserve. But do all those sick and suffering people deserve to die when Specimen 1 could have saved them? Seeing how well our patients are recovering—the transplant patients don't even need medications to prevent their immune systems from attacking their new organs—it gives me hope for Yuki.

28 June 2035 Continued:

Barrowman and Lawson came and went. The two were shown Specimen 1, and they expressed their awe, even checking their teeth like a damn horse. They're so impressed by our work that they want to expand our human trials. They want us to be drawing Specimen 1's blood to be sent out to the Red Cross for transfusions and to send daily tissue samples to pharmaceutical and biotechnology corporations for further experimentation. Additionally, they want to continue human trials with organ donations.

"That's a lot," I said, "Right now, Specimen 1 is stable, but accelerating our trials might—"

"Mrs. Thompson, I can't believe I forgot to say this, but I'm so sorry to hear about your wife," Director Barrowman said. "It must be so difficult to be working on a miracle cure she probably will never receive. If you keep pushing forward with the trials, we can move her to the top of the list of participants."

The bribe was transparent but effective. I know lung transplants aren't common for cancer, but Specimen 1's organs and tissue have cancer fighting properties that extend to the rest of the body. I can have her for the rest of our lives. "Okay," I said, refusing to look at Specimen 1 in the two-way mirror, "I'll accelerate the trials."

"Excellent," Crain said, "I'll send you a list of interested parties and what you're to supposed to send to them. Do you think she'd be ready by next week?"

"I, um, I can try," I said.

After they left with their chests puffed and visions of dollar signs dancing in their heads, I entered Specimen 1's cell alone for the second time. I sat down on the bed, and they put the rabbits in my lap before resting their ever-shifting head on my shoulder. I'd never hated myself more than in that moment.

In high school, I read Ursula K. Le Guin's short story, "The Ones Who Walk Away from Omelas." In it, she asks you to imagine a perfect society—one free from pain, disease, or want, with festivals every day and love abounding—but it holds a dark secret. In a basement somewhere, a child experiences all the pain and suffering so that the town does not. Everyone sees the child once, and they get a choice: stay in this city knowing the source of its prosperity or walk away to some great unknown.

But now imagine you're the jailer administering the beatings and pouring rotten gruel down its throat for the sake of the community. Unlike everyone else, you're confronted with the source of the city's prosperity every day. How can you possibly stay?

But here I am, the jailer torturing the child for the good of everyone else. I used to like to think I'd walk away, but now I know I wouldn't. Instead of being just complicit in its suffering, I'd choose to inflict it for the greater good.

The greater good. What a phrase. Ever notice that people only say it when they're about to do something heinous? It's never, "I'm recycling for the greater good," or "I'm volunteering at the homeless shelter for the greater good." Instead, it's always "I'm experimenting on people without their consent for the greater good" or "I'm enslaving these people for the greater good."

Sensing my growing distress, Specimen 1 sat up and took my hand, placed it on their chest so I could feel them breathe in and out. Their eyes met mine, and I studied the shifting colors. A deep feeling of peace washed over me, giving me the sense that everything would be okay.

29 June 2035:

I talked to Yuki last night about the experimental lung transplant. Even though it's highly classified, I came clean about the project I'd been working on.

"So, if I'm understanding you correctly," she said, her voice dangerously low, "You've been lying to patients by telling them you're implanting 3D printed organs when they're really from this miracle alien."

"I know it's not ethical, but—"

"Not ethical is the understatement of the century! This is horrifying!" At that last exclamation, she doubled over coughing.

I rushed to her side, but she shrugged me off. "Yuki..."

"You, of all people..."

"I know," I closed my eyes, willing the tears back. I'd wanted to tell her all this time, to talk to her about my conflicts and guilt, get her advice on what I should do, but it's all classified. So classified, in fact, that not even all of Congress is aware of Specimen 1's existence. If they find out I told her anything at all, I could be kicked off the project or worse.

"I want to see them," she said.

My jaw dropped. "What? I can't—"

"I'll only agree to this if I see them for myself." She had that steely look in her eyes, the kind that told me she'd made her choice and will not budge. She's stubborn like that.

"I'll see if I can clear it," I said.

I couldn't, in fact, clear it. As expected, my superiors laughed in my face. I came prepared, though. Two years ago, when Yuki was going through a photography phase, I bought her a polaroid camera for her birthday. Today, I brought it in with me and took it out as soon as they were done calling me an idiot for even thinking about showing her the specimen.

Specimen 1 sat in their cell with their rabbits. When they saw me holding a camera, they smiled and posed with its bunnies and stuffed animals. I snapped a few pictures and showed them to Specimen 1. They seemed delighted by them and the camera, trying to take it apart to see how it worked. The nice thing about polaroid is that it leaves no digital footprint. All it will take is a match to get rid of the evidence. It's the same reason I'm writing this in a physical journal rather than on a computer. I know Yuki wanted to meet them, but this is the best I can do without sending a government assassin after us.

30 June 2035:

I showed Yuki the photographs. She's still not happy about my ethics, but in all fairness, neither am I. After staring at the polaroids, she asked me a few questions about Specimen 1, mostly their behavior and how other patients have reacted to its tissue.

"I haven't seen anyone suffering adverse effects," I said, "In fact, most recover quickly, don't need to take medication to prevent the body from rejecting it, and are overall healthier than their previous peak."

She frowned, staring at the pictures of them holding the rabbit up to the camera with a big smile on their face. "I feel bad. I know they'll heal, but it's like you're asking me to let you torture a puppy to cure my cancer."

I took her hand. "If it makes you feel better, they seem intelligent enough to consent, and have done so already for all the patients we've had."

"It doesn't," she said, sliding the polaroid back to me, "but I'll do it."

We burned the photos immediately after. As I watched the fire consume them, I prayed that Specimen 1 would perform a miracle again and give us a future.

04 July 2035:

It's done. Yuki is resting in the recovery room, and I am exhausted. Specimen 1 is exhausted too. They're curled up around their rabbits, and asleep. Funny, I didn't know they did that.

We'd tried to make the removal quick without damaging the organs, but it was still open lung surgery without anesthetic. I held their hand as the surgeon cracked open their chest. They remained still, tears streaming down their face as the lungs were removed. As they gasped for air where there was none, I saw something in their eyes that I'd never seen in any of our other procedures—fear. The inability to breathe had awakened an animal terror that I didn't think they had. The lungs were growing back almost as soon as they were taken out, but there clearly wasn't enough oxygen going in. The surgeons closed their chest, and with an agonizing slowness, their breathing returned to normal. As soon as it had, I let out I breath I hadn't realized I'd been holding.

Yuki was in surgery for eight hours in total. Early scans so far look good. She's breathing unassisted and the cancer already seems to be retreating. It's now after dinner, and I've sat down for the first time since arriving in the building before the crack of dawn. The news is on in the background. It seems the president is hosting a Fourth of July ball. Most of Congress is in attendance, as are diplomats and CEO's of Fortune 500 companies. So much for keeping the money out of politics. He's about to give a big speech before the fireworks. One set off a little early, though, and—Oh God. That wasn't a firework. It was a bomb. Now multiple bombs are going off at once. I'm just sitting here in frozen shock. I know my superiors will call me in soon. Me and Specimen 1.

06 July 2035:

I can't do this anymore. For the past two days, I've been at Specimen 1's side, holding their hand as they tore them apart like vultures picking out the liver of Prometheus. Right now, they're back in their cell sobbing into their rabbits. I keep staring at the cat Beanie Baby stained irrevocably with their blood. They took so much from them—removing their heart, spleen, lungs, kidneys, eyes, and peeling off large swaths of skin for grafting. They even cut off limbs and attached them to the amputees. Apparently, Specimen 1's extremities can be grafted onto people like cuttings on a tree. They even adapt skin color and length so that only a scar indicates that the limb was removed at all.

Forty-eight hours of this. By the time we were done, Specimen 1 was practically exsanguinated. They now walk on shaky legs and have this haunted look in their kind eyes. I think we've finally broken them. I want to go in there and comfort them as best I can, but when I tried to steady the, Specimen 1 flinched away from my touch. I don't blame them. I'm glad they at least have their rabbits and stuffed animals for comfort.

As painful as these past two days have been, I'll give them this—Specimen 1 has not lost a single patient. Sure, there was a death toll. We couldn't get to everyone in time, but every person we were able to treat—even the ones in critical condition—pulled through. It feels weird seeing the President's literal guts instead of just his metaphorical ones. I'm still getting used to that knowledge.

We did a lot of good that day—I know we did—but I'm done. Specimen 1's screams still echo in my ears, and I can't hear them again. I'm walking away from Omelas and the destruction of my soul for the greater good. I know it seems hypocritical to do that now after directly benefitting from Specimen 1's suffering, and maybe it is, but I'm going to make things right.

You see, when I first read the story, I admired the ones who could pick up their lives and leave Omelas and thought they'd redeemed themselves by no longer participating in the child's direct suffering. But now, I've realized that they're no less complicit than the ones that stayed. They may have cast themselves out of paradise for the sake of their morals, but none of them actually helped the child. It stays trapped and miserable in its cell. I can't do that. I can't be complicit anymore.

I'll stay and play along until I can figure out how to help them escape.

29 July 2035

Apparently, there are side effects to Specimen 1's tissue. It makes people more altruistic. For some, it's subtle. Yuki has become more involved in activism and community outreach. When I'm not around, she's usually volunteering at the local homeless shelter. She's always cared about these issues, but the new lungs seem to be the push she needed to get involved. It's mostly harmless, maybe even good.

Mostly. It seems that, for some, the altruism is on pain of bodily rejection. The CEOs and politicians we treated after the July Fourth white supremacist bombing are finding certain tasks difficult. The CEO of an oil company that shall not be named, for example, has been experiencing chest pain that can only be alleviated by him decreasing his fossil fuel drilling and investing in clean energy.

A number of politicians report pain when they consider cutting taxes on the rich and creating legislation that limits the rights of queer people. They're all scared, and people have been whispering about the imminent ending of the program.

I'm sorry, but I have to laugh. The wealthy and powerful are terrified of being forced to put people over profit. Some of the biotech corporations are even ending their experiments on Specimen 1's tissue. After all, what's the point of a miracle cure-all if it won't make them money by creating a false scarcity?

I've been thinking about how I can help Specimen 1 escape. The best time would probably be when they're in transport for surgery offsite. They have a heart donation coming up for a CEO more scared of his mortality than the forced altruism. That could be my best chance.

17 August 2035

I need to get this down before I burn the whole book just to get the secret out of my system.

They're gone. I don't know where, but they're gone—free. Freer than we'll be if we get caught. Right now, I'm on a secluded beach in Montenegro. I won't say more than that. The country hits that sweet spot of being safe for gay people, just diverse enough that a black woman and an Asian woman wouldn't be too unusual and having no extradition treaty with the US. We're staying at least for ninety-days, and beyond that...we'll think of something.

As it turns out, lying in a hospital bed recovering from a lung transplant is a great opportunity to plan a successful heist. Yuki's been thinking about it ever since she woke up with her greater sense of altruism. All in all, it was a relatively simple plan.

A few days before Specimen 1 was to be taken offsite for the heart transplant, I took the rabbits from their cell. I knew that they would be devastated if we left them behind.

When I entered with the cage, they huddled in the corner, holding them both close. I knelt down in front of them.

"I'm going to take your friends in for a vet checkup. Make sure they're up to date on their shots and healthy, okay?" I said, mentally pushing a desire for their trust towards them and hoping they would pick up on those feelings with their empathic abilities.

They eyed me suspiciously but relinquished their grip on them.

I put them in the cage and said, "This may take a few days, but I promise you'll see them again."

Their only reaction was to watch me intently as I left them alone with their stuffed animals. I wonder what was going through their head. Did they trust me? Or did they just feel too powerless to fight back?

Phase Two required a lot of luck and timing on the day of surgery. Because the average citizen would panic at the sight of a shape-shifting humanoid, we always enter through the morgue with Specimen 1 in a body bag. Convenient that my wife's a mortician then, right?

In my experience, security tends to be more lax on the way back than the way there. It's the Everest principle: people expend most of their energy reaching the mountain peak and are therefore more likely to die on the return when their guard is down.

The removal of Specimen 1's heart took an hour. We waited another hour for it to regrow and fully heal. While the surgeon drew blood for emergency transfusions, I texted Yuki our code, "Did you take the pork out of the freezer for dinner?"

When she texted back, "Shoot! Sorry, doing that now!" I knew she was in position.

It was around lunch by the time we were heading out. To not appear too suspicious, I was accompanied by two armed guards dressed like nurses. One walked ahead of me, the other behind. In that final corridor, I spotted Yuki casually pushing a gurney with a body bag. An underrated skill of a mortician? Makeup. With the magic of bronzer and contouring, she'd completely changed her face shape. Her usually round face was now more chiseled and masculine, and her lips were now fuller with a defined cupid's bow. Up close, it wouldn't stand to scrutiny, but with her hair up, she could easily be mistaken for a man. When we reached the door, there were two nondescript white vans—the government's and Yuki's. And the government's had a flat tire.

"Oh, come on," the guard in front exclaimed.

"Wait here," the other said, pushing past me. That morning, I had left a nail behind one of the back tires. The van ran over it, and the puncture slowly let out air so that we could get to the hospital without raising suspicions. While they debated what to do, Yuki walked up beside me from behind.

I glanced up at the security camera, and praying I was in a blind spot. Casually, we swapped places. She continued on with Specimen 1's gurney while I pushed forward with the decoy body. As soon as she pulled away, I went up to the guards struggling with replacing a tire.

"Hey, I'm starving," I said, "Do you think I have time to run to the Subway and get something to eat?"

He shrugged. "Yeah, probably. Just don't be too long."

"Thanks," I said, and headed back inside.

Meanwhile, Yuki had driven around to the main entrance. I walked there and hopped in the back with Specimen 1 and the rabbits. As she drove out of the parking lot, I unzipped the body bag and Specimen 1 sat up in confusion. I lifted the cage, showing it the bunnies while Yuki exclaimed, "Prison break!"

For the first time since Fourth of July, Specimen 1 smiled.

We let them go in a national park. With the cage in one hand, they pressed another to my cheek and then to Yuki's, and I felt this great warmth come from within. They shimmered, light bending around them like a prism, and then vanished.

Angel or alien, I don't think I'll ever know the whats and the whys. Were they a gift from God? A test? If it was the latter, did we pass it by letting Specimen 1 go or fail by not using them to their fullest potential? Even sitting here on this beach, matchbook in my front pocket, I don't know if I made the right choice. I doubt I ever will.

About the Author

Kay Hanifen was born on a Friday the 13th and once lived for three months in a haunted castle. So, obviously, she had to become a horror writer. Her work has appeared in over forty anthologies and magazines. When she's not consuming pop culture with the voraciousness of a vampire at a 24-hour blood bank, you can usually find her with her black cats or at kayhanifenauthor.wordpress.com.

Sedative

Booker G. A. Feniks

CW: Needles, restraints, non-consensual drug use
Whumpee: Man, Whumper: Unspecified, Caretaker: N/A

He shrieked and cried and kicked when they strapped him to the table. The cuffs formed grooves in his skin, and his joints felt stretched beyond their breaking point. There were tingles traveling all over the base of his skull from where his tail was being pulled on.

"Hold it down, I need to administer the sedative." The cold voice washed over him like a wave, slightly muffled beneath the heavy-duty masks the scientists wore. A scientist grabbed at his jaw when he gnashed his teeth at them, sinking a single canine into the delicate, meaty flesh of a human hand.

"I said *hold* it *down.*" Another wave of fear brought a sob to his trembling lips, his jaw forced open so wide that his serpentine tongue had no purchase anywhere.

"I'm administering the sedative." A prick, the tingling feeling of warmth spreading beneath his skin, beneath the scales of his elongated throat. A second, and then the world began growing dark at the edges, the smells of the laboratory began growing dull.

A third prick, and he was gone.

About the Author

Booker-Garet August Feniks is a queer, disabled writer of fantasy, comedy, and poetry. He writes stories that pull directly from their experiences as a queer immigrant. Originally from Poland, Kielce, Booker writes primarily in English, and has a passion for storytelling and linguistics as a whole.

Settling the Little Albert Debate

Aiden E. Messer

CW: Phobias, unethical science

Whumpees: Men and women, Whumper: Unspecified, Caretaker: N/A

Introduction

Much has been written about Little Albert's experience in inducing phobias (Watson & Rayner, 1920), and any student of psychology will have heard of it. Yet, this experiment has never been replicated, and its results are highly debated. Indeed, the experiment was carried out on a single subject, and although a phobia of white rats and, by extension, of furry objects in general, was instantiated, no attempt was made to desensitize the subject. Moreover, Little Albert left the hospital with his mother shortly after the experiment, and his identity remains unconfirmed. It is therefore impossible to know whether the phobia lasted over time or disappeared on its own, or whether Dr. John B. Watson would have been able to decondition it as he believed.

The aim of the present study is to rectify these shortcomings, and to investigate in detail the conditioning and deconditioning processes involved in phobias.

Our hypothesis is that, as Dr. Watson believed, a phobia can be conditioned and deconditioned using appropriate stimuli.

Methodology

Participants

For ethical reasons, it was impossible to carry out this experiment on babies of Little Albert's age. Instead, we selected 60 undergraduate students who agreed to take part in exchange for extra credit. The subjects, 24 women and 36 men aged 18 to 25, were not told the exact purpose of the study, so as not to bias the experiment. They believed they had been selected for a study on memorization.

Method

Participants were divided into two groups of 30: a test group and a control group. The test group had to watch and memorize images displayed on a screen. Each time an image of a red apple (neutral stimulus) appeared, a painful electric shock (unconditioned stimulus) was sent through electrodes to their stomachs. This method is inspired by Burrhus Skinner's theory of operant conditioning (Skinner, 1963) and the concept of aversive electrical shock (Busch & Evans, 1977).

The control group was subjected to the same images, without the electric shocks.

The test group was then split into two groups of 15: again, a test group and a control group. The test group was subjected to a desensitization process consisting of associating apples (conditioned stimulus) with a sweet food reward (unconditioned stimulus). The control group did not experience any desensitization.

In other words, the apple was first associated with a positive punishment (the addition of physical pain), then to a positive reward (the addition of sweet food) (Skinner, 1963).

Results

	Test (18M, 12F)	Control (18M, 12F)
Phobia of apple developed	93.3% (18M, 10F)	0% (0M, 0F)
Phobia generalized to other fruits	73% (15M, 7F)	0% (0M, 0F)
Phobia generalized to other red elements	60% (12M, 6F)	0% (0M, 0F)
Phobia generalized to the laboratory itself	73% (14M, 8F)	0% (0M, 0F)

Fig 1: subjects' initial reaction

Almost all test subjects developed aversive reactions to the sight of the apple. We suspect that the two test subjects on whom this did not work might have had an earlier experience with pain that they did not disclose during the screening process, or a higher-than-normal resistance to pain, though this could not be verified. All test subjects but the two previously mentioned asked to leave the study before the end, but a reminder of the effect this would have on their grades and academic future changed their minds.

One month after the experiment, the rate of phobia had fallen significantly in the test group, particularly with regard to generalizations of phobia to other elements. This effect was also present in the control group, albeit to a significantly lesser extent.

There is one notable exception to this trend. Surprisingly, aversion to the laboratory itself seems to have increased in both the test and control groups. Further research is needed to understand the reasons for this phenomenon.

Discussion

In this study, we wanted to find out whether, as Dr. Watson believed, it was possible to induce a phobia and then make it subside. The answer seems to be positive; we have indeed succeeded in inducing a phobia of red apples, and the first results seem to indicate that we can make it disappear. Further tests will be carried out on subjects in 1, 5 and 10 years' time to confirm this hypothesis. It will also be interesting to conduct another study to understand the strange effect that the laboratory itself seems to have had on the test subjects.

	Test (9M, 6F)	Control (9M, 6F)
Negative response to apple	66,6% (7M, 3F)	86,6% (8M, 5F)
Neutral response to apple	26,6% (2M, 2F)	13% (1M, 1F)
Positive response to apple	6,6% (0M, 1F)	0% (0M, 0F)
Negative response to other fruits	46,6% (5M, 2F)	46,6% (6M, 1F)
Neutral response to other fruits	46,6% (4M, 3F)	53,3% (3M, 5F)
Positive response to other fruits	6,6% (0M, 1F)	0% (0M, 0F)
Negative response to other red elements	20% (2M, 1F)	20% (1M, 2F)
Neutral response to other red elements	66,6% (6M, 4F)	73,3% (8M, 3F)
Positive response to other red elements	2% (1M, 1F)	6,6% (0M, 1F)
Negative response to the laboratory itself	100% (9M, 6F)	100% (9M, 6F)
Neutral response to the laboratory itself	0% (0M, 0F)	0% (0M, 0F)
Positive response to the laboratory itself	0% (0M, 0F)	0% (0M, 0F)

Fig 2: desensitization

Conclusion

In conclusion, although it's still too early to claim a definitive answer, it seems clear to us that Dr. Watson was right. Phobias can indeed be induced and treated through operant conditioning.

Bibliography

Busch, C. J., & Evans, I. M. (1977). The effectiveness of electric shock and foul odor as unconditioned stimuli in classical aversive conditioning. *Behaviour Research and Therapy, 15*(2), 167-175

Skinner, B. F. (1963). Operant behavior. *American psychologist, 18*(8), 503.

Watson, J. B., & Rayner, R. (1920). Conditioned emotional reactions. *Journal of experimental psychology, 3*(1), 1.

About the Author

Aiden E. Messer does not exist. Are they an illusion, a ghost, a mere thought? No one knows. If we are to believe one of the children they seem to work with, if they were a teacher, they would be as tall as a human. They are not a teacher. According to various sources, they have studied psychology, and have always had a penchant for horror and the macabre. They like to combine these subjects in their books.

The Boy of Theseus

Zipper

CW: Gore, limb amputation

Whumpee: Man, Whumper: Man, Caretaker: N/A

For what felt like the thousandth time, Axel sat back in the chair while the doctors strapped him in. The familiarity of the situation didn't stop him from trembling like he'd caught a chill. The doctors hadn't told him what was coming; they never did anymore. They'd grown weary of his pleading. It didn't help, though, not being told—Axel could imagine what was coming well enough to make himself sick with anticipation.

By now, he knew better than to beg. Or, at least, he thought he did. When a lab tech raised the rubber bit toward his mouth, he spoke up. "Can—can you please use anesthetic this time?"

He worried that his small voice would get lost amongst the bustle of preparation, but Dr. Brenner, the head doctor on today's experiment, paused and turned to him. He'd always been one of the kinder ones. He looked sympathetic now as he said, gently, "Axel, you know it wears off too quickly."

"I know," he whispered. His metabolism flushed drugs out of his system faster than they could be used. It would be a waste to dose him with anything when it wouldn't last half as long as he needed it to. "But—but—"

Dr. Brenner gave him a smile that was probably meant to be reassuring. "We've just got this one experiment lined up for today, okay? Then we'll be out of your hair till next week, I promise."

The doctors said that every time. Axel didn't think any of them realized how short a week was. "Okay," he said quietly.

Dr. Brenner patted him on the shoulder, almost fatherly. "You're a pro at this, Axel. It'll be over before you know it."

Over like a nightmare—a handful of excruciating minutes that stretched until they felt like hours. Axel opened his mouth and let the bit slide between his teeth. He clamped down tight and closed his eyes.

It never helped. When the bone saw sliced his skin, just below his shoulder, his eyes flew open of their own volition. His body jerked, but hands and straps held him steady, and the bone saw glided back and forth, blood spraying the doctors' scrubs, gushing down his arm, his fingers twitching and convulsing until he finally couldn't feel them anymore, couldn't feel anything except pain, pain, *pain*.

Through a haze of tears, Axel watched as someone unstrapped his right wrist and transferred his arm to a metal tray. It sailed out of the room, disappearing into the depths of the lab. The worst part was over, but Axel couldn't stop sobbing, molars clenched on the bit, wishing for morphine or numbness or unconsciousness. His vision refused to go dark, only smudged with watery blurs as the doctors cleared out of the way.

"Good job, Axel." The voice seemed to come from some distant island of reality. Axel lifted his head to see Dr. Brenner smiling at him, his blue surgical scrubs smattered with blood. "Just hold still for the camera, okay?"

Axel always forgot the camera. It was aimed at the stump of his right arm, watching it regenerate. The gush of blood was already slowing to a trickle, and he felt the burn of his skin suturing itself back together, cells multiplying to replace what was taken away. His entire right side felt warm and sticky. He looked away, to his left, and realized that his gown was flecked with red over there, too. His cheeks were gritty with salt. Nothing was clean after these experiments.

A damp cloth passed over his face. "Axel?" Dr. Brenner's voice sounded closer now, less echoey, but the man himself was still standing in the same place. "Are you with me?" Axel nodded, focusing his gaze across the room, so that he wouldn't have to look at the doctor or his own blood-soaked lap. "Do you want the bit out?" His teeth ached with the pressure of his clenched jaw. He shook his head. "Alright, just hang in there. Looks like the arm's already growing back." Axel felt it: nerve endings springing to life, bone and sinew progressing downward as if to fill the invisible mold his old arm had left behind.

His old arm. How old was it, really? A few months? He couldn't remember. All he knew was that it wasn't the arm he'd been born with. That one was taken years ago, the first time the doctors had performed this experiment. But then, every person's cells were constantly dying and replacing themselves. No one *really* had the same arms they were born with, even if theirs hadn't been sawn off in a lab.

The Axel of Theseus. He was light-headed enough that the thought made the corner of his mouth twitch. How many parts of a ship can you replace before it's not the same ship anymore? How many parts of a boy can you chop off before he becomes a different person altogether?

The answer was disappointingly simple, for a philosophical question. Axel's body grew the cells; it wasn't as though new genetic material was being introduced. No matter how often his limbs were chopped off, his organs removed, his hair plucked or shaved, it was always him. The doctors hadn't touched anything as fundamental as his brain yet. That would be a real philosophical predicament. If the doctors cut off his head, would his body grow a new head? Would his head grow a new body? Which one would be him? Both of them?

It would be more interesting to him, he supposed, if the question were strictly theoretical. Now all he could think about was how it would feel if that throbbing pain in his right arm were happening to his neck.

A dry cloth wiped the tears from Axel's face, and a hand patted his good shoulder. "You're always such a good sport, Axel. We'll be done soon."

Until next week, Axel wanted to remind him. *You'll be done until you need me again.* Him and his brand-new right arm, flowing into the space where its predecessor had been.

About the Author

Zipper is from the east coast, USA. They're currently studying writing of all kinds at [REDACTED] College. When they're not writing, you can find them thinking about writing.

Human

Konn Lavery

By Konn Lavery
CW: Character death
Whumpee: Man, Whumpers: Man, Woman, Caretaker: Woman

Confinement in a cage drives any being to insanity. The lack of connection mutates civilized people into wild beasts. Even well-trained animals will revert to their primal ways if locked away. Jackson finds himself an excellent candidate for the effects, for he sits naked in his concrete box, day in, day out, with nowhere to go and no one to talk to.

His mind rots, little by little, as he squats in the corner relieving himself, staring at the light grey box on the opposite side of the ceiling with a red light flashing each second. It's the ever-alert eye, informing the Watchers what he does inside his concrete prison. Since he was born, the box has been there, and there isn't a damn thing he can do about it.

Jackson isn't naïve to the outside world. He may have grown up in this cage, but he has seen wildlife. There's a tree out there, tall and beautiful, reaching for the blue skies. Other than the one time, the closest possession he has to the wild is his stuffed rabbit toy.

The Watchers decide when he is worthy to leave his confinement. Unfortunately, it has only been the single encounter. That glimpse from his childhood is forever ingrained into his memory. Of course, it mirrors the photos he has seen during his learning sessions, curated by the Watchers.

Being outdoors changed him by providing hope for something better. The smell of open space under the tree ignited a burning desire to be there again, underneath the large tree with a broad base and lush dark green leaves. The experience lasted a blink of an eye, and then he was brought back into the concrete maze with cold lights illuminating from the ceiling. Why the Watchers took him beyond was a mystery. He has never touched nor tasted the outside.

This burn made him disobedient, rebelling against the Watchers. He screamed, throwing his stuffed rabbit at the light grey box. He threw his food at the ever-alert-eye. He even launched his own excrement at the red light in hopes to cover it. Jackson has damaged his hands from punching against the solid walls, smearing them red. He wanted his outside.

The violence forced the Watchers to take action. Three arrived from the cold steel door with their usual strange white rubber skin and soulless black faces staring at him. Their breath ended in a hissing exhale. The tubes around their throats swayed side to side.

Jackson attempted to attack the group with his damaged fists, sprinting towards them. A projectile needle met his neck before he could even blink. Its poison was instant and caused him to stumble for several steps and collapse onto the ground, sliding inches from the black feet of the three Watchers.

The following day Jackson woke up on his soft mattress in the corner of his prison with his stuffed rabbit beside him. All the blood on the walls was removed, the light grey box was no longer covered in feces, and a fresh breakfast bowl awaited him by the steel door. His efforts were futile. It belittled Jackson, making him wish he could end his miserable existence. There was no tool to perform the task. The Watchers broke the poor soul.

Jackson has broken a total of twelve times in his life. He's good at counting.

The burning memory of being outside with the crisp air and that magnetic tree resurfaces in his dreams. In his slumber, he attempts to see how high he is able to climb. It's as close to the beautiful greenery as he can get.

All Jackson can do is sit here and stew in his own misery until the Watchers provide him with food, a new learning session, or until he falls into a deep sleep. The memory of the tree lives on, despite the Watchers breaking him into their will.

Time is difficult to tell considering there is no sun nor seasons. Jackson repeats his miserable daily routine. He doesn't understand their strange technology or most of the language they speak.

Each day his physical checkup occurs after he has breakfast. The white-suited humanoids enter his prison with a chrome wheeled tray filled with tools. They take his blood sample, weigh him, check his reflexes, and analyze his eyes with a bright light. Once they deem him worthy, his educational sessions may begin.

The first group of Watchers left, and a new one enters, rolling in the learning box. Its bright curved glass illuminated brightness with a speaker just below. It made strange sounds, trying to communicate with him as it showcases a series of photos within the screen. The display highlighted the tree outside and rabbits, like his stuffed toy. He was unfamiliar with what they were attempting to say and does his best to imitate the learning box to create a form of communication with the Watchers.

The voice said the exact phrases on repeat. Its sounded identical to the Watchers, and Jackson couldn't mimic the complex vocals they produce. He felt a hot rage inside him and punched the speaker from time to time. By mimicking certain noises, he earns a sweet reward that is released from the bottom of the learning box.

Today, the light displayed illustrations of unclothed pale beings. They looked similar to him. There were two drawings on the screen. The first was rounder with curves creating the complete form with long brunette locks, while the second looked more like Jackson: broader and sharper angles.

Both images had far less hair than he, only existing on their heads and pelvic region. The learning box projected sound. Jackson couldn't understand what it said. It became clearer, changing from:

HOO-AN

HOO-MAH-AN

HOO-MAN

Human.

"HUMAN," Jackson said. The bottom tray opened, providing him a sweet treat to enjoy.

Then, the screen changed to a new illustration of a single human with much more hair and muscles. The box spoke, giving him a different phrase far more complex:

NEE-AN-HALL, JACKSON

NEE-AN-DA-HALL, JACKSON

NEE-AN-DA-ERA-HALL, JACKSON

Jackson couldn't comprehended what the learning box was trying to say with the first word. He didn't get a second candy.

One morning, he woke to find his food bowl with a scrap piece of paper tucked underneath it with a crude drawing. The illustration was of a tree. Not any old tree, but the exact one he saw outside with the broad base and thin top.

He looked up at the alert light grey box, remembering its watchful blinking red eye. He shifted his back to it and stared at the torn document, flipping it over to see if there was anything of value. It had no clue, smell, or taste, just a tree drawing. He ate the paper with his bowl of mush, knowing there must be no evidence of this strange message for the Watchers to find. Too often, they clean his prison.

The dish was taken away each day, and the Watchers perform a physical health checkup. He is obedient and does not fight back. There is a sliver of hope in his mundane existence. The message stirred in his mind without end, and he toyed with the possibility that it was a strange experiment by the Watchers. Only time would tell the true nature of the image.

Five days went by before Jackson got a second letter under his bowl. Goosebumps rose on his skin as he held the paper in excitement. This sheet was another crude drawing of a door and one of the Watchers with a heart beside it. He ate the message and the food after.

The steel door opened, and a single Watcher entered the room. Their black rubber hands raised, taking slow steps towards Jackson. The right thumb pressed against the palm, holding a piece of paper. Jackson's pulse raced, scanning the Watcher's white plastic skin, tubes, boots, their whole form to determine if there's a hidden trick up their sleeve.

The blackness of the face made it impossible to know what emotion they were feeling. Only the hissing snake exhale filled the room. Jackson remained by his bowl, waiting to see what the Watcher would do.

They spoke a muffled, inaudible phrase that Jackson wished he could understand. The tone was higher pitched, friendly, far less hostile than the usual Watchers. The being reached several paces from Jackson when he rose from his seat. He took his first lumbering steps towards them. The being froze as Jackson approached and said something understandable:

JAH-CH-SHON

Jackson knew it was his name. The voice was feminine in tone, similar to the learning box. He patted his chest and tried to mimic the exact phrase, but his tongue and throat did not create the same sound, producing a strange groaning, "*AH-CH-HOHN.*"

The Watcher, in slow motion, unfolded the piece of paper in their hand, showing a picture of the tree. Jackson smiled, clapping.

This newcomer raised their hands to their black face, moving around the tubes to the back of their head, pulling on the rubber and lifting the mask off. The new face was of a female, much like the illustration on the learning box. The bright blue eyes stunned him as he analyzed her entire facial complexion. The skin was far softer than his own, and the hair is long, wavy and blonde. It struck him was a strange sense of wonder he hadn't felt before, similar to the tree, but its own potent emotion.

"COME JAH-CH-SHON," the Watcher said, waving.

Jackson looked to his bed and stuffed rabbit once they reached the steel door-frame leading to a bright white hallway. A calm wind came from beyond the prison, causing him to shiver. He ran his hand along with the passage, sensing the cold steel, recalling this corridor from when he was a child. It had been so long.

The Watcher said something that he couldn't understand. The only words he caught were *"CAM-EH-AH"* and *"COME."*

The Watcher picked up her pace and Jackson followed through the bright hallway. They move past expansive glass windows peering into a dark room with chairs and an oval wooden table. His attention was brought to the dim reflection of himself. He paused, looking at it face on.

Unlike the Watcher, his face was far flatter. The nose had a wide bridge, and his eyebrows widen above the eyes. The ears were more prominent, from his sockets and down to his jawline. His shaggy brown hair ran from his chin, coarser, up to his scalp. Most of his neck, shoulders, and chest were covered in the same tangled strands.

He placed his hand against the reflection, getting a clear look at himself for the first time. He's always speculated and could only see his face in the water bowl that distorted his image. He looked so different than the beautiful Watcher.

"COME JAH-CH-SHON," the Watcher urged.

The white hallway turned red as loud sirens erupted. The sound blasted into his eardrums, causing him to cover them and squat downward. The blaring noise bounced off the walls, piercing his senses, making it impossible to tell its origins.

A soft, warm hand grabbed his rough fingers and pulled his forearm. The motion triggered Jackson's impulsive, defensive nature, and he let out a fierce cry. He yanked on his arm, pulling the blue eyed Watcher. She flung in the air, passing Jackson to the other side of the hallway. The Watcher slammed onto the ground, sliding into the wall. Her head made a loud thump against the concrete. Red liquid drizzled out from under her wavy hair, eyes closed.

Jackson breathed in rapid sessions, feeling his hairs stand on his body. He killed her, he knew it. He burst from his frozen stance. The blaring siren continued echoing through the halls, never lessening. The harshness and volume disoriented Jackson, but he kept running, taking a left turn, then right, straight, and zigzagging through this maze of uncertainty.

One hall had a new window showing a concrete room that looked identical to his prison. Inside this space was another naked being. Their hairy form and wide nose bridge reminded him of himself. They used their own learning box, unaware of the sirens.

Jackson took a few steps back and bumped into the opposite wall against a different window. He turned to face a second concrete room with a new being who looked just like Jackson. This being was sleeping, unalarmed, on its mattress with its own stuffed rabbit. The similar characteristics ramped his instincts to run.

He dashed from the glass and down the long hall housing more windows on each side of him. Each one presented the same room with hairy clones of himself. A T-intersection confronted Jackson after the last window. This panel showcased large cylinders filled with water and tubes coming out of them. Inside each tank was a being. These ones were smaller, semi-formed, with shrivelled arms and legs. Cold lights illuminated the tanks, forming elongated shadows on their flat-nosed faces.

Jackson didn't stop and ran until he reached the intersection with heavy stomping. Three Watchers appear from the left hall. A sharp turn down the opposite end, Jackson came face-to-face with a new window, a bright one with plenty of blue and green. Outside.

The vibrant sky contained fluffy white clouds hovering above the concrete pathway with lush thick grass on each side. The path led to the wide-brimmed base of a trunk. The tree thinned at the top with umbrella branches covered in rich dark leaves.

Jackson smiled. Outside. Tree.

"*JAH-CH-SHON!*" shouted one of the Watchers piercing through the sirens.

Jackson pounded his rough fists on the pane. Outside! He persisted in punching with all his might, watching the window wobble with each hit. Outside!

Cracks appeared on its surface with wet smears from his split knuckles. Outside! The glass gave way, and shards scattered onto the ground. They cut into his hands, causing the skin to shred. He kept striking, ignoring the burning pain, moving the barrier out of the way until there was enough room for him to make it through.

A whizzing sound soared by his ear as one of the projectile needles hit the window frame. Jackson leaped forward, bursting through the remaining broken glass. Outside!

Gravity accelerated his fall, and he had no knowledge of how high he was until his face collided with the hard surface below. His neck bent in a new way as the rest of his form toppled. He rolled several times until his back lay flat on the concrete. His body didn't respond; it was numb to all senses. He saw liquid running along his skin and onto the ground.

Above is the shattered window where the three Watchers stood. Each one took off their mask. Their human faces were wide-eyed, mouths hanging open, staring at Jackson.

Jackson's vision saturated as he looked to see the base of the large tree. It reached for the sky as the branches extended outward to him. The leaves blew in the wind as he attempted a good whiff of oxygen.

The fresh air tingled his mouth as a weak smile lifted on his upper right lip.

He felt tired.

His lids closed for a peaceful nap, outside.

About the Author

Konn Lavery is a Canadian author whose award-winning fiction has reached the bestselling charts on Amazon and in his hometown, Edmonton. His work has been described as uncanny and immersive in the Dark Fantasy and Horror genres. Each of his stories are housed within the Macrocosm universe

If They Won't Give Us Our Humanity, We Will Take It

Lux Thorn

CW: coercive medical treatment, nonconsensual drug use, fear of needles
Whumpee: Man, Whumper: Man, Woman, Caretaker: Man

John woke all at once, emerging from dark unconsciousness into sharp light and pain. Harsh fluorescent lights glared down at him from above. He hurt everywhere, but especially in his abdomen—just under the rib cage, where the bullet had gone in. Pain was an improvement, though. He hadn't thought he would wake up at all.

His neck was too heavy to lift, but he struggled to look around. He was indoors somewhere, with other beds to the left and right, which held unconscious or weakly twitching figures of their own. The air was sterile and cool, every drop of humidity and every smell of illness and injury filtered away. This wasn't the makeshift medical tent he had expected to wake up in if he survived. This was a hospital. Where was he?

He frowned as he turned his attention inward. The bullet wound hurt—of course it did—and with a sharpness and immediacy that told him he was going to need more pain medication soon. But it didn't hurt as much as it should have. He had been shot before. It should have taken a week or two for the pain to dial down to this amount, especially with whatever pain medication they had given him rapidly leaving his system. How long had he been out?

He tried to sit up. His muscles quivered, but he pushed through it—only to hit unexpected resistance. He couldn't lift his arms. And his chest... there was something heavy across it, like someone had sat a stack of books there.

He craned his neck as far as he could to get a look at himself. No—it wasn't a stack of books. It was a thick vinyl strap, holding him down as tightly as if it were made of iron. Matching straps restrained his arms at the wrists and his legs at the ankles.

A sharp surge of fear shot through him, sending the pain into the background. He struggled. The straps didn't budge. They only chafed against his bare skin like a rug burn.

Bare skin... was he naked *all over?*

"Oh, don't do that." A smiling ginger-haired man walked unhurriedly across the room to him. He looked young, as young as John had been when he had first put on his uniform.

"Who... what..." John's voice was gravelly, as if he hadn't used it in weeks. He struggled to make his heavy tongue form words.

"Glad to see you're awake," said the man. "We like to keep you people asleep as much as possible for the healing process, but we do need you awake for the trials. Fully awake and aware—that means no more pain medication for you, either. Sorry about that." He didn't look very sorry.

John fought against the straps again. If he could just get one hand free, he could loosen the other straps, find something to use as a weapon... The man waggled a finger at him.

John's weakened muscles quivered. A stabbing pain shot through his abdomen. He collapsed back onto the bed. "Where... am I?"

The man's grin broadened. "You're home," he said. "The good old US of A. Welcome home, by the way. Officially, though, you're dead, which might put a damper on the whole homecoming thing. My condolences." He shook his head slowly. "Killed in action. Body unrecoverable. A tragedy. You'll be mourned, I'm sure."

Panic prickled down John's immobilized limbs. "I don't... understand."

"We have an arrangement to take custody of a certain percentage of soldiers with severe injuries like yours. Since there's a good chance you would have died without our state-of-the-art treatment anyway, it's not like you've really lost anything. In fact, this is a gain for you. Think of it this way—you're not done serving your country. You're just going to do it in a different way from now on. We're working on some real wonder drugs here—drugs to help soldiers like you fight longer and harder. But we've got to test them somehow, hammer out all those pesky side effects. That's your job now."

Was this all some kind of nightmare, a hallucination before death? From the sharpness of the pain, and the vividness of the sparkle in the man's eyes, John didn't think so. This was real.

"And hey, you might even survive," the man continued. "Some do. Not many. But if you don't, you can know you died as noble a death as you would have on the battlefield."

"Who... do you work for?"

"The US military, of course. Same as you?" He frowned, tilting his head to one side. "Did you really think your bosses would have made that agreement with anyone else?"

"You're lying."

The man shrugged. "Believe what you like. It's not like it'll make much of a difference to you. I just thought you might like to know your sacrifice will mean something."

Before John could spit an answer at him, an older woman with black hair pulled into a severe bun strode over, face creased in a disapproving frown. "Don't *talk* to them," she said, shaking her head at the man. Her eyes slid over John as if he wasn't there. "Haven't I warned you about this before? If we were working with actual guinea pigs, you'd be the type to name one and take it home as a pet, wouldn't you?"

"I just think he should know where he is," the man protested. "And that he's going to serve a good purpose. It might calm him down, you know?"

His eyes met John's. His lips curved upward. John met his gaze with a steady stare.

That wasn't the look of someone who wanted to calm him down. That was the look of someone who wanted to see him squirm.

"Just wait," John vowed. "Wait until you make a single mistake. One day soon, you'll leave one of these straps a little too loose, or turn your back on me a second too long. It *will* happen. And when it does—"

The older woman pressed her lips together in irritation. "We don't need to listen to that while we're working." She grabbed a roll of gauze from a nearby table and wrapped it around John's mouth—once, twice, three times. He twisted his neck back and forth, trying to free himself from her grip, but her hands were as strong as steel. And as cold.

She held a syringe up in front of him. It was filled with a muddy brown liquid. The gauze muffled his noise of protest. He tried to squirm away, but the straps held him fast.

"Time for this one to make himself useful," she said to the man. Without ceremony, she jabbed the syringe into John's upper arm.

The liquid was molten lava as it spread down his arm and up his shoulder. He yelled into the gauze.

"Keep a close eye on him for the next hour," the woman ordered. "Note down any physical reactions. And no more making conversation, you hear me?" She gave the man a stern look. "Ungag him in an hour and ask him about his experiences. If he won't say anything helpful, put the gag on him again. I don't want you making friends."

The younger man screwed up his face. "You actually think I would get *attached* to one?"

"What am I supposed to think, when I find you chatting away like—"

Then the real pain hit, and John couldn't follow their conversation anymore. All he could do was thrash uselessly against the straps and scream as the fire consumed him.

***

John's imagined version of hell had always been something straight out of Sunday school. It would be hot, of course, too hot to bear, hot enough to melt the flesh from one's bones. The air would be thick with smoke and ash and the smell of sulfur. The sky would be dark, lit only by the red glow of the flames.

He had been wrong.

This cold and sterile room, with its bright fluorescent lights glaring down on him day and night... this was hell.

The screams, though... they could have been straight out of the Sunday-school stories. There was always someone screaming. Or begging. Or calling out for their mother. But mostly screaming. The screams kept him from sleep, even when the pain receded enough that he could have drifted off. He prayed for the experimental drugs to kill the others just so they would fall silent and he could sleep, and then he lay awake under the weight of his own guilt.

And sometimes, he was the one screaming.

Today wasn't one of those days. Today, he had no screams in him. It was all he could do to breathe, with his muscles clenched painfully tight around his ribs. Dr. Kiyoshi, with her black bun and cold hands, walked up to him as he struggled to draw in breath.

"How are we doing over here?" She directed the question at him, but he knew from experience that she didn't want an answer. She swept her gaze with professional efficiency over his nude body, never once looking him in the eye.

He knew what a visit from Dr. Kiyoshi meant. He knew what came next.

"No," he whispered with what little breath he had in him. "No, no, please. No more."

He had once been captured by a squad of enemy soldiers for two weeks. They had tried to beat his mission out of him, and when that hadn't worked, they had moved onto knives. He still had the scars. And yet, in all that time, he had never begged.

He was begging now.

"No more. No more..."

She took out her tablet and started tapping out notes. "Still experiencing periodic muscle contractions, I see," she said—to herself, clearly, not to him. "They've grown strong enough to cause bruising—I see a bruise on the upper thigh and another on the lower left abdomen. Looks like six centimeters and eight centimeters, respectively." She used a ruler to measure as she spoke, then nodded as her estimates were confirmed.

Her fingers brushed the larger of the bruises. John's whole body flinched. It made no difference. The straps held him firmly in place. The skin around them was rubbed raw now, and the slightest movement made the swollen friction burns erupt in agony.

She moved on to feeling his ribs. He gasped out a yelp as her fingers found a sharp center of pain, undiscovered until now. "At least one cracked rib," she reported. She frowned at the monitors next to his bed. "Heartbeat is showing irregularities," she said, tapping out another note. "I'll need to run some tests to check for damage. Assuming the next phase of the trial doesn't render the point moot."

Finally, she met his eyes. Her gaze was cold and clinical, as if she were staring down at a not-particularly-interesting specimen in a petri dish. "How do you feel?"

"Fuck... you," he gasped.

She clucked her tongue at him. "If you're going to be here anyway, you may as well give me some useful information. It would make your sacrifice mean more. But I suppose I should know better than to expect cooperation from any of you.

It's like expecting a rat not to bite your finger when you're stupid enough to stick your hand in the cage."

"Go to hell." A useless curse. She was already there. They both were.

"That's enough of that." She took a length of gauze in her hands and wrapped it around his mouth. He struggled—he always did—but he was weaker now than he had been on the first day. His pathetic thrashing didn't even slow her down.

She pulled out another syringe filled with the now-familiar muddy liquid. "Voice note," she said, shifting into the clipped tone she used for dictation. "After twice-daily injections for seven days, subject 72's muscle contractions are growing progressively worse. Please see detailed notes in the subject's file. This will be the subject's fifteenth injection. In accordance with study protocol, along with this injection he will also receive the compound designed to counteract these side effects. He will receive a half dosage, in the hope of avoiding the negative outcomes we've seen with previous subjects."

She set the tablet down. The syringe came closer. He moaned through the gag.

She let out an exasperated sigh. "Why do they always have to be so loud?" she muttered. "I've got half a mind to suggest removing their vocal cords as soon as they're brought in."

The needle bit into his arm. The flesh was bruised and torn from all the previous injections. But that pain was quickly swallowed by the burning that engulfed him.

The flames of hell. This, too, was like the stories.

She pulled out another syringe. This one was only half full. The liquid was a cloudy white. Without a word of warning, she pierced his skin with the needle, just below where the first drug had gone in.

Blessed cold flooded his body, quenching the flames wherever it touched. He moaned again—this time in pure relief. The pain was fading... fading... it was *gone.* For the first time since the initial injection, the pain was gone.

He had time for a single slow breath.

Then a new pain erupted from his gut. Not fire this time. Something worse. Like he was splitting open from the inside.

He screamed—and choked on a mouthful of blood. It soaked through the gauze gag and poured out his nose. It wet his face and dribbled down his neck as he tried to cough it out, struggling in vain for breath. His insides twisted and convulsed.

Dr. Kiyoshi noted his distress with a sigh and a small shake of her head. "Not again," she muttered. "Well, so much for that subject." She waved across the room to the ginger-haired man from the first day. "We've got another subject dying from the second drug," she said. "Half dose, this time. Same result." She kept talking as the ginger-haired man hurried over. "Watch him. Take notes on how his condition deteriorates. We might still be able to get some useful data from him."

The pain clawed its way up John's chest. His whole body shook with his coughs and gags. Blood leaked out around the gauze. His vision grew dim around the edges.

"What useful information?" the man protested. "We already know how this progresses. We've seen it happen with a dozen subjects already. And I was in the middle of something."

"It's important to be thorough," Dr. Kiyoshi lectured. "Whatever else you were doing can wait ten minutes until he—"

A crash like thunder drowned out the rest of her words.

The doors slammed open, and a hurricane of figures in black tactical gear swept in. The thunder turned to shouts. "Freeze! FBI!"

John caught the outrage on Dr. Kiyoshi's face as she turned away from him to face the intruders. "You can't do this." Even her anger was cold. "This facility is under the jurisdiction of the US military—"

She yelped as one of the black-clad figures slammed her against a wall and twisted her hands behind her back. Handcuffs clicked shut around her wrists.

Even though John couldn't draw a breath, even though all the color had leached from his vision and turned the world of sickly gray, he still managed a weak smile through the blood-soaked gag.

The woman who had handcuffed Dr. Kiyoshi brought a hand to her mouth as she looked around the room. She looked like she was going to be sick. "I can't believe it's real," she murmured to the man next to her. "I was sure we weren't going to find anything." Her eyes landed on him—and widened in horror. "Is that one dead or alive?"

I'm alive, he wanted to say, but he didn't have the breath. He tried to clear his lungs with another violent cough, knowing it was no use.

The cough tore something new in his chest. A fresh gush of blood rushed up from his throat. His vision turned from gray to black.

As he went limp against the straps, he knew he wouldn't wake up this time.

***

John was in a hospital. He knew because someone had told him so as they had rushed him in on the stretcher under the bright white lights. If they hadn't, he would have assumed nothing had changed—because the hospital was exactly the same as the other place.

The same searing fluorescent lights. The same sterile-smelling air, slightly too cool for comfort. The same figures in scrubs hurrying back and forth, prodding at his body without speaking to him directly or looking him in the eye. The same mechanical beeps and sharp orders shouted back and forth, rousing him from sleep every time he started to drift out of consciousness again. The same pain.

The only thing missing was the screams.

The pain wasn't as bad now. They must have given him something. But the medication made him feel like he was thinking through a fog. He would have expected to be ecstatic for the chance to make that trade-off after a week of near-constant excruciating pain. But he needed to be able to think. To move. To make his escape.

But he didn't need to escape, did he? Not anymore. He was free.

Free—and alive. Somehow, his rescuers had saved him.

He wished he felt a little more relieved, and a little less sick to his stomach.

Two blurry figures in blue scrubs paused next to his bed. "What did they do to *this* one?" one of them asked. A woman.

The second figure answered in a deeper male voice. "Whatever they did, it practically turned his organs to soup. We've got him stable for now—barely. But between you and me, I don't think he stands a chance."

John's stomach twisted. From the man's words or from what the other place had done to him, he wasn't sure.

Maybe they hadn't saved him after all.

He blinked at the two figures until their faces started to come into focus. Neither of them seemed to notice. The woman hung her head, looking like she was going to cry. "He doesn't deserve that." Her voice trembled. "After what he's been through... I thought we could give them all a happy ending. Like an abused dog who finally finds a good home, you know?"

"Don't get attached," the man warned. "Not to any of them, and especially not to him. They're all in bad shape, and he's worse off than any of the others."

The woman crossed the short distance to John's bed. He tried to meet her gaze, but his eyes wouldn't focus. And she wasn't really looking at him anyway, as she wiped away her tears with the back of her hand.

She took John's hand in hers. Her skin was almost painfully warm against his—just how cold was he? He tried to pull away, but he didn't have the strength to so much as twitch a finger. He might as well have still been strapped down.

She squeezed his hand. "You poor thing," she murmured. "We'll take good care of you. I promise."

The man shook his head and sighed. "Don't say I didn't warn you."

John tried to speak. All that came out was a low, rasping moan. His throat felt like someone had rubbed it down with sandpaper. His mouth still tasted like blood.

The woman jumped back, startled. She let go of his hand like it was a hot potato.

He tried again. "Where..." That one word prompted a coughing fit. Pain shot through his insides in a dozen places, too strong even for the medication to overcome. He felt like an army of porcupines was rolling around inside him.

The coughing subsided. He lay back, gasping. The woman leaned over his bed, her blue eyes wide and bright with concern. "Don't try to talk," she warned him.

But he had spent too long gagged to be quiet now. "Where... am I?" he managed. "What's going on?"

"It's all right," she assured him. "It's going to be all right. Just rest." She wiped her eyes again, then curled her fingers insistently around his. Her hand was wet with her tears.

She hadn't answered him. "What's... happening... to me?"

She squeezed his hand until he winced in pain. "Don't worry about it." Her voice wobbled.

Standing back from John's bed, the man gave his head another slow shake. "Bad idea," he muttered. "Bad, bad idea. Never get attached to the hopeless cases."

John shifted his gaze to the man, who avoided his eyes. "You said... I'm dying."

The man pressed his lips together and didn't answer. The woman made a strangled noise in the back of her throat, like she was the one in pain. "We'll take good care of you," she promised.

John tried to sit up. He couldn't even lift his head. "That's... not... an answer." The last word scraped at his throat in just the wrong way, prompting another round of painful coughing.

The woman squeezed his hand harder. "Don't get yourself worked up," she said. "It will only make it harder for you to get better."

"He's not *going* to get better," the man muttered.

She ignored him as she let go of John's hand and walked to a nearby counter. Unable to move, he couldn't see what she was doing as she rattled around in the overhead cabinet. Not until she came back to his bedside, holding something between her fingers.

A syringe.

He jerked away. His shoulder found the edge of the bed. He slipped, teetered, began to fall. A wave of queasy dizziness spread over him, vertigo and panic rolled into one. He couldn't take his eyes off the syringe.

She grabbed for him, holding him in place. "That's what I mean about getting yourself worked up." She brought the syringe closer, still holding him down. "This will help calm you down."

"No," he rasped. "No, no more, please..."

The syringe slid into his arm, a sharp bright burst of pain. He screamed.

There was no burning this time. Only a thick cotton blanket that tightened around him, invisible, as the drug spread through his veins. Warming him. Slowing his thoughts. Holding him down.

"No," he said in a thready whisper. "No..."

His eyelids fluttered shut. The thick blanket of the drug stole his vision and then his words.

"There you go," she murmured, patting his chest. "Just sleep. We'll take good care of you." Her last words followed him down into uneasy dreams. "You're safe now."

***

John hated the flowered curtains.

The flowers were big, droopy blue things that looked like a six-year-old had drawn them. The curtains were thin enough that they did nothing to block the light early in the morning, but thick enough that the room was always too dim during the day unless he switched on the overhead light. There was a fraying hem at one corner, and his eyes kept coming back to it as he wished he could muster up the strength to heave himself out of bed and cut off the offending loose threads.

As it was, he could barely make it out of bed to piss without one of the nurses to help him. And it wasn't as if they allowed him *scissors*.

At least he had a private room in wherever this place was that they had moved him. That meant no screams to keep him awake. Not that he would have been able to stay awake regardless, with the amount of sedatives they gave him to knock him out at night. Those drugs could have dropped a full-grown grizzly bear into a full hibernation.

The quiet was nice. And he wasn't strapped down. He didn't have to eat through a tube. That was where the good points of his new room ended.

He had been here six weeks. In that time, he had memorized every crack in the ceiling, every wrinkle in the dated wallpaper. He had grown to know those horrible flowered curtains better than he had known some of his lovers. When the nurses wheeled him out of his room for more tests, he always knew whether the room had been cleaned when he came back, because the cloying lilac spray they used lingered like bad gas.

He might not have been in hell anymore, but now he was in jail—a soft, smiling, cozy jail. He couldn't say it was all that much of an improvement.

"Knock knock!" a voice outside his door chirped. The door opened before he could answer. Daisy, his morning nurse, walked in with a spring in her step and a breakfast tray in her hands. Judging by the smell, it was scrambled-eggs day. The kind that came from a jug. Fantastic.

When Daisy saw him, her lips curved downward in an exaggerated pout. "Oh, my," she said. "It looks like you just woke up. You're not even sitting up yet, poor thing. Let me help you up so you can eat."

Daisy Wachter, with her cloud of rust-red curls and a face that made her look about twelve years old, reminded him of a kindergarten teacher. From the beginning, that hadn't boded well for their relationship. In kindergarten, he had been sent to the principal's office almost every day.

She set the tray down on the side table and shifted his pillow up against the headboard, prompting a grunt of annoyance from him. She slipped one hand under his back to help him up.

He flinched away. "I can do that myself, you know."

Shifting himself to a seated position took him longer than it should have, and of course she was watching him the whole time. He was sure he could see every flinch of pain that crossed his face, too, and hear every swallowed whimper. To her credit, she left him alone for the first thirty seconds or so. Then she just couldn't help herself. Ignoring his glare, she shifted him upright the rest of the way.

She wheeled the table over to the bed and whisked the cover off the plate of food with a flourish. "Eat up!"

As he suspected—scrambled eggs. He stared them down as if waiting long enough would turn them into something else.

"I can help you if you want," Daisy offered in the same cheery chirp. "But you really should feed yourself. It's the small things that will do the most to help you get your strength back."

He transferred his glare from the meal to her. "I wasn't waiting for you to feed me," he informed her. "I'm not very hungry this morning."

Not for reconstituted scrambled eggs, at least.

"You need to eat," she said, sounding as if he had suggested walking around nude in the nearest downtown. "How else are you going to heal up?" She loaded scrambled eggs onto the fork and lifted it to his mouth.

He snatched the fork out of her hand. With a grimace, he brought it to his lips. Better to force down the eggs than endure any more of her trying to feed him.

His fingers trembled with the effort of holding the fork. His arm felt like a wet noodle. He clenched his jaw.

"How are you feeling this morning?" Daisy chose that moment to ask.

John glanced over at the flowered curtains. "Like a prisoner," he said bluntly. "When can I get out of here?"

"Cabin fever," she said, with a sugary smile of sympathy. "I understand."

No, she most certainly did not. She got to walk out of this place every night when she was done helping her patients against their will.

"I have an idea!" she exclaimed. "Maybe we can go out in the garden later today."

"That's not what I mean," John said, setting the fork down with a clang. "I want to know when I'll be done with the treatments. The tests. The surgeries. The physical therapy. All of it. When can I go home?"

She patted his shoulder. "One step at a time." Pat, pat, pat. Like he was one of those little purse dogs.

"All I want to know is what's going on with my own body," he said. "I want to know what my life looks like from here. But no one will give me a straight answer."

"I hear your frustration. It's understandable, after what you went through. But I have good news for you! I hear they're going to have a therapist come in and talk to all of you who came out of... that place. You'll be having regular weekly sessions. That should help you deal with your anger."

Right now, he felt like what would help him deal with his anger was throwing the plate of scrambled eggs across the room. "Weekly sessions? How many more weeks do you expect me to be here?"

"Finish those eggs," Daisy urged. "They're getting cold."

John did not throw the plate across the room. But he did shove it to the far end of the table, prompting a disapproving frowned from her. "I have the right to refuse treatment," he said. "Don't I?"

Her eyes went wide with alarm. "I think you ought to have a realistic view of what you're capable of," she said carefully.

"But technically," he said, "I can leave whenever I want. Isn't that true?"

"Yes," she said, drawing out the word on a tight breath. "But most doctors won't be equipped to handle your unique case. And you're going to need specialized care for the rest of your life."

John tensed, sending a spike of pain down his limp-noodle arm. "What kind of care?" The kind where Daisy fed him eggs every morning?

Daisy bit her lip. "It's like I keep telling you," she said. "It's best to take these things one step at a time. You don't need to think that far ahead just yet."

"Answer the damn question," he snapped.

Her eyes went round at the language. It took her a few seconds to recover. "There's a good chance you'll need to live in a facility like this long-term—"

"Like hell," he interrupted.

"Hopefully one that understands your situation," she continued.

"My *situation?* It can't be that complicated. I almost died. I'm getting better." Not fast enough. Never fast enough. "What more is there to know?"

"Those experimental drugs did a lot of damage," said Daisy. "In fact, one of the doctors is going to be talking to you about that—when you're feeling a bit better, of course. We're hoping you'll sign an agreement so we can study the effects of what they did to you."

The hair on the back of his neck stood on end. "Study me? So you want me to be *your* guinea pig now?"

Daisy clucked her tongue at him. "It's not like that, John," she said reproachfully. "I would hope you would know that, after everything we've done to help you. All we want is to find better ways to support you and everyone who came in with you. And of course we won't do anything without your consent."

"You won't get it," said John. "I don't want to be anyone's guinea pig anymore. All I want is to leave."

He started to swing his legs over the side of the bed. Then a wave of exhaustion overcame him, and he sagged bonelessly into the pillow.

"And you're free to do that anytime, of course," Daisy said softly, her eyes shining with pity.

The pity wasn't just because a brief argument and a forkful of breakfast had worn him out, he knew. It was because he *couldn't* leave, and she knew it. He couldn't take care of himself in the state, and he had no one waiting at home to take care of him. That meant he was stuck. If they wanted him as their guinea pig, he didn't have any other choice.

He glared at the scrambled eggs, an easier target for his fury. "Take that away. I'm not hungry anymore."

"You can't recover if you don't fuel your body." She loaded more eggs onto the fork and held them out to him.

"The way you're talking, it sounds like I can't recover no matter what."

"That's not what I—"

"No more. I'm done." He turned away.

With a sigh, Daisy lowered the fork. "From what I understand, these bursts of rage are to be expected. Talking to that therapist will help—I'm sure of it." She patted his shoulder again. "Would you like to take that trip out to the garden now?"

He couldn't answer through his clenched teeth.

"All right," she chirped. "I'll check in with you later. Maybe you'll be feeling more up to it after a nap." She picked up the tray and left the room.

Only then did John let out his breath.

But he didn't even have time to be properly grateful for her absence before the door opened again. "What now?" he snapped.

But it wasn't Daisy who walked in. It was a lanky man with a beard down to his chest and a limp that made his hips twist every time with every step he took. And—the part that lifted John's heart—he was scowling.

He might have been the first person John had seen in this whole candy-colored jail who hadn't greeted him with a smile.

The man closed the door and leaned against it, wincing as his shoulder struck the wood with a heavy thump. "Isn't this just the most charming prison you've ever been in?" he drawled.

***

All John could do was blink at the intruder. "Who are you?"

"A prisoner here, same as you." The man shrugged. One of his shoulders started moving half a second later than the other, and lifted at an angle that wasn't quite right. "Or a patient, if you prefer." He smiled at that, but his smile was lopsided and cynical.

"Were you..." John's voice trailed off. He didn't know how to ask about the hell he had been in—didn't know if this man would want to talk about it if he had been there, wasn't sure he himself wanted to explain it if he hadn't.

"A guinea pig? Yep. But they were testing something different on me." He lifted one arm. His sleeve slid down to reveal a waxy white prosthesis. Now that John was looking closely, he could see that the other man's hand was made of the same shiny material, the fingers frozen in a slight curve.

"They're not pretty, but they're supposed to be more advanced than anything on the market today," the man said. "Wired directly into the brain. The reality is... a little different."

As if to demonstrate, he wiggled the fingers of his prosthetic hand in a half-wave. Four of them came down smoothly; the pinky finger stayed jutting jauntily up. On the way back up, one finger got stuck halfway, and two more didn't come up at all.

"The leg works about as well," he said, patting one thigh. "It likes me today—I was able to walk all the way here. Crossing my fingers it'll still like me on the way back." He crossed the fingers on his prosthetic hand, then rolled his eyes. "I'm going to regret that. They'll be stuck like that for the next twenty minutes."

John brought a hand to his abdomen, feeling the last echo of the pain of the gunshot wound he had thought would kill him. "You lost your arm and leg," he guessed. "That's how you ended up with them." Because they had looked at his injuries and seen someone who could be useful to them. His gut clenched.

But the man shook his head. "Nope," he said, with another of those cynical smiles. "That didn't stop them, though."

John shook his head. "And I thought what they did to me was sick."

The man held up a hand—his real one this time. "Don't," he warned. "Don't do the thing our jailers do. That thing where they look right through you with pity in their eyes. I get enough of that from them. I'm guessing you do, too."

"You got a name?" John asked.

"Torrance," he said, with no indication of whether it was his first name or last. "Pleasure to meet you. I'd shake hands, but..."

"Looks like you've been here a bit longer than me," John said. "If you're up and walking around."

The man shrugged—with only his real arm this time. "A bit. But also, I think you had it worse than most. You're the one whose insides were basically sludge when you got to the hospital, isn't that right?"

John answered with a small shrug of his own, unwilling to say more about it. At least Torrance's blunt honesty was an improvement over Daisy's smiles and careful euphemisms.

"So then you know a bit more about this place than I do," said John. "Seeing as I can't go anywhere without a nurse by my side." He met Torrance's dark eyes. "You called this place a prison. Is that a metaphor, or..."

"That's not a simple question." Torrance crossed the room and started to sit at the edge of John's bed. He shot John a questioning look. When John nodded, he lowered himself to the thin mattress.

"I think, for the most part, they believe the things they tell us," he said. "That they want the best for us. That everything they do, they're doing to take care of us. But that's not the whole story. Did any of them talk to you yet about wanting to study you?"

"To help figure out how to treat us, they said," John answered, feeling the same prickle of unease as when Daisy had brought it up.

Torrance nodded. "It makes things easier for them if they can convince themselves that what they want happens to be what's best for us. But ask them sometime about how we ended up with them in the first place."

"The nurse also said we can leave anytime we want." Not that it made a difference to John. Not when he had nowhere to go in his current state.

"Well, sure." The cynicism was back in Torrance's smile, in full force. "Bet she didn't tell you about all the fine print. I tried it, you know. Said I was done. That I wanted out before the end of the day. They were quick to remind me that I didn't have anyone waiting back home to take care of me, let alone a doctor who could really understand the... renovations those people made." He waved his prosthetic arm. "But I insisted."

"But you're still here," John said, pointing out the obvious.

"Yep. Here I am." He gestured to himself with a flourish—or tried. His hand got stuck halfway through the gesture, making him look like an awkwardly posed dummy. "If you try it, you'll find out the same thing I did: that they can find one medical justification after another to keep you. Maybe you need a mental health evaluation before they can release you. And as soon as that happens, oops, they've just started you on a new course of drugs, and it would be too medically risky to release you before the treatment is finished. And by the time that's finished... well, you get the idea."

"They can't hold us here," John said. "Not legally."

"You just try telling them that. No, really—try. I'd like to hear how it goes for you." He held John's gaze. "And after you do, I've got a proposal for you." Torrance lowered his voice. "We escape. Make a run for it."

John stared. "What?"

Torrance slapped his prosthetic thigh. "Well, however much running the two of us can do. Might look more like making a crawl for it."

"It seems awfully drastic, is all. You're that sure they won't let us go?"

Torrance looked at him grimly, all traces of his cynical smile gone. "I'm that sure."

John looked down at his own body—at the limp-noodle arms, still worn out from feeding himself a couple bites of breakfast, and his legs, which had threatened to collapse on him the last time he had ventured across the room. "Even if you're right... say we made it out. Where would we go from there? You said you don't have anyone waiting for you. Neither do I."

"We can figure that out when we get there," Torrance said. "I'm not saying it'll be easy. I'm just saying that if we don't do it, we'll be here for the rest of our lives. Listen to me—they will never let us go."

John shivered at the intensity in his voice. "Why ask me? We've known each other for five minutes."

"You'll find you don't get much opportunity to make friends in here," Torrance said. "Five minutes may be all we get. As for why... well, I haven't been able to convince anyone else to go with me. And I still haven't gotten up the nerve to go on my own." He shook his head ruefully. His beard quivered.

"Maybe they won't do it because they know it's a bad idea," said John. "I don't like feeling like I'm back in kindergarten any more than you do, but you're talking about giving up the only help we've got. And we're not prisoners. No matter how it feels." He was, he realized, trying to convince himself.

"Like I said," said Torrance, "you go ahead and tell them you want to leave. Tell them you're going to walk right out the door, and see what they do."

"I can't leave yet," said John, feeling the bitter truth of those words. "I can barely make it to the bathroom by myself."

"They want you to believe you can't leave," said Torrance. "But ask yourself this: can you afford to stay?"

John tried to put the thought of Daisy's words about his future out of his mind. "I won't stay. Not forever. I'll let them do what they can to patch me up, and then I'll go."

"You just keep telling yourself that." With a disappointed sigh, Torrance stood up off the bed. Or one of his legs did. He grabbed the table to keep his balance, and gave the other leg a couple of smacks before it jerked itself to a standing position.

He walked to the door. "When you change your mind," he said over his shoulder, "you let me know."

***

Escape. What a ridiculous thought.

He couldn't deny that a part of him saw the appeal. Especially when faced with the prospect of months, years... a lifetime?... in this place. But it was a petulant fantasy, the dream of a child who didn't want to take his medicine. And if he was stupid enough to give in to that temptation, there was nothing waiting for him on the other side even if he made it out. Unable to work, he'd end up homeless, and dead shortly after that. Surely enduring Daisy for a little while longer was better than that.

And it would only be a little while longer.

He would make sure of that. He would do everything this place asked of him. He would get back to his former self, no matter what it took.

He would prove Daisy wrong.

And then, finally, he would earn his freedom.

He woke the next morning full of fresh determination. When Daisy walked in with his breakfast—a pair of greasy sausage patties, a stack of dry and tasteless pancakes—he startled her by greeting her with a smile. He shocked her even more by eating every last bite of his breakfast, even though no amount of maple syrup could breathe life into those pancakes.

For the first time ever, when she cheerily suggested a round of affirmations, he said them right along with her. He didn't even roll his eyes as he repeated after her, *I am stronger than I have ever been. The strength of the universe flows through me.* The strength of the universe—what even was that? But if there was the slightest chance Daisy was right and saying the cheesy words would speed up his healing by the smallest fraction, he would parrot the dumb lines every single day.

Whatever it took.

"I'm so proud of you, John," she said with one of her tooth-rotting smiles when they were done. "You really seem like you've turned a corner with your attitude. I can see you're ready to get better."

As if he hadn't been ready the second he had woken up in this bed. But he tried to return her smile. "I don't plan on staying here for the rest of my life."

Her smile grew strained around the edges. "That's some great positive thinking, John."

He forced himself to keep up his smile. He *would* prove her wrong, if he had to eat a mountain of dry pancakes to do it. He would just see what she had to say *then.*

Someone knocked at the door. A man in scrubs with a neatly trimmed beard, wheeling one of those ubiquitous medical carts full of unpleasant tools, barged in without waiting for a response. Like everyone did in this place. Why did they even bother to knock? John's smile became a grimace.

"Right on time!" Daisy chirped. "It's time for more blood tests!" She said it like she was announcing a trip to Disney World.

Whatever it took, John reminded himself. He held his arm out to the bearded nurse.

The nurse grabbed John's arm and prodded it like he was testing a cut of meat at the grocery store. His fingers were reptilian—cool and dry, slightly rough to the touch. "He's got terrible veins," he groused to Daisy. "You could have warned me."

Of course he didn't speak to John directly. But it didn't matter, because he was getting out of here—and the more he went along with them, the faster it would be. So he didn't pull away, didn't so much as scowl at the bearded nurse. Even when the nurse wrapped a tourniquet around his upper arm tightly enough to draw a grunt of pain from him.

The nurse kept poking and prodding at John's arm, squeezing the flesh in different directions. He tapped a vein and frowned. "I guess this is the best we're going to get." With no further, he pulled out a syringe—

—*no, please, no more*—

—and slid it under John's skin. John yelped in pain—the man hadn't been gentle about it.

"Oh, you poor thing," said Daisy. "That one hurt, didn't it? You're doing so well." Her hand came down on his shoulder. Pat, pat, pat.

"Thank you," he said to her with gritted teeth.

The bearded nurse replaced the full vial of blood with an empty one. He drew a second vial of blood, a third, a fourth. "Just how many of those do you need?" John couldn't resist asking.

Immediately, he wished he hadn't, because it prompted another round of patting from Daisy. "It's all right," she assured him. "You're doing fine." Which was not what he had asked.

After enough vials of blood that John lost count, the bearded nurse finally withdrew the needle—which, of course, caused a fresh burst of pain. This time, he swallowed his yelp, just so Daisy wouldn't start patting his shoulder again. But he didn't hide it well enough to avoid her pitying smile.

"Is that all for now?" Daisy asked. "I think he's pretty tired." She squeezed his shoulder in what John was sure she thought was sympathy. John clenched his jaw and said nothing.

The bearded nurse untied the tourniquet. It left a red ring that John was certain would turn into a bruise. "He's due for an injection," he said, digging around in the second shelf of his cart. His hand came up clutching another syringe, this one twice the size and full of liquid—

—*no, no, no*—

"No," John said in a ragged whisper, but the syringe had already pierced his flesh. He gritted his teeth as the cold liquid spread through his veins. He couldn't speak. He couldn't breathe.

Only when the bearded nurse withdrew the needle did John draw in a gasping breath. The bearded nurse rolled his eyes. "Some people never get over being babies about needles, I guess," he said—to Daisy, not to John.

Daisy's hand tightened on John's shoulder. "Go easy on him. He's been through a lot. They all have."

The bearded nurse had already turned away. He wheeled his cart out the door, and was gone.

"The next time someone sticks a needle in me without asking, they're going to find that needle somewhere they really don't want it," John said, scowling at the closed door. Yes, he had said he would do whatever it took, but there had to be limits.

Daisy clucked her tongue at him. "He could have been nicer about it, I'm sure. But he just wants to help you get better. We all do. And that's what you want, too, isn't it? You had such a good attitude this morning."

"I might have a better attitude if that guy hadn't jabbed me with a needle with no warning. And without bothering to tell me what was in it."

"You need something to cheer you up," Daisy declared. "I know! We could play a few rounds of checkers, if you don't think you're too tired."

She really did think he was five years old, didn't she? He hadn't played checkers since he had hit double digits. "I wouldn't mind meeting some of the other—" He stopped himself before he could say *prisoners*. "The other people who were rescued from the same place I was."

Daisy's brow creased. "Oh, I don't think that's such a good idea."

"I met one of them yesterday," he said. "Torrance."

Daisy's frown deepened. "He came to see you? We'll need to look into that."

"Are you saying we're not allowed to talk to each other?"

"Oh, of course you're *allowed*. But it just isn't the best thing for your recovery. And that one, in particular, is a difficult case. Very uncooperative. I don't want him infecting you with all that negativity of his. Especially considering how well you're doing today."

She crossed the room to the small closet and dug around until she pulled out a battered board game box. She turned back to him with a bright smile, all traces of her frown gone. "Now, how about that game?"

This time, he didn't return the smile. "Then how about you tell me more about what you mentioned yesterday? You said you people want to study us. What will you be studying, exactly?"

"We'll need to take a comprehensive look at all your physical systems. After all, we can't know what those drugs affected unless we look! The people who had you destroyed all their files before we could get to them, so the only information we have is inside your bodies."

"And how long do you plan on doing this?" John pressed. "If any of us consent, that is."

"It's too early to say," Daisy said with a vague wave of her hand. "But definitely a few years at minimum."

At *minimum?* "You don't think you'll have learned everything you need to learn about how to treat us before then?" He couldn't speak for the others, but he certainly didn't intend to be here for *years*.

"Well, the hope is for our work to eventually have benefits beyond you," Daisy said. "Of course you'll be the first to benefit, as we use what we learn to help you recover. But despite the monstrous things those people did, there might be something to be learned from their work—and like I said, right now all that's left of that work is inside your bodies." Another sugary smile; another pat to his shoulder. "It may be that some good could come of all this pain and tragedy."

This time, John flinched away from her hand. At the movement, a sharp spike of pain shot down his chest to rest in his abdomen like a burning coal. He ignored it.

He met her wide, bright eyes. "You're recreating their research?"

She pulled her hand away. "Well, you'd have to ask the doctors about the specifics," she said, in that same careful tone she had used when he had told her he didn't plan on staying here for the rest of his life. "I'm just one of the nurses here. My only job is to help you get better."

"You sounded like you were pretty cozy with them a minute ago," John said. "You said *we* when you were talking about them."

"You'll have to ask them for the specifics," she repeated. From the look in her eyes before she turned away, John had a suspicion it would be a long, long time before he got a chance to speak to one of the doctors. If he ever did.

"Who are you, anyway?" John asked. "You've never said."

"I told you, I'm the nurse whose job it is to help you get—"

"I don't mean you personally," he interrupted. "I mean whoever you work for. Who exactly is taking care of me? Who's paying my medical bills?"

She hesitated just long enough for him to notice. "I work for a medical innovations company—"

"Medical *research*, you mean." John went cold all over.

"They've generously agreed to pay for all your treatments."

"To get your hands on what's left of the drugs those other people used on me."

Daisy gave him an I'm-disappointed-in-you look. "To put the company's commitment to humanitarian action into practice," she corrected.

"Do you really believe all that?" John tried to sit up straighter in the bed. It was the next best thing to getting up and striding for the door, which he knew would end with him in a sad wet-noodle heap on the floor. "I'm done," he said. "I'm signing myself out of this place *now*. Bring me the paperwork."

Daisy set the game down with a sigh. "Of course," she said. "If you're sure that's what you want."

"I'm sure."

"You know, of course, that you're going to need specialized medical—"

"I said I'm sure."

"Then we'll get you that paperwork right away," she promised. "Just as soon as we have a complete psychological evaluation done. We have to make sure you're in a suitable mental condition to be released—it wouldn't be medically responsible otherwise. That shouldn't take too long, though—maybe a couple of weeks." She held out the game box. "But for now... checkers?"

***

Up until now, John had been so focused on how physically difficult it would be for him to leave his room, he hadn't considered how impossible it would be in other ways. Not until he made the decision to push past his body's weakness and find Torrance again. He waited for his chance... and waited... and waited. But there were always eyes on him here. Why had he never noticed that before?

There was Daisy, of course. Always Daisy, hovering with a cheery smile to make sure he ate his lunch and then his dinner. To give him a pep talk about the importance of a positive attitude. To offer him another round of checkers. Then there was physical therapy, with his every motion scrutinized and criticized by a deceptively baby-faced drill sergeant. There was a round of full-body scans—no one bothered to tell him what they were for, of course. And then, once Daisy went home for the night, there was Gina, her replacement, to help him to the bathroom and get him a glass of water before bed.

He watched the clock with growing frustration. At nine-thirty exactly, yet another nurse would come along with the medications that would send him into a sleep so deep it felt like death. And there was no way to avoid taking them—they always checked. If John didn't swallow the pills on command, they threatened him with an injection instead. That was always enough of an inducement for him to swallow them down, as much as he dreaded the suffocating sleep they wrapped him in.

Nine-thirty. Never a moment later. It was nine twenty now. He had ten minutes.

As Gina smiled beatifically down on him, he affected a slight frown. Gina's sharp eyes caught it immediately, of course. "Does something hurt?" she asked. "I can ask the other nurse to bring extra pain medication with your sleeping pills."

"Just hungry." John offered her a slight smile, even though it made him sick to do it. "Any chance of a late-night snack?" As if nine at night counted as late anywhere but here.

Gina frowned thoughtfully. "You're really not supposed to have snacks after bedtime... but... I know Daisy has worried about your appetite. So have the doctors. I'm sure they'd be glad to see you eating." She gave a decisive nod, as if she had agreed to take part in a serious act of rebellion. If only she knew. "I'll see what I can find."

As soon as the door closed behind her, John swung himself out of bed.

For a moment, all he could do was sway in place. His legs, weakened by the experiments and weeks of lying in bed for days on end, trembled ominously. He caught himself against the edge of the bed and willed himself not to fall. That was just what he needed—not only for his mission to end before it had begun, but for Gina to find him lying on the floor and give him those pitying eyes.

He glared down at his legs, and at his chest, where his heart beat in as frantic a rhythm as if he had attempted to climb Everest. He didn't have time for this. At this rate, he wouldn't make it to the door before Gina came back.

He let go of the bed and took a wobbly step forward. Then another. Faster this time. Faster. His legs trembled. His heart beat against his ribcage like a bird caught in a fist.

He made it to the door. It felt like reaching the finish line at the end of a marathon. But he didn't let himself stop there. He clutched the wall as he emerged into the hallway.

He had been down this hallway with Daisy many times, but now, on his own, the white tile seemed to stretch into infinity. The walls seemed to warp, first widening and then narrowing in around him. Where were the other patients' rooms? They had never told him. He had never thought to ask.

His thoughts grew woozy, losing coherence. Who was he looking for again? Why had he dragged himself out of bed? What—

His hand, slick with sweat, slowly slid down the wall. His legs trembled harder, the way they did when they were about to give out under him. Sharp pain spiked through his abdomen.

One more step, he promised himself. One more. And then one more after that.

He took that one step—and slid in slow motion down the wall to the floor.

Footsteps echoed too loudly in his ringing ears. Gina. She was back. He was too late.

But when he looked up, ready to be softly but insistently dragged back to bed and sedated for the night, it wasn't Gina's face he saw. It was Torrance.

There was a blessed lack of pity in the other man's eyes as he offered John a hand. "You're lucky I came along," he said. "I'm dodging a meditation session—the nurse says it's supposed to help with sleep. Of course it doesn't mean she'll let me skip the sedatives, or I'd consider it. How about you?"

"All... of it," John managed. "You said... you had a plan to get out of here. I'm ready."

"Oh, really?" Surprise flared in Torrance's eyes. "Then I guess we better go somewhere we can talk."

He leaned down and wrapped an arm around John's shoulders. His arm was cool to the touch, and more solid than it should have been—it was the prosthetic arm. "I apologize in advance if this thing decides it doesn't like you," Torrance said.

Sure enough, as soon as he said it, his hand clamped down on John's shoulder hard enough to leave a bruise. John swallowed his pain and used Torrance's grip to haul himself to his feet. "If it gets me up off the floor," he said, "I'm not complaining."

Torrance led him, step by careful step, into a small room a few doors down. It turned out to be a storage closet, small and crowded and smelling of bleach. Torrance gave his prosthetic leg a few smacks until it obediently folded under him, lowering him to an awkward seat on the floor. John joined him, leaning heavily against the wall.

"So," Torrance said. "You're ready to run, huh?" He didn't look as happy as John had expected, or as vindicated. Mostly, he looked confused.

John nodded. "You were right. They're not going to let me go. And I don't plan on staying here a moment longer than I have to. So let's go. Tonight."

Torrance held up a hand. "Hang on. It's not that simple. We can't just—"

"You said you had a plan, right?" John interrupted.

"Yes, but—"

"So what's the plan?" John asked, his voice tight with impatience.

"Sorry," said Torrance. "I just wasn't expecting you to come around this fast. Maybe not at all. You're the first person who—"

"The *plan*."

"Right." Torrance swallowed, looking as queasy as John felt. Why? Wasn't he getting what he wanted? "Here's what I was thinking. We each pretend to have some kind of medical crisis—something too serious for them to treat here. They'll have to take us to the nearest hospital, unless they want to risk us dying. Then we escape from there."

That was his plan? John swallowed down a bitter surge of frustration. "It won't work."

Torrance frowned. "I've been thinking about this for—"

"I don't care. It won't work. First of all, with all the tests they run here, they'll know right away if we're faking. All they'll have to do is draw more blood, or stick us under their scanners, or whatever."

"If they think it's urgent enough—"

"They'll still make sure before risking letting us out of here. Also, they might believe a sudden crisis from one of us, but not both at once. That'll be a dead giveaway that we're faking, unless there's real evidence to back us up. Evidence that shows up on their tests. Which we won't have."

Torrance opened his mouth to argue. This time, John didn't let him get a word out before continuing. "And finally, do you really think they'll let us out of their sight, even in the hospital? One of their nurses will be at our bedside day and night—at minimum. We're too valuable to them—otherwise they wouldn't be paying for all this."

Torrance opened his mouth. He closed it again. His pathetic hand waggled back and forth, as if on its own. He glowered at it.

"You're right," he finally said. "It's a bad plan. I should have seen it." He smacked the wall with his prosthetic hand, hard enough to make the shelves rattle. This time, John was fairly sure the movement had been intentional. "Well, so much for escape, I guess."

The walls of the small storage closet seemed to draw in closer. "No," he said quickly. "We're not giving up that easily. We're doing this."

"I told you, I've been thinking about this practically since I got here. And that's the best plan I've been able to come up with."

"How about this?" John suggested. "One of us dresses as a nurse. The other one fakes some kind of medical crisis, like you said. The one in disguise gets the other one out before anyone can run any—"

But Torrance was already shaking his head. "Their security is too good. Even if no one noticed a nurse they've never seen before—a nurse who moves like we do..." Here, he transferred his glare to his prosthetic foot, which was doing a small twitching dance all on its own. "The staff still have to show ID on the way in *and* out."

John slumped against the wall. "There's got to be a way to make this work."

"It was a dream," Torrance said heavily. "A way to make the days more bearable. But it's time to wake up."

"No," John said. A quiet protest, as futile as his pleas back in that cold and sterile hell. Then, louder—"No. I've got it."

Torrance looked up at him, his eyes devoid of hope.

But John had enough hope for both of them. "You almost had it. But we don't fake medical crises. We *have* crises. Real ones."

"I don't know about you, but I can't have a stroke on command."

"They've got enough drugs in here to fuck up just about anybody's body," John said. "It can't be that hard to get our hands on some of them. At least not for you—you seem to have the run of the place."

"And roll the dice with the effects of an overdose on god-knows-what?"

"We already know what they plan on doing to us here. Sounds an awful lot like what we left behind. I say we take a gamble on the unknown."

Torrance was silent for a moment—a tacit agreement. "There's still the problem of the hospital," he pointed out. "Like you said, they won't risk taking their eyes off us, even there."

"Which is why we won't go to the hospital," John said. "They'll load us up in an ambulance, right? Or maybe drive us there themselves. Either way, we take control of the vehicle, and then we drive ourselves wherever we want to go. Someplace far away from here."

Torrance raised a skeptical eyebrow. "While in the middle of a medical crisis bad enough to make them risk taking us to the hospital?"

"I never said it was a perfect plan. But it'll give us a chance. What do you say?"

Torrance thought about it for a long moment. Then, abruptly, he shook his head. "No."

John frowned. "What do you mean, no?"

"I mean it won't work, all right? I was wrong. Escaping was a stupid idea. I've admitted it. Why can't you do the same?"

John opened his mouth to argue. He closed it without speaking, studying Torrance's face. Taking in the queasy look that had been there since John had said he was ready.

"You never thought you were actually going to do it, did you?" John asked. "It was always just talk. You never thought you'd have to put your money where your mouth was—and you liked it that way."

"Now hang on just a minute. You know how long I've been planning this? You know how many people I've tried to talk into it?"

"If you've been planning for so long," said John, "why not try on your own? Your plan would be easier with one person than two—more believable."

"I told you, I couldn't get up the nerve to do it on my own."

"I don't think you could have gotten up the nerve to do it no matter who you talked into it. And I don't think you ever planned to. It was easier to blame everyone who wouldn't go along with you, wasn't it?"

Anger burned in Torrance's eyes. Then, like a pinched-out candle flame, the fire went dark. "Maybe," Torrance said to his still-twitching foot. "Maybe you're right."

"Well, now you've got a choice to make," said John. "Because I think there's a chance my plan could work. Maybe not much of a chance, but it's more than what we've got right now."

Torrance shook his head. "I can't. I'm sorry."

"I'm not finished," said John. "I'm doing this—no matter what you decide. But hijacking that ambulance is going to be next to impossible with just one of us. So are you finally going to get up the nerve to do something? Or are you going to stay here and leave a fellow soldier in the lurch?"

Torrance heaved a sigh. "See, here's the problem with not having a chance to get to know each other better," he said. "I never would have come to you if I'd known you were the type to fight dirty."

John knew what he was really saying. He was in.

"So that's that," said John. "Same time tomorrow. We'll make plans. For now, let's think up a good excuse to give the nurses when they track us down tonight."

***

John slid the white checker across the board without really paying attention to where it was going. His focus was on what was happening inside his body—his rhythmic breathing, the steady beating of his heart. There—had his heart gone off-rhythm for a second?

No, there it was, ticking away like a metronome as always. Was his throat tight at all? Was his skin flushed? But he drew in his next breath easily. And when he looked down at his hands, they still had the pallor of someone who never went outside except for brief walks in the garden.

"Got you!" Daisy exclaimed, jumping over the piece he had just moved with one of her black checkers. "Better be careful, or I'm going to beat you again."

He muttered something noncommittal as he made his next move. His heart kept ticking away. He didn't feel so much as a bead of sweat on his forehead.

After all the drugs he and Torrance had stolen, surely *something* was about to go wrong. Any minute now. He had spent the past few weeks railing against his body's weakness. Now he cursed his sudden attack of good health.

Torrance had stolen everything he could get his hands on. John hadn't asked how. There had been big pills, small pills, white pills and colorful ones. A handful of vials of liquid medicine, too, and the syringes to go with them. John had gulped down the pills by the handful, right along with Torrance, who had shooed them like they were candy.

They didn't know what any of the drugs were, or what they were intended for. They didn't care. Unspoken between them had been the understanding that if the mystery cocktail killed them, it would be preferable to what awaited them here.

But John hadn't gotten up the nerve to inject himself with any of the liquids. He hadn't let Torrance inject him, either, although Torrance had offered. Maybe that was why he remained so frustratingly healthy.

He wiped his brow, checking for sweat. Nothing. His vision swam for a second, and he looked up hopefully—was he starting to get dizzy? But whatever it had been, it disappeared as quickly as it had appeared.

Daisy frowned. "Are you feeling all right?"

He blinked rapidly and shook his head, trying to bring on another wave of dizziness. Nothing. Just his mind playing tricks on him, manifesting phantom symptoms when all he needed was something real. Daisy's frown grew.

"I'm fine," he said with a sigh. He slid another checker across the board, not caring that it was moving right into the path of one of Daisy's pieces.

Before he could lift his hand off the piece, something gripped his chest, like a hand had reached through his rib cage and tightened into a fist around his heart. He gasped, suddenly unable to breathe.

Despite the pain, he had to fight to suppress a smile as he toppled sideways, scattering the pieces across the floor.

A heart attack? He hoped so.

Then the pain spread outward through his chest, reaching tendrils into his mind and wringing it free of thoughts like it was a wet washcloth. But the triumph, the relief—those remained.

As if from far away, he heard Daisy yelling for help. A flurry of activity filled the room. Strong hands lifted him onto a stretcher; an oxygen mask came down over his face as the hallway whizzed by. Faces leaned in close to his, eyes wide with alarm, barking rapid questions he couldn't answer.

A different room. Different hands. Needles piercing flesh—*no, not that, anything but that.* They gave up on asking him their questions, and exchanged short, brisk comments with each other instead.

"He collapsed suddenly. No warning."

"It's not just his heart. Check out his liver numbers."

"Not only that—the initial bloodwork says he's dying in a dozen different ways."

"What *happened?*"

"He needs a hospital."

He was glad the oxygen mask was there to cover his smile. *Yes,* he silently urged. *Take me to a hospital. Get me out of here.*

"A hospital will see the irregularities from the drug the military tested on him," someone pointed out. "And they'll want to know who we are and how he ended up with us. They'll have questions." A slight pause. "We can't trust him to give the right answers."

A sudden silence fell over the room. The hovering faces all looked at each other. No one wanted to be the first to speak. No one looked directly at him.

"He needs a hospital," a familiar voice said firmly. Daisy's voice, devoid of its usual kindergarten chirpiness. When John blinked up at her, she wasn't smiling. She met the eyes of the others one by one, as if daring them to argue with her.

The tension went out of the air, as if the whole room had breathed a sigh of relief at once. The assembled doctors and nurses, who no doubt all had seniority over Daisy, nodded. Their relief that someone had made the decision for them was plain on their faces.

For the first time, John felt a hint of genuine warmth for Daisy.

Someone called an ambulance. The others watched him, watched the monitors, waited in tense silence. He heard the fears they didn't voice aloud. They were afraid he was going to die. Afraid of losing the key piece of research he represented.

If he'd had the strength to speak, he could have reassured them that he wasn't planning on dying today.

As the distant sound of sirens announced the arriving ambulance, the room filled with activity again. Another stretcher rattled across the floor. Doctors and nurses conferred in tense voices.

Torrance, on the other stretcher, waggled his prosthetic fingers at John. He managed a half-smile before his eyelids fluttered and he lapsed into half-consciousness.

"Same symptoms with this one," a bewildered voice reported.

"He wasn't even part of the same trial as the other one, was he?"

"What is going on here?"

John tensed—but at that moment, the paramedics rushed in, and any potential speculation on the part of the doctors and nurses dissolved into silence.

There was a brief moment of confusion when Daisy had to tell the paramedics that they no longer had one patient, but *two*. But the paramedics quickly took the change of plans in stride, and wheeled both stretchers out the doors. John's bones rattled as the stretcher raced across uneven pavement. He tried to keep his eyes on Torrance, but Torrance was behind him now, out of sight.

The stretcher tilted, then stabilized. Tight walls closed in around him. The ambulance. He wasn't trapped, he reminded himself. This wasn't a cell. It was freedom.

But he had thought he was free once before.

Torrance's stretcher came in a few seconds after his, and John let out his breath in relief. Torrance gave him a hazy wink.

The paramedics started to close the doors. Two figures in scrubs shoved their way in before they could. "We'll be riding with the patients," one of them said. "They're our responsibility, as the paperwork shows." The other figure in scrubs held out a messy pile of papers, hastily gathered.

The paramedics looked at each other. John silently willed them to argue. But apparently they weighed the cost of having two extra warm bodies in the back with them against the hassle of looking through those papers, because they gave their only-slightly-annoyed agreement.

The doors closed—this time with the two nurses in back with them.

Neither of them had anything resembling Daisy's cheer. Their faces were grim, their eyes cold, their arms muscular under their scrubs. John revised his assessment of them. Nurses? They looked more like guards to him.

The ambulance started moving. The paramedics did all the familiar things—hooking up monitors, checking vital signs. John, expending all his energy on fighting off the gray cloud of unconsciousness stealing in around the edges of his vision, tuned it all out. It was just more of the same. Background noise.

Until one of them brought out a syringe.

His eyes went wide. He shook his head.

"It's all right," the paramedic said in a soothing voice that reminded him of Daisy. "This will help you get some sleep."

A fresh bolt of alarm shot through John. This time, it had nothing to do with his bad memories. If the paramedics sedated them, they would lose their chance.

He squirmed away from the syringe as his eyes searched for Torrance. Torrance looked back, his gaze unfocused but present. Good—they hadn't gotten to him yet either. But the paramedic's hand came down on John's arm, his grip soft but insistent. "It's all right," he repeated as the syringe moved closer.

John tried to pull away. Payne seized his heart. His limbs froze along with his breath.

From the other side of the ambulance, a blur of motion. Then a heavy *thwack*. The paramedic toppled sideways, landing between the two stretchers. The other paramedic turned, eyes wide—just in time to see Torrance's heavy prosthetic arm swing at his head. A second later, the second paramedic dropped on top of the first.

"Sorry about that," Torrance said, his voice tired but blessedly clear. "None of this is *your* fault."

A grunt from below told John one of the paramedics was still awake. The first paramedic squirmed and struggled, trying to free himself from his unconscious comrade.

John rolled off the stretcher and hit the floor heavily. Pain exploded through his body; he ignored it. He didn't have time for that. His fingers fumbled for the fallen syringe. His fingers went cold and prickly when he took hold of it, but he pushed the panic back ruthlessly as he slid the needle under the paramedic's skin.

The paramedic's protest died on his open lips. His eyes rolled up in his head, and he went still.

"What's going on back there?" The driver asked. John met startled eyes in the rearview mirror. No one answered him.

The guards hadn't moved. They stared at the scene playing out in front of them, frozen in confusion. Apparently *this* wasn't the threat they had been sent along to guard against.

They looked at each other. The confusion on their faces turned to grim determination.

Torrance raised his prosthetic arm again. He started to swing it at the closer of the guards—but it froze straight out in front of him. He cursed at it, but it didn't move. His pinky finger gave a jaunty waggle, but that was it.

One of the guards picked up the vial that had fallen next to the paramedics. He fumbled through a drawer until he found a syringe.

The driver looked nervously over his shoulder. "Should I... should I pull over?"

"No," snapped the guard holding the syringe. "Keep driving."

Torrance kicked out at the guard with his prosthetic leg. It, too, locked up halfway through the movement, sticking out at a diagonal. Torrance wobbled, toppled, fell.

As John looked on helplessly, the guard slid the syringe into Torrance's arm. Torrance's curses trailed off into nothing as his eyes fluttered shut.

Both guards advanced on John.

John tried to haul himself to his feet, grasping onto the stretcher for purchase. The stretcher wobbled sideways, then toppled to the floor. John rolled aside before it could land on him.

The falling stretcher caught one of the guards in the leg. The guard shouted in pain, but it only stopped him for a second. And John was still on the floor, helpless. His chest ached. His muscles quivered.

He was too weak. Too damaged. He couldn't fight his way out. That chance had died when the military had destroyed his body with those drugs.

One of the guards had filled another syringe. He held it out in front of him as he closed in on John.

John eyed the ambulance doors. Better to take a chance on the hard pavement then let that syringe pierce his skin. But the guards were between him and the doors. He had as much chance of reaching them as he did of fighting the two guards off on his own.

He rolled sideways and opened every drawer within reach. He rifled through them frantically. There had to be something in here he could use as a weapon. But all he found was gauze, medical tape, a spare blanket. Nothing sharp. Nothing—

Then he saw it. The long plastic cylinder, the orange cap. An EpiPen. His little cousin used to have to carry one of those around with him all the time.

Which was how he knew they were designed to inject adrenaline directly into your body. Could he—

No, one part of him whispered. *Not right after a heart attack. It's too dangerous.*

No! Another part of him screamed. *Not more needles—not more drugs—no, please, please—*

He told both voices to shut up. He wasn't going back.

He pulled off the safety cap and tossed it aside. Without letting himself think about what he was doing, he swung the tip of the cylinder down into his thigh.

He felt a sharp pain first. Then a strange sensation came over him, like time was simultaneously racing by and crawling along with unbearable slowness. A sharp pain shot through his chest. *Not now,* he ordered his body. *Keep going just a little longer.*

His limbs trembled harder. But when he tried to get his feet, his legs obeyed. He stumbled forward, into the arms of the guard holding the syringe. He ducked away from the sharp tip and clutched at the guard's fingers, prying the syringe from his hand.

The guard's grip released. The syringe nearly slipped from John's sweaty fingers, but he flipped it around and plunged it into the guard's shoulder.

As the guard fell, the other guard lunged for John. John let momentum carried him forward, half running and half falling into the doors. His fingers felt for the latch. He didn't let himself think about the risk. The greater risk was going back to the place he'd escaped.

The latch released. The doors yawned open. The roar of the wind and the rattle of the wheels filled the back of the ambulance. The pavement sped by underneath them, dizzyingly fast. John wobbled, clutching at the closest cabinet handle, feeling himself teeter on the brink of oblivion.

He grabbed blindly for the other guard. His hand caught a handful of shirt. And he *shoved*.

The guard grabbed for the swinging door. His hands caught nothing but empty air. There was a thump as he hit the pavement. Then nothing, as the ambulance sped away.

The driver gave a shout of alarm. "Did someone just fall?"

"Keep driving," John demanded. His voice didn't sound like his own.

He looked at the swinging doors, thought about trying to close them. No—too risky. He stumbled away from the doors instead, pausing only to make sure Torrance was in no danger of sliding toward the back.

The ambulance veered to the side and came to a screeching halt. Torrance slid perilously toward the open doors.

"I said keep driving!" John barked—or he tried. The words came out in more of a wheezing whisper. Time was still moving both impossibly slowly and fast enough that everything had become a blur.

The front door slammed as the driver got out. John searched again for a weapon. But everything was so blurry. His heart convulsed in his chest.

A figure stepped into the back, making the floor wobble under him. He clutched at the wall.

John blinked, trying to see more clearly. The driver seemed to split into two, and both men had identical frightened expressions on their faces.

"Get back... behind the wheel," John gasped. "Keep... driving. Or I'll..." Another sharp pain shot through his rib cage like a bolt of lightning, stealing his words. He sagged against the side.

The fear on the driver's face didn't abate. But he took a step closer to John. "You look like you need help more than you need to get to wherever you want me to take you. Because judging by what just happened, I'm guessing you're not going to ask me to take you to the hospital as planned."

"I don't want... your *help*," John spat. "The last people... who promised to help me... just put me in a prettier cage. Now get back up front and *drive*."

At the last word, lightning seared through his chest again. He slid to the floor.

"I don't know what's going on here," said the driver, "but I've seen enough medical crises to know what one looks like. You're going to die without my help." He looked past John to Torrance's unconscious form. "Maybe your friend, too."

John couldn't answer. He could only clench his jaw against the pain and his own desperate panic, tightening his hands into useless fists.

"But I also know what someone desperate looks like," said the driver. "Someone with no options left. You see a lot in this job." He took another step forward. Too close. "You've been through some bad things, haven't you?"

Even through his panic, John found room for a surge of anger. Here was where the pity would start. Like Daisy, the man would lavish him in it, drown him in it, even as he forced his help on him.

"And I'm guessing those bad things had to do with that guy you pushed out the back," the driver continued. "And this other one here." He looked down at the unconscious guard. "Now, maybe you had the right of it in that fight, or maybe not. No way for me to know." Another flash of fear shot across the man's face, but he didn't back away. "But either way, my job is helping people who need it."

"I don't... want..."

Now, finally, the driver took a step back. But he didn't look ready to run. Determination shone in his eyes, stronger than his fear.

"I don't want to let you die," he said. "But I won't help you unless you want it. You've got to say it."

John felt the truth of the man's earlier words—felt it in every exhausted fiber of muscle, in every irregular beat of his struggling heart. He was dying.

But the thought of ending up in another cage... Maybe death would be better. He lay still under the driver's gaze, unable to surrender, equally unable to say no and seal his fate.

The man sighed, as if he already knew what John's answer would be and didn't like it much. "Whether you want my help or not," he said, his voice gentle and resigned, "would you mind telling me your name? I like to know who I'm talking to."

He met John's eyes. Maybe it was the blur in John's vision, but John could have sworn the man was looking at him like the answer mattered. Like John was a real human, with a name, a past, a life. With a will of his own.

He had forgotten what it was like for someone to look at him like that.

John gathered the last of his strength to speak. "John," he whispered.

He drew in a gasping breath.

"Please... help me."

About the Author

A hermit at heart with a twisted mind, Lux Thorn is a lifelong whump enthusiast with a weakness for death scenes. They live in northern New England with their partner and child. They love swimming in the ocean, staying up late reading, and big floofy dogs.

My heart beats on

Aiden E. Messer

CW: Nail whump, live vivisection, dehumanisation, body decomposition, sexual assault

Whumpee: Man, Whumpers: Man, Woman, Caretakers: Man, Woman

Elio was sitting on his bed, holding his head between his hands. His phone vibrated incessantly at the other end of the room where he'd thrown it in a fit of rage, not wanting to deal with the endless questions and remarks that would undoubtedly come. He didn't want to think, didn't want to talk, and definitely didn't want to see his reflection. Nothing made sense. He just wanted to wake up in the warmth of his bed, realizing that it had all been a weird dream, but deep down, he knew that wasn't going to happen.

It all started with that strange sand dust that covered the streets, he was sure. Yes, sand clouds sometimes arrived from the Sahara, but there was something wrong with this one. It hadn't been announced, and the sand looked... off, for lack of better word. What else could explain what had happened? He was enjoying his meal, sitting on one of the campus lawns in the shade of the trees with his friends, as he did every Tuesday when their lunch break fell at the same time, when he felt itching on his head, his fingers, then his arms and all the rest of his body. His friends had stopped eating and were staring at him in shock, one of them even dropping her sandwich. Elio didn't know what was happening. He ran his hand through his long, curly auburn hair and felt something soft that didn't belong there. At the same time, he withdrew his hand with a small cry of pain and looked at his finger with incomprehension. In place of his nails were curved white claws, slender and sharp. A small drop of blood covered one of them where he had accidentally scratched himself. A crowd was forming around them, the other students whispering and pointing. Some had even pulled out their phones to film or photograph him.

Elio got up briskly, grabbed his bag and hurried off. He made his way through the main building and out of the campus as quickly as possible. All heads turned as he passed, and he wished he'd been invisible. His face was reflected on the glass of the sliding door leading outside, and he saw for the first time what he looked like: pointed ears had appeared on his head, the same color as his hair. His eyes had become bright yellow, his pupils vertical slits. Out of the corner of his eye, he saw a hairy auburn tail protruding from his shorts.

A catboy.

He had turned into a fucking catboy.

What the actual hell?

Fortunately, he didn't live too far from the university. He went home, ignored his parents' questions and their shocked expressions, and locked himself in his room.

He was still prostrated on his bed, doing his best not to think about anything, when he heard unfamiliar voices downstairs followed by footsteps on the stairs. He raised his head and opened his eyes when he heard the sound of a metal object falling to the ground. The key to his door was lying on the floor, and something seemed to be tampering with the lock from the outside. Elio froze, biting his lip piercing anxiously. His breath caught in his throat as the door opened, revealing three men in white lab coats. His parents watched the scene wordlessly from the hallway. His mother was tugging nervously at her blouse, while his father wrung his hands uncomfortably. Elio couldn't understand what was going on. Had they called them? Were they doctors there to treat him? Why wasn't anyone saying anything? He felt a tingling sensation in his neck and realized too late that one of the men was holding a syringe and had just injected him with something. He tried to stand up, his instincts screaming at him to run away, but his legs wouldn't respond. His vision blurred, and everything went black.

***

The first thing Elio was aware of when he woke up was his throbbing head. He grunted and tried to move his arm to massage his skull, but something prevented him from doing so. It was then that he noticed the sensation of cold metal against his bare skin, and his complete inability to move. Memories of his transformation, the doctors and the syringe hit him like a freight train, and his eyes flew open. He immediately closed them again as the harsh light of a lamp blinded him, then forced himself to open them again, more slowly this time. After blinking a few times, he was finally able to make out some of his surroundings, and what he saw caused fear to grip his heart like a vise. Men and women in white lab coats bustled around him, typing on a computer, manipulating eerie equipment, and observing a vial filled with red liquid. He himself was strapped to what appeared to be an operating table, restraints holding his wrists, ankles, abdomen and neck firmly in place.

"What's going on? What do you want?" Elio asked. He was trying to sound confident, but his voice came out as nothing more than a pathetic squeak.

The men ignored him, focused on their tasks. Elio knew that if he opened his mouth again he would cry, so he remained silent.

"There is an abnormal number of stem cells in his blood," an old scientist with a gray beard announced, "but that is the only element out of the ordinary."

"That could explain tumoral growth, but why would they take such a shape?" a blond woman replied.

"We have to wait for the DNA results," a short bald man interjected. "Surely, they will give us more answers."

"I don't know if the fact that he's not the only one with a similar mutation makes this more or less freaky," a young man with short black hair added softly. "God, this makes no sense!"

Elio hated hearing them talk about him as if he wasn't there. Why did this have to happen to him? He was just a normal art student, he always tried to be kind to people around him, he didn't deserve this!

"Give me the pliers, please," the blond woman's voice sounded again.

Elio watched in horror as she clamped the pliers onto one of his claws. An excruciating pain followed, and the claw slowly separated from his finger, leaving only a bloody trail behind.

The woman carefully placed it in a small plastic bag that the young man handed her, and the two of them moved out of his sight, leaving him shaking and sobbing.

The scientists went back to ignoring him, focusing on their notes and the blinking equipment, until an old woman with brown hair gasped in surprise.

"His claw! Look, it grew back!"

All the scientists -there must have been a dozen of them- crowded around him, chatting rapidly and excitedly.

Elio turned his head towards his hands and saw that all his claws were indeed there again. Yet the pulsing pain in his finger where one had been torn off was still present. He was too exhausted to think about what it meant. He just wanted to curl up and forget everything, but with the restraints, that was not an option.

"The original claw is still in the bag," the young scientist said. "That shouldn't be possible!"

"None of this should be possible," the old man added.

"The stem cells!" the blond woman exclaimed. "That has to be what causes the rapid regeneration."

"We need to study this more closely," the bald man added. "If he really can heal in an accelerated way, it could save millions of human lives."

Elio squeezed his eyes shut. Human lives. So they didn't consider him to be human anymore. Elio suspected it, but hearing it said like that hurt more than he would have imagined.

A sharp pain in his arm made his eyes snap open again. The bald scientist was cutting his arm with a scalpel. Everyone looked intently at the shallow wound, and victorious cries resounded through the laboratory as it began to close by itself. The bald scientist made a second, deeper cut, causing Elio to scream in pain. A few moments later, this one too healed, but the pain remained. Elio felt a new rush of panic invade his body as the scientist approached with the blade again.

"No! Please, no more! It hurts! It hurts too much!"

The man ignored his desperate pleas and cut deeper, scratching the bones. Still, the wound healed but the pain remained.

"Fascinating," the blond woman whispered. "Would his limbs grow back too, or does this ability limit itself to minor wounds?"

Despite knowing that it was useless, Elio couldn't stop himself from begging and crying. In response, the woman took out a bone saw from a drawer and began to cut off one of his fingers. The pain was overwhelming. The woman picked up the severed finger with her gloved hands and put it in a plastic bag similar to the one where his claw was. Searing agony pounded where Elio's digit had been. His cries had turned into choked sobs, and his whole trembling body was covered in sweat. He couldn't fathom how anyone could treat someone else so cruelly. Even if they didn't see him as a person anymore, he was still a living, breathing being. Even animals weren't supposed to be experimented on like that! At least, he didn't think so.

Enthusiastic gasps and frenzied typing indicated to him that his finger was growing back, but what good did it do him if the pain didn't fade?

"It's getting late. I think we've seen enough for today," the old scientist stated. "Tomorrow, the analyses of the various tissues we've collected will be ready, and we'll find out more. For now, we'd better get some rest. It's been a long day."

A long day for them? Was that a fucking joke? Elio would have laughed if he wasn't too busy crying.

The scientists undid his restraint and dragged him out of the room. He tried to fight them, but he was too weak. They shoved him in a small metal cage, barely high enough for him to crouch. Inside were two bowls: one with water, the other with some kind of unappetizing gruel. His stomach churned at the idea of eating anything, but his throat was parched from all the screaming, so he drank the water and left the other bowl untouched. He curled up against the cold metal floor, his tail wrapped around his body, doing his best to find a comfortable position in this cramped space where he couldn't even stretch his legs. Soon, exhaustion caught up with him and he fell into a nightmare-filled sleep.

Elio had no way of knowing how long he slept. The laboratory's industrial neon lights gave no indication of the time, and there was no window. All he knew was that he was still exhausted when the scientists came back to take him out of his crate, and that his body was aching. As soon as his feet hit the ground, he tried to make a break for it, but a prick in his neck swept away his thin hope: they had drugged him again. This time, he didn't lose consciousness, but his limbs grew heavy, and the slightest effort felt like running a marathon. Elio expected to be strapped back on the metal slab, but instead, he was shoved into a plexiglass tank that was promptly closed and locked. Before his numbed brain could process this new turn of event, the tank started filling with water. This shook him out of his drugged-induced stupor and he struggled to break free, screaming and banging on the walls. The scientists looked at him with professional interest and, for some, a hint of giddy excitement like he was a shiny new toy. Water soon reached the top of the tank. Elio held his breath, fighting back the panic threatening to crush him. He could see the scientist taking notes. Were they going to just watch him drown? How could they not feel guilty?

Elio's chest felt as if it was on fire, he tried to hold on, but eventually his natural reflexes took over and he took a deep breath, filling his lungs with water. He couldn't hold the panic back any longer. His heart beat furiously, his head felt as if it was about to explode, and more and more water swept through his mouth and nose. His vision became blurry, and he was sure that he was going to pass out anytime now, but unconsciousness seemed determined to deny him that mercy. Minutes passed, maybe hours, Elio couldn't tell anymore. He was drowning, he was hurting, but he wasn't dying and somehow that made it worse.

Then, the tank was opened and rough hands pulled him out of the water. He coughed and gasped, throwing up all the water he had inhaled. From the corner of his eyes, he saw that the brown-haired woman had written: *'Can't breath but can't die. Eternal asphyxiation?'* on her notepad.

He was put back in his crate with some fresh food and water, and the scientist left again. The mere sight of the water made his heart race, and he threw the bowl against the bars. That reminded him of when he'd thrown his phone, just after his transformation, one day ago. A lifetime ago. Would things have been different if he'd picked it up? He'd never know. He curled up on himself, sobs racking his soaked body, his auburn hair sticking uncomfortably to his face.

Hours later, footsteps brought him out of the hopeless stupor he had fallen into. A wave of nausea swept over him at the thought of what they were going to do to him next. This time, however, the young scientist was alone and looked uneasy. Could he be having second thoughts? Even remorses? Maybe he was there to set him free? Despite himself, Elio began to hope again.

The man opened the crate, and Elio's hopes were brutally shattered as he sedated him once more.

"A fucking real-life catboy," the scientist muttered to himself, "I can't let an occasion like that pass. I just can't."

Elio's eyes widened as he saw him take a condom out of his pocket. He couldn't let that happen, he just couldn't!

"Please, man don't do this! I beg you!" Elio said, his voice weak and shaky. "You know it's wrong! I don't know what happened to me, but I'm still a person, you can't do this."

This didn't get any more reactions than all his previous pleas. The scientist ran his fingers over Elio's cat ears and tail, marveling at how soft they were. Elio's skin crawled in disgust. He tried to claw at the man, but the drug was too strong and his hand fell pathetically back to the ground.

The scientist moved behind him, and a red hot pain invaded his inside. A strong hand pressed on his neck, preventing him from crawling away.

It burned.

It burned so much.

Then, the pain got worse as he felt something inside him tear. The scientist didn't slow down. Why would he care anyway? It would heal, and Elio would be left to deal with the pain. He felt as if he was watching the scene from the outside. The scientist's free hand was playing with his furry ears and tail, but they didn't feel like his. He stared absently at the white wall in front of him. Nothing felt real anymore.

A grunt. The thrusts stopped, leaving an empty ache behind them. Something cold against his skin. The scientist wiping off the blood that had pooled between his legs. His crate again, locked. Alone.

Was it the same day? The next? Elio didn't know. He didn't fight when he was dragged out of his cage and strapped to the operation table again, this time attaching sensors to his body. What would be the point? They were stronger than him anyway. He was just a helpless little lab rat here.

"Is everyone ready?" the blond woman asked.

"Are we sure about this?" the old brown haired scientist said slowly, her voice heavy with doubt. "This could kill him. We don't know when we'll be able to catch another one."

"We need to know for sure," the bald scientist responded. "The sample results have been very enlightening, but we won't get any further if we don't test this theory. Even if he doesn't survive the operation, we'll have learned something and will still be able to dissect his body."

Elio heard their words, but they seemed distorted, as if his head was still underwater. The prospect of death didn't scare him as much as it had before. Actually, he hoped he'd die. He didn't want to live like this anymore.

A sharp pain spread across his sternum as one of the scientists made a deep incision. Metal clamps were hooked to the flesh, spreading the edges of the wound and preventing it from closing. An electric noise filled the room, and something cut through the sternum. Elio's vision went black, and he thought he was going to faint from pain, but once again he remained cruelly awake.

His sternum was split open. Hands rummaged inside his chest. More cuts. When his vision came back, the blond scientist was holding his still-beating heart in her gloved hands.

"Incredible, he's still breathing," the bald scientist remarked.

Elio's heart was placed in a jar filled with formaldehyde. The scientists were congratulating each other, frantically taking notes, and talking about the possibilities this opened up for science and medicine. Elio couldn't keep his eyes off the pulsing heart in the jar. His pulsing heart. But was it still his if it could keep beating without him?

***

Elio was rotting. He was still alive, or at least still conscious, but his body was decaying steadily. It had been days since they removed his heart, and the organ seemed to taunt him, pulsing steadily in the yellowish liquid. The scientists hadn't unstrapped him from the table. They occasionally checked on him, taking more notes and looking at the sensor's data, but his body seemed to hold less interest to them than the samples they already had collected.

The operation wound hadn't healed. Blood was no longer pumped through his veins. Even without the restraints, he wouldn't have been able to do much more than slowly clench and unclench his hands. His skin was blackening, tissues liquifying. He could even see bits of bones appear on his arms, and he suspected the same would be true for the rest of his body if he was able to move enough to see it. Every nerve ending was in constant agony, yet he felt nothing but a numb emptiness. He would close his eyes, but his eyelids had already melted. Would he finally be able to rest in peace when he was nothing but a skeleton, or would his mind remain stubbornly attached to his withered bones?

He didn't flinch when the door opened. He was used to it by now. They would look at him as if he was some mildly interesting specimen, take some more notes, and leave.

"Shit, they really did a number on him!" a voice Elio didn't know sounded.

A man about his age stood next to the operating table. It took Elio's decomposing brain several seconds to register that he had long, rabbit-like ears.

"There, that must be his heart!" another voice. More feminine this time.

Elio couldn't comprehend what was happening. Those weren't the scientists. What were they doing here? More subjects?

The woman was now next to the rabbit man. Small round ears protruded from her short brown hair, and the jar was clutched between the black claws of her hands. A bear girl, maybe? Did it matter anymore?

More people gathered around, all adorned with various animal-like features. They looked at him with concern and sympathy.

"I'm going to put this back in his place," the rabbit man said, taking Elio's heart out of the jar. "You should start healing again. I think."

Elio tried to say something, but his mouth wouldn't work. He didn't know what he would have said anyway. He was just so tired.

More soothing words came from the others, but he couldn't make them out, there were too many. Then, his heart was back in his chest. The mere proximity seemed to be enough, as it started attaching itself back to Elio's arteries. Soon, the wound was closing, and the decomposed tissues were growing back. A warm glow flooded Elio's body, not dissipating the pain but making it somewhat more bearable. His brain began to function at a normal speed again, and some of what everyone was saying made its way into his mind. They were here to help him. They had rescued others before him. They would bring him somewhere safe. An incredulous smile spread across his face despite the pain in his body and soul as the bonds came undone.

Free.

He was free. And more importantly, he wasn't alone anymore.

About the Author

Aiden E. Messer does not exist. Are they an illusion, a ghost, a mere thought? No one knows. If we are to believe one of the children they seem to work with, if they were a teacher, they would be as tall as a human. They are not a teacher.

According to various sources, they have studied psychology, and have always had a penchant for horror and the macabre. They like to combine these subjects in their books.

Live

Pier

CW: Attempted suicide, non-consensual drug use
Whumpee: Man, Whumper: Woman, Caretaker: N/A

37 rested his head against the cool metal of the wall behind him and brought a hand to his nose. It came away bloodied.

That wasn't a surprise. Withdrawal was a bitch.

"37? 37!"

37 would've laughed if he had the energy for it. He closed his eyes instead and immersed himself in the pounding headache taking over his brain. He ran a hand through his hair– the bloody one, he realized belatedly– and felt for the scar on the side of his head. Maybe he could try bleeding out the headache.

A hand squeezed his neck, feeling for a pulse. *Klos,* his mind registered before he reached up and yanked her away by the wrist. He forced himself to open his eyes, ignoring how his vision swam dangerously at the edges, and glared at her.

"Don't," he snarled. "Don't you fucking dare–"

Klos's face was grim. "I told you you'll die if you don't take it," she said.

37 barked out a laugh. "Why do you think I stopped? Cure me or kill me," he said. "But I'm not going to be one of your fucking experiments, Klos." The ringing in his ears was growing louder. He was running out of time.

Klos shook off 37's grip and began rolling up his sleeve. 37 closed his eyes as the needle slipped underneath his skin.

"I hate you," he said as his body began to relax, the drugs entering his bloodstream.

"I love you too," Klos replied.

About the Author

Pier is a writer, artist, and creator based in the US. His passions outside of art include history and linguistics. He spends most of his time reading, hyper-fixating, or playing with the little characters inside his head. His current goal is to become fully fluent in Cantonese and finish the novel he has been working on for the past year.

Project: Valeriana

Booker G. A. Feniks

CW: Forced pregnancy, transphobia, forced detransition, sexual assault
Whumpee: Man, Whumper: Man, Woman, Caretaker: N/A

I

"Please! You're making a mistake!" Shepherd begged the two of them but was ignored. He was dragged towards the depths of the facility by the very men who were once created to serve him, whom he had trusted with his own life.

"It's what the boss wants, Shepherd." Ace's voice was cold, emotionless. Titan, as always, said nothing.

"You have to listen to me!" Shepherd sobbed, yanking and ripping at his chained arms.

"It's what the boss wants, Shepherd." Ace repeated, bringing his free hand up. His fingers curled around the back of Shepherd's neck; he squeezed. Shepherd felt the pressure, heard his pulse beating beneath the taut skin of his neck. One second, two, and he was out cold.

***

He awoke to a blinding white light; he awoke to blinding white walls; he awoke to a blinding white ceiling and floor. Shepherd awoke to the beating pain within his shoulders and the constricting heat of leather that bound his arms tightly behind him. His head was pounding, and there was a sharp pain behind his eyes from the bright lights.

There was a muzzle around his face. He wasn't sure how that had escaped him on waking up. There was a cold, metallic muzzle fastened to his face. He felt the clip at the back of his neck, beneath his long hair. It went under his chin, just below his nose, and stretched across his cheeks. It confused him, unnerved him. He felt pinpricks of pain alongside his entire jaw, as if it was wired shut, as if the muzzle was wired into his skin and muscles. Every subtle movement of his jaw sent shocks of pain through his nerves. He couldn't even call for help. There *was* no one to call for help.

***

He lost count of how long it had been since he awoke. There was just him, the white everything, the muzzle, and his tightly bound arms. The floor beneath his feet was lukewarm, the walls against his forehead were no different. The air felt stagnant as he breathed it in through his nose, and yet something within it burned his nasal cavities, travelling upwards and then down to scorch his throat. It became unbearable after just a few minutes, until he was screaming through his wired-shut jaw and muzzled mouth, screaming and screeching like a soul from the deepest circles of hell. He screamed until the burn ate away at his skin, and his nose began spurting out blood. Onto him, onto the white floors and the white walls. It was blazing when he pressed his bare chest against his own bloodstains, the warmth finally a change, finally a difference. He rubbed it over his chest, over the muscles of his shoulders, over his stomach and down to his legs, until he was covered in the burning blood that spurted out of his burning nose like lava out of the mouth of a volcano.

"How are we feeling, Shepherd?" The man that walked into his tomb had a smile like a serpent, and a face like a chimaera. The name eluded him in that moment, he hadn't even realised he was being talked to. 'Shepherd' didn't register as a name to him, not even as a real word. But something within his ribcage told him to defy.

"I see you've still not learned your lesson," The man hummed, his smile twisting into a sneer. "Well, no matter. Once I'm done with you, you'll wish you had been obedient from the start."

II

He had been alone. There had been a fire in his lungs. The white light of God behind his eyelids. An emptiness within his mind.

When he had come to his throat had been thick with the blood from where he had bitten through his tongue. The taste had been sweet in a way he hadn't noticed before; almost comforting. It had taken his mind off the full body ache that had made his entire being convulse, rhythmically, his naked back pressed to a cold, metallic surface.

"Shepherd, how do you feel?" The voice had come from his right, a breath ghosting over his cheek. He had thought he only blinked; had moved in the span of the second it had taken him to swallow down his own blood. But the shock of the cold floor against his soles had pulled him back to the buzzing of medical equipment, and the blinding white of the overhead lamps. It had pulled him back into his body, where his palm had been warm against the throat of a portly, balding man in a lab coat. The doctor... scientist's legs had been dangling a good few inches off the floor. His arm hadn't even shaken, he hadn't even felt the weight.

"Please..." The scientist had croaked out, a tear running down from one of his warm brown eyes. The scientist's blue lips had barely formed the individual syllables.

His fingers had released one by one, as if pried open by an invisible force. The scientist had dropped heavily to his knees, his hands flying up to grasp at his throat. Colour had slowly returned to the scientist's face, and he had watched it do so, the thoughts, the sensations, solidifying within his mind.

The lab hadn't been big, a simple square room. In the corner, by the door, had stood a heart rate monitor snuggled up to a coat hanger, and in the very centre had stood a bed next to an operating table. The white light above had dribbled out of a swinging light bulb; there had been no other exits but the metal door by the corner.

"I see... I see that you're doing much better now," the scientist had gasped, "That's very good, very promising." His hand had shot out, and the scientist had flinched back. He had flinched in turn, pressing his offered arm against his bare chest, watching dejectedly as the scientist had clambered back onto his feet.

"Where am I?" he had whispered, his throat feeling as if it was stuffed with cotton.

"You're safe, Shepherd," The scientist's voice had been gentle, a slightly nasally timber that had made him feel warm inside, but his words had made his blood run cold, "You were terminally ill, but we managed to bring you back. You're alive, Shepherd, and better than ever, all thanks to Mr Fergusson."

"That's not my name." A flash of fear had passed over the scientist's face. He hadn't known what that meant, all he had known was that Shepherd wasn't his name. He had a name; one he had chosen for himself. He could no longer remember it.

"It is your name now, my boy." The man's voice had still been gentle, still calming, "You have lost your memory, but you are a new man now."

But that wasn't his name. He had one before. He couldn't remember, why couldn't he remember.

"Come along, my boy. Mr Fergusson will explain everything to you. I am Dr Gok Man Shik, by the way. I will take care of you."

III

They blindfolded him for his second torture session. He refused to call it 'reha-bilitation' or 'breaking' like Leif Fergusson did. He wouldn't be broken, and then fixed into whatever Fergusson wanted him to be. He was being tortured; he would die before he let them break him.

The muzzle was still attached to his face by the hooks embedded in his cheeks. The gurgling breaths he let out of his raw nose hurt, and they filled up his ears in the complete darkness.

His arms were chained to the chair he sat upon. The metal encased his wrists and his ankles, and not even his superhuman strength could free him. It was cold; the metal refused to warm up.

The seat beneath him was hard and cold too. Everything in the facility was metal. The doors, the walls, the floors. And the chairs, like the one he sat upon.

There was no draft in the room, no sound of the wind except for his laborious breaths. And yet he was still cold, the stagnant air around him making the hairs upon his bare body rise.

The darkness was penetrating. It was almost as if he and his chair were floating in space. There were bright spots exploding in his eyes before long, electric fire-works of colourless light.

He was cold; he heard his own heartbeat in his ears; there was only darkness. And yet the worst thing about all this was his mind. There was nothing to grasp onto, nothing to focus on. Just the darkness and the cold air, and the emptiness in his eyes and ears. His mind raced in circles around his metal chair like a wild sparrow, frightened of its own shadow. His mind was a shadow in the corner of his eyes, chased by the wild sparrow. He was the wild sparrow, chasing his own shadow, chased by the wild sparrow with a hummingbird heart that drummed a beat like a freight train. He faced a freight train and its lights exploded in his eyes. His eyes exploded within their sockets, the whistle of the train exploded in his ears, the wild sparrow flew onto the track and exploded before the train. The wild sparrow was him, and the freight train was him, and they both chased the shadow that was him in the darkness before his eyes. And the shadow dove behind his metal chair and his body was part of the chair, his body was cold metal and black darkness, his mind was the wild sparrow chasing after the metal chair, flying in circles around the metal chair. His mind was the metal and the cold and the darkness and the wild sparrow chased around it and the shadow chased after it and the freight train chased after him and it and them and after his very *self*.

***

Hours passed before someone entered the dark, empty room he was chained within. The blindfold had long since dried from where his tears wet it, his head hanging limp against his chest. And the wild sparrow still tried to escape its own shadow within his empty mind.

IV

Titan and Ace were their names. The only other men who had survived Project: Valeriana.

Titan was bigger than life, true to his name. A Hispanic man who stood at 7 feet tall, with bulging muscles that were bigger than Shepherd's head. The story had been that he was brought to Mr Leif Fergusson by his wife, after a car accident had left him paralysed and comatose. She had pleaded with the businessman to save her beloved's life with his Gladiolus serum, and it *had* saved his life. However, Fergusson always said, it had done little for Titan's body, his strength and size had been a gift from nature itself. The Valeriana serum, on the other hand, had worked wonders, Fergusson claimed. And yet Titan still struggled with his memory.

Ace was an African American man who had the look of a scholar, rather than a fighter. His name 'Ace' had come from the fact that he had taken to the two serums the best, and yet he barely looked the part. A weak, sickly young man who had been brought before Fergusson by his weeping father, hellbent on saving his precious baby boy's life despite the high mortality rates of Project: Valeriana. He was the silent type, but exceptionally intelligent, and yet he had gotten along with Shepherd like they were a pair of long-lost friends. The brief mentions of their past, and the rare bursts of memory, did little to piece together a supposedly shared history.

Shepherd had taken to the Gladiolus serum the best. His muscle mass had increased alongside his considerable strength. He had been the fastest, most agile of the Project: Valeriana soldiers. The serum had given him a body that the others considered worthy of a Greek god, a small penis included. There had been a sense of confusion whenever he thought about his body and those of Titan and Ace. Fergusson had called him the pinnacle of male physique, but his words had always been coloured by a sneer. Dr Gok had prattled on, constantly, about how well Shepherd's 'feminine' body had taken to the Gladiolus serum, how the regimen of testosterone exemplified both his natural abilities and his new powers. And yet there had been confusion on his end. His body, the body of a man, had been a surprise to the scientists and the leaders of the Project. His body, that had been changed to be even better than before, had confused people who called him 'female', 'feminine', who had looked at him like he was a freak.

He had taken badly to the Valeriana serum, and his failing memory was supposed to be a testament to that. He knew not his name, his age, his nationality. He knew he was a man, that Shepherd wasn't his real name, and that there was an emptiness within him whenever he tried to think further than the day he woke up beneath Dr Gok's knife. He had to be told that he was 43 years old, a second-generation Polish immigrant to Canada, and that he was 'transgender'. In his mind he was simply a man, a nameless one, who loved his body but wished he remembered if any of this was his own choice. He wanted to know that he *had* a choice, and what his decisions had been.

That had been another failure of the Valeriana serum. He had made too many independent choices; he had refused to bow down to Leif Fergusson.

V

"Let me tell you, my Harbinger, I like you a helluva lot." Leif Fergusson was a thin, sickly-looking man with a blond quiff and a threadbare moustache. He had a pleasant smile on the rare occasion he was actually happy. His other smiles, however, never failed to frighten Shepherd.

"What's that you're saying, Sheppy boy?" Fergusson leaned in, almost pressing his ear up against Shepherd's muzzle. He paused for a second, and then burst out into raucous laughter. That sound reminded Shepherd of a donkey, and yet it was almost flattering on Fergusson. Shepherd had to wonder who hurt this man so much; he was almost bearable when happy. Almost.

"Or do you prefer me call you girl? I could never figure it out with you." He was tied down to another one of the metal chairs in the facility, his arms tied behind its back in a way that made his chest protrude. The look Fergusson aimed his way was one of disgust, and his bluish-grey eyes never left Shepherd's face.

"I gave you the sort of body real men would kill for, fåne! I was an Aphrodite, I fixed you right up, I made you my Adonis! But all you wanted to be was Hermaphroditos! And you thought Gok your Hermes, but he was your Salmacis instead!" Fergusson's thick Swedish accent only reared its head when talking about Man Shik, and Shepherd had been subject to it often over the past few months. Shepherd often wondered where the poor doctor had disappeared off to. Fergusson refused to say.

"Really, you're so ungrateful. Both of you. I gave you everything you could have wanted, even though I was being paid to kill you off and bury your body under a pile of paperwork that no one ever looked at. You caused me far more trouble than you should be worth, my Harbinger." The space between Shepherd's legs was growing wet, blood dripping down his thighs. Fergusson scrunched up his face but seemed to pay it no mind. He was closer to him again, and his breath stank of alcohol. There was a moment in which Fergusson tried catching his eye, blue to green, but he failed and dropped the attempt. Up close, Shepherd could count each and every discoloured spot on his front teeth, coffee stains and the wet film of high percentage vodka.

"You would've made a pretty woman, my Harbinger. Never understood why you wanted to ruin..." Fergusson's teeth let out a resounding *CLACK*, his head snapping backwards with such force that his chair tipped backwards. His thin, gangly body sprawled out on the floor in a boneless heap, and Shepherd felt the space between his eyes sting something awful.

Fergusson lay there for what felt like hours, unmoving. Shepherd almost thought he had killed him, Fergusson's dainty chest looking as if it wasn't rising and falling anymore. With his cuffed hands he had aimed, spritzing Fergusson in the face, droplets of water dripping from his fingers. Fergusson had given him these powers, and what good were they, really? The drunken bastard just lay there, still as a corpse.

So, Shepherd just sat there, because he had nothing else to do, but realise that his second official kill as a superhuman soldier was his former boss who had a transphobic streak when drunk.

But Fergusson eventually woke up and climbed to his feet. There was no fanfare, no evil looks or promises of further torture. The Swede turned on the balls of his feet and stumbled out of the room without so much as a glance at his prisoner.

The blood still dripped down Shepherd's thighs.

VI

"Sparkplug, don't leave me here." Shepherd's hand had wrapped around Ace's warm wrist, tugging at him gently. The light from the overhead lamp had filtered through his eyelids, making the darkness take on a sun-like consistency. The bunk above him had been empty, and the blanket beside him had been cold as Ace had begun flitting about the room aimlessly.

"Shep, I don't want Mr Fergusson to find us like that." There had been no windows in the three-bed barrack room they shared, and yet the clinical white light had made Ace's hair shimmer like a halo around his head. They had been the favourite children, the three of them, so Ace wore his hair in tight curls that bounced slightly as he walked; Titan preferred his hair in a buzz cut, like the regular soldiers; Shepherd had his in a low ponytail at the base of his neck.

"You're beautiful, Ace." And he truly had been, with the slight smile on his dark red lips, and the faint bags underneath his beer-brown eyes. His dark brown skin had glowed from the yellow light on their InfoPad's screen. And yet when he had looked at Ace it felt as if something was missing. Another name starting with A had floated around in the back of his mind, but each time he had reached out for it, he had been met with a spreading pain within his chest.

There had been something so familiar about the way they had made love to each other long after Titan had fallen asleep. A sharing of bodies and souls, a merging of the very essences of their beings. And yet, they were missing something, Shepherd was missing something, and it had refused to leave him alone.

"Take your pills, lamb." The smile on his lips had been shy, small. His voice was deep and bassy; his Southern accent had made the nickname 'lamb' sound like a prayer, and Shepherd had always wanted to know how Ace would sound pronouncing his real name. But then there had been that reminder, a hand outstretched with a circular, white pill on his palm, the other holding an empty plastic cup for him to fill up. It had been the reminder that Ace had fully succumbed to the Valeriana serum, that he had become fully subservient to Fergusson.

"Yes, yes." Shepherd had sucked the water out from the air around them, directing it into the cup the same way their training instructors had taught him. He had grasped at the Plan B, fumbling with the tiny tablet between his fingers. Man Shik had bought him those pills after the first scare, the first mistake caused by his failing memory. When had Shepherd began calling the doctor Man Shik instead of Dr Gok? Sometime around the Investor Scandal, possibly, although he couldn't be sure. It was around that time he had stopped calling Fergusson 'Mr'.

A pair of warm lips had pressed against his forehead when he had leant over to take a sip, "Hurry up, my lamb. I'll see you in the training grounds." Ace had left before Shepherd had the time to kiss him back, or even look up at him. He had heard the buzz of electricity when Ace had activated the door controls, and that had been it. Shepherd had already begun feeling empty, already missing him.

No matter how much control Fergusson had over their lives, when they ate and slept, when they trained and how they worked, Shepherd had still been Ace's lamb. He had been the shepherd to lead his flock of soldiers; he had been a king to his generals, the one they would both die for. But he had also been 'lamb' to Ace, the most important person to him, more important than Fergusson. Someone Ace had promised to always protect.

He had swallowed the pill, and it had dropped into his stomach like a stone. He had been the most important person in Ace's life, and yet something felt wrong. Something didn't quite add up.

VII

They had strapped him to a table, spread eagle and naked. There were bits of metal between his teeth forcing his mouth open. The wounds upon his cheeks left from the mask were weeping.

"A lengthening of the canine teeth corresponds with the increased need of the subjects to consume red meat. Higher protein consumption causes an increase in muscle mass. Really, it's all linked as you can see, Mr Fergusson." The doctor hovering over Shepherd's body wore a papery face mask, but his voice was uncomfortably high-pitched, and his eyes were squinty black dots lost within the folds of his weathered face. Dr Owen was Dr Gok's replacement, Fergusson had said. He still didn't know what had happened to Man Shik. Did his family know? His wife, his daughter? Did Fergusson keep it a secret from them too?

"Yeah, yeah, I know. Anything new you can tell me?" Fergusson was in the corner in his business suit. He looked like an ostrich in a field of flamingos, as tall and gangly as 90% of the doctors milling around, but his beige suit made Shepherd's eyes hurt after looking at the scientists' bright blue scrubs for so long.

"Well, there is an increase in speed that can be…" Fergusson cut him off with a wave of his hand, "There is also a toughening of the skin and increase in healing…" Again, Fergusson interrupted, "The subject has heightened senses compared to that of…" And again, "I…"

"Dr Owen," Fergusson began with a sickly-sweet smile, "Have you read the documents I sent over to you at the beginning of our partnership?" The look in his eyes had Shepherd shivering.

"I, uh, never received the documents, sir." Dr Owen's eyes flitted between him and Fergusson. Each time he focused on Fergusson he would flinch. Each time he focused on Shepherd he would shudder and let out a sigh that sounded half-pleased. The metal in his mouth pressed deeper into his cheeks, and goose flesh rose across the entire length of his prone body.

"Time to fire Sergei, then." Shepherd knew that he was the only one to hear Fergusson's angry muttering. But the rest of the scientists reflexively tensed.

"There... there is a curious side effect of the serum where the patient's body seems to have synthesised with the testosterone injections to start producing higher levels of it, naturally, than a biological female. Not nearly as much as a biological male, but this almost resembles the symptomatology of PCOS without the negative effects of..."

"I KNOW THAT!" Fergusson's roar had Owen flinching, and Shepherd spied a dark patch forming at the front of his scrubs. Another doctor bumbled over to Shepherd, sticking him in the arm with something that burned when it entered his veins.

"Sir, the subject's eggs are still viable." A blond-haired nurse came up beside Fergusson. They looked like father and son, with near identical hooked noses, and gaunt faces beneath sheets of stretched, pale skin.

"And how does that help us, Arne?" The look within the young Fergusson's eyes mirrored the venom-filled gaze of his father.

"Sir, we could breed soldiers for Project: Valeriana that are born with the superhuman abilities we are looking for." Shepherd's blood ran cold.

"Arne, son, you just got your first raise." Arne, with his blueish-grey eyes, identical to his father's, leered over at Shepherd. His smile was too wide, showed too many teeth. Unlike his father, he completely refused to look Shepherd in the face.

VIII

"Mrs Agustina Windisch, it is a pleasure." Mr Fergusson had given the petite, smartly dressed woman one of his famous faux smiles. She was hardly tall enough to reach Shepherd's chest, and he was only 5'7" himself. Her lips were thin and so red that they looked more like a sliced open wound, than a mouth. Her eyes were painted with dark brown eyeshadow and pitch-black eyeliner, making her dull brown irises seem almost as black as the pupils.

"The pleasure is all mine, Mr Fergusson." She had a high-pitched, breathy voice with a thick accent that had made it hard for Shepherd to understand her. She had shaken Mr Fergusson's hand with enough force to make the man visibly wince.

"Don't break there, boss. It's not appropriate." Shepherd had worn a grin on his face, and Mrs Windisch almost seemed to be smiling back at him. At his sides, Titan and Ace had tensed. They had stood in a line, the three of them, their chests thrust out and their arms rigid at their sides.

There had been a rumour floating around that Mrs Windisch had arrived at the facility in a black limo. She had arrived before the rest of the investors, taking even Mr Fergusson by surprise. Whether the rumours had been true or not, the soldiers within the windowless facility had no way of telling, but some had been more vocal about it than others, Shepherd being one of them.

"This, Mrs Windisch, is Shepherd," Mr Fergusson had seethed, "We call him that because he has a way with words." With Mrs Windisch's back turned to him, Mr Fergusson had glared at Shepherd. His lip had curled in a way that had made his moustache squirm like a caterpillar.

Shepherd had done a little bow, putting on his most disarming smile, "Far be it for me to be rude to a lady of such high status." Mr Fergusson had looked about ready to strangle him with his bare hands.

"Oh, danke, young man," Mrs Windisch had said in her thickly accented voice, before turning back to Mr Fergusson, "I can see that. But is he truly strong and fast above human capability?" She had been studying him with a look like one of the doctors, but there had been a warmth to her eyes that reminded him of Dr Gok. She still had that small, hidden smile on her face.

"Yes, he is, as are all three of them. Why, Mrs Windisch, why don't I show you? How about a durability test?" Mr Fergusson wasn't a tall man, nor was he very imposing. He wasn't scary, he didn't command the respect of others with just his presence. And yet Shepherd had felt the cold sweat pool in the small of his back as Mr Fergusson had approached him with a knife. A knife was overselling it. It had been a pocketknife that was hardly as long as his pointer finger, and yet when it had sunk beneath his skin it stole the air out of his lungs. The cold metal had penetrated him with all of its length, and then Fergusson had twisted the handle and Shepherd had been scared he would faint.

He vaguely remembered hearing Mrs Windisch's shriek of horror, and Ace's terrified yell. He had felt Titan's arms encircle him when his knees had buckled. And when the cold metal had been removed, it was replaced by a shuddering burn. The burn had spread from his stomach and the wound to his chest where a hot fury had sizzled within his breast.

"As you can see, Mrs Windisch, he might be a bit dazed, but he has already healed." A cold snap of air and his shirt had hung limply off his shoulders. The stab wound had been, indeed, already healed, but that wasn't where Mrs Windisch had looked.

"I... I'll take him to the, the medbay, boss." Shepherd had hardly heard Titan speak. His eyes had met those of Mrs Windisch, and he had seen pity within their depths.

IX

There was a doctor who visited him the most. She was a pretty, young thing. There was a mole above the right corner of her rose-coloured lips; lips which she painted to be more bow shaped. She had thick lashes decorating big, brown doe eyes. Her hair, falling in luscious locks around her frail shoulders, was the colour of burnt caramel, and she smelled like fudge.

She was the cruellest, most evil creature Shepherd had ever met.

"How are we feeling today, mutt?" Her lips twisted into a smirk, her perfectly threaded eyebrows turned down into an expression that almost seemed angry. Klara appraised his body, spread out upon a metal table, needles stuck into his skin.

"Such a shame." She mused. He bit down on his tongue behind the steel protection of his muzzle. A hand, dainty and frail, caressed the inside of his thigh. He felt the shiver ripple through his body. Bile began to rise in his throat and his hands tingled with a surge of power. He clenched them into fists, feeling the wetness drip down onto the table and pool around his wrists.

"I never understood why Mr Fergusson let you ruin yourself. He could have made you strong and powerful without ruining your perfect, female form. He could have made a goddess out of you, waxing and waning like the moon, the tides at your command. A healing, feminine force to offset the destructive male powers of the other two." Shepherd tried not to listen. Klara never talked to him, but always at him, with a voice like silk drifting over him in a gentle whisper. The Gladiolus serum could not let him be, he could hear every venom-filled word that dripped past her rosy lips.

"What a waste." Her off-key humming was distracting, it wouldn't let him fall asleep to the rest of her droning speech and dulcet tones. Her hand rubbed deeper, higher, leaving goosebumps in its wake beneath the softness of her hands. Shepherd kept his eyes shut and his body taut, biting down on his tongue and digging his nails into the palms of his hands.

"I could have fixed you, mutt." That word was almost affectionate, almost like a pet name shared between lovers. "If I got to you first, I could have fixed you. Made you realise how much you were missing, before. Made you into a goddess. Now, it's too *late*, mutt." Her fingers curled around the slight length between his legs. Shepherd loved that length. The day he had woken up and felt it gently swing against his upper thigh had been the day he had fallen in love with the body he was given.

"You are ruined!" A keen was squeezed out of his clenched lips when she yanked on his self-made manhood, the Greek sculptor's religion, the marvel of science that was the only thing Fergusson had ever given him. It burned, the thin skin at its base burned and ached and Shepherd was scared that it would rip, that Klara wanted to rip his dick away, rip it out alongside his very soul.

"What a waste." She whispered, from the doorway. A tear; a single, salty tear slipped down Shepherd's cheek and pooled beneath his head. The next moment, Klara was already gone.

X

Titan rarely spoke. That was the thing everyone in Project: Valeriana knew: Titan didn't speak, didn't like to speak. When he did, he had something of a British accent, but with the trilling Rs of Spanish.

If Ace was 'the silent type', Titan was functionally mute. That's why Shepherd felt almost honoured every time he could hear the man speak.

"I... I have... I *had* a dau...aughter." They had been sitting on the bottom bunk of the bed Shepherd shared with Ace. Titan's bed was across from them, covered by data sheets and workout equipment. Their shoulders had been pressed together to the point that the pressure had almost hurt, but Shepherd hadn't cared to move away. The barracks always grew cold in the evenings, and Titan always ran so warm.

"You did?" There had been fear, at first, that if Shepherd spoke he would frighten Titan too, back into silence. He had kept his face impassive, a rarity, like an action someone would take to not scare off a baby deer.

"Yes. A... a little baby girl. With, uh, the...ese huge, bro...own eyes. And... and little pudgy hands... hands." There had been the barest hint of a smile on Titan's face, a mere shadow of his usual toothy grin. It had been unsettling, and Shepherd wished he would have stopped. At the same time, he had wanted to keep listening to Titan's deep, bassy voice go soft at the memories of his little girl.

"Do you remember her?"

"I... I just remembered, jus...just now! A...and my wife, she... Shep, she...e was beautiful!" Titan had grabbed him by the shoulders, had angled him upwards so that they could look into each other's eyes.

"Then why are you crying?"

There had been tears streaming down Titan's face, fat crocodile tears staining his red face, "Cause... cause she left me. A...and took my baby girl. I... I remember, so mu...uch!"

Shepherd had felt trapped, "Why did she leave?"

"I... I didn't want... didn't like sex. Didn't wa...ant more kids, or the...e sex. Bu...ut I loved her, I... I did!" Shepherd had felt trapped at his inability to help Titan, when the other had begun sobbing. He had felt trapped when Titan's voice grew thick with tears, and whatever pleas for comfort existed in his words, Shepherd hadn't understood him.

"You loved her but didn't want to have sex with her?" Shepherd hadn't understood then. To join your body with that of another was like joining your souls. To love without sex or to have sex without love were foreign concepts to him. And yet, to abandon someone you love, because you both loved differently, seemed even worse.

"I... I'll never see my...y daughter aga...ain!" Shepherd hadn't known what to do. There had been a hole in his own heart that wept silently for whatever it was missing. All he could have done, really, was hold onto Titan, let him cry into a friendly shoulder. His friend had sobbed, and sobbed, and Shepherd's heart broke with every fresh wave of tears.

XI

Arne visited him once outside of the entourage of Dr Owen. He never looked Shepherd in the face, never met his eyes, simply scanned his body.

Shepherd's body was muscular and toned. The fat around his hips had shifted years ago, leaving him with a well-proportioned figure and a noticeable V-line. His shoulders were broad, his legs and arms were thick. His face had also become more angular over the years, with a sharper jawline accentuating his long, sharp nose. A slight beard was even growing over his chin, that he had kept well-trimmed once upon a time. The way his body looked, felt, moved, he was in love with it in ways he hadn't been before the Project. Now, however, he felt as if it was perfect, as if Project: Valeriana had made him perfect, moulded him in the image of godly perfection.

But there were parts of him that made people think he was a woman. There was an opening a few centimetres below his T-dick (which had grown girthier from the serum, longer) that people called his vagina. He didn't call it anything, just an extra orifice he had that he had liked using for pleasure. Then there were his breasts, the two sacks of fat upon his chest that were covered in stretch marks and scars and veins. They were ever so slightly flatter than they should have been thanks to his musculature, but were big enough to be visible beneath his clothing if he chose to forgo a binder. He didn't see these parts of himself as 'woman', they were just as much 'man' parts as his cock and beard, as his broad shoulders and lower voice. They were parts of him that he loved just as much as he loved all the other parts of himself, and looking at himself in the mirror in the days prior had always brought a joy to his mind that Man Shik had told him was called 'euphoria'.

Euphoria. The word sounded so beautiful to him.

***

Arne always looked at his body whenever he came along with Dr Owen. He seemed intrigued by Shepherd's musculature, by his sex characteristics, and the way his body worked. He always ignored Shepherd's face, muzzled and hidden as it was. Only his body mattered.

The first time Arne visited him alone, he was drunk. Shepherd had experience with a drunk Fergusson Sr visiting him every so often, sitting him down on a metal chair where the cuffs dug into his wrists and ankles, and talking to him incessantly. Arne was different.

Where Fergusson Sr was bigoted and cruel. Arne was loving and gentle. Where Fergusson Sr demeaned him, Arne only had kind words for him. Arne was different, but the sound of his heels distinctly clacking against the tiled floor sent a shiver throughout Shepherd's body that Fergusson Sr could never get out of him.

"Hi, Shepherd. Hi, beautiful," Arne mumbled in a voice that lacked a rhythm, an accent, or much intonation. It was like listening to a recording, Arne's voice seemed so far away. Shepherd couldn't reply, he simply watched Arne mill around the room, getting his fumbling hands on surgery tools and stationery, playing with the medical equipment.

"I need another name for you, gorgeous. Shepherd sounds too military and your classified name too masculine," Arne spoke with a soft whisper, so quietly that anyone other than Shepherd wouldn't have heard, "My father calls you his Harbinger, but you're not really his, are you? How about Lucy? I like Lucy. I'll call you Lucy from now on. My Lucy." There was a smile on his face, something lopsided that almost looked like one of Fergusson's real smiles. Except for the eyes that didn't smile, that stayed as stony and cold as every other time.

"My father thinks you'll help him save the world, Lucy," he cooed, and suddenly Arne was by Shepherd's side, "I want to help you help my father. Will you let me help you?" Shepherd was cuffed to the metal table that served as his bed, utterly naked. There was a long gash down the front of his belly that had been healing for the past few days, but was still raw and achy. Arne leaned over him, hands fumbling at his own belt while his lips brushed over the stitches in Shepherd's stomach.

"You would look so beautiful full of my seed. A Mother goddess, birthing the next generation of superhumans. I, your humble servant, would sire an entire army of demigods, while you did nothing but sat on your throne, worshipped by all." His fingers traced over the skin on Shepherd's thigh, Arne's thumb digging into the supple muscles of his leg.

A scowl came over his face, lopsided from the alcohol as he sneered, "My father would never let me do this, he thinks our bloodline is weak. But he doesn't have to know, it can be our little secret, Lucy. Just mine, and yours." His tongue was warm and wet as it circled Shepherd's belly button, pulling painfully at the stitches as it dragged over his skin. Arne's breathe stank of cheap beer when he moaned, his breath ghosting over Shepherd's naval.

There was a voice screaming in his head, pounding at the edges of his skull until he thought he could hear it reverberating in the air around him. It might have just been his own muffled scream from beneath the muzzle. His eyes were blurring at the edges when Arne began to fully remove his trousers, and Shepherd realised he couldn't breathe. The air filtering in through his nose was but a sliver of the air he needed, and the cold made his nasal ducts ache with each gasping breath he was failing to take in.

Arne's mouth travelled higher until it latched onto one of his nipples and the sound that followed was certainly a scream, "I could fix you, beautiful. I could ask my father and I could fix you, Lucy. If this is what the Gladiolus serum did to you, I'm sure I could create one that could reverse it, turn you even more beautiful than you already are. Serum Rosaceae, what do you think? Or maybe you would prefer Serum Ambrosia, my sweet?" The darkness at the edges of his eyes was growing, and his head felt light as if he was resting on a cloud. There was a sensation somewhere deep within him, something that felt like panic. He couldn't hear Arne anymore, he couldn't see him through the grey haze and shadowy corners, he couldn't feel Arne's hands on his body.

At some point he stopped feeling the violent rise and fall of his heaving chest, and there was this tiny voice in the back of his head that told him he was safe, that it was ok.

There was pain, and then nothingness.

XII

Dr Gok and Mr Fergusson had stood in front of a whiteboard, one prim and proper, the other dishevelled but excited. They had been separated by at least two feet, as if unable to bare the idea that they should touch. On the other side of

Dr Gok had stood two other scientists, a Fijian woman and an Indian man, one scientist assigned to each of the three super soldiers.

"I am glad to see you three up and running," Mr Fergusson had said with what amounted to glee, despite the fact he wouldn't deign them with even a small smile, "I see that none of you are about to kick the bucket any time soon, and that you all are getting used to your new superhuman abilities well."

"As well as we can, really," Shepherd had snarked back, holding up the broken off armrest of his chair. It had been wooden, glazed and dark, but the wood at the broken off junction had been a pale brown. Dr Gok had looked at him with something that amounted to pride in his black eyes, while Mr Fergusson had just scowled. The other two scientists had said nothing and didn't react. 'Not their charge, not their business,' Dr Gok had told him later on, in secret.

"M'yes, I can see that, Shepherd. But that, luckily for you, isn't the reason why you're here." That day had been the first time Shepherd had met Mr Fergusson. It had been before he was just Fergusson, before Dr Gok was Man Shik, before Titan was friend, and Ace was beloved. It had been the first time Mr Fergusson had met him after his transformation, and the man had already been twisting his moustachioed lips into a displeased grimace that told of the turbulent times to come.

Shepherd had wanted to say something again, but a glare from Dr Gok had made him clamp him mouth shut with an audible clack.

At a nod from Mr Fergusson, Dr Gok had spoken up, "As I'm sure the three of you know already, you are part of Project: Valeriana, a secret, scientific experiment aiming to create superhuman soldiers to protect the world." Titan and Ace had listened enraptured as Dr Gok talked, but all Shepherd had thought about was the fact he hadn't felt much like a hero. He had felt like an experiment, that was true, but more like the chronically or terminally ill people who agreed to experimental cures and tests. Because someone had to do it, right? And they already had nothing more to lose.

"We are currently situated in Canada," the Fijian woman had continued, "As we are close enough to the United States to monitor its military. The United

Nations have authorised us to carry out this project in the eventuality of a nuclear war."

"There is a sister Project currently working from Kazakhstan," the Indian man had spoken up next, "Monitoring Russia for the same reasons. Unlike us, they haven't had any luck yet." The three scientists then had gone quiet, each turning to look at Mr Fergusson.

"That is where you three come in." A smile had returned to his face, as fake as the previous one. "You three are the first, ever, genetically modified super soldiers. You are the first men to survive being injected with the Valeriana and Gladiolus serums."

"The what and what serums?"

"Don't interrupt, please." Dr Gok had gently admonished him, making Shepherd flush in shame. A vein had pulsed in the space above Mr Fergusson's right eyebrow, and it had only seemed to pulse at the sound of Dr Gok's voice.

"As I was saying," Mr Fergusson had cleared his throat, "You three are genetically modified super soldiers. Over the course of the next few years, as we are waiting for news from our sister facility, Project: Gladiolus, you are going to go through extensive training to help you learn how to control your newfound strength, speed, and any other powers we find out about along the way."

"Powers like this?" A shiver had run down Shepherd's spine at the sound of Ace's voice. It was almost as if his body had recognised it, somewhere deep within his consciousness. But there had also been confusion beneath that feeling of déjà vu. He had turned to look at Ace, and had jumped when he realised he was seeing sparks fly out from the tips of his fingers.

The Fijian woman had pulled out a pen and notepad from one of the pockets of her lab coat, scribbling something down at lightning speed, "The ability to control electrical charges within the air! That's amazing!"

"That was one of the three powers we predicted!" The Indian man had grabbed at the hems of his lab coat, an awestruck look on his face. He had been holding himself back, but sent looks of envy towards the Fijian woman, Ace being *her* charge.

"So fast, too. Mr Fergusson did good naming you Ace." Dr Gok had rubbed at the pudgy underside of his chin, a thinking look coming over his face that Shepherd had recognised. Ace at his side had seemed pleased with the attention, the sparks still flying from the tips of his fingers. Titan, sitting on the other side of Shepherd, had seemed just as intrigued by the display of power. He had been snapping his fingers to the rhythm of the sparks fizzling out in the air, when suddenly there was a hiss and a terrified shriek.

"Shepherd, your hair!" The smell of burning hair had been sickly, growing overwhelming within seconds, and the heat in the small of his back had made him jump out of his chair and panic.

"Fuck, kurwa, shit, cholera! What do I do? What do I do!" In the ensuing panic, Shepherd had ended up yanking at his braid, sending it flying forward and landing on his shoulder. He had fanned at the flames that seemed to eat away at his hair and the sleeve of his shirt, frantically blowing at it without abandon.

"Titan, do something!" Then there had been another hiss, and then a sizzle, and the burn upon his shoulder had filled with cool relief. All around his body, he had felt a thin mist of water droplets forming, and a thin streak of steam had risen from the tip of his braid.

Dr Gok had been panting, the other two scientists had also been calming down, but Mr Fergusson had fumed. Titan had seemed both in awe and apologetic.

"Well," Dr Gok had begun, once he had gathered his breath again, "Seems like the other two predictions were also true. Thank you, Titan, for demonstrating your control over fire and heat. And thank you, my boy, for demonstrating your control over water."

XIII

Ace and Titan weren't allowed to visit him. Fergusson never said why. Klara and Arne and Dr Owen were all as quiet as ever. He had an inkling of a feeling that it had something to do with the memories. Fergusson had to isolate his loyal soldiers for them to stay loyal. At least until he managed to break his Harbinger.

"How much pain do you think a human body can take before it shuts down, my Harbinger?" Fergusson was leaning over him. There were wires taped to Shepherd's skin, over his abdomen and chest. Fergusson was playing with one of those wires, twirling its dark length around his slim fingers. He seemed mesmerised.

"Of course, you can't answer me." He sneered; it sometimes felt as if Fergusson regretted fitting him with the muzzle that only one of his scientists could remove. "But you're a smart kid and I know that you know that your body can take much more pain than the average human." The wire dropped back down into Shepherd's lap, and Fergusson straightened back up, sneering down at Shepherd's bound body. The chair beneath his ass was wonderfully wooden that day, still hard but much warmer than the metal ones.

"I don't want to kill you. You *know* that." Standing in the doorway of the theatre-like room, Fergusson gave him a smirk, "But I am mighty curious how far I can push you, my Harbinger."

The door shut and the lights went out. The glare of the overhead lamps had made Shepherd's eyes ache, but in the pitch blackness he bemoaned the lack of comfort they provided him. The air was, as always, cold against his bare skin, his entire body breaking out in goosebumps. He could, ever so faintly, hear people milling around on the other side of the wall, somewhere to his right where he knew stood a one-way mirror. He often wondered if Ace and Titan were ever brought to his torture sessions, sitting just out of sight. He wondered if Fergusson ever used him as an example.

A minute passed and there was still nothing. During long training sessions Man Shik would often tell him to do something to occupy his mind. Counting had been his favourite, so he began counting down.

10... 9... 8... 7... 6... 5... 4... 3... 2... 1... Nothing. He knew there would be nothing. Fergusson loved making him wait. Shepherd felt the warm sweat cool as it trailed down his back.

10... 9... 8... 7... 6... 5... 4... 3... 2... 1... Still nothing. He was breathing harder through his nose now than he was before. His head swam, there were lights at the edges of his vision that he couldn't be sure were actually there. Maybe he was going mad again, maybe they were planning to break his mind first, maybe the talk of pain was meant to frighten him. They had done it before, and the counting hadn't helped. But they had failed each time, so why should they try again?

Fergusson was playing him for a fool.

Come on, Shepherd, Stay focused. 10... 9... 8... 7... 6... 5... 4... 3... 2... 1...

His body registered it before his mind did. His abdominal muscles clenched, and then pain shot through his spine. It was a single, simple shock, he hardly let out a grunt when it hit him.

10... 9... 8... 7... 6... 5... 4... 3... 2... 1... The next shock came, and Shepherd felt as if the air had been squeezed out of his lungs. His pectorals clenched so hard he thought his heart would stop, but it wasn't unbearable yet. Another 10 seconds, another shock had him wriggling in his seat. Another 10, and he was gasping for air, but had enough time to suck some O2 through his nose before the next shock came.

10... 9... 8... 7... 6... 5... 4... 3... 2... The next shock made him feel as if his spine would snap with the force that his muscles clenched at. One of his legs was shaking, the muscles beneath his skin jumping like an earthquake through his nerves.

10... 9... 8... 7... 6... 5... 4... 3... He clenched his hands at the next jolt of pain, water soaking out from between his fingers. In a last ditch effort he shot at the wires, but they held strong, plastered to his now wet skin.

10... 9... 8... 7... 6... 5... 4... A scream followed the next shock, a cry so loud Shepherd could hear it echoing in his skull for minutes afterwards. The shocks were intensifying, and the sweat and water coating his body only made it worse.

10... 9... 8... 7... 6... 5... At the next shock he threw his head back and wailed like a banshee, a prediction of his own end. This latest jolt of electricity reminded him of when Ace shocked him once during training. The way Ace's fingers curled around his wrist afterwards, his other hand pressed tightly to Shepherd's hot and sweaty cheek. The next wail he let out was one of anguish.

10... 9... 8... 7... 6... The legs of his chair clattered against the floor beneath him. He thought he could feel blood cascading down his chest, over the swell of his breasts and down the taut skin of his stomach, but maybe that was just more water. He wondered if someone's skin could rip simply from how tightly their muscles were clenching. He wondered when his skin would begin to burn. He still had enough of his mind left to wonder, to think.

10... 9... 8... 7... There was a white light behind his eyes, and there was pain.

10... 9... 8... There was nothing but pain. There was piss running down his leg and he was choking on his own spit, but he couldn't feel any of it.

10... 9... There was pain.

10... There was pain.

10... There was pain.

10... There was pain.

10... There was pain.

10...

10...

10...

10...

There was nothing.

***

He knew he had been crying because the skin around his eyes was dry and crusty. It made it hard to blink, but when he did, he was met with the glaring white lights of one of the facility's laboratories.

"Don't move, now." Owen's high-pitched voice met him from far away, as if Shepherd was hearing him from the other side of a tunnel. There was an ache deep within him somewhere, but there was also one on the very surface of his skin. It felt as if his entire torso had been dipped into acid.

"I said, don't move." Owen's hand roughly pushed Shepherd back down onto the table. In his other hand the doctor held something that vaguely registered as burn cream in Shepherd's mind. Somewhere in the back of his mind he also realised he hadn't been tied down. Another movement from him had Owen pressing his thumb into one of Shepherd's burns, and the bright flashes of light before his eyes made him feel dizzy. There wasn't even any new pain there, not when everything was already so painful.

"There. If you behave so nicely for me in your upcoming procedures, then we're going to be very good friends." Owen's hand was hard and heavy as it passed over Shepherd's body, spreading the cream over the burns left by the wires. Owen lingered and lingered over his chest; his beady-black eyes ogled the scars surrounding Shepherd's breasts. There was something in those eyes that almost reminded him of Arne, but there was also so much of Klara in them.

A flood of relief washed over him when Owen left. He couldn't remember what happened next, either way. Fergusson came in soon after, and had him sedated.

XIV

"Do you see them, my boy?" Man Shik had a voice that was ever so slightly breathy, and an accent that was just vague enough that Shepherd couldn't place it. It reminded him sometimes of the voice of an old grandpa from a children's cartoon.

Thinking about children always brought on a sense of melancholy within him.

"I see them." He had been leaning over Man Shik's shoulder, peering into the glass. The sight on the other side had been truly grand. A great atrium, a theatre whose ceiling was held up by colossal columns, and rows and rows of soldiers marching upon its polished wooden floors.

"You are going to lead these people, one day." Man Shik had a hand on Shepherd's shoulder. It had been the welcome hand of a comforting friend, not the heavy load of a keeper and handler. The drumbeat of the soldiers' stampeding feet had synched up to Shepherd's heartbeat, and he had imagined what it would be like to lead his own army for the good of humanity.

"Are you sure they can't see us?" The glass had been warm when Shepherd put his hand against it. He hadn't known then what a one-way mirror was supposed to look like. To him, it had just looked like a regular window.

"I'll show you what it looks like from the other side when they're done with training, OK?" The doctor had smiled. He had an easy-going smile, one with bared teeth and exposed gums. His monolid eyes always wrinkled in the corners when he smiled, and there were permanent laugh lines embedded into his cheeks, growing deeper with age. Shepherd, as always, had gladly smiled back.

***

The other side of the one-way glass had looked immaculate. It had been a simple mirror, albeit big enough for a good two dozen people to comfortably see themselves within it while standing shoulder to shoulder. Shepherd had pressed a hand against its surface, as if expecting it to move, bend, maybe ripple beneath his fingers. He had traced the shape of his head upon the mirror, leaving behind his finger a trail of condensation.

"Something isn't right with it. My reflection doesn't quite connect." When he had looked at his hand, tracing the outline of his left ear, the tips of his finger and that of his reflection's, hadn't quite met. It had been as if there was a thin sheet of something between them, as if he had been looking at his twin on the other side of a glass wall.

Man Shik had stepped up to him and gave a hollow tap on the glass, "Very perceptive of you, my boy. A one-way mirror can never function fully as a real mirror because of how it's constructed." The doctor had a wedding ring on the hand he pressed against the glass. Shepherd hadn't noticed it until that moment.

"Is that why you told me not to use the mirror in my cell?" Man Shik had smiled again, one of those toothy smiles that had made the corners of his eyes wrinkle.

"As I said, my boy," his smile had only grown wider, "Very perceptive of you." Shepherd had turned his head away from the imposter in the mirror, and gave Dr Man Shik a sharp-toothed grin of his own.

XV

Fergusson didn't stop trying to break him.

"Look, boy," his voice was uncomfortably soft and gentle, his hands were wiping the stray tears trailing down Shepherd's cheeks, "You're going to work for me one way or another. I want you by my side, my Harbinger, doing what is right." There was a smile curling the blond pencil moustache above Fergusson's lips. It was as genuine as his smiles got without being fully real.

"Don't make me, Fergusson." Shepherd's voice cracked when he spoke. His tongue was bone dry, and his lips bled with every formed syllable. It pained him simply to move his mouth, much less to talk.

"Harbinger," Fergusson sounded almost paternalistic, almost like a normal man, "I don't like Arne's idea any more than you do. The boy's a freak, like his mother. But you leave me no choice."

Shepherd forced himself to look Fergusson in the eyes. "There's always a choice." He found nothing within them but disgust and contempt.

"Yes, and the choice is yours. Either you continue fighting, and I continue trying to break you, or you relent. You relent and the torture stops, and I will take you back. Ace and Titan will take you back." Fergusson brushed his hand through Shepherd's long, tangled hair. The motion was almost soothing, a fragile comfort that threatened to send Shepherd into another bout of tears.

"If, by the end of the year, you don't choose, I'll be forced to relent myself. If in three months you still fight me, I'll let Arne do with you whatever he wants. You will work for me one way or another, my Harbinger." He stood up, his warm hand retreated from Shepherd's hair. There was a moment, a single heartbeat, in which the two men looked at each other, truly *looked*. Shepherd held Fergusson's gaze bravely, with watery eyes full of tears that threatened to blind him. It was the Swede who gave it up first, turning away with a sharp twist of his head as if ashamed. His quick step echoed within the confines of Shepherd's head long after Fergusson was gone.

***

"That's... that's not me." It took him a while to blink the tears away, to lift his heavy head up from his chest. There was a mirror behind Fergusson, unobstructed now that he had left. Shepherd had been cuffed in front of it, left in a prostrate position with his back against a metallic cross. He was standing upon his own two feet for the first time in months.

"That's not me..." He sobbed. The figure in the mirror wept, trying to curl up into herself, to hide herself from the view of the man on the other side of the window. Because it had to be a window, it couldn't be a mirror.

Shepherd couldn't look away from the woman in the mirror. She had his blueish-green eyes, and his sharp, long nose. Her hair was a dark chestnut shade, falling around her shoulders in waves, reaching just slightly above her naval. Fergusson had him shaved before tying him up in front of the mirror, and now he was forced to look at a soft-faced, round-cheeked woman of middle age, with laugh lines in the corners of her lightly pinkish lips.

"That's not me!" He shrieked into the dark room, and the woman on the other side of the mirror yanked at her chains in a feeble attempt to escape. She sobbed, and he cried for her sake.

"That's not me..." Dr Owen had been injecting him with *something* for weeks now, and he finally knew what it was. The woman on the other side of the mirror had big, curvy hips and thick thighs. The swell of her breasts was highly noticeable beneath the long tresses of her hair. There was a visible swell to her stomach that confused him. The paunch was surrounded by old stretch marks and fading scars, but it was clearly there.

"Are you... am I?" No, it couldn't be, Arne's seed couldn't have taken, not that quickly, not after a single drunken tryst. The woman in the mirror had a perfectly rounded stomach from where her organs sat inside her, but it still disconcerted him. It was there, pressing against her skin, and Arne and Fergusson knew that it worked, that it was still fully functional, and they had been pumping him full of oestrogen to prove it. They were trying to undo every miracle the testosterone had brought about.

"That's not me!" he roared. He pulled on the reinforced chains with all of his might, listening to them creak. They had taken so much from him, but they couldn't take away his voice. When the woman in the mirror unhinged her jaw, a low baritone fell from her trembling lips. When she twisted against her bonds, he felt the thick hair upon his arms and legs tangle in the chains. When she hiked up her legs, there hung a cock between her thighs. It was still him, the woman in the mirror was still him.

"That's me..." he sobbed, feeling the hot tears run down his face and softly drop onto his chest. His heaving sobs displaced the hair hanging across his torso and he got to take a proper look at his breasts. They were covered in scars, many from the torture, but many from his training as well. No matter how much Fergusson tried to hide it, it was the chest of a man who knew how to protect himself.

"It's me," he kept mumbling, the mirror shivering before him.

"It's me. It's me. It's me." It was him. He was a man with long hair and breasts and both a vagina and a cock. He was a man who had stood up against Leif Fergusson and was still alive to talk about it. He was a man who had built himself up from the ashes of a woman that had been gone for years. Cruel experiments changed nothing.

"It's me. I'm a man. I *am* a man. It's me. I'm a man and my *name* is..." Water coalesced upon the pearly surface of the mirror, and then it shattered with a deafening *bang*. The scientists burst into the room seconds after, and the flash of the overhead lamps blinded him. The cameras in the corners beeped and went offline, and the doctors buzzed around him like obedient worker bees, cowering and trembling at the shouting coming from Fergusson.

"That didn't fucking work, Holečková," Fergusson shrieked at Klara, "You told me that would fucking work, you shrink bitch! I need him broken. Fucking *break him* for me already!"

His name wasn't Shepherd. He wasn't a woman. He wasn't broken. He would never let himself be broken.

XVI

Shepherd knew all of Ace's tells.

"What did Mr Fergusson tell you?" He had asked as Ace exited the office. A slip of paper had slid into his back pocket, too fast for Shepherd to see what it said.

"Nothing much. He just wanted to catch up and see how I was coming along with getting my memory back." Ace's nose had flared just the slightest bit, a silent intake of breath. That had been his tell for lying. Shepherd knew all of his tells, from the way his eyebrows would twitch before he smiled, to the small massaging of his thumb and pointer finger together whenever he was nervous. There was very little that got past Shepherd, he knew Ace too well.

"Alright, then. The docs say we have the evening off, you want to go cuddle?" And yet Shepherd had never brought any of it up.

***

"I'm getting my memory back." Ace's voice had rumbled beneath Shepherd's cheek. They had been curled up together on Shepherd's bunk in the barracks, Ace's back to the headboard and Shepherd snuggled up in his lap. The position had been awkward, maybe even enough to be painful as Shepherd's legs had been squished beneath him and his bulk had been pressing down on Ace's body. And yet neither of them had moved; Shepherd always knew it was because Ace wanted to feel like the bigger, stronger party.

"What are you remembering?" The question had been simple enough, but Shepherd had immediately angled up his head to stare, enraptured, at Ace.

The other man had chuckled, brushing a hand through Shepherd's hair making his scalp tingle. "I remember my father, the one who brought me to Project: Valeriana in the first place. I remember that we... never really got along." A frown had creased his face, his nose scrunching up in that familiar way it always did whenever something went wrong, like Titan setting some training equipment on fire.

"Why is that?"

Ace's nostrils had flared, "Don't really know why. Might've had something to do with my brother. He was always the older, taller, better brother. Maybe father wanted me to be as good as him. Dunno." Shepherd had been certain that his eyes were sparkling. They had so little of their old selves, knew so few details of their lives before the Project. They hadn't even known if they had families, truly had them despite Fergusson's assurances that they were loved, once. It had been like opening a present on the morning of the 6th of December, whenever the other two had told him of their memories.

"I remembered you, too." The silence that followed had been deafening. Shepherd's fists had balled up in the front of Ace's shirt. He couldn't place the emotion that had stabbed away at his heart in that moment, but he had felt Ace's warm hands sliding up the back of his shirt and he shuddered from the electrifying contact of his skin.

"You remember me?"

"We were in love, Shepherd," The smile that had graced Ace's face was beautiful, distracting enough to almost miss the way his nostrils had flared with a silent intake of breath, "We were a couple, we lived together, and loved one another. We had a life together, my little swallow."

"Sparrow."

"What?" The smile had left Ace's face.

Shepherd had gulped, "Sparrow. My parents used to call me wróbelek when I was younger, which means 'little sparrow'. H... you started calling me 'little sparrow' when we first started dating, because I would always sing for..." The pain in his chest had worsened, it had taken his breath away. Ace hadn't looked angry or annoyed, just confused, but Shepherd's breathing had taken a while to grow steady again.

"Well," Ace had finally started up after a moment, "that's behind us, isn't it? Swallow, sparrow, I don't really get the difference, they're both just birds. Oh, I know, I'll just call you my little lamb instead." Ace's large hand had gone back to rubbing the space above Shepherd's left hip, right over the small, monochrome tattoo of a House Sparrow. It had been the first time he remembered what the round, white-breasted bird sitting on his hip was. Każik. The name of the little sparrow he had saved at the age of six, one beautiful summer's day when he was visiting family in Poland.

The grip on his hip had tightened. "Lamb fits too." The smile he had gotten in return had made him feel hollow. "You trust Mr Fergusson, don't you, spark-plug?"

Ace's nose had not flared when he answered the question, "Completely."

XVII

He lied. It was easier to lie to himself than force himself to remember.

Arne visited him biweekly, exactly seven days after Fergusson Sr himself would drunkenly stumble into his room and berate him about his choices. Fergusson Sr never touched him, however; he found Shepherd too disgusting to touch.

Arne didn't rape him again for months, but he would touch him. He hid it behind a facade of 'medical checkups', like the ones Man Shik did after a particularly gruelling training session. Arne's checkups were far more in depth than anything Man Shik ever put him through.

"Lucy." Arne sounded very pleased with himself, almost stooping low enough to use a sing songy voice to greet Shepherd. He was wearing a fresh lab coat. The previous one had been stained by Shepherd's blood and cum, just like every lab coat he wore before that. This one would, inevitably, join its brethren in the incinerator.

"You'll never guess what happened today, my love." He placed a kiss on Shepherd's forehead, brushing hair out of his face and staying bent over the metal operating table. Shepherd had long since gave up fighting against his bonds. But neither did he give Arne the satisfaction of a reaction.

"Doctor Owen is dead." The glee within his voice was paired with a hand between Shepherd's thighs, rough fingers pushing his cock out of the way to get at his opening. He felt none of it, and reacted accordingly.

"He was found dead beneath his desk with his head cracked open." Shepherd could see Arne's hand pumping in and out of him, his other hand idly playing with one of his breasts. He couldn't feel that either.

"Everyone agreed that it was an accident." He let out a dark chuckle, a sound that could almost rival Fergusson's own laugh. "There was no one who thought otherwise. The old fool tripped, maybe slipped on some spilled coffee, and took himself out." The fingers sped up, Arne's other hand clutching at his breast so hard that the scarred skin was turning white. Shepherd didn't react.

Arne's breath ghosted over the side of his face, "I'm slowly moving up the ranks, my darling Lucy. Soon, I'll have you all to myself, my goddess." A wet tongue dragged up the sliver of his cheek unobstructed by the muzzle, leaving a steaming trail of saliva in its wake.

"And the next person on my list is that shrink bitch, Klara. She knows what she did." The movement was almost imperceptible. Arne's scrawny arms flexed beneath his shirt sleeves, and the next thing Shepherd knew the man was buried wrist deep in his vaginal canal, a mask of cold fury covering his face. Only the slight tremble of his upper lip told Shepherd that the young Fergusson had any sort of emotion.

"If she gives you anaesthesia one more time before one of our meetings, I will cut off her tits and shove them down her throat." He pulled his fist out of Shepherd, the entire limb covered in slime and fresh blood. He shucked off his coat and wiped his hand on the material, before bundling it up under his arm and leaving the room, switching the lights off as he walked out.

And with him, went another piece of Shepherd's soul.

XVIII

"We're going to be listening to a freak?" The woman's voice had cut through the warm haze that had settled over Shepherd. His belly had been full of warm stew that day, and the sun beating down on him had been neither oppressive nor shy. The blue sky had made his eyes ache after so many months shut up inside the

Project: Valeriana facilities, but the way the great, fat clouds above him had rolled lazily by made him smile. That had been when the woman; a nameless, masked soldier, had barked at him.

"Freaks? Who are you calling freaks?" A man, another one of the higher-ranking human soldiers, had yelled at the woman, pushing a finger into her chest. "These three men are the strongest people on this base. They are martyrs who died and came back from the dead as super soldiers, capable of withstanding anything! They are the future of the world, the only force capable of preventing a nuclear war!"

"The white one ain't a man, though." Another nameless, faceless soldier had spoken up. He had a similar accent to the woman to his right, something European that contrasted to the French-Canadian inflection Shepherd usually heard from the human soldiers.

"You got a problem with women leaders, comrade?" The soldier had flinched, and his similarly accented companion had grabbed at his arm. Both of them had been looking at Shepherd, their helmets angled in just the right way to have him guessing they were avoiding his eyes.

"You're not a woman either, are you though?" The woman had hissed out, yanking her companion forwards again as he had started walking backwards. The high-ranking official before them had worn a loose jaw and eyeballs the size of dinner plates, completely silent.

"One way to find that out, sweetheart," Shepherd had growled. He had stood with his arms held behind his back, and he could feel his knuckles going white with how hard he had been holding onto his shirt sleeves.

"See, captain? That thing's a freak. I don't want to work under it." The rest of the little squad had bristled around her, her companion trying and failing to pull himself out of her grasp with each word she spoke. The high-ranking official had stood still, dumbfounded, his hands shaking at his sides.

"Ask Fergusson to move you, then," Shepherd had replied dismissively. He had seen the way her companion had been pawing at her hand, heard the way he had whimpered when she tightened her grip. In one swift motion, her helmet had flown in an arc above their heads. It had landed right where Shepherd had stood just seconds before. He had seen the way the muscles in her jaw danced, he had heard her panting breaths like those of a caged animal, he had smelled the fear permeating from her sweating body. A hand had clutched at the front of her jacket, her toes had left the floor.

"You are a freak. Picsa!" She had snarled, hanging limply in his grip. He had watched her, exploring her face. Small lips, hollow cheeks, big forehead. And those eyes, so full of hatred.

"And you're dismissed, złotko. I don't need someone this green on my team." He had dropped her. Fat, angry tears had begun rolling down her cheeks, and she had swatted away the hands of her companion with such force that he had whimpered again.

XIX

Sometimes he wasn't sure if Klara hated him because she was jealous, in love with him, or saw herself within him. He wasn't sure which of these he would have preferred.

"Arne is pissed at us, mutt," she told him with glee as she caressed his hip. Her small, dainty hand balled into a fist, which she drove right into his stomach. He was tied to the iron cross again, but this time with his legs cuffed to the bottom of it. He couldn't even flinch away from her.

"Oh, how I love that idiotic fool, sometimes. He is so easy to get a rise out of." They had been through this before. She would visit him the day after Arne, she would shove a tool up his vagina and forcefully scoop anything and everything that Arne could have left inside him. The man could no longer control his lust. Fingers no longer cut it.

"Don't worry, mutt," She cooed, going up onto her tiptoes to place a kiss against his cheek, "I'll murder that little Swedish freak before the three months are up." She traced a finger up and down the muscles of his stomach. The oestrogen regimen was working wonders, and yet he could still feel the muscle definition beneath this new layer of fat, especially when Klara poked and prodded at him cruelly. Sometimes, however, he looked down at himself and wondered if he was getting bigger, if he was getting rounder. He wasn't sure what truth he preferred, that he was pregnant with Arne's demon spawn, or that he was becoming paranoid.

"I would still have to deal with Fergusson Sr, but I have ways around that." A shiny, glass vial waved before his eyes, a gleaming white liquid dancing around within it. Behind it, Klara stared at him with a smile that was all teeth, her eyebrows downturned as if she couldn't decide if she was angry or happy. For the first time in months, Shepherd felt himself perk up. His muscles tightened, his breathing quickened, his head shot up as he looked at the little vial. In the back of his ruined, unused throat, he let out a sound that was something between a whimper and a 'hmm'.

"I want you to kill Arne for me, and in turn, I'll make sure that the seed that will birth Fergusson's army will belong to Ace." Her voice was a low, seductive purr. Beneath the metal mask and the painful hooks stuck in his cheeks, Shepherd felt the corners of his mouth pull up into a smile.

XX

"Dammit, Shep! How did you do that?" Some of the lower ranking soldiers had gotten used to calling him 'Shep'. Like it was cute, like they were friendly. Shepherd had never deigned them with a response, switching the safety back onto his gun. He had slipped the weapon back into his pocket, turning on his heel to look at Ace.

Ace had smiled at him. "Share your secrets with us, Sheep." Ace had liked teasing him. 'Lamb' had been too intimate for the moments outside of the barracks, 'Shep' had often been too casual. It had annoyed Shepherd to no end, yet he had never said anything about it. It had been Ace, after all; he could get away with anything back then.

"Not my damn fault none of you know how to properly aim." The haughty upturn of his nose had been a bit much, Shepherd thought. Ace had chuckled anyway, and Titan had cracked a small smile behind him as well. Shepherd hadn't missed the slight crease to Titan's eyebrows, however. The giant hadn't quite learned how to hide his jealousy yet, not like Ace had. Sometimes, Shepherd would forget that Ace got jealous of him. But only sometimes.

There had been a scuffle in the corner of the room, the booming voices of excited soldiers. Shepherd's gaze had travelled over to the crowd gathering beneath a banner carrying the Valeriana and Gladiolus flowers.

"Make way, please!" That had been Man Shik's voice, his head peeking in between the bodies of the soldiers. He had pushed through with whatever strength he had in his short, stout body, an equally short woman trailing behind him with a flushed face and a pleased smile.

"Misters Ace, Titan, and Shepherd!" Agustina Windisch had approached them all, reaching out her dainty hand for the three of them to shake. Man Shik had stood at her side, a pleased expression on his face.

"To what do we owe the pleasure?" Shepherd had attempted a smile, but had ended up with something between a pained grimace and a frown. The businesswoman had seemingly paid no mind to it, smiling at him with a smile brighter than the ones she gave Ace and Titan.

"Mr Shepherd, what amazing form, what magnificent show of skill," her voice had risen in pitch with her compliments, "Would I be able to pull you aside for a minute?" When Shepherd had looked over, Man Shik had nodded, and the jealous look Titan gave him hadn't dissuaded him from following behind the petite, older woman.

"Are you feeling alright?" Had been the first question out of her mouth, her smile dissolving into a frown.

"Yes, ma'am. Why wouldn't I be?"

"Last time I saw you face to face…" She hadn't continued. She had simply stared at him.

Shepherd had taken in a deep breath, "Don't you worry about that, ma'am. That was a planned show between me and Mr Fergusson."

"Did he tell you to say that?"

"Yes." Mrs Windisch had sighed, rubbing the bridge of her nose over the indents left behind by reading glasses.

"Mr Shepherd." He had waited, and waited, and Mrs Windisch had stayed silent, simply thinking. "Were you aware, sir, that you come from Toronto, in Ontario, Canada?" Something within his mind had suddenly clicked. A pit had opened up within his stomach, nausea coming over him.

"How do you know what? What more can you tell me?" He had crowded in around her, and she had just lifted her chin and stared up at him.

"I cannot say more, or tell you how I got the information I have now. But do be aware, Mr Shepherd, that there is much you do not know yet, and I advise you to be careful." She had turned on her heel and left, leaving Shepherd standing there with his shoulders hunched forward as if there was still a smaller body pressed up against his own.

XXI

He was sure Fergusson would be his first kill. He wanted Fergusson to be his first kill.

Murdering Arne was even better.

Klara had left him ready in the room Arne always visited. He felt every twitch of his muscles, felt the cold metal of the table spreading against his back. The straps around his arms and legs were loosened.

Arne arrived in the room with his usual air of self-importance. He regarded Shepherd with a cold look, and yet his eyes roved over the prone body upon the examination table. Everything seemed to happen so slowly. Arne approached the table as if walking through molasses, his hands moving over Shepherd's body as if he were trapped underwater. His climb upon the table happened even slower, tantalising. Shepherd hardly even felt the breach of Arne's penis within his hole.

"Lucy. Oh, goodness. Lucy!" Arne's wanton moaning sharply cut off. His face slammed against Shepherd's exposed chest, his hands flying up to the taller man's shoulders. His blueish eyes briefly shone with confusion, before his face twisted into a mask of horror.

Shepherd had the fake muzzle discarded, smiling down at Arne with sharp fangs. He could see his reflection in the shiny metal of the examination table, and the murderous glint in his eyes terrified him. It seemed to terrify Arne even more.

"Did you piss yourself inside me, freak?"

Arne shivered. Shepherd's voice was raw, his throat burned with every forced-out sound, but the deep rumble of his words warmed him up on the inside. They couldn't take this away from him.

"I... I..." Arne cut himself off with a pathetic squeal, his body going limp in Shepherd's grasp. In seconds, he was thrown onto the floor of the examination room. The air around them felt heavy as Shepherd climbed off the table, collapsing to his knees in a way he hoped looked purposeful. The young Fergusson whimpered when Shepherd's bulk settled across his chest.

Shepherd leant forward, dragging his nose from the softness of Arne's jaw to the blond fuzz at his temples. The man shivered beneath him; quiet, mewling whimpers fell out of his mouth as Shepherd's broad, calloused hands dragged up his chest. The hands settled upon the delicate skin of Arne's neck.

"A kiss, my love," Shepherd whispered against Arne's cheek, raising his voice into a soft, high-pitched croon, "From your Mother goddess, your darling Lucy." His voice dropped into its lowest octave like a stone dropped into a roiling sea. His lips pressed faintly against the pale, trembling cheek beneath him, and his hands began tightening. Arne's eyes began to bulge, his hands flailed wildly and grasped at Shepherd's arms. It was the most intimate thing Shepherd had ever done, with any man. He could almost feel Arne's soul leaving his body with every squeeze, and Shepherd gleefully took it into his lungs, holding it there like a prisoner. One more exhale, and he was ready.

3... 2... 1... snap.

Arne's movements stilled, and Shepherd stilled with him. He could still feel Arne's warm piss dripping out of his abused cunt.

"Look! I told you he was a danger! Seize him before he kills anyone else!" Klara's voice came to him as if through a fog. The words sounded nonsensical, the arms that smacked against his head and his shoulders felt irrelevant. The ropes snaking around his arms and legs didn't matter.

Arne Fergusson was dead. And yet Shepherd didn't feel saved.

XXII

"For your first mission, you are being sent to Toronto in Canada." Shepherd had felt the air rush out of his lungs, as if Fergusson himself had sucked all of it out.

"What are we meant to do, sir?" Ace had asked, standing to Shepherd's right. The three of them had their arms crossed behind their backs, shoulders pulled backwards, and chins thrust out forward. The uncomfortable position was meant to make up for the lack of respect Fergusson tended to receive from his soldiers.

"A protest has broken out within the city, some sort of march aimed at Project: Valeriana. Your job will be to protect the citizens affected by the march, and to show the dissidents that they are wrong about the purpose of our experiments." Fergusson's upper lip had been curled into a sneer, his eyes impassively holding Shepherd's gaze.

"We need you all to be on your best behaviour, boys," Man Shik had said from Fergusson's right, smiling at the three soldiers as if he was sending them off to school for the very first time.

"Yes, sir!" a three-voiced chorus had come back. Shepherd remembered the way the words had tasted on his tongue, the bile that had refused to return to his stomach. The tightness of his throat had made it hard to speak, as if he had been trying to swallow a knife.

Man Shik had still been smiling at the three of them, and as Fergusson had left, the portly scientist waved them all over to a table. The three had rushed towards him, Ace and Titan almost pushing each other out of the way. Shepherd had let them fight, silently approaching Man Shik and filtering out the explanations he had for the other two soldiers.

"My boy," Man Shik had greeted him with familiar enthusiasm, that same grandfatherly smile still plastered to his round face, "I am so proud of you for getting this far. Your first mission! So exciting! Here." Shepherd wasn't very familiar with guns. He had once had the best aim of the three super soldiers, he knew how to clean his training gun and how to dis- and reassemble it. But he couldn't tell the difference between SMGs, AKs, rifles. He hardly remembered the difference between pistols and revolvers.

The pistol that Man Shik had handed to him had a sleek, black body, a typically short barrel, and a comfortably moulded grip. It had looked, to his untrained eye, like a standard issue military pistol. There had been letters on the underside of the grip, however, that spelled out the word 'S.H.E.P.H.E.R.D'.

"Can I name it?"

"I don't see why not."

"Euphoria."

***

The cacophony of screams and shouts had made Shepherd's teeth itch. He had thought the police were doing a good enough job at beating the protesters, he hadn't really understood what Fergusson wanted from him and his teammates. If the man had expected them to join in with the brutality, he had certainly chosen the wrong taskforce for the job.

"Aren't... sho...ouldn't we be...e, uh, protecting these... these people?" Titan's voice had rumbled through Shepherd's bones, the giant bending down at the shoulders to whisper into his ear.

"Not our job, big guy. Just hold your gun tight and act like you know what you're doing." Titan had straightened back up, just as Ace had returned from wherever he had run off to.

"Are they dispersing yet?" He had stopped beside Shepherd, and his breath had stank of vomit.

"Slowly, yeah." Shepherd had scanned the crowds once more, watching as they petered out to a handful of stubborn protestors. The ambulances at the edge of his vision had been idling, the taste of engine smoke had hung heavy in the air.

"Whoever tipped Mr Fergusson off about this should be fired," Ace had grumbled at his side. "Forcing us, the saviours of humanity, to have to watch helplessly as some clueless officers beat back a harmless protest. Mr Fergusson will hear of this." A full body shudder had gone through Shepherd in that moment, one he had barely held in as he watched Ace's impassive face.

***

Crowds had flown in to cover the scene of the former protest, stamping over dropped banners and discarded signs. Shepherd had lost sight of Ace and Titan, scanning the crowd for his lost companions. The van they had arrived in, had stood a few streets away, but it wouldn't have been appropriate for him to return to the van by himself.

"Lucas?" A hand had wrapped around his bicep, he had felt his entire body stiffen and reach for Euphoria at his side. A woman had pushed her way to stand before him, beaming like the sun.

"Lucas! It *is* you!" She was a pretty, young thing with long, straight black hair, a round face, and earthy brown, almond-shaped eyes. Her other hand had flown up to his shoulder, before she had yanked him forward in a crushing hug.

"I... Miss, please let go. I don't know you." May hadn't let go, and Lucas had quickly realised he didn't want her to. Lucas... May...

"It's me, Kas. May." Her eyes had filled up with tears when she looked back up at him. Something within him had told him May was just a nickname. There were syllables missing, and specific sounds, and... It had disturbed him that he knew all this. He knew *her*.

Lucas hadn't fit quite right, either. There was a W sound missing there, maybe a SH sound too.

"Łukasz," And there it had been, a burst of warmth spreading through his chest, "We've been looking all over for you. We've all been so worried!" Łukasz had held her at arm's length, bringing one hand up to brush a tear away from May's cheek.

"I'm sorry, I don't remember. Who is 'everyone'?" Her upper lip had trembled, she had sniffled, but she hadn't outright cried when she reached into her bag and brought out a photograph for him to see.

"Your family, Kas." There was him... Shepherd, Lucas, Łukasz. He was smiling at the camera with a little boy, no more than two years old, sitting on his hip. The boy had his face, the brown locks that curled around his head, and skin so dark that it made Łukasz look pale. Beside him stood a man with an identical little boy nestled against his chest, and all four of them were smiling. At first Łukasz thought that the other man was Ace, with dark red lips and beer-brown eyes, hair cut into tight ringlets around his head. But the man was taller than Ace, taller than even Łukasz himself, sporting a neatly trimmed beard and much broader shoulders.

"Who are these people?" Łukasz had pointed at the little twin boys.

"Your sons, Brandon and Logan. Remember?" The heat within his chest had spread, making it almost painful to breathe.

"I... I used to call them Bolek and Lolek, like that Polish kid's cartoon my dad had VHS tapes of." Lolek was the shy one, curled up against his father's chest. Bolek had always been the braver one, the rambunctious one as he wiggled in his dad's arms.

"Alexander's been calling them that in your stead." A soft, sad smile had graced May's face for a fraction of a second, before she was crying again, shoving the torn up, little photograph into his hands. "Oh, Lucas, he's been going mad with grief after you disappeared! And then his brother went missing too."

"He... He has a brother?" Ace, Ace, Ace, Ace. His mind had screamed at him, the heat within his chest had burned him alive from the inside.

"Yes, Tristan, remember? The nerdy, quiet one who you were best friends with in school." Her voice had been like honey, her Chinese accent just subtle enough for Łukasz to take a moment to realise it was there, before losing himself in it.

"I don't... I... I only remember snippets, and only when you keep talking. When you stop, it's all just blank." The pain had intensified. May had begun to blur around the edges, her eyes growing watery and black.

"Łukasz... Oh, we need to get you out of there, wherever you are. Alex misses you so much." It had been like a rubber band had stretched within his chest. With those final words, it had snapped, and Shepherd was plunged into darkness.

XXIII

Fergusson had met him with a sneer that slowly, subtly grew into a manic grin.

"Shepherd, what brings you here?" He had known. The bastard had known long before Łukasz had dragged his aching, ailing body to him. He hadn't been sure what was wrong with him, he had guessed that the Valeriana Serum was fighting him, fighting against his memories.

"You lied to me, Fergusson." About his family, about his past. About the people who had loved him and the people he had called his friends. May hadn't been the only one, flashes of familiar faces keeping him up at night.

"I did, Harbinger. I very much did." That grin had stayed frozen on Fergusson's face, even as Łukasz had slammed the door behind him, even as Łukasz had marched up to the desk, even as Łukasz had leaned over Fergusson's body and roared at him.

"I had a FAMILY, you monster! A husband who loved me! Children I had birthed with my own body! I had friends who searched for me the entire time I was gone! You took me away from my children!" Łukasz hadn't realised he was crying until he felt the tears softly fall onto Fergusson's desk, soaking his fingers where he was leaning on the smooth wood.

"And now you no longer do, Harbinger." Fergusson had placed his hands on the desk, framed by Łukasz's own, much larger palms. His grin had grown so wide it no longer looked human.

Łukasz had hated how weak he had sounded. "Why?"

"You want to know the truth, Shepherd? You want to know why you're here, Lukas Pasterski?" The laugh that had breached past Fergusson's lips was a chilling thing, tinged with cruel undertones. "Your older brother. Your little Matty. Matthew Pasterski, does that ring a bell? He brought you here. He was my old best friend. You knew this, once, that we used to be college roommates. Ah, those were the days. But you weren't expecting that, were you? Because I took those memories away from you. Plucked them out of your brain like worms from the earth." Łukasz had felt as if his entire body had frozen over. Matthew, Mateusz, the little twerp who had always complained that his younger brother was getting too big, getting too much attention, getting too many awards at school. A bearded face had flashed before his eyes for a split second, pale-skinned and brown-haired, before the visage had solidified into that of Ace. Of Tristan.

"But why?"

Fergusson had laughed again. "Because your brother hated you. Because he saw you as an abomination and your children as his salvation. You are the Shepherd of the Damned, the Harbinger of the End times, that's what he always called you. And your brats? He saw it as his mission to convert them, have them turn their backs on you, so that he could get into heaven and sit beside his beloved god. Nonsense, if you ask me, but then again, I was never religious." Flashes of Matt's face, green with jealousy, were interspersed with memories of his little boys growing up. How old would they be now? Three years old? Four?

"I was never terminal, then."

"Oh, no, not physically at least." The grin had dropped into a disgusted snarl, Fergusson's hand shooting up to grope at the softness beneath Łukasz's shirt. "He saw it as a sickness of the mind, told me to fix it. If anything, I think I just made you better than you were before. A freak to rule all my other freaks." His grin had returned, even as he had been shaking his hand off from the slap it had received.

With one hand suspended in mid-air, Łukasz's other hand had only tightened upon the desk, and he had felt it splinter. "A freak, because what? Because of how my body is? Because of my mind?"

"More or less. Ah, but this always amuses me. You see, your brother was right in a sense. Why do you think I gave you the name Shepherd?" Fergusson's hand had snaked its way through the air, hovering just millimetres from Łukasz's stubbled cheek. "Because you were always going to lead my army, your flock. Because, in a sense, your brother was right that you would bring about the End Times. You, not Ace, not Titan, not even me. It was always you, Harbinger."

The second slap had sent Fergusson reeling, the wheels of his chair squeaking as he was sent back against the wall.

"If you think I'm going to go along with your sick plan!"

"Don't worry, I've got time." His grin had turned darker, but Łukasz was there to meet it with a snarl full of fanged teeth, his hands fumbling at his side for Euphoria. "Maybe today you don't like the idea of making the world your own, but you'll come around eventually. One day, however long it takes to break you. And break you I shall, my Harbinger. Ace, Titan! You know what to do." A sharp prick had sent a jolt through Łukasz's body, the lights and sounds and colours around him crashing down into a blurry, muffled mess. Through the fog he had felt hands grasp at his arms, and Fergusson's laugh had echoed between his ears. In the stiff grip of his paralysed hand, he had held onto the thin photograph from May.

"No. No! You can't do this! NO!"

"I very well can, Mr Pasterski. I can, and I just *did.*"

XXIV

His body hurts.

There is a cacophony of sounds outside of his cell.

His tongue feels like sandpaper, and hooks are digging into his cheeks, a muzzle clamps his mouth shut.

The meagre light from outside of his cell filters through the window at the top of the door.

His chest aches; each breath sends a stabbing pain through his ribs as warm liquid runs down the front of his torso.

The sounds outside his cell are meaningless babble, a raised voice and loud banging that means nothing to him.

His hair lays in clumps around his shoulders; it does nothing to protect his decency.

The sounds vaguely coalesce into a recognisable phrase, 'doc, over here!', before they once more turn into nonsense and gibberish.

His arms are forced back at an angle, tied tightly together with a long since familiar sleeve, and he can no longer feel his fingers.

The scream outside his door sounds familiar, but the bang that precedes it haunts his nightmares.

His body no longer sweats; he can no longer feel the power coursing through his veins; he has become an empty reservoir, filled by something crawling and gnawing instead.

The banging outside his cell gets louder, the shouting becomes more frantic, the light is ever so often broken up by a shadow passing before the window.

His stomach lays distended beneath him, a solid weight that rests upon his bent and crooked legs, and every so often he feels the thing inside him move and squirm.

The light outside his cell is suddenly cut off entirely, and the darkness he is plunged into sooths his aching eyes.

His cell door opens with a shrill shriek, and he curls up into himself as best he can, shivering in the cold of the cell.

The silhouette in the doorway stands there, as if frozen in time, but behind it he can see other nondescript figures moving around, bustling in the hallways.

His ears pick up a subtle hitch of a breath, a soft sniffle followed by the quietest of sobs.

The figure steps forward, and its voice fills up the silence like a gunshot in an empty field. "Łukasz. Sparrow?"

His body aches.

Alex.

About the Author

Booker-Garet August Feniks is a queer, disabled writer of fantasy, comedy, and poetry. He writes stories that pull directly from their experiences as a queer immigrant. Originally from Poland, Kielce, Booker writes primarily in English, and has a passion for storytelling and linguistics as a whole.

Pygmalion's Folly

Coy Chambers

CW: body horror, medical ableism, eye trauma, gore
Whumpee: Man, Whumper: Woman, Nonbinary, Caretaker: N/A

Elian didn't so much "open his eyes" as he "became conscious." His eyes didn't close anymore. Hadn't for a week or so. Not since the silver-haired doctor had poured stuff in them. It had hurt, a lot, and he'd screamed, a lot, but eventually the pain had faded and he hadn't gone blind, so there was at least one upside to the situation. There weren't many, but at this point he'd have to take what he could get.

"Good morning Elly! How are we feeling today?" This was the smiling doctor. He couldn't move his eyes to look at her, but he knew she would be smiling. She always did. She was kind to him, always trying to make him more comfortable with blankets and stuffed toys and decorating his room. Not that he could really feel softness on his skin anymore. He liked her, even though he was pretty sure this whole thing was her idea. She seemed to be the one in charge.

"I'm... fine..." he murmured through the stiffness of his jaw. He was fine. The drugs they had him on made sure of that. He'd done a lot of crying and begging in the beginning, but once the drugs started he hadn't been able to muster the will to care. "Please let me go," he added, for the sake of it. The smiling doctor ignored him.

She cupped his cheek in her hand. It was warm, and he wanted to cry when she pulled it away, but he couldn't do that either. "Excellent. We just have a few tests to run this morning, all right? And then we'll be right back to making you beautiful."

He would have blinked against the sudden flash of a penlight in his eyes, but of course he couldn't. "Pupillary response normal. The resin ought to have cured enough to be scored and restore range of motion. Is that the color you would prefer? I will be unable to alter it later." The silver-haired doctor was speaking now. Elian didn't like them. They were always the one who hurt him. They put in the port in the back of his neck that delivered the drugs and God knew what else. They did the injections that felt like they were tearing his veins to shreds. They weren't kind either. It didn't seem like they wanted to be there at all, they were always cold with him and addressed him like an object.

"It's gorgeous. I don't want to change it, do I, Elly? Aren't your eyes the prettiest things ever?" He'd learned by now that she didn't want a response to those questions. He remained silent until she continued speaking. "How are we with everything else? It's an injection day, isn't it?"

The silver-haired doctor nodded. "I will conduct the elasticity tests, and if all goes well, we can do an injection this morning and install the rigging in the afternoon." Rigging? What was that? After nine weeks, he still had no idea what they were doing to him.

The smiling doctor squealed with delight from her position outside of Elian's field of view. "Hear that, Elly? You're almost complete! Just a few more steps and you'll be perfect. When can I do the painting, Rowan? I think I've found the perfect shades."

Rowan was what the smiling doctor called the silver-haired doctor. They didn't seem to like it very much. Their face would always crease into more of a frown for a few minutes after she did it. "If his body does not reject the implants, then he should be ready to paint and lacquer the following week, after the last injection.

And then I can wash my hands of this whole thing," they added under their breath. The smiling doctor ignored this, too.

"Delightful! Run your tests, and I'll check in on his nutrition." Right. Something must have been keeping him going. They hadn't fed him in at least a month. His jaw couldn't open wide enough. The smiling doctor made clicking sounds at a computer that Elian guessed showed some kind of information on him, and the silver-haired doctor began the test.

They did this test every day, and it was the only time their hands on him were gentle. They pressed into every portion of his skin and muscle, cold, gloved fingers making him shiver less and less as whatever transformation they were working in him progressed. He didn't like how it felt. As his flesh compressed under the doctor's hands, he could feel each individual muscle fiber sliding and straining against the next. The surface of his skin felt oily, tugging at the rubber gloves when they moved across it. He felt like he was made of plastic. Or fiberglass. Fragile strands that shredded him as they snapped and scraped across each other. It was miserable.

"Skin surface is showing precipitated resin," the silver-haired doctor commented, deep in thought.

The smiling doctor came into Elian's view for the first time. Still smiling, but smaller and with concern on her face. "Is that good or bad? I don't want delays, Rowan."

They frowned again. "Neutral. I may alter the serum delivery ratio if his body is rejecting excess material. The animal testing showed no adverse effect to the timeline." So they'd tested this stuff. He supposed that made sense. The thought of an animal going through this made him sick. "Even if it would affect it, a delay is more acceptable than experiment failure, is it not? You chose this subject specially. Surely you would not like to have to find another."

Elian barely remembered his capture, didn't know when the smiling doctor had set her sights on him. He'd made himself a picnic in the park, maybe, and fallen asleep in the sun. It didn't matter. He'd woken up here. They'd had the decency to bring his chair along. Not that he'd used it in weeks. Or moved under his own power at all.

"He's not a subject. He's a sculpture." She put her (also gloved) hands on either side of his face, and though he could no longer see her, he could hear the doting grin in her voice. "And of course I don't want to replace him. He's nearly perfect already, aren't you, Elly?" No response needed. He remained still.

The silver-haired doctor's mood was only getting worse. "*Helvete*. Just get the seven-devilled infusion over with."

Oh, no. This was always the worst part of the week. Elian had learned to mark the time passing by when the silver-haired doctor would bring the thick syringes made of metal and glass and connect them to the IV ports on his right arm and left foot (the silver-haired doctor had been annoyed that he didn't have a left arm to put a needle in). They'd been left in since the second week, when the needles started bending on the way into his skin. He hadn't wanted to think about what that meant, then. He still didn't want to think about it. Didn't want to know what he was becoming. (The smiling doctor had hinted at it. A... sculpture?)

The syringes were filled with a clear, off-yellow liquid that flowed like glue. The silver-haired doctor would screw them into the ports and flip a switch that Elian guessed heated whatever was inside so that it flowed better. It definitely felt hot when it went into him. It burned and it cut and it seared and it sliced. He felt every millimeter of condensed, vitreous agony as it crawled through his veins until it faded into a more general ache at the elbow and knee. He couldn't cry, but he did emit a keening wail that increased in pitch and volume as the plungers went down.

The smiling doctor always petted his hair during this, whispering soft encouragement and running her fingers in soothing circles on his scalp. It was the only thing that made the experience even vaguely bearable. How could she be so kind to him and so cruel all at once? She seemed to love him, in her own way, even if that manifested as whatever sick experiment she was running. The silver-haired doctor hummed some vaguely unsettling tune that he didn't know, and he got the idea it was more for their own amusement or to cover up the sound of his cries than for any benevolent purpose.

"He's sweating resin, Rowan," the smiling doctor noted a few minutes in.

"Yes, I noticed. I have already slowed the infusion rate." More of this? Elian didn't think he could bear it. "Odd, really. None of the prior testing showed this issue..."

The smiling doctor's hand tightened in Elian's hair for a moment before relaxing and giving him an apologetic stroke. "Surely he's not rejecting the serum?" Her tone made it sound as if someone would be losing an eye if that were true.

The silver-haired doctor hummed consideringly. "No... I do not believe that to be the case. When we place the rigging in a few hours, I shall do a core sample, and that should explain a few items. We may have merely supersaturated his tissues, and the rest of the hardening process will need to be completed externally."

Elian didn't understand most of those words, but none of them sounded good. Part of him was disappointed at the idea that he might be failing whatever experiment they were doing on him. Why did he want to succeed at this horrible change? Was it the way the smiling doctor looked down at him while the infusions ripped through him, soothing and gentle and with something akin to love? She seemed to see some sort of purpose in him, to have specially picked him out as perfect for whatever this was. He... didn't want to disappoint her. Not while she was so kind.

The pain faded, settling into his bones and leaving a heavy fatigue in its wake. That was normal. Once the fluid wasn't pushing its way into his body anymore, he was always worn out. The smiling doctor was the one to flick the penlight in his eyes this time. "Pupillary response normal, still, though I think he'll be going to sleep soon. Isn't that right, Elly? Tired, are we?"

He was. His eyelids would be fluttering if they could close at all. "It will be just as well to sedate him," the silver-haired doctor said. "Brady will be here soon, and I will need to cure this resin before the installation."

"Better for him to sleep until that's finished, I agree. Just a little bit of diazepam for you, dearie, that's the ticket."

"You will want propofol and most likely ketamine after the fact."

"Don't tell me how to do my job, Rowan. Just finish your injections." She never did stop smiling, even when she was annoyed.

Elian felt his consciousness sliding away from him gradually, and didn't bother fighting it. There was no point in fighting any of this, really.

***

When Elian woke, it was to white-hot agony. Like someone had put a metal rod into a fire and poked him with it all over. His upper arm, his wrist, his thighs, his calves. Even his hips had circular patches of burning pain. He made a mewling sound in his dry throat. What had he done to deserve this?

"Elly? Shit. Rowan, he's waking up—"

"Ahead of you. Adding ten ccs of—"

"Wait! Hold on." Elian recognized this voice. The engineer. He was American, while the silver-haired doctor was probably British (though some of their pronunciations threw that into doubt), and the smiling doctor seemed to be Spanish. Elian had only seen him twice, both times to measure his arms and legs. "I'm testing something. Need him awake and aware."

The silver-haired doctor made a disapproving sound in their chest. "Very well, but finish quickly. If his nervous system goes into shock I will have to take drastic measures to correct it."

"No delays, Warren, you'd damn well better do this right..." She didn't sound like she was smiling now.

"Patience, Dr Salazar. Isn't that what Dr Fairbank is always saying?" he shot back with a grunt, and whatever he did made Elian feel as if he were being ripped apart. His arm and legs moved of their own accord, as if hauled upward by some force, amplifying the pain in each of the points he'd identified earlier tenfold and sending his joints into a spiderweb of fractured agony. His vision was blurred, whether by tears or something else, he didn't know, and he couldn't tell what was going on. He wailed through his locked jaw, abjectly miserable.

"It will do you well to keep my words from your mouth," the silver-haired doctor snapped. "Are you mad? Let the bone ossify around the grafts before you add load! You will break him in half!" They injected something into his neck port that lessened the pain, but only a little.

The engineer scoffed. "Live a little, doctor! If the grafts ossify and *then* the metal snaps, you'll be blaming me, and it'll be a hell of a delay. Might even ruin the damn thing. More than it is already, I guess." Elian's limbs lowered back to the table and he could have sobbed with relief. "I'm done, anyway, you can knock it out if you want."

The smiling doctor carded her fingers through Elian's hair encouragingly. "Easy, sweetheart, just a little more." Then, in a much less soothing tone, "Where are those drugs, Rowan? Why do I even have you here?"

"You are trying my patience, Salazar. Anaesthesiology is not exactly facile. Would you rather I left you to do it yourself?" Despite their words, cool liquid flooded Elian's neck port, leaving behind a tingling sensation. A dense fog settled gradually over his senses, and whatever the smiling doctor retorted with was muffled as he slipped into unconsciousness.

***

The cycle continued after that. Waking up, elasticity tests, drifting in limbo as his pain waxed and waned. He didn't even have the energy to be terrified when the silver-haired doctor used a drill bit to score the resin and carefully machine his eyes back into working order. The movement was as smooth and painless as he remembered it being, so really, it must have been all right. They even gave him a new arm at one point and he barely noticed. It wasn't as if he could move either of them on his own.

Today was more of the same. He became aware of sound before his eyes opened, the smiling and silver-haired doctors' familiar voices discussing something. Elian inhaled deeply, almost involuntarily, before blinking his eyes open under the harsh exam table lights. The silver-haired doctor was mixing something in a large basin, and Elian could identify the acrid smell of paint thinner, though it was hard to pick out over the ever-present chemical sweetness of his own resin-skin.

"Your 'muse' is awake," they commented sardonically, only barely looking up. They were never pleased to see him.

The smiling doctor's hands were in his hair again. "Good morning, Elly! We've got very exciting work to do today! The last step in making you truly beautiful!" He leaned into her hand, his scalp the only remaining portion of his skin that could still feel properly. Making him "truly beautiful"? He couldn't understand what she meant by that. All he could feel was that she was destroying his body for her own purpose. And still, somehow, she loved him. He couldn't hate her for that.

The silver-haired doctor sighed. "Are you ready? The varnish is properly mixed. I will apply it when you are satisfied with the appearance."

The smiling doctor gave Elian's hair a final pat and withdrew. "Yes, I feel inspired. This will be my best work yet, I think. It's the least I can do for such an incredible canvas. He's been so good to us, hasn't he?"

"He is not violent. That is a welcome change. Otherwise, he is perfectly ordinary, if not borderline defective, and I cannot comprehend your obsession with him." Elian couldn't either, though he bristled at the idea that he was defective. He'd been perfectly fine the way he was before anyone had interfered. "Regardless, my purpose here is not to understand your motivations, it is to ensure the procedure is carried out properly. Do your 'art' and I will do mine." They seemed in an even worse mood than usual.

The smiling doctor was a brunette woman in her early forties, with dark eyes that crinkled when she smiled (which was most of the time). Elian didn't see her as often as she was present, she had a tendency to stand behind him, just out of his eyeline, though he was very familiar with her voice and her touch. This time, she stood in front of him, looping her back-length hair into a messy bun and rolling up the sleeves of her lab coat. It wasn't her usual one: this one was already flecked with paint and stained with watercolor, and looked to be much older than any of the others he'd seen her in over the weeks he'd been here. She seemed more comfortable in it.

The tray she rolled next to the exam table held no surgical tools. Instead, carefully mixed cups of paint and a stack of palettes occupied the space. "Rowan, the music, please," she murmured, gaze already distant, appraising Elian with the critical eye of a sculptor choosing which slivers of stone to remove from a block of marble. Her smile had faded, giving way to a look of intense concentration as she mixed her first set of colors. The silver-haired doctor dropped the needle on a record player in the corner and then vanished from Elian's eyeline as violin music began to play.

"Good. I think we'll be productive today." The smiling doctor collected pigment on her brush and began to paint.

It was watching a master at work. In other circumstances, Elian would have been awestruck to watch the way she assembled color out of pigment, building light colors onto dark bases in each section of his skin until it replicated the original tone. She moved like a virtuoso, weaving seemingly-random patches of hue into a tapestry so realistic he almost didn't notice how hauntingly flawless it was. As it was, it made his stomach twist in odd ways to watch every one of his scars (of which there were many), marks (also numerous), and blemishes (few) melt away into painted smoothness. She was "making him beautiful," whatever that meant.

He didn't like how long the silver-haired doctor had remained out of sight. That was never a good sign for him, and even if he couldn't hear them talking or laughing to themselves, it didn't mean he was safe from whatever they were doing next. Elian tried tilting his head up to see if he could catch sight of them again, his atrophied muscles protesting even the slight movement.

"Ah-ah, Elly, hold still, dearie." The smiling doctor was painting Elian's chest, and caught him by the chin to bring it back to its original position. "I'll change the angle when I want it changed and not before. Art takes time."

The silver-haired doctor knew what he was after. "I am over here, preparing for the next stage. You need not look for me, I will neither be moving nor cooking up new torments for you." He had been worried about that, but he wasn't exactly sure he trusted them.

"Hush, Rowan. The sound of your voice makes it difficult for me to focus." The silver-haired doctor said something in a language Elian didn't understand, though it sounded mocking, and was silent.

This made Elian a bit bolder, though. While the doctor took a moment to clean her brush, he looked up at her and asked, "Please, doctor, can't I know what's happening to me?" Both of them liked being called doctor. He'd learned that early.

She hummed softly, considering, then chuckled, "I've already told you, love. We're making you beautiful. You were quite lovely before, of course, I just thought I could make a few small improvements."

This didn't seem like an improvement, he was in even more daily pain than he'd been before and he couldn't even eat on his own. He wanted to be back at home, in his room with his own comforts instead of the smiling doctor's hollow reassurance. She wasn't a person who took kindly to being disagreed with though, her interactions with the other two had told him that much, and she didn't seem likely to give him a better answer. She liked playing coy, teasing him. He lapsed into silence.

It was almost meditative, the faraway feeling of the doctor's brush as she painted over his skin. The music transported him to an alternate reality in which he wasn't being tortured for his utility in some sort of modern art piece. He could have fallen asleep if it weren't for the almost-ticklish sensation of his freckles being filled in with a detailing brush. Telling time was impossible here, he had no way of knowing how many hours the doctors worked, he only knew how often they gave him his nutrition supplement, which seemed to be twice a day if the injections really were weekly. It could have been one hour or ten that the smiling doctor spent on her work.

Focusing on the words the two doctors were speaking to each other was difficult through the haze of soothing fatigue. He caught things like "sedate him" and "for the best" and "breathe the fumes," which didn't exactly sound good, but then another burst of liquid came through his neck port, and he found himself caring very little. He caught a glimpse of the silver-haired doctor wearing a gas mask and assembling some sort of spraying device.

"Easy, there, Elly. Just go right to sleep while we protect your skin, all right?" The smiling doctor petted his hair again before withdrawing. Elian was able to identify the smallest fraction of a second of searing agony being sprayed over his arm before the sea of unconsciousness closed over his head.

***

He was surprised that they'd put him in his chair today. He hadn't seen it since the first week he'd been here, after the first round of injections when the silver-haired doctor had declared his skin too fragile for him to be allowed to move freely. Elian hadn't seen *them* since the last coat of material went onto his skin. He guessed their part in it all must be finished.

The smiling doctor had wheeled him down a set of hallways he hadn't seen before and into multiple elevators until he was questioning how impossibly large the building must be. These people must have so many resources, if they could afford a base this size and kidnap him in broad daylight, not to mention all of the equipment. How many others might they be keeping here? Not worth thinking about.

Now, she'd brought him into what looked like a dressing room and was comparing several different satin fabrics to his new skin tone. "Want to set off your eyes..." she murmured to herself, along with other similar musings. In Elian's opinion, pink was his best color, but the smiling doctor seemed to dislike how his already-pink hair contrasted with the soft rose of the fabric she had, and finally chose to dress him in azure instead. His limbs were articulated again, which made moving much smoother and less painful than it had been at certain points, and the smiling doctor manipulated Elian's body to dress him fairly easily. He thought he could probably stand and dress on his own if he really tried, but she was a perfectionist and insisted on doing most things herself anyway. What good would standing do him? It wasn't as if he had the faintest idea where the exit was.

"There! I think that does it. Have a look, Elly, darling. See what you think." That was odd. She'd never asked him what he thought about anything before.

The smiling doctor rolled a large, floor-length mirror in front of Elian's chair, and he saw himself in his entirety for the first time since being brought to the lab. He recognized the face in the mirror as his own, but... altered. His usually pale skin was nearly luminous, highlighted on the cheeks and nose to emphasize the glossy sheen of the varnish. He'd known he must have been covered with the stuff, the silver-haired doctor hadn't spared a square inch of him from the sprayer, but he hadn't realized how artificial it made him look. His eyelids were solid pieces that raised and lowered themselves as the doctor tilted his head for him, and they opened much wider than usual, giving him an air of perpetual innocence. He was smiling, and a pang of dissonance ripped through him when he realized he couldn't even feel it. It had been ages since he could feel his face. There was a plastic fitting over his teeth, preventing airflow and his mouth drying out. He would have thought she'd fix the gap between the front ones, but she must have found it charming. She'd rearranged the pattern of his freckles.

His arms perfectly matched on both sides, including the ring finger on his right hand he hadn't noticed had been replaced. Articulated like doll's limbs, with full range of motion, and those strange metal rings the engineer had installed on the day Elian had woken up during the procedure. The doctor had put him in a tutu, far from his first, with his hair arranged into a neat bun and tied with a ribbon in the same pastel blue as his clothes. He'd never danced ballet, though this ensemble was reminiscent of what he'd been wearing that day in the park. Was that why she'd taken him?

"Well?" she asked, bending to put his feet into pointe shoes, her ribbon technique showing she had experience doing so. His left ankle wasn't articulated at all, but rigid, fixed in a pointed position, and the corresponding knee had several positions it could be locked into rather than a full range of motion like the other.

"I-" It came out more clearly than he expected. There seemed to be some kind of microphone set up that projected his voice past the veneers. "I don't... understand..." It was still difficult to form consonants with his jaw and lips stuck fast.

"You were nearly perfect when I found you. All you needed was a few minor adjustments to be flawless. Some color correction here, a functional repair there. The smallest detail makes the work, after all. Wouldn't you agree you're much improved?"

Disagreeing with her didn't seem like a safe thing to do, but how could he agree that being turned into a china-doll mockery of himself was an *improvement*? The image in front of Elian wasn't truly of *him* at all, it was more of a sculpture vaguely modeled after him. The smiling doctor seemed enamored with it, though, and she played with his hair and beamed with delight while they looked in the mirror together. "Thank you, doctor. I'm perfect now." The words made him sick to his stomach.

Another indulgent smile. "I'm so glad you feel that way. Now, the final step."

She pushed his chair again, more long hallways and turns, until she finally brought him to a stop at the center of a stage in a small theater. The engineer was here, too, tinkering with some equipment. "Doctor Salazar. Everything ready?"

"Everything. Can I trust you not to damage him or will I have to monitor you? I'd hate to have to adjust the decorations again."

The engineer shrugged. "If that stuff Doctor Fairbank put in him works right, there probably isn't anything I *could* do to damage him. I'll be alright."

Her smile tightened. "He's art, not equipment. Treat him as such."

"Yeah. Right. Will do." Elian was beginning to think he'd rather have the silver-haired doctor.

The engineer spent several minutes connecting carabiners to the ring-like shapes screwed into Elian's bones. That horrible shattering sensation came back again whenever the cables took up the weight of his limbs and lifted them even slightly into the air, and by the time the engineer declared all of his testing complete, Elian felt as if he'd run a marathon. The pain alone was exhausting, and he'd been seated the whole time. That didn't last long, though.

The engineer gave a signal to someone Elian couldn't see, and all at once the cables hauled him up out of his chair and into a standing position, balanced on the point of his fused leg. It felt precarious, and he swayed dangerously, but the metal ropes held him in place. The engineer wheeled Elian's chair off stage, and he mentally reached out, insecure without it. He breathed heavily through his nose, anxiety fluttering in his chest. Was this the end goal of it all?

The curtain went up, the lights flared to life, and Elian squinted out at the empty chairs, save one, where the smiling doctor seemed nearly manic with excitement as she took her seat. Music began to play, the charmingly off-key notes of a music box, and the rigging pulled his limbs up and into the motions of a dance he wasn't familiar with, rotating him delicately around his central axis and extending and retracting his leg to the rhythm. His muscles felt tense and stiff after weeks of disuse and the glass, each smooth-yet-awkward movement was utter agony and thick tears made of resin torturously gathered in his glazed eyes. He thought he could hear the crackling scrape of vitreous muscle all the way in his teeth. He wanted to scream, but the sound choked and died in his chest.

Elian looked out at Doctor Salazar, alone in the audience, the rictus grin lacquered onto his face. What was he looking for, some hollow comfort? Some indication that his life was not now meaningless? *Are you happy now? Am I what you wanted?* Despair pooled in his gut as he watched the affection die in her eyes along with the smile on her face.

About the Author

Coy Chambers (they/them) is fictional, a Time Lord, and able to lick their own elbow. A queer writer of color, they write science fiction and fantasy short stories and nibble at the occasional novel.

Elian belongs to Bones @delaureyjournal-whump on tumblr and is used with permission.

The Blanket

Scarlett Skyes

CW: Mentioned laboratory testing, vomiting
Whumpee: Man, Whumpers: Unspecified, Caretaker: N/A

If nothing else, at least the blanket was warm.

It didn't matter that the rest of the lab felt like ice, nor did it matter that the lights were like a thousand suns above him. The tubing connected to his arm was uncomfortable whether he stayed completely still or moved around, but hardly mattered either because the blanket was *warm*.

His throat would burn when he inevitably brought up whatever he tried to eat, yet they still coaxed him to have the next meal anyway. The scans that they said would not be painful were loud, louder than he had ever thought possible, echoing in his head hours after being returned to his room.

The procedures that had been deemed necessary hurt regardless of what medications they used to dull his senses, and he would often shake for hours after, but the blanket was warm so surely everything else was manageable.

After something went wrong with a test, and he ended up coughing for hours and hours and hours even after he was put into a full oxygen mask, that blanket had been a lifeline that surpassed all others.

No matter how much pain ripped through him, no matter what they did to him, the blanket was right there with him through it all.

It had been there since the very first day, the dark blue fabric soft and familiar, tied with a little red bow and a note to say that this was all temporary. The note was long since gone, having been torn up in a fit of anger as the days dragged into weeks into eternity, but the warm blanket remained his closest companion.

When the oxygen mask had become too much and he tried to rip it off his face, his cold hands had been guided away, placed onto the soft fabric and he had felt all of his pain and stress melt away.

Temporary. All of this was temporary.

The thin scratchy fabric gowns they kept him in did little to protect against the unending clinical coldness of the laboratory, but once again the thick blanket was his respite. He would clutch onto it tightly, keeping it as close to his chest as he could even as his body ached.

Impossibly, it still smelled like her.

The only scent that was more powerful than that of the antiseptic the Doctors used each time they entered the room, then again if they dared touch his skin even if they had used gloves. Surely by now her perfume of sandalwood and vanilla would have faded, and yet whenever he felt like this unending suffering had become too much, he would remind himself that the blanket smelled like her.

The masks the Doctors wore made hearing their words difficult, though he had come to care less and less about what they had to say as the endless time wore on. Whatever warnings they tried to give him, a small scratch here or a new possible symptom there, hardly seemed to matter when his whole body had become little more than pain no matter how gentle they were with him.

No, the warnings did not matter. It was hardly like they listened to him if he tried to ask for a reprieve anyway, why fight when he knew how willing they were to strap his wrists and ankles to the guardrails of the bed if that is what it took to do their tests?

At least if he went along with whatever it was they were doing, he could keep the warm blanket.

The familiar comfort was grounding, even in a sea of whiteness and tests and sensations that made it as though his very blood had become acid. The blanket was *everything* to him. So when he woke with a start, vomiting onto it before he could stop himself, he damn near fell apart completely.

He had screamed, he had cried, he had beat hard hands onto the chest of the Doctor that had rushed in, begging them to just let it end, begging them to just let him die already. He had cried himself to exhaustion, slowly waking hours or maybe even days later on that very same bed.

The lights were bright.

The thin fabric of his clothing scratched his too sensitive skin.

New bandages covered his newest scars from procedures he couldn't even remember.

But most important of all was that the blanket was warm. It had been washed, and yet somehow it still had the smell of her. The smell of his sister, the sister they claimed time and again was still alive. She was alive because of what they were doing to him, they claimed, she was alive because of his noble sacrifice.

She was alive and that was all that mattered and so when the doctors came for the newest tests, he willingly held out his arm.

This would all be temporary, he told himself, and even if it wasn't, at least the blanket was warm.

About the Author

Scarlett is an Australian writer who loves all things Whumpy. With a particular focus on family based comfort, whether that be biological or found family, she loves to have a fun mix of angst and heartfelt moments where even at their lowest, a Whumpee's family is right there for them!

His Lake

Booker G. A. Feniks

CW: Character death

Whumpee: Man, Whumper: Man, Caretaker: N/A

For centuries it had only been darkness. The water had invaded every single one of his crevices, the fish had made a home of his ribcage, the algae floated off his limbs. The gentle rippling of the sunlight above didn't reach his eyes, it was just him within the darkness of His Lake.

He called it His Lake. He knew every corner, every bend, every critter that lived around him. Hermit crabs liked hiding in the ports on his back, guppies would dart between their birthplaces beneath his feet. Minuscule vertebrates used his exoskeleton as temporary shells, and young river sharks liked playing in the bubble streams created by his leather lungs.

And he still lived on. Days passed, and years, and centuries, but he had no concept of time anymore, he no longer knew when it was night or day. He no longer knew of the world outside of His Lake. He no longer knew of the growth pains of society, his own aches were all he felt. He no longer knew how many descendants he had, to him there were only the fish.

Then, one day, he saw sunlight again.

***

The burn behind his eyes was excruciating, but the water within his lungs did not let him scream. His body convulsed and each movement sent volts of pain through his joints. There was the familiar darkness at the edges of his vision, an unattainable comfort.

"It's alive, fuck me!" The voice came from his left, from his right, from above and below him. It encompassed him so thoroughly, so completely, that he thought he could hear it within his own mind, rattling around in his skull in the space between his copper ears.

"Call the boss, idiot!" Warm air ghosted over his taut skin. His face burned as if a hot iron was being dragged over his cheeks. The cables beneath his flesh sizzled and protested, crying out when a hand pressed against his forehead.

"A cyborg, my god. Exactly where that old man said it would be."

***

His Lake stood empty since 1819, the day his body had crashed into it and flooded the nearby fields. No one who remembered it was still alive. *He* remembered it, the flashes of memory bursting like fireworks behind his eyelids. His metallic spine cradled the nerves that encircled his brain, and each twinge of his heaving lungs made a connection spark. These flashes were brief, but they were grand.

He had been a dead man shot through the spine by a man of the law. There had been no trial, the price on his head had been high enough to make the saints cry. He remembered the way the bullet felt as it entered his breast and exited through his back; he felt the way the guppies nibbled exploratorily over the rough edges of the holes. He remembered the way his body had begun growing numb like a wave, gradually spreading from his toes to his neck; he felt the way his metallic joints creaked and the way his leather lungs constricted around the water that threatened to choke him again.

A woman had saved him, a sister to him in all but blood. A man had brought him back to life, taking everything but his body as payment. He remembered the way the cold of the metal operating table had gradually spread from his back to the tips of his fingers and toes; he felt the cold of His Lake penetrate him to the heart beating beneath his chest helped along by canvas pumps. He remembered the way the knife had made incisions along his abdomen and the blood drained from each slice as if he were a gutted fish; he felt the way the water danced through the holes in his body, filtering in and out with the movement of the waves.

The shabby shed the man called his laboratory had once been home. There had been three of them in the days before his death. He remembered the operating table shimmering in the light of a gas lamp; he felt the gentle caresses of the sun above him without seeing it. He remembered the chains and the cuffs that encircled his body; he felt the algae curled around his body, entangling him in the plants at the bottom of His Lake.

These flashes came briefly, alongside the pain and the aches. All other times, he was empty, blank. His mind was darkness.

***

"What a marvel. What an amazing specimen. The augmentations are dated to at least the early nineteenth century, if not earlier."

"What shall we do with it, Doc?"

"Why, open it up, of course! Such a marvel of modern science must be studied! Hold it down, dammit! Those lazy idiots didn't tie it down tight enough."

"You heard the boss, tighten the bonds."

"I can't have it messing up my incisions."

"There. Go ahead, Doc. Brilliant."

"Someone shove something down its throat, goddammit! Its screaming will wake up the neighbours and we can't have those old fishermen knowing that we're here. They're fools and barbarians, but not idiots."

"Boss, boss!"

"What?"

"I... I don't think it's alive anymore."

"All the better, at least it won't get in the way. If we do this fast enough, we may still see how its internal parts work."

"Got it, Doc. You heard him, hurry it up!"

"What's this? A hole?"

"Don't stick your fingers in there, idiot!"

"It's... boss, it's woken up!"

"Boss!"

"God have mercy on us, GOD HAVE MERCY ON US!"

"Doc... Oh god, it crushed his head. Oh god."

"Run, idiot! RUN!"

***

Another century passed, and then another. His wounds healed, the new holes in his body created homes for new species of fish.

His Lake's waters lapped at the banks; the algae swayed gently in the current upon his body. Hermit crabs hid in the ports on his back; young river sharks nibbled at his hair.

And so it was, until the very end.

About the Author

Booker-Garet August Feniks is a queer, disabled writer of fantasy, comedy, and poetry. He writes stories that pull directly from their experiences as a queer immigrant. Originally from Poland, Kielce, Booker writes primarily in English, and has a passion for storytelling and linguistics as a whole.

Sunlight

Kailey Alessi

"You're an old man now, ya know that?" Cal leaned against the doorframe, smirking. Renn rolled his eyes.

"You're older than me."

"Exactly. Welcome to the old man club, where our favorite activity is napping and complaining loudly about the weather." Cal crossed the room and ruffled Renn's hair. Renn slapped his hand away playfully.

"But seriously, Renn. Happy birthday."

"Thanks," Renn said. "I honestly can't believe I'm twenty. Part of me didn't think we'd live this long."

Cal sighed. "Wow, way to bring down the mood." He wrapped Renn in a hug. Renn closed his eyes and squeezed his brother back. They were dhampirs, half human and half vampire. They weren't supposed to exist. If the authorities ever discovered them, they would be executed. There had been several close calls over the years, but they had so far evaded detection.

"Boys! Dinner is ready," Sylvie called from downstairs. She was the human housekeeper who had taken care of them for the past few years. Ever since things with their vampire parents had gone sour.

The two boys tromped downstairs. Renn breathed in the scent of rosemary roasted chicken. It was his favorite meal.

"It smells delicious in here." Renn pulled out his chair and settled in, Cal in the chair across from him.

"I would hope so. I've been slaving away at the stove all day. There's mushroom soup, rosemary chicken, mashed potatoes, and a lemon cake for dessert." Sylvie put a dish of butter on the table, removed her apron, and sat down.

Renn's mouth watered at the feast. He started to fill his plate. "Thank you, Sylvie. Everything looks amazing."

"Anything for you, Renn. Happy birthday."

They talked and laughed as they ate. Renn drank the cup of blood Sylvie had provided for him to wash down his dinner.

Sylvie brought out the cake and she and Cal fussed over how best to arrange the twenty candles on top.

"Well make a wish," Cal said.

Renn stared at the flickering flames, contemplating. Then he blew out the candles. *I wish for twenty more years just like this.*

The cake was, of course, heavenly. Renn leaned back in his chair. "I pronounce this birthday feast a success." He got to his feet and started to gather the dirty dishes.

"Hey, I got those," Cal said as he swatted Renn's hand away. Renn let his brother have the dishes. Cal was at the sink when Renn noticed Sylvie crying.

"What's wrong?" Renn pulled out a chair next to her, his brow pinched in concern. She looked at her lap and sniffled into a handkerchief.

"Oh, nothing. You boys are just both so grown up." Sylvie looked at him with a sad expression. "It feels like it went by so fast." She stroked his cheek. "I'll miss you."

"What do you mean?" Renn asked. "I'm not going anywhere."

Sylvie's eyes widened. "I mean . . . I'll miss the little boy you used to be."

Renn couldn't suppress his snort. "Really? I think I single-handedly gave you at least three-quarters of your grays."

Sylvie laughed. "You weren't that bad. I only got half from you, the other half came from your brother."

"I don't know what you're talking about," Cal called from the sink. "I'm an angel."

"What about that time you brought an entire bucket of frogs into the house?" Renn asked.

Cal spun around. "It was freezing outside! I was trying to save them."

Sylvie chuckled. "I swear my heart almost gave out when I woke up to a frog on my pillow."

The rest of the evening passed quietly. Renn changed into his nightclothes and climbed into bed. It was early spring and he left the window cracked open to get the cool night breeze. The only sounds were the chirping of the crickets and the wind whooshing through the leaves. Renn, Cal, and Sylvie lived in a little house out in the country, far away from prying eyes. It hadn't always been that way. Renn shook off the memory. They were here now, that's what mattered. He was just about to put his candle out when there was a knock at his door.

"Come in."

Sylvie came in, a candle in one hand and a cup in the other.

"I brought you some tea," she said as she set the candle on the table. "I know how much you like the chamomile."

Renn sat up in bed and took the teacup. "Thanks. Does it have-"

"Yes, I put in two dollops of honey."

Renn grinned. "You're the best, Sylvie."

Renn took a sip of the tea. He sighed at the sweetness. Sylvie sat down on the edge of his bed.

"I love you, Renn. Please always remember that."

Renn's forehead creased. "I love you too. Are you alright? You've seemed sad today." He took another sip of his tea. He could feel a headache coming on.

"You've always been such a sweet boy. I asked them for more time, but they said it had to be now."

"Wh-what are you talking about?" Renn asked. His vision blurred and his head pounded. He suddenly was so, so tired. Sylvie took the cup from him as he fell back against the pillows.

"I'm sorry," Sylvie said. Renn's eyes widened. She had drugged him. But why? He tried to move away from her but his limbs were as heavy as lead. Sylvie shifted his head into her lap. "Don't fight it. It's no use. Just relax, Renn." Renn's eyes drifted shut. He forced them open. He had to get away. He had to warn Cal. He attempted to yell but all that came out was a strangled sob. He was going to die. He had always thought he would burn to death. That someday the authorities would discover him and Cal and have them burned at the stake for being monstrosities. He had never thought it would be like this. Drugged by the woman who he loved as if she was his own mother.

"It's okay, honey, it's okay," Sylvie soothed as she ran a hand through his hair. "You're just going to sleep for a little bit." Renn wanted to pull away from her, but he was completely helpless. The last thing he saw before the darkness claimed him was the tear sliding down Sylvie's face.

***

Renn floated in the darkness for what felt like eternity.

"He's more sensitive than Callum," a voice said. "She should have given him a smaller dose."

"She had no way of knowing that," another voice replied. "He'll be fine. It'll just take a little longer to get through his system."

Renn whimpered. His head pounded and he had never felt so sore in his life. He blinked his eyes open. The light burned and he snapped them shut again with a groan.

"Ah, you're awake!"

"W-" Renn coughed. His tongue felt thick and a bout of dizziness washed over him. He tried again. "W-where am I?"

"You're home, my beautiful boy. You're finally home." That voice. Renn knew that voice. With enormous effort, he opened his eyes.

"Mother?"

"Yes, baby, I'm here." She looked just like he remembered. Long black hair pulled back into a sensible bun, a no-nonsense gray dress, eyes that sparkled with what he had once thought was love. He knew better now.

"You had Sylvie drug me," he said, the pieces falling into place.

His father spoke up. "I'm sorry about that, it must have been unpleasant. But you never would have come home otherwise."

"Of course not!" Renn yelled. His heart pounded and he was hit by the instinct to flee. He had never wanted to see them again. Not after he had seen them murder his human mother and Cal's human father in cold blood. "You killed them. You killed our parents right in front of us."

Father sighed. "For what it's worth, we didn't intend for you and Callum to see that. The only reason we eliminated them was to protect you two."

Renn let out a deep breath. "Why am I here? Where's Cal?" He tested his limbs and found he could barely move a finger.

"Callum's downstairs. We've already spoken with him," Mother said. "As for why you're here, you'll be helping us to push the boundaries of modern science. You and Callum are the first dhampirs to make it to maturity in generations. We know next to nothing on dhampir anatomy and physiology, so we'll be studying you two."

Renn's throat went dry. "You're going to dissect us?"

Father had the audacity to laugh. "Oh no, of course not. We're much more interested in how your bodies work than what they look like on the inside." *That* wasn't very reassuring.

"You're too special to waste on something as unrefined as dissection," Mother pitched in. Renn closed his eyes as tears burned. "You must be exhausted. Let's take you downstairs."

Renn couldn't fight back as Father picked him up and carried him to his fate.

***

"Good morning, boys!" Cal flinched at Father's voice and Renn wrapped his arm around him protectively. "We have a big day planned," Father continued. "But first things first - breakfast."

He opened the door to the cell and set down a tray with toast and two mugs of blood.

They ate slowly, Renn keeping one eye on their parents as they moved about the lab. The experiments were starting today, and Renn was ashamed to admit how scared he was.

"All done?" Mother asked. Renn and Cal both nodded. "Perfect, time to go outside." Renn blinked. He couldn't have heard that right. But Father unlocked the cell and motioned for the boys to follow them up the stairs.

Cal stumbled on a step and fell to his knees. Father sighed. He grabbed Cal by the elbow and supported him the rest of the way. As they emerged on the first floor for the first time in weeks, Renn was hit by the urge to run. He was fast, and if he could make it to the forest he could lose them. But there was no way Cal would be able to get away too, and he couldn't leave him. Renn's heart sank as his hopes of escape dwindled down to zero.

They led them outside. Renn breathed in deeply. The smell of the grass and flowers filled his lungs. It was just before dawn and the sky to the east was a light gray.

Renn stopped walking when he saw the chains on the lawn. "What?"

Father grabbed his shoulder, his grip like iron. "Keep going." He led him closer to the chains. There were four of them, with one end staked into the ground and a metal shackle on the other end.

"Take your shirt off." Renn shook his head, fear closing up his throat.

"Fine." Father grabbed Renn's shirt and yanked it over his head. With his next breath he forced Renn onto his stomach.

"Let go of me!" Renn yelled. But Father was stronger than him and just snapped the shackles shut around his wrists. "Please!" Renn begged, panic building as his ankles were secured in shackles. They were going to leave them here to see how the sun affected them. Renn struggled against the shackles but it was no use. Cal was restrained the same way. He was shaking.

"The sun will be up within the hour," Mother said. "We will come check on you throughout the day."

"You'll kill us! Mother, Father, please don't do this." Renn sobbed, the panic clawing at his throat.

"Don't worry," Mother said, kneeling down and cradling Renn's cheek in her hand. "We won't let you die. You're too important. We'll check on you every hour. If the burns become too severe we'll end the experiment and bring you inside."

With that, they headed back to the safety of the house. Renn strained against the shackles as the world grew brighter. He had only been in the sun once before, when he was twelve and had fallen asleep on the window seat reading. He had forgotten to close the curtains, and when the sun came up he had awoken to burning pain on his face. A chill went up his spine as he remembered how attentive his parents were to his injury. They had been waiting for this moment.

The first rays of sunlight reached down. Renn gasped at the warmth on his back.

"It's okay, Renn," Cal said. Renn looked at him. Cal gave him a tight smile. "We'll get through this. Together, alright?"

Renn nodded. He tried to steady his breathing as his back heated up. It didn't hurt. Not yet.

An hour in, their parents came out to check on them. Renn envied their sun cloaks.

"How do you feel, loves?"

"It stings," Ren said.

"How long ago did it start stinging?" Father asked.

"About ten minutes," Ren said.

"Interesting." Father paused and his pencil scratched across his notebook. "What about you, Callum?"

"I don't feel any pain," he said. "At least not yet."

"Fascinating." Father wrote something else down. "Renn's back is turning a pinkish color while Callum's is the same as it was when we started. I can't wait to see how things progress over the day."

Renn choked on a sob. It was going to get worse.

Their parents left them again. "Do you really not feel anything?" Renn asked.

"I mean, my back is warm, but it's not unpleasant," Cal said.

"Lucky bastard," Renn muttered.

"I'm sure my turn will come."

Another hour passed. Renn squirmed on the ground. Now it *burned*. He groaned.

"Oh my." He hadn't even heard Mother approach. "Renn, you're almost as red as my roses."

"It-it hurts," he stammered. "It hurts so much." He didn't attempt to stop the tears from rolling down his cheeks. "Please let me come inside. Please."

"I'm sorry, I can't do that, sweetie. We need to test the limits of what your body's capable of. Cal, how do you feel?"

"It's starting to sting," he said. "I can handle it for now. But please, please let Renn go inside. You have enough data."

"No," Father said. "We need to know when the third degree burns start. For vampires, it sets in within the first hour. You two are entering hour number three. It looks like Renn is still experiencing first degree burns, and you have barely started to burn yet."

"Stay strong, boys," Mother said.

Then they left them again.

Renn was on fire. He was going to burn to death, here in the sun. It wasn't just his back. It was his arms, the backs of his hands, his neck. Everywhere the sun touched was like fire on his skin.

Renn's forehead rested on the ground and he took in a shaky breath. They would see reason soon, right? They would realize that these were their children that they were torturing, and they would come out and get them.

The hours passed slowly. Renn started screaming at noon. The fire was under his skin. It felt like his muscles were roasting on his bones. He sobbed and pulled at the restraints. He rubbed his skin raw and blood trickled down his wrists and ankles, but it was no use.

Their parents came back. Mother knelt down in front of Renn. "You're doing so well. I'm so proud of you."

Renn sobbed. He hated her. He hated both of them. "Please, Mom, please make it stop." His throat was raw from screaming but he managed to croak out the plea.

"I'm sorry, my beautiful boy, I can't do that," she said. "But you can bite down on this to help with the pain." She had a wooden spoon. Renn almost refused it. He didn't want a fuckin' spoon. He wanted to be inside, safe from the sun. But that obviously wasn't an option. He opened his mouth and bit down on the offered spoon handle.

Cal was feeling the burn now too. His face was coated in sweat and he whimpered. "It won't last forever," he whispered. Renn didn't know if Cal was talking to him or to himself. "It won't last forever."

Renn felt the skin on his back crack and hot blood bubble to the surface. He bit down as hard as he could and screamed.

The next time they came to check on him, Renn was barely conscious. The pain was being replaced with numbness. He had given up trying to escape and just lay there in the grass, forehead on the ground as he burned alive.

They asked him something, but he couldn't hear the words. All he heard was the pounding of his heart, which he was sure would burst soon.

He shrieked when a hand touched his wrist, and tried to jerk away. The sudden movement split his burnt skin open and Renn blacked out for a second. They set some sort of fabric on top of him. He should have felt relief because of the protection from the sun's rays, but instead the fabric scratched his wounds and tore another scream from his throat. He bit down and the spoon cracked in half.

"We're taking you inside," Mother said. "You did so good. We're taking you inside now, love."

Renn shook, feeling both like he was burning and like he was frozen as Father carried him inside. Father had an arm under his thighs and another gently supporting his neck so he was leaning over his shoulder. That meant that Renn had a clear view of Mother kneeling next to Cal, taking notes as he burned and begged for mercy that wouldn't come.

About the Author

Kailey Alessi is the founder and editor-in-chief of the Whumpy Printing Press, a publishing company whose mission is to publish the work of the whump community. She is also the author of the Of Vampires and Men dark fantasy series, and her short fiction has appeared in numerous anthologies. She is an archaeologist by day, and by night she writes all sorts of dark fiction. You can find her on tumblr @whumpy-writings

Acknowledgements

First and foremost, I would like to thank the authors who contributed stories to this anthology. I loved reading your work!

Thank you to our lovely graphic designer, Nicole, for the awesome cover. You took my vague idea of "blood" and "laboratory" and created a piece of art. You rock!

And thank you, dear reader, for picking up this book. I started WPP because I wanted to see more whumpy books out in the world, and every time someone picks up a copy I know that I'm not the only one! I hope you've enjoyed reading this book as much as I enjoyed putting it together.

Now, if you don't want the lab whumperflies to end, turn the page for an excerpt from WPP's next book. I hope you like vampires!

An Excerpt from Savage Sunset

Nox Spacey

The *captivity* was not what made Lex feel guilty. If they had just been keeping him *captive*, Lex would have felt A-OK about that. No, it was the sounds she heard every time she passed the basement, the pitiful muffled screams and Nick's soft yet merciless voice. The rattling of chains and the sobbing she heard *every time*, because you had to pass the basement to enter and exit the building. Occasionally there would be the smell of something burning.

She tried not to think about it too much. *Just ignore it. You know he deserves it. This is an emotional reaction, not a logical one. He's a monster that's in the shape of a human to hunt more efficiently, he's like a parrot, he's mimicking the sounds that evoke the urge to help in humans.*

But she couldn't just *ignore* it when Nick started showing up to their weekly all-hands meetings to report the results of his experiments. He brought photos, which he proudly reported he developed himself in the dark room. He arranged them in a notebook alongside his notes and the results, like a ghoulish scrapbook.

The first week, he showed them all a photo of the gradient of burns from his first experiment. Nick proudly reported that he'd discovered that a weapon with a coating that was sixty percent silver and forty percent steel yielded results that weren't significantly different from a weapon that was one hundred percent silver, and since silver was getting harder and harder to find, this could save the hunters quite a lot of money. The steel also made the weapons more durable and more effective in combat.

The second week, he reported that he'd tried a variety of sedatives, poisons, and anesthetics and found that none of them were successful, as he'd suspected. He did, however, develop a type of dart that delivered a shot of silver colloid into the bloodstream, which was as close as he'd gotten to a poison and which caused seizures when administered.

The third week, he reported he'd developed a device that could replicate the effects of sunlight, which could be effective in a situation where silver bullets weren't available. Nick pointedly did not show any pictures that time. Lex later found out that was because the pictures were so incredibly graphic that even Nick knew they wouldn't be well-received; the charred flesh was so melted and burned away that bone was visible at certain points.

It went on and on like this. The experiments started to get gradually less justifiable.

I've found out vampires hold up better under extreme cold than extreme heat. It was seven minutes till loss of consciousness in flames, but three hours in an ice bath. This could be useful for choosing where to stage fights and for incorporating fire into hunting.

I've found out a vampire can hold its breath for fourteen minutes before its body begins to shut down. This could be useful if we were somehow able to trap one underwater long enough as an alternative method of subduing them.

I've found out a vampire can have forty percent of its brain removed and still remain conscious. Non-silvered weapons to the head can potentially be effective if they remove more than this.

I've found out that starving a vampire slows its healing capacity by two percent for every day it's gone without feeding, at least for open wounds. I'm still testing if this is true for broken bones.

According to my calculations, a vampire's strength is lost at a rate of about one point five percent for every day gone without feeding, judging by ability to lift objects with the pectoral muscles. Walking speed and balance are lost at three percent per day without feeding.

I've discovered that a silver bullet in the lung will immobilize as much as three elsewhere in the torso, and that bullet wounds can close up without removing the bullet.

After a week where he showed a picture that included what was *clearly* flayed skin, as well as whip marks, and was interrogated about when and why the marks had been left, Nick stopped bringing pictures.

Ari was stoic about it, but Lex knew her well enough to know how her discomfort manifested: she ruthlessly criticized every new development Nick brought to the table.

And how's that supposed to help us?

That's all you found out? Were you just sitting around with your thumb up your ass the whole week?

Big whoop, the world is saved! Three percent per day. We've got them on the run now, boys!

Nick claimed vampires didn't feel pain the same way humans did. That since they were sturdier, they didn't have any use for such a sensitive nervous system; it would only hamper their supernatural physical prowess.

Nobody was buying it. Nobody was thrilled with what Nick was doing, even though it did occasionally provide some very useful information, and even though the director – who, notably, was rarely at the actual physical location to hear the screaming – ended up being pretty pleased by it, since it led to improvements in the way they hunted vampires.

There was a reason for it, but it was still torture. And vampires didn't die easily, not at all, so there was no way for this vampire to escape it – not even by dying. It made the situation even more gruesome, knowing this vampire would be forced to endure whatever abuse was heaped onto it without concern of accidentally killing it.

Despite the fact that most of the hunters at their base had been hurt by vampires in very personal ways and hated the creatures, few of them thought *torturing* one was okay. Even the ones who found satisfaction in killing vampires did so because it meant taking out threats and serving justice. Some could call this justice … but most wouldn't. Anyone who heard about what was happening and laughed or said *Good, that thing deserves it* immediately fell silent upon seeing the photographs and hearing the sickening sounds.

But … none of them wanted to be the one to pull the trigger on saying it needed to be stopped. Nobody wanted to be the one defending a cannibalistic serial killer. Nobody wanted the others to see them saying *This monster deserves kindness despite the earth-shattering abuse it's propagated*, but more than that, nobody wanted to carry the emotional burden of *extending* said kindness to said monster. Being a conscientious objector was easy. It was easy to walk past quickly and keep telling yourself *He deserves it he deserves it he deserves it.* Being an active participant in helping someone who'd hurt you and your family so badly was quite another matter.

Most of them were like Lex and had either been attacked, almost snatched away or taken and escaped, or had loved ones disappear. It was … hard to extend sympathy to someone who did that, even if not to them personally.

But still. The pool of humans willing to watch Nick do what he was doing shrank. About half a dozen told Nick they would from here on out refuse his requests to open the coffin the day after Lex had done so. Nick started having trouble getting enough coverage to satisfy the "two people present when the coffin is open" rule.

Lex saw Valen less and less – she avoided it on purpose – but every time she did see him, he looked worse. Eventually she refused to go down in the basement at all, and rejected Nick's requests to help bring the coffin upstairs.

She walked past the basement quickly these days. Everyone did. They tried to ignore the sounds and go about their business. They still had vampires to hunt. People to save. Most of them weren't there that often, or for that long, and the discomfort hearing it was only temporary.

Except for Lex. The guilt settled in her stomach permanently.

Also by The Whumpy Printing Press

Anthologies

Hurt and Comfort

Once Upon a Blade

The Whumpboratory

High Stakes and Bloody Business

www.ingramcontent.com/pod-product-compliance
Lightning Source LLC
Chambersburg PA
CBHW052027240626
47153CB00006B/1982